THE HORNED GHOSTS . . .
THE COLD WATER GANG . . .
IGLI THE GOLEM . . .

They were the first of the perils Scar Gordon faced on the Glory Road . . . but not the last or the worst. That came *after* he had saved a farflung star-civilization and won his lady and his empire. . . .

A tougher Tolkien or an urbane Burroughs *might* have written GLORY ROAD—but only Heinlein could have carried it off as perfectly as he has!

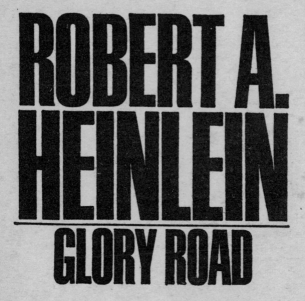

ROBERT A. HEINLEIN

GLORY ROAD

BERKLEY BOOKS, NEW YORK

This Berkley book contains the complete
text of the original hardcover edition.
It has been completely reset in a type face
designed for easy reading, and was printed
from new film.

GLORY ROAD

A Berkley Book / published by arrangement with
G. P. Putnam's Sons

PRINTING HISTORY
G. P. Putnam's Sons edition published 1964
Berkley edition / March 1970
Twenty-second printing / February 1981

ISBN: 0-425-04865-9

A BERKLEY BOOK ® TM 757,375
Berkley Books are published by Berkley Publishing Corporation,
200 Madison Avenue, New York, New York 10016.
PRINTED IN THE UNITED STATES OF AMERICA

For
George H. Scithers
and
the regular patrons
of the
Terminus, Owlswick, & Ft. Mudge
Electrick Street Railway

BRITANNUS (shocked):
      Caesar, this is not proper.
THEODOTUS (outraged):
      How?
CAESAR (recovering his self-possession):
      Pardon him Theodotus: he is a barbarian, and thinks that the customs of his tribe and island are the laws of nature.

Caesar and Cleopatra, Act II
—George Bernard Shaw

GLORY ROAD

I

I KNOW a place where there is no smog and no parking problem and no population explosion ... no Cold War and no H-bombs and no television commercials ... no Summit Conferences, no Foreign Aid, no hidden taxes—no income tax. The climate is the sort that Florida and California claim (and neither has), the land is lovely, the people are friendly and hospitable to strangers, the women are beautiful and amazingly anxious to please—

I could go back. I could—

It was an election year with the customary theme of anything you can do I can do better, to a background of beeping sputniks. I was twenty-one but couldn't figure out which party to vote against.

Instead I phoned my draft board and told them to send me that notice.

I object to conscription the way a lobster objects to boiling water: it may be his finest hour but it's not his choice. Nevertheless I love my country. Yes, I do, despite propaganda all through school about how patriotism is obsolete. One of my great-grandfathers died at Gettysburg and my father made that long walk back from Chosen Reservoir, so I didn't buy this new idea. I argued against it in class—until it got me a "D" in Social Studies, then I shut up and passed the course.

But I didn't change my opinions to match those of a teacher who didn't know Little Round Top from Seminary Ridge.

Are you of my generation? If not, do you know *why* we turned out so wrong-headed? Or did you just write us off as "juvenile delinquents"?

I could write a book. Brother! But I'll note one key fact: After you've spent years and years trying to knock the patriotism out of a boy, don't expect him to cheer when he gets a notice reading: GREETINGS: *You are hereby ordered for induction into the Armed Forces of the United States—*

Talk about a "Lost Generation"! I've read that post-World-War-One jazz—Fitzgerald and Hemingway and so on—and it strikes me that all they had to worry about was wood alcohol in bootleg liquor. They had the world by the tail—so why were they crying?

Sure, they had Hitler and the Depression ahead of them. But they didn't know that. *We* had Khrushchev and the H-bomb and we certainly did know.

But we were not a "Lost Generation." We were worse; we were the "Safe Generation." Not beatniks. The Beats were never more than a few hundred out of millions. Oh, we talked beatnik jive and dug cool sounds in stereo and disagreed with *Playboy's* poll of jazz musicians just as earnestly as if it mattered. We read Salinger and Kerouac and used language that shocked our parents and dressed (sometimes) in beatnik fashion. But we didn't think that bongo drums and a beard compared with money in the bank. We weren't rebels. We were as conformist as army worms. "Security" was our unspoken watchword.

Most of our watchwords were unspoken but we followed them as compulsively as a baby duck takes to water. "Don't fight City Hall." "Get it while the getting is good." "Don't get caught." High goals, these, great

12

moral values, and they all mean "Security." "Going steady" (my generation's contribution to the American Dream) was based on security; it insured that Saturday night could never be the loneliest night for the weak. If you went steady, competition was eliminated.

But we had ambitions. Yes, sir! Stall off your draft board and get through college. Get married and get her pregnant, with both families helping you to stay on as a draft-immune student. Line up a job well thought of by draft boards, say with some missile firm. Better yet, take postgraduate work if your folks (or hers) could afford it and have another kid and get safely beyond the draft—besides, a doctor's degree was a union card, for promotion and pay and retirement.

Short of a pregnant wife with well-to-do parents the greatest security lay in being 4-F. Punctured eardrums were good but an allergy was best. One of my neighbors had a terrible asthma that lasted till his twenty-sixth birthday. No fake—he was allergic to draft boards. Another escape was to convince an army psychiatrist that your interests were more suited to the State Department than to the Army. More than half of my generation were "unfit for military service."

I don't find this surprising. There is an old picture of a people traveling by sleigh through deep woods—pursued by wolves. Every now and then they grab one of their number and toss him to the wolves. That's conscription even if you call it "selective service" and pretty it up with USOs and "veterans' benefits"—it's tossing a minority to the wolves while the rest go on with that single-minded pursuit of the three-car garage, the swimming pool, and the safe & secure retirement benefits.

I am not being holier-than-thou; I was after that same three-car garage myself.

However, my folks could not put me through college. My stepfather was an Air Force warrant officer with all he could handle to buy shoes for his own kids. When he was transferred to Germany just before my high school senior year and I was invited to move in with my father's sister and her husband, both of us were relieved.

13

I was no better off financially as my uncle-in-law was supporting a first wife—under California law much like being an Alabama field hand before the Civil War. But I had $35 a month as a "surviving dependent of a deceased veteran." (Not "war orphan," which is another deal that pays more.) My mother was certain that Dad's death had resulted from wounds but the Veterans Administration thought differently, so I was just a "surviving dependent."

$35 a month did not fill the hole I put in their groceries and it was understood that when I graduated I would root for myself. By doing my military time, no doubt— But I had my own plan; I played football and finished senior year season with the California Central Valley secondary school record for yards gained and a broken nose—and started in at the local State College the next fall with a job "sweeping the gym" at $10 more a month than that pension, plus fees.

I couldn't see the end but my plan was clear: Hang on, teeth and toenails, and get an engineering degree. Avoid the draft and marriage. On graduation get a deferred-status job. Save money and pick up a law degree, too—because, back in Homestead, Florida, a teacher had pointed out that, while engineers made money, the big money and boss jobs went to lawyers. So I was going to beat the game, yes, sir! Be a Horatio Alger hero. I would have headed straight for that law degree but for the fact that the college did not offer law.

At the end of the season my sophomore year they de-emphasized football.

We had had a perfect season—no wins. "Flash" Gordon (that's me—in the sports write-ups) stood one in yardage and points; nevertheless Coach and I were out of jobs. Oh, I "swept the gym" the rest of that year on basketball, fencing, and track, but the alumnus who picked up the tab wasn't interested in a basketball player who was only six feet one. I spent that summer pushing an idiot stick and trying to line up a deal elsewhere. I turned twenty-one that summer, which chopped that $35/month, too. Shortly after Labor Day I fell back on a previously prepared position, i.e., I made that phone call to my draft board.

I had in mind a year in the Air Force, then win a competitive appointment to the Air Force Academy—be an astronaut and famous, instead of rich.

Well, we can't all be astronauts. The Air Force had its quota or something. I was in the Army so fast I hardly had time to pack.

So I set out to be the best chaplain's clerk in the Army; I made sure that "typing" was listed as one of my skills. If I had anything to say about it, I was going to do my time at Fort Carson, typing neat copies while going to night school on the side.

I didn't have anything to say about it.

Ever been in Southeast Asia? It makes Florida look like a desert. Wherever you step it *squishes*. Instead of tractors they use water buffaloes. The bushes are filled with insects and natives who shoot at you. It wasn't a war—not even a "Police Action." We were "Military Advisers." But a Military Adviser who has been dead four days in that heat smells the same way a corpse does in a real war.

I was promoted to corporal. I was promoted seven times. To corporal.

I didn't have the right attitude. So my company commander said. My daddy had been a Marine and my stepfather was Air Force; my only Army ambition had been to be a chaplain's clerk Stateside. I didn't like the Army. My company commander didn't like the Army either; he was a first lieutenant who hadn't made captain and every time he got to brooding Corporal Gordon lost his stripes.

I lost them the last time for telling him that I was writing to my Congressman to find out why I was the only man in Southeast Asia who was going to be retired for old age instead of going home when his time was up —and that made him so mad he not only busted me but went out and was a hero, and then he was dead. And that's how I got this scar across my broken nose because

I was a hero, too, and should have received the Medal of Honor, only nobody was looking.

While I was recovering, they decided to send me home.

Major Ian Hay, back in the "War to End War," described the structure of military organizations: Regardless of T.O., all military bureaucracies consist of a Surprise Party Department, a Practical Joke Department, and a Fairy Godmother Department. The first two process most matters as the third is very small; the Fairy Godmother Department is one elderly female GS-5 clerk usually out on sick leave.

But when she is at her desk, she sometimes puts down her knitting and picks a name passing across her desk and does something nice. You have seen how I was whipsawed by the Surprise Party and Practical Joke Departments; this time the Fairy Godmother Department picked Pfc. Gordon.

Like this— When I knew that I was going home as soon as my face healed (little brown brother hadn't sterilized his bolo), I put in a request to be discharged in Wiesbaden, where my family was, rather than California, home of record. I am not criticizing little brown brother; he hadn't intended me to heal at all—and he would have managed it if he hadn't been killing my company commander and too hurried to do a good job on me. I hadn't sterilized my bayonet but he didn't complain, he just sighed and came apart, like a doll with its sawdust cut. I felt grateful to him; he not only had rigged the dice so that I got out of the Army, he also gave me a great idea.

He and the ward surgeon— The Surgeon had said, "You're going to get well, son. But you'll be scarred like a Heidelberg student."

Which got me thinking— You couldn't get a decent job without a degree, any more than you could be a plasterer without being a son or nephew of somebody in the plasterers' union. But there are degrees and degrees. Sir Isaac Newton, with a degree from a cow college such

16

as mine, would wash bottles for Joe Thumbfingers—if Joe had a degree from a European university.

Why not Heidelberg? I intended to milk my G.I. benefits; I had that in mind when I put in that too hasty call to my draft board.

According to my mother everything was cheaper in Germany. Maybe I could stretch those benefits into a doctor's degree. Herr Doktor Gordon, mit scars on der face from Heidelberg yet!—that would rate an extra $3,000 a year from any missile firm.

Hell, I would fight a couple of student duels and add real Heidelberg scars to back up the dandy I had. Fencing was a sport I really enjoyed (though the one that counted least toward "sweeping the gym"). Some people cannot stand knives, swords, bayonets, anything sharp; psychiatrists have a word for it: aichmophobia. Idiots who drive cars a hundred miles an hour on fifty-mile-an-hour roads will nevertheless panic at the sight of a bare blade.

I've never been bothered that way and that's why I'm alive and one reason why I kept being bucked back to corporal. A "Military Adviser" can't afford to be afraid of knives, bayonets, and such; he must cope with them. I've never been afraid of them because I'm always sure I can do unto another what he is planning to do unto me.

I've always been right, except that time I made the mistake of being a hero, and that wasn't too bad a mistake. If I had tried to bug out instead of staying to disembowel him, he would have chopped my spine in two. As it was, he never got a proper swing at me; his jungle cutter just slashed my face as he came apart—leaving me with a nasty wound that was infected long before the helicopters came. But I never felt it. Presently I got dizzy and sat down in the mud and when I woke up, a medic was giving me plasma.

I rather looked forward to trying a Heidelberg duel. They pad your body and arm and neck and put a steel guard on your eyes and nose and across your ears—this is not like encountering a pragmatic Marxist in the jungle. I once handled one of those swords they use in Heidelberg; it was a light, straight saber, sharp on the edge, sharp a few inches on the back—but a *blunt* point! A toy, suited only to make pretty scars for girls to admire.

I got a map and whaddayuh know!—Heidelberg is just down the road from Wiesbaden. So I requested my discharge in Wiesbaden.

The ward surgeon said, "You're an optimist, son," but initialed it. The medical sergeant in charge of paper work said, "Out of the question, Soldier." I won't say money changed hands but the endorsement the hospital's C.O. signed read FORWARDED. The ward agreed that I was bucking for a psycho; Uncle Sugar does not give free trips around the world to Pfcs.

I was already so far around that I was as close to Hoboken as to San Francisco—and closer to Wiesbaden. However, policy called for shipping returnees back via the Pacific. Military policy is like cancer: Nobody knows where it comes from but it can't be ignored.

The Fairy Godmother Department woke up and touched me with its wand.

I was about to climb aboard a bucket called the *General Jones* bound for Manila, Taipei, Yokohama, Pearl, and Seatle when a dispatch came granting my every whim and then some. I was ordered to HQ USAREUR, Heidelberg, Germany, by available military transportation, for discharge, at own request see reference foxtrot. Accumulated leave could be taken or paid, see reference bravo. Subject man was authorized to return to Zone Interior (the States) any time within twelve months of separation, via available military transportation at no further expense to the government. Unquote.

The paper-work sergeant called me in and showed me this, his face glowing with innocent glee. "Only there ain't no 'available transportation,' Soldier—so haul ass aboard the *General Jones*. You're going to Seattle, like I said."

I knew what he meant: The only transport going west in a long, long time had sailed for Singapore thirty-six hours earlier. I stared at that dispatch, thinking about boiling oil and wondering if he had held it back just long enough to keep me from sailing under it.

I shook my head. "I'm going to catch the *General Smith* in Singapore. Be a real human type, Sarge, and cut me a set of orders for it."

"Your orders are cut. For the *Jones*. For Seattle."

"Gosh," I said thoughtfully. "I guess I had better go cry on the chaplain." I faded out fast but I didn't see the chaplain; I went to the airfield. It took five minutes to find that no commercial nor U.S. military flight was headed for Singapore in time to do me any good.

But there was an Australian military transport headed for Singapore that night. Aussies weren't even "military advisers" but often were around, as "military observers." I found the plane's skipper, a flight leftenant, and put the situation to him. He grinned and said, "Always room for one more bloke. Wheels up shortly after tea, likely. If the old girl will fly."

I knew it would fly; it was a Gooney Bird, a C-47, mostly patches and God knows how many millions of miles. It would get to Singapore on one engine if asked. I knew my luck was in as soon as I saw that grand old collection of masking tape and glue sitting on the field.

Four hours later I was in her and wheels up.

I checked in aboard USMTS *General Smith* the next morning, rather wet—the *Pride of Tasmania* had flown through storms the night before and a Gooney Bird's one weakness is that they leak. But who minds clean rain after jungle mud? The ship was sailing that evening which was grand news.

Singapore is like Hong Kong only flat; one afternoon was enough. I had a drink in the old Raffles, another in the Adelphi, got rained on in the Great World amusement park, walked through Change Alley with a hand on my money and the other on my orders—and bought an Irish Sweepstakes ticket.

I don't gamble, if you will concede that poker is a game of skill. However this was a tribute to the goddess of fortune, thanks for a long run of luck. If she chose to answer with $140,000 US, I wouldn't throw it in her

19

face. If she didn't ... well, the ticket's face value was one pound, $2.80 US; I paid $9.00 Singapore, or $3.00 US—a small gesture from a man who had just won a free trip around the world—not to mention coming out of the jungle still breathing.

But I got my three dollars' worth at once, as I fled out of Change Alley to avoid two dozen other walking banks anxious to sell me more tickets, Singapore dollars, any sort of money—or my hat if I let go of it—reached the street, hailed a cab, and told the driver to take me to the boat landing. This was a victory of spirit over flesh because I had been debating whether to snatch the chance to ease enormous biological back pressure. Good old Scarface Gordon had been an Eagle Scout awfully long and Singapore is one of the Seven Sinful Cities where *anything* may be had.

I am not implying that I had remained faithful to the Girl Next Door. The young lady back home who had taught me most about the World, the Flesh, and the Devil, with an amazing send-off the night before I was inducted, had "Dear-Johnned" me in basic training; I felt gratitude but no loyalty. She got married soon after, now has two children, neither of them mine.

The real cause of my biological unease was geographical. Those little brown brothers I had been fighting, with and against, all had little brown sisters, many of whom could be had for a price, or even *pour l'amour ou pour le sport*.

But that had been all the local talent for a long time. Nurses? Nurses are officers—and the rare USO entertainer who got that far from Stateside was even more thoroughly blocked off than were nurses.

I did not object to little brown sisters because they were brown. I was as brown as they were, in my face, except for a long pink scar. I drew the line because they were *little*.

I was a hundred and ninety pounds of muscle and no fat, and I could never convince myself that a female four feet ten inches tall and weighing less than ninety pounds and looking twelve years old is in fact a freely consenting adult. To me it felt like a grim sort of statutory rape and produced psychic impotence.

Singapore looked like the place to find a big girl. But when I escaped from Change Alley, I suddenly didn't like people, big or little, male or female, and headed for the ship—and probably saved myself from pox, Cupid's catarrh, soft chancre, Chinese rot, salt-water itch, and athlete's foot—the wisest decision I had made since, at fourteen, I had declined to wrestle a medium-sized alligator.

I told the driver in English what landing I wanted, repeated it in memorized Cantonese (not too well; it's a nine-toned language, and French and German are all I had in school), and showed him a map with the landing marked and its name printed in English and drawn in Chinese.

Everybody who left the ship was given one of these maps. In Asia every cab driver speaks enough English to take you to the Red Light district and to shops where you buy "bargains." But he is never able to find your dock or boat landing.

My cabbie listened, glanced at the map, and said, "Okay, Mac. I dig it," and took off and rounded a corner with tires squealing while shouting at peddle cabs, coolies, children, dogs. I relaxed, happy at having found this cabbie among thousands.

Suddenly I sat up and shouted for him to stop.

I must explain something: I can't get lost.

Call it a "psi" talent, like that stuff they study at Duke. Mother used to say that sonny had a "bump of direction." Call it what you will, I was six or seven before I realized that other people *could* get lost. I always know which way is north, the direction of the point where I started and how far away it is. I can head straight back or retrace my steps, even in dark and jungle. This was the main reason why I was always promoted back to corporal and usually shoved into a sergeant's job. Patrols I headed always came back—the survivors, I mean. This was comforting to city boys who didn't want to be in that jungle anyhow.

21

I had shouted because the driver had swung right when he should have swung left and was about to cut back across his own track.

He speeded up.

I yelled again. He no longer dug English.

It was another mile and several turns later when he had to stop because of a traffic jam. I got out and he jumped out and started screaming in Cantonese and pointing at the meter in his cab. We were surrounded by Chinese adding to the din and smaller ones plucking at my clothes. I kept my hand on my money and was happy indeed to spot a cop. I yelled and caught his eye.

He came through the crowd brandishing a long staff. He was a Hindu; I said to him, "Do you speak English?"

"Certainly. And I understand American." I explained my trouble, showed him the map, and said that the driver had picked me up at Change Alley and had been driving in circles.

The cop nodded and talked with the driver in a third language—Malayan, I suppose. At last the cop said, "He doesn't understand English. He thought you said to drive to Johore."

The bridge to Johore is as far as you can get from the anchorage and still be on the Island of Singapore. I said angrily, "The hell he doesn't understand English!"

The cop shrugged. "You hired him, you must pay what is on the taximeter. Then I will explain to him where you wish to go and arrange a fixed fee."

"I'll see him in hell first!"

"That is possible. The distance is quite short—in this neighborhood. I suggest that you pay. The waiting time is mounting up."

There comes a time when a man must stand up for his rights, or he can't bear to look at himself in a mirror to shave. I had already shaved, so I paid—$18.50 Sing., for wasting an hour and ending up farther from the landing. The driver wanted a tip but the cop shut him up and then let me walk with him.

Using both hands I hung onto my orders and money, and the Sweepstakes ticket folded in with the money.

But my pen disappeared and cigarettes and handkerchief and a Ronson lighter. When I felt ghost fingers at the strap of my watch, I agreed to the cop's suggestion that he had a cousin, an honest man, who would drive me to my landing for a fixed—and moderate—fee.

The "cousin" turned out to be just coming down the street; half an hour later I was aboard ship. I shall never forget Singapore, a most educational city.

II

TWO months later I was on the French Riviera. The Fairy Godmother Department watched over me across the Indian Ocean, up the Red Sea, and clear to Napoli. I lived a healthy life, exercising and getting tan every morning, sleeping afternoons, playing poker at night. There are many people who do not know the odds (poor, but computable) for improving a poker hand in the draw, but are anxious to learn. When we got to Italy I had a beautiful tan and a sizable nest egg.

Early in the voyage someone went broke and wanted to put a Sweepstakes ticket into the game. After some argument Sweepstakes tickets were made *valuta* at a discount, $2.00 USA per ticket. I finished the trip with fifty-three tickets.

Hitching a flight from Napoli to Frankfurt took only hours. Then the Fairy Godmother Department handed me back to the Surprise Party and Practical Joke Departments.

Before going to Heidelberg I ducked over to Wiesbaden to see my mother, my stepfather and the kids

—and found that they had just left for the States, on their way to Elmendorf AFB in Alaska.

So I went to Heidelberg to be processed, and looked the town over while the red tape unwound.

Lovely town— Handsome castle, good beer, and *big* girls with rosy cheeks and shapes like Coca-Cola bottles— Yes, this looked like a nice place to get a degree. I started inquiring into rooms and such, and met a young kraut wearing a *studenten* cap and some face scars as ugly as mine—things were looking up.

I discussed my plans with the first sergeant of the transient company.

He shook his head. "Oh, you poor boy!"

Why? No G.I. benefits for Gordon—I wasn't a "veteran."

Never mind that scar. Never mind that I had killed more men in combat than you could crowd into a—well, never mind. That thing was not a "war" and Congress had not passed a bill providing educational benefits for us "Military Advisers."

I suppose this was my own fault. All my life there had been "G.I. benefits"—why, I had shared a bench in chem lab with a veteran who was going to school on the G.I. Bill.

This fatherly sergeant said, "Don't take it hard, son. Go home, get a job, wait a year. They'll pass it and date it back, almost certainly. You're young."

So here I was on the Riviera, a civilian, enjoying a taste of Europe before using that transportation home. Heidelberg was out of the question. Oh, the pay I hadn't been able to spend in the jungle, plus accumulated leave, plus my winnings at poker, added up to a sum which would have kept me a year in Heidelberg. But it would never stretch enough for a degree. I had been counting on that mythical "G.I. Bill" for eating money and on my cash as a cushion.

My (revised) plan was obvious. Grab that trip home before my year was up—grab it before school opened. Use the cash I had to pay board to Aunt and Uncle, work next summer and see what turned up. With the

25

draft no longer hanging over me I could find some way to sweat out that last year even if I couldn't be "Herr Doktor Gordon."

However, school didn't open until fall and here it was spring. I was damn well going to see a little of Europe before I applied nose to grindstone; another such chance might never come.

There was another reason for waiting: those Sweepstakes tickets. The drawing for horses was coming up.

The Irish Sweepstakes starts as a lottery. First they sell enough tickets to paper Grand Central Station. The Irish hospitals get 25 percent and are the only sure winners. Shortly before the race they draw for horses. Let's say twenty horses are entered. If your ticket fails to draw a horse, it's wastepaper. (Oh, there are minor consolation prizes.)

But if you do draw a horse, you still haven't won. Some horses won't start. Of those that do, most of them chase the other horses. However, any ticket that draws any horse at all, even a goat that can barely walk to the paddock, that ticket suddenly acquires a value of thousands of dollars between the drawing and the race. Just how much depends on how good the horse is. But prizes are high and the worst horse in the field has been known to win.

I had fifty-three tickets. If one of them drew a horse, I could sell that ticket for enough to put me through Heidelberg.

So I stayed and waited for the drawings.

Europe needn't be expensive. A youth hostel is luxury to a man who has come out of the boondocks of Southeast Asia and even the French Riviera isn't expensive if you approach it from underneath. I didn't stay on La Promenade des Anglais; I had a tiny room four floors up and two kilometres back, and the shared use of some plumbing. There are wonderful night clubs in Nice but you need not patronize them as the floor show at the beaches is as good ... and free. I never appreciated what a high art the fan dance can be until the first time I watched a French girl get out of her clothes and into her bikini in plain sight of citizens, tourists, gendarmes, dogs —and me—all without quite violating the lenient French mores concerning "indecent exposure." Or only momentarily.

Yes, sir, there are things to see and do on the French Riviera without spending money.

The beaches are terrible. Rocks. But rocks are better than jungle mud and I put on trunks and enjoyed the floor show and added to my tan. It was spring, before the tourist season and not crowded, but it was warm and summery and dry. I lay in the sun and was happy and my only luxury was a deposit box with American Express and the Paris edition of the N.Y. *Herald Tribune* and *The Stars & Stripes*. These I would glance over to see how the Powers-that-be were mismanaging the world, then look for what was new in the unWar I had just been let out of (usually no mention, although we had been told that we were "saving civilization"), then get down to important matters, i.e., news of the Irish Sweepstakes, plus the possibility that *The Stars & Stripes* might announce that it had all been a hideous dream and I was entitled to educational benefits after all.

Then came crossword puzzles and "Personal" ads. I always read "Personals"; they are a naked look into private lives. Things like: *M.L. phone R.S. before noon. Money.* Makes you wonder who did what to whom, and who got paid?

Presently I found a still cheaper way to live with an even better floor show. Have you heard of l'Île du Levant? It is an island off the Riviera between Marseilles and Nice, and is much like Catalina. It has a village at one end and the French Navy has blocked off the other for guided missiles; the rest of it is hills and beaches and grottoes. There are no automobiles, nor even bicycles. The people who go there don't want to be reminded of the outside world.

For ten dollars a day you can enjoy luxury equal to forty dollars a day in Nice. Or you can pay five cents a day for camping and live on a dollar a day—which

27

I did—and there are good cheap restaurants anytime you get tired of cooking.

It is a place that seems to have no rules of any sort. Wait a minute; there is one. Outside the village, Heli opolis, is a sign: LE NU INTEGRAL EST FORMELLEMENT INTERDIT. ("Complete nakedness is strictly forbidden.")

This means that everyone, man or woman, must put on a little triangle of cloth, a *cache-sexe*, a G-string, before going inside the village.

Elsewhere, on beaches and in camping grounds and around the island, you don't have to wear a damned thing and nobody does.

Save for the absence of automobiles and clothes, the Isle of the Levant is like any other bit of back-country France. There is a shortage of fresh water, but the French don't drink water and you bathe in the Mediterranean and for a franc you can buy enough fresh water for half a dozen sponge baths to rinse off the salt. Take the train from Nice or Marseilles, get off at Toulon and take a bus to Lavandou, then by boat (an hour and a few minutes) to l'Île du Levant—then chuck away your cares with your clothes.

I found I could buy the *Herald-Trib*, a day old, in the village, at the same place ("Au Minimum," Mme. Alexandre) where I rented a tent and camping gear. I bought groceries at La Brise Marine and camped above La Plage des Grottes, close to the village, and settled down and let my nerves relax while I enjoyed the floor show.

Some people disparage the female form divine. Sex is too good for them; they should have been oysters. All gals are good to look at (including little brown sisters even though they scared me); the only difference is that some look better than others. Some were fat and some were skinny and some were old and some were young. Some looked as if they had stepped straight out of Les Folies Bergères. I got acquainted with one of those and I wasn't far off; she was a Swedish girl who was a *"nue"* in another Paris revue. She practiced English on me and I practiced French on her, and she promised to cook me

a Swedish dinner if I was ever in Stockholm and I
cooked her a dinner over an alcohol lamp and we got
giggly on vin ordinaire, and she wanted to know how I
had acquired my scar and I told some lies. Marjatta was
good for an old soldier's nerves and I was sad when she
had to leave.

But the floor show went on. Three days later I was
sitting on Grotto Beach, leaning against a rock and
working the crossword puzzle, when suddenly I got
cross-eyed trying not to stare at the most stare-able
woman I have ever seen in my life.

Woman, girl—I couldn't be sure. At first glance I
thought she was eighteen, maybe twenty; later when I
was able to look her square in her face she still looked
eighteen but could have been forty. Or a hundred and
forty. She had the agelessness of perfect beauty. Like
Helen of Troy, or Cleopatra. It seemed possible that she
was Helen of Troy but I knew she wasn't Cleopatra
because she was not a redhead; she was a natural blonde.
She was a tawny toast color all over without a hint of
bikini marks and her hair was the same shade two tones
lighter. It flowed, unconfined, in graceful waves down
her back and seemed never to have been cut.

She was tall, not much shorter than I am, and not too
much lighter in weight. Not fat, not fat at all save for
that graceful padding that smoothes the feminine form,
shading the muscles underneath—I was sure there were
muscles underneath; she carried herself with the relaxed
power of a lioness.

Her shoulders were broad for a woman, as broad as
her very female hips; her waist might have seemed thick
on a lesser woman, on her it was deliciously slender. Her
belly did not sag at all but carried the lovely doubly-
domed curve of perfect muscle tone. Her breasts—only
her big rib cage could carry such large ones without ap-
pearing too much of a good thing. They jutted firmly out
and moved only a trifle when she moved, and they were
crowned with rosy brown confections that were frankly
nipples, womanly and not virginal.

Her navel was that jewel the Persian poets praised

Her legs were long for her height; her hands and feet were not small but were slender, graceful. She was graceful in all ways; it was impossible to think of her in a pose ungraceful. Yet she was so lithe and limber that, like a cat, she could have twisted herself into any position.

Her face— How do you describe perfect beauty except to say that when you see it you can't mistake it? Her lips were full and her mouth rather wide. It was faintly curved in the ghost of a smile even when her features were at rest. Her lips were red but if she was wearing makeup of any sort it had been applied so skillfully that I could not detect it—and that alone would have made her stand out, for that was a year all other females were wearing "Continental" makeup, as artificial as a corset and as bold as a doxy's smile.

Her nose was straight and large enough for her face, no button. Her eyes—

She caught me staring at her. Certainly women expect to be looked at and expect it unclothed quite as much as when dressed for the ball. But it is rude to stare openly. I had given up the fight in the first ten seconds and was trying to memorize her, every line, every curve.

Her eyes locked with mine and she stared back and I began to blush but couldn't look away. Her eyes were so deep a blue that they were dark, darker than my own brown eyes.

I said huskily, *"Pardonnez-moi, ma'm'selle,"* and managed to tear my eyes away.

She answered, in English, "Oh, I don't mind. Look all you please," and looked me up and down as carefully as I had inspected her. Her voice was a warm, full contralto, surprisingly deep in its lowest register.

She took two steps toward me and almost stood over me. I started to get up and she motioned me to stay seated, with a gesture that assumed obedience as if she were very used to giving orders. "Rest where you are," she said. The breeze carried her fragrance to me and I got goose flesh all over. "You are American."

"Yes." I was certain she was not, yet I was equally

30

certain she was not French. Not only did she have no trace of French accent but also—well, French women are at least slightly provocative at all times; they can't help it, it's ingrained in the French culture. There was nothing provocative about this woman—except that she was an incitement to riot just by existing.

But, without being provocative, she had that rare gift for immediate intimacy; she spoke to me as a very old friend might speak, friends who knew each other's smallest foibles and were utterly easy tête-à-tête. She asked me questions about myself, some of them quite personal, and I answered all of them, honestly, and it never occurred to me that she had no right to quiz me. She never asked my name, nor I hers—nor any question of her.

At last she stopped and looked me over again, carefully and soberly. Then she said thoughtfully, "You are very beautiful," and added, *"Au 'voir"*—turned and walked down the beach into the water and swam away.

I was too stunned to move. Nobody had ever called me "handsome" even before I broke my nose. As for "beautiful"!

But I don't think it would have done me any good to have chased her, even if I had thought of it in time. That gal could swim.

III

I STAYED at the *plage* until sundown, waiting for her to come back. Then I made a hurried supper of bread and cheese and wine, got dressed in my G-string and walked into town. There I prowled bars and restaurants and did not find her, meanwhile window-peeping into cottages wherever shades were not drawn. When the bistros started shutting down, I gave up, went back to my tent, cursed myself for eight kinds of fool—(why couldn't I have said, "What's your name and where do you live and where are you staying *here?*") —sacked in and went to sleep.

I was up at dawn and checked the *plage*, ate breakfast, checked the *plage* again, got "dressed" and went into the village, checked the shops and post office, and bought my *Herald-Trib*.

Then I was faced with one of the most difficult decisions of my life: I had drawn a horse.

I wasn't certain at first, as I did not have those fifty-three serial numbers memorized. I had to run back to my tent, dig out a memorandum and check—and I had!

It was a number that had stuck in mind because of its pattern: #XDY 34555. I had a horse!

Which meant several thousand dollars, just how much I didn't know. But enough to put me through Heidelberg . . . *if* I cashed in on it at once. The *Herald-Trib* was always a day late there, which meant the drawing had taken place at least two days earlier—and in the meantime that dog could break a leg or be scratched nine other ways. My ticket was important money only as long as "Lucky Star" was listed as a starter.

I had to get to Nice in a hurry and find out where and how you got the best price for a lucky ticket. Dig the ticket out of my deposit box and sell it!

But how about "Helen of Troy"?

Shylock with his soul-torn cry of "Oh, my daughter! Oh, my ducats!" was no more split than I.

I compromised. I wrote a painful note, identifying myself, telling her that I had been suddenly called away and pleading with her either to wait until I returned tomorrow, or at the very least, to leave a note telling me how to find her. I left it with the postmistress along with a description—blond, so tall, hair this long, magnificent *poitrine*—and twenty francs with a promise of twice that much if she delivered it and got an answer. The postmistress said that she had never seen her but if *cette grande blonde* ever set foot in the village the note would be delivered.

That left me just time to rush back, dress in off-island clothes, dump my gear with Mme. Alexandre, and catch the boat. Then I had three hours of travel time to worry through.

The trouble was that Lucky Star wasn't really a dog. My horse rated no farther down than fifth or sixth, no matter who was figuring form. So? Stop while I was ahead and take my profit?

Or go for broke?

It wasn't easy. Let's suppose I could sell the ticket for $10,000. Even if I didn't try any fancy footwork on taxes, I would still keep most of it and get through school.

But I was going to get through school anyway—and did I really want to go to Heidelberg? That student with the dueling scars had been a slob, with his phony pride in scars from fake danger.

Suppose I hung on and grabbed the big one, £50,000, or $140,000—

Do you know how much tax a bachelor pays on $140,000 in the Land of the Brave and the Home of the Free?

$103,000, that's what he pays.

That leaves him $37,000.

Did I want to bet about $10,000 against the chance of winning $37,000—with the odds at least 15 to 1 against me?

Brother, that is drawing to an inside straight. The principle is the same whether it's 37 grand, or jacks-or-better with a two-bit limit.

But suppose I wangled some way to beat the tax, thus betting $10,000 to win $140,000? That made the potential profit match the odds—and $140,000 was not just eating money for college but a fortune that could bring in four or five thousand a year forever.

I wouldn't be "cheating" Uncle Sugar; the USA had no more moral claim on that money (if I won) than I had on the Holy Roman Empire. What had Uncle Sugar done for *me?* He had clobbered my father's life with two wars, one of which we weren't allowed to win—and thereby made it tough for me to get through college quite aside from what a father may be worth in spiritual intangibles to his son (I didn't know, I never would know!)—then he had grabbed me out of college and had sent me to fight another unWar and damned near killed me and lost me my sweet girlish laughter.

So how is Uncle Sugar entitled to clip $103,000 and leave me the short end? So he can "lend" it to Poland? Or give it to Brazil? Oh, my back!

There was a way to keep it all (if I won) legal as marriage. Go live in little old tax-free Monaco for a year. Then take it anywhere.

New Zealand, maybe. The *Herald-Trib* had had the

usual headlines, only more so. It looked as if the boys (just big playful boys!) who run this planet were about to hold that major war, the one with ICBMs and H-bombs, any time now.

If a man went as far south as New Zealand there might be something left after the fallout fell out.

New Zealand is supposed to be very pretty and they say that a fisherman there regards a five-pound trout as too small to take home.

I had caught a two-pound trout once.

About then I made a horrible discovery. I didn't want to go back to school, win, lose, or draw. I no longer gave a damn about three-car garages and swimming pools, nor any other status symbol or "security." There was *no* security in this world and only damn fools and mice thought there could be.

Somewhere back in the jungle I had shucked off all ambition of that sort. I had been shot at too many times and had lost interest in supermarkets and exurban subdivisions and tonight is the PTA supper don't forget dear you promised.

Oh, I wasn't about to hole up in a monastery. I still wanted—

What *did* I want?

I wanted a Roc's egg. I wanted a harem loaded with lovely odalisques less than the dust beneath my chariot wheels, the rust that never stained my sword. I wanted raw red gold in nuggets the size of your fist and feed that lousy claim jumper to the huskies! I wanted to get up feeling brisk and go out and break some lances, then pick a likely wench for my *droit du seigneur*—I wanted to stand up to the Baron and *dare* him to touch my wench! I wanted to hear the purple water chuckling against the skin of the *Nancy Lee* in the cool of the morning watch and not another sound, nor any movement save the slow tilting of the wings of the albatross that had been pacing us the last thousand miles.

I wanted the hurtling moons of Barsoom. I wanted Storisende and Poictesme, and Holmes shaking me awake to tell me, "The game's afoot!" I wanted to float down the Mississippi on a raft and elude a mob in company with the Duke of Bilgewater and the Lost Dauphin.

I wanted Prester John, and Excalibur held by a moon-white arm out of a silent lake. I wanted to sail with Ulysses and with Tros of Samothrace and eat the lotus in a land that seemèd always afternoon. I wanted the feeling of romance and the sense of wonder I had known as a kid. I wanted the world to be what they had promised me it was going to be—instead of the tawdry, lousy, fouled-up mess it is.

I had had one chance—for ten minutes yesterday afternoon. Helen of Troy, whatever your true name may be—And I had known it . . . and I had let it slip away.

Maybe one chance is all you ever get.

The train pulled into Nice.

In the American Express office I went to the banking department and to my deposit box, found the ticket and checked the number against the *Herald-Trib*—XDY 34555, *yes!* To stop my trembling, I checked the other tickets and they were wastepaper, just as I thought. I shoved them back into the box and asked to see the manager.

I had a money problem and American Express is a bank, not just a travel bureau. I was ushered into the manager's office and we exchanged names. "I need advice," I said. "You see, I hold one of the winning Sweepstakes tickets."

He broke into a grin. "Congratulations! You're the first person in a long time who has come in here with good news rather than a complaint."

"Thanks. Uh, my problem is this. I know that a ticket that draws a horse is worth quite a bit up until the race. Depending on the horse, of course."

"Of course," he agreed. "What horse did you draw?"

"A fairly good one, Lucky Star—and that's what makes it tough. If I had drawn H-Bomb, or any of the three favorites— Well, you see how it is. I don't know whether to sell or hang on, because I don't know how to

36

figure the odds. Do you know what is being offered for Lucky Star?"

He fitted his finger tips together. "Mr. Gordon, American Express does not give tips on horse races, nor broker the resale of Sweepstakes tickets. However— Do you have the ticket with you?"

I got it out and handed it to him. It had been through poker games and was sweat marked and crumpled. But that lucky number was unmistakable.

He looked at it. "Do you have your receipt?"

"Not with me." I started to explain that I had given my stepfather's address—and that my mail had been forwarded to Alaska. He cut me off. "That's all right." He touched a switch. "Alice, will you ask M'sieur Renault to step in?"

I was wondering if it really was all right. I had had the savvy to get names and new billets from the original ticket holders and each had promised to send his receipt to me when he got it—but no receipts had reached me. Maybe in Alaska—I had checked on this ticket while at the lockbox; it had been bought by a sergeant now in Stuttgart. Maybe I would have to pay him something or maybe I would have to break his arms.

M. Renault looked like a tired schoolteacher. "M'sieur Renault is our expert on this sort of thing," the manager explained. "Will you let him examine your ticket, please?"

The Frenchman looked at it, then his eyes lit up and he reached into a pocket, produced a jeweler's loupe, screwed it into his eye. "Excellent!" he said approvingly. "One of the best. Hong Kong, perhaps?"

"I bought it in Singapore."

He nodded and smiled. "That follows."

The manager was not smiling. He reached into his desk and brought out another Sweepstakes ticket and handed it to me. "Mr. Gordon, this one I bought at Monte Carlo. Will you compare it?"

They looked alike to me, except for serial numbers and the fact that his was crisp and clean. "What am I supposed to look for?"

"Perhaps this will help." He offered me a large reading glass.

A Sweepstakes ticket is printed on special paper and has an engraved portrait on it and is done in several colors. It is a better job of engraving and printing than many countries use for paper money.

I learned long ago that you can't change a deuce into an ace by staring at it. I handed back his ticket. "Mine is counterfeit."

"I didn't say so, Mr. Gordon. I suggest you get an outside opinion. Say at the office of the Bank of France."

"I can see it. The engraving lines aren't sharp and even on mine. They're broken, some places. Under the glass the print job looks smeared." I turned. "Right, M'sieur Renault?"

The expert gave a shrug of commiseration. "It is beautiful work, of its sort."

I thanked them and got out. I checked with the Bank of France, not because I doubted the verdict but because you don't have a leg cut off, nor chuck away $140,000, without a second opinion. Their expert didn't bother with a loupe. *"Contrefait,"* he announced. "Worthless."

It was impossible to get back to l'Île du Levant that night. I had dinner and then looked up my former landlady. My broom closet was empty and she let me have it overnight. I didn't lie awake long.

I was not as depressed as I thought I should be. I felt relaxed, almost relieved. For a while I had had the wonderful sensation of being rich—and I had had its complement, the worries of being rich—and both sensations were interesting and I didn't care to repeat them, not right away.

Now I had no worries. The only thing to settle was when to go home, and with living so cheap on the island there was no hurry. The only thing that fretted me was that rushing off to Nice might have caused me to miss "Helen of Troy," *cette grande blonde! Si grande ... si belle ... si majestueuse!* I fell asleep thinking of her.

I had intended to catch the early train, then the first boat. But the day before had used up most of the

38

money on me and I had goofed by failing to get cash while at American Express. Besides, I had not asked for mail. I didn't expect any, other than from my mother and possibly my aunt—the only close friend I had had in the Army had been killed six months back. Still, I might as well pick up mail as long as I had to wait for money.

So I treated myself to a luxury breakfast. The French think that a man can face the day with chicory and milk, and a croissant, which probably accounts for their unstable politics. I picked a sidewalk café by a big kiosk, the only one in Nice that stocked *The Stars & Stripes* and where the *Herald-Trib* would be on sale as soon as it was in; ordered a melon, *café complet* for TWO, and an *omelette aux herbes fines;* and sat back to enjoy life.

When the *Herald-Trib* arrived, it detracted from my Sybaritic pleasure. The headlines were worse than ever and reminded me that I was still going to have to cope with the world; I couldn't stay on l'Île du Levant forever.

But why not stay there as long as possible? I still did not want to go to school, and that three-car-garage ambition was as dead as that Sweepstakes ticket. If World War III was about to shift to a rolling boil, there was no point in being an engineer at six or eight thousand a year in Santa Monica only to be caught in the fire storm.

It would be better to live it up, gather ye rosebuds, carpe that old diem, with dollars and days at hand, then— Well, join the Marine Corps maybe, like my dad. Maybe I could make corporal—and keep it.

I refolded the paper to the "Personals" column.

They were pretty good. Besides the usual offers of psychic readings and how to learn yoga and the veiled messages from one set of initials to another there were several that were novel. Such as—

REWARD!! *Are you contemplating suicide? Assign to me the lease on your apartment and I will make your last days lavish. Box 323, H-T*

Or: *Hindu gentleman, non-vegetarian, wishes to meet cultured European, African, or Asian lady owning sports car. Object: improving international relations. Box 107*

How do you do that in a sports car?

One was ominous— *Hermaphrodites of the World, Arise! You have nothing to lose but your chains. Tel. Opéra 59-09*

The next one started:

ARE YOU A COWARD?

Well, yes, certainly. If possible. If allowed a free choice. I read on:

> ARE YOU A COWARD? This is not for you. We badly need a brave man. He must be 23 to 25 years old, in perfect health, at least six feet tall, weigh about 190 pounds, fluent English with some French, proficient with all weapons, some knowledge of engineering and mathematics essential, willing to travel, no family or emotional ties, indomitably courageous and handsome of face and figure. Permanent employment, very high pay, glorious adventure, great danger. You must apply in person, 17, rue Dante, Nice, 2me étage, appt. D.

I read that requirement about face and figure with strong relief. For a giddy moment it had seemed as if someone with a skewed sense of humor had aimed a shaggy joke right at me. Somebody who knew my habit of reading the "Personals."

That address was only a hundred yards from where I was sitting. I read the ad again.

Then I paid the *addition,* left a careful tip, went to the kiosk and bought *The Stars & Stripes,* walked to American Express, got money and picked up my mail, and on to the railroad station. It was over an hour until the next train to Toulon, so I went into the bar, ordered a beer and sat down to read.

Mother was sorry I had missed them in Wiesbaden. Her letter itemized the children's illnesses, the high prices in Alaska, and expresed regret that they had ever had to leave Germany. I shoved it into my pocket and picked up *The Stars & Stripes.*

Presently I was reading: ARE YOU A COWARD?—same ad, right to the end.

I threw the paper down with a growl.

There were three other letters. One invited me to con-

40

tribute to the athletic association of my ex-college; the second offered to advise me in the selection of my investments at a special rate of only $48 a year; the last was a plain envelope without a stamp, evidently handed in at American Express.

It contained only a newspaper clipping, starting: ARE YOU A COWARD?

It was the same as the other two ads except that in the last sentence one word had been underlined: *You must apply in person—*

I splurged on a cab to rue Dante. If I hurried, there was time to untangle this hopscotch and still catch the Toulon train. No. 17 was a walk-up; I ran up and, as I approached suite D, I met a young man coming out. He was six feet tall, handsome of face and figure, and looked as if he might be a hermaphrodite.

The lettering on the door read: DR. BALSAMO—HOURS BY APPOINTMENT, in both French and English. The name sounded familiar and vaguely phony but I did not stop to figure it out; I pushed on in.

The office inside was cluttered in a fashion known only to old French lawyers and pack rats. Behind the desk was a gnomelike character with a merry smile, hard eyes, the pinkest face and scalp I've ever seen, and a fringe of untidy white hair. He looked at me and giggled. "Welcome! So *you* are a hero?" Suddenly he whipped out a revolver half as long as he was and just as heavy and pointed it at me. You could have driven a Volkswagen down its snout.

"I'm not a hero," I said nastily. "I'm a coward. I just came here to find out what the joke is." I moved sideways while slapping that monstrous piece of ordnance the other way, chopped his wrist, and caught it. Then I handed it back to him. "Don't play with that thing, or I'll shove it up your deposition. I'm in a hurry. You're Doctor Balsamo? You ran that ad?"

"Tut, tut," he said, not at all annoyed. "Impetuous youth. No, Doctor Balsamo is in there." He pointed his eyebrows at two doors on the left wall, then pushed a bell button on his desk—the only thing in the room later than Napoleon. "Go in. She's expecting you."

" 'She'? Which door?"

"Ah, the Lady or the Tiger? Does it matter? In the long run? A hero will know. A coward will choose the wrong one, being sure that I lie. *Allez-y! Vite, vite! Schnell!* Get the lead out, Mac."

I snorted and jerked open the right-hand door.

The doctor was standing with her back to me at some apparatus against the far wall and she was wearing one of those white, high-collared jackets favored by medical men. On my left was a surgeon's examining table, on my right a Swedish-modern couch; there were stainless-steel and glass cabinets, and some framed certificates; the whole place was as up-to-date at the outer room was not.

As I closed the door she turned and looked at me and said quietly, "I am very glad that you have come." Then she smiled and said softly, "You are beautiful," and came into my arms.

IV

ABOUT a minute and forty seconds and several centuries later "Dr. Balsamo-Helen of Troy" pulled her mouth an inch back from mine and said, "Let me go, please, then undress and lie on the examining table."

I felt as if I had had nine hours of sleep, a needle shower, and three slugs of ice-cold akvavit on an empty stomach. Anything she wanted to do, I wanted to do. But the situation seemed to call for witty repartee. "Huh?" I said.

"Please. You are the one, but nevertheless I must examine you."

"Well . . . all right," I agreed. "You're the doctor," I added and started to unbutton my shirt. "You *are* a doctor? Of medicine, I mean."

"Yes. Among other things."

I kicked out of my shoes. "But why do you want to examine *me?*"

"For witches' marks, perhaps. Oh, I shan't find any,

I know. But I must search for other things, too. To protect you."

That table was cold against my skin. Why don't they pad those things? "Your name is Balsamo?"

"One of my names," she said absently while gentle fingers touched me here and there. "A family name, that is."

"Wait a minute. *Count Cagliostro!*"

"One of my uncles. Yes, he used that name. Though it isn't truly his, no more than Balsamo. Uncle Joseph is a very naughty man and quite untruthful." She touched an old, small scar. "Your appendix has been removed."

"Yes."

"Good. Let me see your teeth."

I opened wide. My face may not be much but I could rent my teeth to advertise Pepsodent. Presently she nodded. "Fluoride marks. Good. Now I must have your blood."

She could have bitten me in the neck for it and I wouldn't have minded. Nor been much surprised. But she did it the ordinary way, taking ten cc. from the vein inside my left elbow. She took the sample and put it in that apparatus against the wall. It chirred and whirred and she came back to me. "Listen, Princess," I said.

"I am not a princess."

"Well ... I don't know your first name, and you inferred that your last name isn't really 'Balsamo'—and I don't want to call you 'Doc.'" I certainly did not want to call her "Doc"—not the most beautiful girl I had ever seen or hoped to see ... not after a kiss that had wiped out of memory every other kiss I had ever received. No.

She considered it. "I have many names. What would you like to call me?"

"Is one of them 'Helen'?"

She smiled like sunshine and I learned that she had dimples. She looked sixteen and in her first party dress. "You are very gracious. No, she's not even a relative. That was many, many years ago." Her face turned thoughtful. "Would you like to call me 'Ettarre'?"

44

"Is that one of your names?"

"It is much like one of them, allowing for different spelling and accent. Or it could be 'Esther' just as closely. Or 'Aster.' Or even 'Estrellita.'"

"'Aster,'" I repeated. "Star. Lucky Star!"

"I hope that I will be your lucky star," she said earnestly. "As you will. But what shall I call you?"

I thought about it. I certainly was not going to dig up "Flash"—I am not a comic strip. The Army nickname I had held longest was entirely unfit to hand to a lady. At that I preferred it to my given name. My daddy had been proud of a couple of his ancestors—but is that any excuse for hanging "Evelyn Cyril" on a male child? It had forced me to learn to fight before I learned to read.

The name I had picked up in the hospital ward would do. I shrugged. "Oh, Scar is a good enough name."

"'Oscar,'" she repeated, broadening the "O" into "Aw," and stressing both syllables. "A noble name. A hero's name. Oscar." She caressed it with her voice.

"No, no! Not 'Oscar'—'Scar.' 'Scarface.' For this."

"Oscar is your name," she said firmly. "Oscar and Aster. Scar and Star." She barely touched the scar. "Do you dislike your hero's mark? Shall I remove it?"

"Eh? Oh, no, I'm used to it now. It lets me know who it is when I see myself in a mirror."

"Good. I like it, you wore it when I first saw you. But if you change your mind, let me know." The gear against the wall went *whush, chunk!* She turned and took a long strip from it, then whistled softly while she studied it.

"This won't take long," she said cheerfully and wheeled the apparatus over to the table. "Hold still while the protector is connected with you, quite still and breathe shallowly." She made half a dozen connections of tubes to me; they stuck where she placed them. She put over her head what I thought was a fancy stethoscope but after she got it on, it covered her eyes.

She chuckled. "You're pretty inside, too, Oscar. No,

45

don't talk." She kept one hand on my forearm and I waited.

Five minutes later she lifted her hand and stripped off the connections. "That's all," she said cheerfully. "No more colds for you, my hero, and you won't be bothered again by that flux you picked up in the jungle. Now we move to the other room."

I got off the table and grabbed at my clothes. Star said, "You won't need them where we are going. Full kit and weapons will be provided."

I stopped with shoes in one hand and drawers in the other. "Star—"

"Yes, Oscar?"

"What is this all about? Did you run that ad? Was it meant for *me*? Did you really want to hire me for something?"

She took a deep breath and said soberly, "I advertised. It was meant for you and you only. Yes, there is a job to do . . . as my champion. There will be great adventure . . . and greater treasure . . . and even greater danger —and I fear very much that neither one of us will live through it." She looked me in the eyes. "Well, sir?"

I wondered how long they had had me in the locked ward. But I didn't tell her so, because, if that was where I was, she wasn't there at all. And I wanted her to be there, more than I had ever wanted anything. I said, "Princess . . . you've hired yourself a boy."

She caught her breath. "Come quickly. Time is short." She led me through a door beyond the Swedish-modern couch, unbuttoning her jacket, unzipping her skirt, as she went, and letting garments fall anywhere. Almost at once she was as I had first seen her at the *plage*.

This room had dark walls and no windows and a soft light from nowhere. There were two low couches side by side, black they were and looking like biers, and no other furniture. As soon as the door was closed behind us I was suddenly aware that the room was achingly, painfully anechoic; the bare walls gave back no sound.

The couches were in the center of a circle which was part of a large design, in chalk, or white paint, on bare floor. We entered the pattern; she turned and squatted down and completed one line, closing it—and it was true; she was unable to be awkward, even hunkered down, even with her breasts drooping as she leaned over.

"What is it?" I asked.

"A map to take us where we are going."

"It looks more like a pentagram."

She shrugged. "All right, it is a pentacle of power. A schematic circuit diagram would be a better tag. But, my hero, I can't stop to explain it. Lie down, please, at once."

I took the right-hand couch as she signed me, but I couldn't let it be. "Star, are you a witch?"

"If you like. Please, no talking now." She lay down, stretched out her hand. "And join hands with me, my lord; it is necessary."

Her hand was soft and warm and very strong. Presently the light faded to red, then died away. I slept.

V

I WOKE to singing birds.

Her hand was still in mine. I turned my head and she smiled at me. "Good morning, my lord."

"Good morning, Princess." I glanced around. We were still lying on those black couches but they were outdoors, in a grassy dell, a clearing in trees beside a softly chuckling stream—a place so casually beautiful that it looked as if it had been put together leaf by leaf by old and unhurried Japanese gardeners.

Warm sunshine splashed through leaves and dappled her golden body. I glanced up at the sun and back at her. "Is it morning?" It had been noonish or later and that sun ought to be—seemed to be—setting, not rising—

"It is again morning, here."

Suddenly my bump of direction spun like a top and I felt dizzy. Disoriented—a feeling new to me and very unpleasant. I couldn't find north.

Then things steadied down. North was *that* way, upstream—and the sun was rising, maybe nine in the morn-

48

ing, and would pass across the *north* sky. Southern Hemisphere. No sweat.

No trick at all—Just give the kook a shot of dope while examining him, lug him aboard a 707 and jet him to New Zealand, replenishing the Mickey Finn as needed. Wake him up when you want him.

Only I didn't say this and never did think it. And it wasn't true.

She sat up. "Are you hungry?"

I suddenly realized that an omelette some hours ago— how many?—was not enough for a growing boy. I sat up and swung my feet to the grass. "I could eat a horse."

She grinned. "The shop of La Société Anonyme de Hippophage is closed I'm afraid. Will you settle for trout? We must wait a bit, so we might as well eat. And don't worry, this place is defended."

" 'Defended'?"

"Safe."

"All right. Uh, how about a rod and hooks?"

"I'll show you." What she showed me was not fishing tackle but how to tickle fish. But I knew how. We waded into that lovely stream, just pleasantly cool, moving as quietly as possible, and picked a place under a bulging rock, a place where trout like to gather and think—the fishy equivalent of a gentlemen's club.

You tickle trout by gaining their confidence and then abusing it. In about two minutes I got one, between two and three pounds, and tossed it onto the bank, and Star had one almost as large. "How much can you eat?" she asked.

"Climb out and get dry," I said. "I'll get another one."

"Make it two or three," she amended. "Rufo will be along." She waded quietly out.

"Who?"

"Your groom."

I didn't argue. I was ready to believe seven impossible things before breakfast, so I went on catching breakfast. I let it go with two more as the last was

49

the biggest trout I've ever seen. Those beggars fairly queued up to be grabbed.

By then Star had a fire going and was cleaning fish with a sharp rock. Shucks, any Girl Scout or witch can make fire without matches. I could myself, given several hours and plenty of luck, just by rubbing two dry clichés together. But I noticed that the two short biers were gone. Well, I hadn't ordered them. I squatted down and took over cleaning the trout.

Star came back shortly with fruits that were applelike but deep purple in color and with quantities of button mushrooms. She was carrying the plunder on a broad leaf, like canna or ti, only bigger. More like banana leaves.

My mouth started to water. "If only we had salt!"

"I'll fetch it. It will be rather gritty, I'm afraid."

Star broiled the fish two ways, over the fire on a forked green stick, and on hot flat limestone where the fire had been—she kept brushing the fire along as she fed it and placed fish and mushrooms sizzling where it had been. That way was best, I thought. Little fine grasses turned out to be chives, local style, and tiny clover tasted and looked like sheep sorrel. That, with the salt (which was gritty and coarse and may have been licked by animals before we got it—not that I cared) made the trout the best I've ever tasted. Well, weather and scenery and company had much to do with it, too, especially the company.

I was trying to think of a really poetic way of saying, "How about you and me shacking up right here for the next ten thousand years? Either legal or informal—are you married?" when we were interrupted. Which was a shame, for I had thought up some pretty language, all new, for the oldest and most practical suggestion in the world.

Old baldy, the gnome with the oversized six-shooter, was standing behind me and cursing.

I was sure it was cursing although the language was new to me. Star turned her head, spoke in quiet reproval in the same language, made room for him and offered him a trout. He took it and ate quite a bit of it before he said, in English, "Next time I won't pay him anything. You'll see."

"You shouldn't try to cheat him, Rufo. Have some mushrooms. Where's the baggage? I want to get dressed."

"Over there." He went back to wolfing fish. Rufo was proof that some people should wear clothes. He was pink all over and somewhat potbellied. However, he was amazingly well muscled, which I had never suspected, else I would have been more cautious about taking that cannon away from him. I decided that if he wanted to Indianwrestle, I would cheat.

He glanced at me past a pound and a half of trout and said, "Is it your wish to be outfitted now, my lord?"

"Huh? Finish your breakfast. And what's this 'my lord' routine? Last time I saw you you were waving a gun in my face."

"I'm sorry, my lord. But *She* said to do it...and what *She* says must be done. You understand."

"That suits me perfectly. Somebody has to drive. But call me 'Oscar.'"

Rufo glanced at Star, she nodded. He grinned. "Okay, Oscar. No hard feelings?"

"Not a bit."

He put down the fish, wiped his hand on his thigh, and stuck it out. "Swell! You knock 'em down, I'll stomp on 'em."

We shook hands and each of us tried for the knuckle-cracking grip. I think I got a little the better of it, but I decided he might have been a blacksmith at some time.

Star looked very pleased and showed dimples again. She had been lounging by the fire, looking like a hamadryad on her coffee break; now she suddenly reached out and placed her strong, slender hand over our clasped fists. "My stout friends," she said earnestly. "My good boys. Rufo, it will be well."

"You have a Sight?" he said eagerly.

"No, just a feeling. But I am no longer worried."

"We can't do a thing," Rufo said moodily, "until we deal with Igli."

"Oscar will dicker with Igli." Then she was on her feet in one smooth motion. "Stuff that fish in your face and unpack. I need clothes." She suddenly looked very eager.

Star was more different women than a platoon of WACs—which is only mildly a figure of speech. Right then she was every woman from Eve deciding between two fig leaves to a modern woman whose ambition is to be turned loose in Nieman-Marcus, naked with a checkbook. When I first met her, she had seemed rather a sobersides and no more interested in clothes than I was. I'd never had a chance to be interested in clothes. Being a member of the sloppy generation was a boon to my budget at college, where blue jeans were *au fait* and a dirty sweat shirt was stylish.

The second time I saw her she had been dressed, but in that lab smock and tailored skirt she had been both a professional woman and a warm friend. But today— this morning whenever that was—she was increasingly full of bubbles. She had delighted so in catching fish that she had had to smother squeals of glee. And she had then been the perfect Girl Scout, with soot smudged on her cheek and her hair pushed back out of hazard of the fire while she cooked.

Now she was the woman of all ages who just has to get her hands on new clothes. I felt that dressing Star was like putting a paint job on the crown jewels—but I was forced to admit that, if we were not to do the "Me Tarzan, you Jane" bit right in that dell from then on till death do us part, then clothes of some sort, if only to keep her perfect skin from getting scratched by brambles, were needed.

Rufo's baggage turned out to be a little black box about the size and shape of a portable typewriter. He opened it.

And opened it again.

And kept on opening it—

And kept right on unfolding its sides and letting them down until the durn thing was the size of a small moving van and even more packed. Since I was nicknamed

"Truthful James" as soon as I learned to talk and am widely known to have won the hatchet every February 22nd all through school, you must now conclude that I was the victim of an illusion caused by hypnosis and/or drugs.

Me, I'm not sure. Anyone who has studied math knows that the inside does not have to be smaller than the outside, in theory, and anyone who has had the doubtful privilege of seeing a fat woman get in or out of a tight girdle knows that this is true in practice, too. Rufo's baggage just carried the principle further.

The first thing he dragged out was a big teakwood chest. Star opened it and started pulling out filmy lovelies.

"Oscar, what do you think of this one?" She was holding a long, green dress against her with the skirt draped over one hip to display it. "Like it?"

Of course I liked it. If it was an original—and somehow I knew that Star never wore copies—I didn't want to think about what it must have cost. "It's a mighty pretty gown," I told her. "But—Look, are we going to be traveling?"

"Right away."

"I don't see any taxicabs. Aren't you likely to get that torn?"

"It doesn't tear. However, I didn't mean to wear it; I just meant to show it to you. Isn't it lovely? Shall I model it for you? Rufo, I want those high-heeled sandals with the emeralds."

Rufo answered in that language he had been cursing in when he arrived. Star shrugged and said, "Don't be impatient, Rufo; Igli will wait. Anyhow, we can't talk to Igli earlier than tomorrow morning; milord Oscar must learn the language first." But she put the green gorgeousness back in the chest.

"Now here is a little number," she went on, holding it up, "which is just plain naughty; it has no other purpose."

I could see why. It was mostly skirt, with a little bodice that supported without concealing—a style favored in ancient Crete, I hear, and still popular in the *Overseas Weekly, Playboy,* and many night clubs. A style that turns droopers into bulgers. Not that Star needed it.

Rufo tapped me on the shoulder. "Boss? Want to look over the ordnance and pick out what you need?"

Star said reprovingly, "Rufo, life is to be savored, not hurried."

"We'll have a lot more life to savor if Oscar picks out what he can use best."

"He won't need weapons until after we reach a settlement with Igli." But she didn't insist on showing more clothes and, while I enjoyed looking at Star, I like to check over weapons, too, especially when I might have to use them, as apparently the job called for.

While I had been watching Star's style show, Rufo had laid out a collection that looked like a cross between an army-surplus store and a museum—swords, pistols, a lance that must have been twenty feet long, a flame-thrower, two bazookas flanking a Tommy gun, brass knucks, a machete, grenades, bows and arrows, a misericorde—

"You didn't bring a slingshot," I said accusingly.

He looked smug. "Which kind do you like, Oscar? The forked sort? Or a real sling?"

"Sorry I mentioned it. I can't hit the floor with either sort." I picked up the Tommy chopper, checked that it was empty, started stripping it. It seemed almost new, just fired enough to let the moving parts work in. A Tommy isn't much more accurate than a pitched base-ball and hasn't much greater effective range. But it does have virtues—you hit a man with it, he goes down and stays down. It is short and not too heavy and has a lot of firepower for a short time. It is a bush weapon, or any other sort of close-quarters work.

But I like something with a bayonet on the end, in case the party gets intimate—and I like that something to be accurate at long range in case the neighbors get un-friendly from a distance. I put it down and picked up a Springfield—Rock Island Arsenal, as I saw by its serial number, but still a Springfield. I feel the way about a Springfield that I do about a Gooney Bird; some pieces of machinery are ultimate perfection of their sort, the only possible improvement is a radical change in design.

I opened the bolt, stuck my thumbnail in the chamber, looked down the muzzle. The barrel was bright and the lands were unworn—and the muzzle had that tiny star on it; it was a match weapon!

"Rufo, what sort of country will we be going through? Like this around us?"

"Today, yes. But—" He apologetically took the rifle out of my hands. "It is forbidden to use firearms here. Swords, knives, arrows—anything that cuts or stabs or mauls by your own muscle power. No guns."

"Who says so?"

He shivered. "Better ask *Her*."

"If we can't use them, why bring them? And I don't see any ammunition around anyhow."

"Plenty of ammunition. Later on we will be at—another place—where guns may be used. If we live that long. I was just showing you what we have. What do you like of the lawful weapons? Are you a bowman?"

"I don't know. Show me how."

He started to say something, then shrugged and selected a bow, slipped a leather guard over his left forearm, picked out an arrow. "That tree," he said, "the one with the white rock at the foot of it. I'll try for about as high off the ground as a man's heart."

He nocked the shaft, raised and bent and let fly, all in one smooth motion.

The arrow quivered in the tree trunk about four feet off the ground.

Rufo grinned. "Care to match that?"

I didn't answer. I knew I could not, except by accident. I had once owned a bow, a birthday present. I hadn't hit much with it and soon the arrows were lost. Nevertheless I made a production out of selecting a bow, and picked the longest and heaviest.

Rufo cleared his throat apologetically. "If I may make a suggestion, that one will pull quite hard—for a beginner."

I strung it. "Find me a leather."

The leather slipped on as if it had been made for me and perhaps it had. I picked an arrow to match, barely looked at it as they all seemed straight and true. I didn't have any hope of hitting that bloody tree; it was fifty yards away and not over a foot thick. I simply intended to sight a bit high up on the trunk and hope that so heavy a bow would give me a flattish trajectory. Mostly I wanted to nock, bend, and loose all in one motion as Rufo had done—to *look* like Robin Hood even though I was not.

But as I raised and bent that bow and felt the power of it, I felt a surge of exultance—this tool was right for me! We fitted.

I let fly without thinking.

My shaft thudded a hand's breadth from his.

"Well shot!" Star called out.

Rufo looked at the tree and blinked, then looked reproachfully at Star. She looked haughtily back. "I did not," she stated. "You know I would not do that. It was a fair trial ... and a credit to you both."

Rufo looked thoughtfully at me. "Hmm— Would you care to make a small bet—you name the odds—that you can do that again?"

"I won't bet," I said. "I'm chicken." But I picked up another arrow and nocked it. I liked that bow, I even liked the way the string whanged at the guard on my forearm; I wanted to try it, feel married to it, again.

I loosed it.

The third arrow grew out of a spot between the first two, but closer to his. "Nice bow," I said. "I'll keep it. Fetch the shafts."

Rufo trotted away without speaking. I unstrung the bow, then started looking over the cutlery. I hoped that I would never again have to shoot an arrow; a gambler can't expect to draw a pat hand every deal—my next shot would likely turn around like a boomerang.

There was too much wealth of edges and points, from a two-handed broadsword suitable for chopping down trees to a little dagger meant for a lady's stocking. But

I picked up and balanced them all...and found there the blade that suited me the way Excalibur suited Arthur.

I've never seen one quite like it so I don't know what to call it. A saber, I suppose, as the blade was faintly curved and razor sharp on the edge and sharp rather far back on the back. But it had a point as deadly as a rapier and the curve was not enough to keep it from being used for thrust and counter quite as well as chopping away meat-axe style. The guard was a bell curved back around the knuckles into a semi-basket but cut away enough to permit full moulinet from any guard.

It balanced in the forte less than two inches from the guard, yet the blade was heavy enough to chop bone. It was the sort of sword that feels as if it were an extension of your body.

The grip was honest sharkskin, molded to my hand. There was a motto chased onto the blade but it was so buried in curlicues that I did not take time to study it out. This girl was mine, we fitted! I returned it and buckled belt and scabbard to my bare waist, wanting the touch of it and feeling like Captain John Carter, Jeddak of Jeddaks, and the Gascon and his three friends all in one.

"Will you not dress, milord Oscar?" Star asked.

"Eh? Oh, certainly—I was just trying it on for size. But— Did Rufo fetch my clothes?"

"Did you, Rufo?"

"His clothes? He wouldn't want those things he was wearing in Nice!"

"What's wrong with wearing Lederhosen with an aloha shirt?" I demanded.

"What? Oh, nothing at all, milord Oscar," Rufo answered hastily. "Live and let live I always say. I knew a man once who wore—never mind. Let me show you what I fetched for you."

I had my choice of everything from a plastic raincoat to full armor. I found the latter depressing because its presence implied that it might be needed. Except for an Army helmet I had never worn armor, didn't want to, didn't know how—and didn't care to mix with rude company that made such protection desirable.

Besides, I didn't see a horse around, say a Percheron or a Clydesdale, and I couldn't see myself hiking in one of those tin suits. I'd be slow as crutches, noisy as a subway, and hot as a phone booth. Sweat off ten pounds in five miles. The quilted longjohns that go under that ironmongery would have been too much alone for such beautiful weather; steel on top would turn me into a walking oven and leave me too weak and clumsy to fight my way out of a traffic ticket.

"Star, you said that—" I stopped. She had finished dressing and hadn't overdone it. Soft leather hiking shoes —buskins really—brown tights, and a short green upper garment halfway between a jacket and a skating dress. This was topped by a perky little hat and the whole costume made her look like a musical comedy version of an airline hostess, smart, cute, wholesome, and sexy.

Or maybe Maid Marian, as she had added a double-curve bow about half the size of mine, a quiver, and a dagger. "You," I said, "look like why the riot started."

She dimpled and curtsied. (Star never pretended. She knew she was female, she knew she looked good, she liked it that way.) "You said something earlier," I continued, "about my not needing weapons just yet. Is there any reason why I should wear one of these space suits. They don't look comfortable."

"I don't expect any great danger today," she said slowly. "But this is not a place where one can call the police. You must decide what you need."

"But— Damn it, Princess, you know this place and I don't. I need advice."

She didn't answer. I turned to Rufo. He was carefully studying a treetop. I said, "Rufo, get dressed."

He raised his eyebrows. "Milord Oscar?"

"Schnell! *Vite, vite!* Get the lead out."

"Okay." He dressed quickly, in an outfit that was a man's version of what Star had selected, with shorts instead of tights.

"Arm yourself," I said, and started to dress the same

way, except that I intended to wear field boots. However, there was a pair of those buskins that appeared to be my size, so I tried them on. They snuggled to my feet like gloves and, anyway, my soles were so hardened by a month barefooted on l'Île du Levant that I didn't need heavy boots.

They were not as medieval as they looked; they zipped up the front and were marked inside *Fabriqué en France*.

Pops Rufo had taken the bow he had used before, selected a sword, and had added a dagger. Instead of a dagger I picked out a Solingen hunting knife. I looked longingly at a service .45, but didn't touch it. If "they," whoever they were, had a local Sullivan Act, I would go along with the gag.

Star told Rufo to pack, then squatted down with me at a sandy place by the stream and drew a sketch map—route south, dropping downgrade and following the stream except for short cuts, until we reached the Singing Waters. There we would camp for the night.

I got it in my head. "Okay. Anything to warn me about? Do we shoot first? Or wait for them to bomb us?"

"Nothing that I expect, today. Oh, there's a carnivore about three times the size of a lion. But it is a great coward; it won't attack a moving man."

"A fellow after my own heart. All right, we'll keep moving."

"If we do see human beings—I don't expect it—it might be well to nock a shaft ... but not raise your bow until you feel it is necessary. But I'm not telling you what to do, Oscar; you must decide. Nor will Rufo let fly unless he sees you about to do so."

Rufo had finished packing. "Okay, let's go," I said. We set out. Rufo's little black box was now rigged as a knapsack and I did not stop to wonder how he could carry a couple of tons on his shoulders. An anti-grav device like Buck Rogers, maybe. Chinese coolie blood. Black magic. Hell, that teakwood chest alone could not have fitted into that backpack by a factor of 30 to 1, not to mention the arsenal and assorted oddments.

There is no reason to wonder why I didn't quiz Star

as to where we were, why we were there, how we had got there, what we were going to do, and the details of these dangers I was expected to face. Look, Mac, when you are having the most gorgeous dream of your life and just getting to the point, do you stop to tell yourself that it is logically impossible for that particular babe to be in the hay with you—and thereby wake yourself up? I *knew*, logically, that everything that had happened since I read that silly ad had been impossible.

So I chucked logic.

Logic is a feeble reed, friend. "Logic" proved that airplanes can't fly and that H-bombs won't work and that stones don't fall out of the sky. Logic is a way of saying that anything which didn't happen yesterday won't happen tomorrow.

I liked the situation. I didn't want to wake up, whether in bed, or in a headshrinker ward. Most especially I did not want to wake up still back in that jungle, maybe with that face wound still fresh and no helicopter. Maybe little brown brother had done a full job on me and sent me to Valhalla. Okay, I liked Valhalla.

I was swinging along with a sweet sword knocking against my thigh and a much sweeter girl matching my strides and a slave-serf-groom-something sweating along behind us, doing the carrying and being our "eyes-be-hind." Birds were singing and the landscape had been planned by master landscape architects and the air smelled sweet and good. If I never dodged a taxi nor read a headline again, that suited me.

That longbow was a nuisance—but so is an M-1. Star had her little bow slung, shoulder to hip. I tried that, but it tended to catch on things. Also, it made me nervous not to have it ready since she had admitted a chance of needing it. So I unslung it and carried it in my left hand, strung and ready.

We had one alarum on the morning hike. I heard Rufo's bowstring go *thwung!*—and I whirled and had my own bow ready, arrow nocked, before I saw what was up.

Or down, rather. A bird like a dusky grouse but larger.

Rufo had picked it off a branch, right through the neck. I made note not to compete with him again in archery, and to get him to coach me in the fine points.

He smacked his lips and grinned. "Supper!" For the next mile he plucked it as we walked, then hung it from his belt.

We stopped for lunch one o'clockish at a picnic spot that Star assured me was defended, and Rufo opened his box to suitcase size, and served us lunch: cold cuts, crumbly Provençal cheese, crusty French bread, pears, and two bottles of Chablis. After lunch Star suggested a siesta. The idea was appealing; I had eaten heartily and shared only crumbs with the birds, but I was surprised. "Shouldn't we push on?"

"You must have a language lesson, Oscar."

I must tell them at Ponce de Leon High School the better way to study languages. You lie down on soft grass near a chuckling stream on a perfect day, and the most beautiful woman in any world bends over you and looks you in the eyes. She starts speaking softly in a language you do not understand.

After a bit her big eyes get bigger and bigger ... and bigger ... and you sink into them.

Then, a long time later, Rufo says, *"Erbas, Oscar, 't knila voorsht."*

"Okay," I answered, "I *am* getting up. Don't rush me."

That is the last word I am going to set down in a language that doesn't fit our alphabet. I had several more lessons, and won't mention them either, and from then on we spoke this lingo, except when I was forced to span gaps by asking in English. It is a language rich in profanity and in words for making love, and richer than English in some technical subjects—but with surprising holes in it. There is no word for "lawyer" for example.

About an hour before sundown we came to the Singing Waters.

We had been traveling over a high, wooded plateau. The brook where we had caught the trout had been joined by other streams and was now a big creek. Below us, at a place we hadn't reached yet, it would plunge over high cliffs in a super-Yosemite fall. But here, where we stopped to camp, the water had cut a notch into the plateau, forming cascades, before it took that dive.

"Cascades" is a weak word. Upstream, downstream, everywhere you looked, you saw waterfalls—big ones thirty or fifty feet high, little ones a mouse could have jumped up, every size in between. Terraces and staircases of them there were, smooth water green from rich foliage overhead and water white as whipped cream as it splashed into dense foam.

And you heard them. Tiny falls tinkled in silvery soprano, big falls rumbled in basso profundo. On the grassy alp where we camped it was an everpresent chorale; in the middle of the falls you had to shout to make yourself heard.

Coleridge was there in one of his dope dreams:

And here were forests ancient as the hills,
Enfolding sunny spots of greenery.
But oh! that deep romantic chasm which slanted
Down the green hill athwart a cedarn cover
A savage place! as holy and enchanted
As e'er beneath a waning moon was haunted
By woman wailing for her demon-lover!
And from this chasm, with ceaseless turmoil seething—

Coleridge must have followed that route and reached the Singing Waters. No wonder he felt like killing that "person from Porlock" who broke in on his best dream. When I am dying, lay me beside the Singing Waters and let them be the last I hear and see.

We stopped on a lawn terrace, flat as a promise and soft as a kiss, and I helped Rufo unpack. I wanted to learn how he did that trick with the box. I didn't find out. Each side opened as naturally and reasonably as opening up an ironing board—and then when it opened again that was natural and reasonable, too.

First we pitched a tent for Star—no army-surplus job, this; it was a dainty pavilion of embroidered silk and the

62

rug we spread as a floor must have used up three generations of Bukhara artists. Rufo said to me, "Do you want a tent, Oscar?"

I looked up at the sky and over at the not-yet-setting sun. The air was milk warm and I couldn't believe that it would rain. I don't like to be in a tent if there is the least chance of surprise attack. "Are you going to use a tent?"

"Me? Oh, no! But *She* has to have a tent, always. Then, more likely than not, *She'll* decide to sleep out on the grass."

"I won't need a tent." (Let's see, does a "champion" sleep across the door of his lady's chamber, weapons at hand? I wasn't sure about the etiquette of such things; they were never mentioned in "Social Studies.")

She returned then and said to Rufo, "Defended. The wards were all in place."

"Recharged?" he fretted.

She tweaked his ear. "I am not senile." She added, "Soap, Rufo. And come along, Oscar; that's Rufo's work."

Rufo dug a cake of Lux out of that caravan load and gave it to her, then looked at me thoughtfully and handed me a bar of Life Buoy.

The Singing Waters are the best bath ever, in endless variety. Still pools from footbath size to plunges you could swim in, sitz baths that tingled your skin, shower baths from just a trickle up to free-springing jets that would beat your brains in if you stood under them too long.

And you could pick your temperature. Above the cascade we used, a hot spring added itself to the main stream and at the base of this cascade a hidden spring welled out icy cold. No need to fool with taps, just move one way or the other for the temperature you like— or move downstream where it evened out to temperature as gently warm as a mother's kiss.

We played for a while, with Star squealing and giggling when I splashed her, and answering it by ducking me. We both acted like kids; I felt like one, she looked like one, and she played rough, with muscles of steel under velvet.

Presently I fetched the soap and we scrubbed. When she started shampooing her hair, I came up behind her and helped. She let me, she needed help with the lavish mop, six times as much as most gals bother with these days.

That would have been a wonderful time (with Rufo busy and out of the way) to grab her and hug her, then proceed ruggedly to other matters. Nor am I sure that she would have made even a token protest; she might have cooperated heartily.

Hell, I *know* she would not have made a "token" protest. She would either have put me in my place with a cold word or a clout in the ear—or cooperated.

I couldn't do it. I couldn't even *start*.

I don't know why. My intentions toward Star had oscillated from dishonorable to honorable and back again, but had always been practical from the moment I laid eyes on her. No, let me put it this way: My intentions were strictly dishonorable always, but with utter willingness to convert them to honorable, later, as soon as we could dig up a justice of the peace.

Yet I found I couldn't lay a finger on her other than to help her scrub the soap out of her hair.

While I was puzzling over this, both hands buried in heavy blond hair and wondering what was stopping me from putting my arms around that slender-strong waist only inches away from me, I heard a piercing whistle and my name—my new name. I looked around.

Rufo, dressed in his unlovely skin and with towels over his shoulder, was standing on the bank ten feet away and trying to cut through the roar of water to get my attention.

I moved a few feet toward him. "How's that again?" I didn't quite snarl.

"I said, 'Do you want a shave?' Or are you growing a beard?"

I had been uneasily aware of my face cactus while I was debating whether or not to attempt criminal assault,

64

and that unease had helped to stop me—Gillette, Aqua Velva, Burma Shave, et al., have made the browbeaten American male, namely me, timid about attempting seduction and/or rape unless freshly planed off. And I had a two-day growth.

"I don't have a razor," I called back.

He answered by holding up a straight razor.

Star moved up beside me. She reached up and tried my chin between thumb and forefinger. "You would be majestic in a beard," she said. "Perhaps a Van Dyke, with sneering mustachios."

I thought so too, if she thought so. Besides, it would cover most of that scar. "Whatever you say, Princess."

"But I would rather that you stayed as I first saw you. Rufo is a good barber." She turned toward him. "A hand, Rufo. And my towel."

Star walked back toward the camp, toweling herself dry—I would have been glad to help, if asked. Rufo said tiredly, "Why didn't you assert yourself? But *She* says to shave you, so now I've got to—and rush through my own bath, too, so *She* won't be kept waiting."

"If you've got a mirror, I'll do it myself."

"Ever used a straight razor?"

"No, but I can learn."

"You'd cut your throat, and *She* wouldn't like that. Over here on the bank where I can stand in the warm water. No, no! Don't sit on it, lie down with your head at the edge. I can't shave a man who's sitting up.".He started working lather into my chin.

"You know why? I learned how on corpses, that's why, making them pretty so that their loved ones would be proud of them. Hold still! You almost lost an ear. I like to shave corpses; they can't complain, they don't make suggestions, they don't talk back—and they always hold still. Best job I ever had. But now you take this job—" He stopped with the blade against my Adam's apple and started counting his troubles.

"Do I get Saturday off? Hell, I don't even get Sunday off! And look at the hours! Why, I read just the other

65

day that some outfit in New York— You've been in New York?"

"I've been in New York. And get that guillotine away from my neck while you're waving your hands like that."

"You keep talking, you're bound to get a little nick now and then. This outfit signed a contract for a twenty-five-hour week. *Week!* I'd like to settle for a twenty-five hour *day.* You know how long I've been on the go, right this minute?"

I said I didn't.

"There, you talked again. More than seventy hours or I'm a liar! And for what? Glory? Is there glory in a little heap of whitened bones? Wealth? Oscar, I'm telling you the truth; I've laid out more corpses than a sultan has concubines and never a one of them cared a soggy pretzel whether they were bedecked in rubies the size of your nose and twice as red . . . or rags. What use is wealth to a dead man? Tell me, Oscar, man to man while *She* can't hear: Why did you ever let *Her* talk you into this?"

"I'm enjoying it, so far."

He sniffed. "That's what the man said as he passed the fiftieth floor of the Empire State Building. But the sidewalk was waiting for him, just the same. However," he added darkly, "until you settle with Igli, it's not a problem. If I had my kit, I could cover that scar so perfectly that everybody would say, 'Doesn't he look natural?' "

"Never mind. *She* likes that scar." (Damn it, he had *me* doing it!)

"She would. What I'm trying to get over is, if you walk the Glory Road, you are certain to find mostly rocks. But I never chose to walk it. My idea of a nice way to live would be a quiet little parlor, the only one in town, with a selection of caskets, all prices, and a markup that allowed a little leeway to show generosity to the bereaved. Installment plans for those with the foresight to do their planning in advance—for we all have to die, Oscar, we all have to die, and a sensible man might as well sit down over a friendly glass of beer

66

and make his plans with a well-established firm he can trust."

He leaned confidentially over me. "Look, milord Oscar ... if by any miracle we get through this alive, you could put in a good word for me with *Her*. Make *Her* see that I'm too old for the Glory Road. I can do a lot to make your remaining days comfortable and pleasant ... if your intentions toward me are comradely."

"Didn't we shake on it?"

"Ah, yes, so we did." He sighed. "One for all and all for one, and Pikes Peak or Bust. You're done."

It was still light and Star was in her tent when we got back—and my clothes were laid out. I started to object when I saw them but Rufo said firmly, "*She* said 'informal' and that means black tie."

I managed everything, even the studs (which were amazing big black pearls), and that tuxedo either had been tailored for me or it had been bought off the rack by someone who knew my height, weight, shoulders, and waist. The label inside the jacket read *The English House, Copenhagen*.

But the tie whipped me. Rufo showed up while I was struggling with it, had me lie down (I didn't ask why) and tied it in a jiffy. "Do you want your watch, Oscar?"

"My watch?" So far as I knew it was in a doctor's examining room in Nice. "You have it?"

"Yes, sir. I fetched everything of yours but your"— he shuddered—"clothes."

He was not exaggerating. Everything was there, not only the contents of my pockets but the contents of my American Express deposit box: cash, passport, I.D., et cetera, even those Change Alley Sweepstakes tickets.

I started to ask how he had gotten into my lockbox but decided not to. He had had the key and it might have been something as simple as a fake letter of authority. Or as complex as his magical black box. I thanked him and he went back to his cooking.

I started to throw that stuff away, all but cash and passport. But one can't be a litterbug in a place as beautiful as the Singing Waters. My sword belt had a leather

67

pouch on it; I stuffed it in there, even the watch, which had stopped.

Rufo had set up a table in front of Star's dainty tent and rigged a light from a tree over it and set candles on the table. It was dark before she came out . . . and waited. I finally realized that she was waiting for my arm. I led her to her place and seated her and Rufo seated me. He was dressed in a plum-colored footman's uniform.

The wait for Star had been worth it; she was dressed in the green gown she had offered to model for me earlier. I still don't *know* that she used cosmetics but she looked not at all like the lusty Undine who had been ducking me an hour earlier. She looked as if she should be kept under glass. She looked like Liza Doolittle at the Ball.

"Dinner in Rio" started to play, blending with the Singing Waters.

White wine with fish, rose wine with fowl, red wine with roast—Star chatted and smiled and was witty. Once Rufo, while bending over to me to serve, whispered, "The condemned ate heartily." I told him to go to hell out of the corner of my mouth.

Champagne with the sweet and Rufo solemnly presented the bottle for my approval. I nodded. What would he have done if I had turned it down? Offered another vintage? Napolean with coffee. And cigarettes.

I had been thinking about cigarettes all day. These were Benson & Hedges No. 5 . . . and I had been smoking those black French things to save money.

While we were smoking, Star congratulated Rufo on the dinner and he accepted her compliments gravely and I seconded them. I still don't know who cooked that hedonistic meal. Rufo did much of it but Star may have done the hard parts while I was being shaved.

After an unhurried happy time, sitting over coffee and brandy with the overhead light doused and only a single candle gleaming on her jewels and lighting her face, Star made a slight movement back from the table and I got up quickly and showed her to her tent. She stopped at its entrance. "Milord Oscar—"

So I kissed her and followed her in—

Like hell I did! I was so damned hypnotized that I bowed over her hand and kissed it. And that was that.

That left me with nothing to do but get out of that borrowed monkey suit, hand it back to Rufo, and get a blanket from him. He had picked a spot to sleep at one side of her tent, so I picked one on the other and stretched out. It was still so pleasantly warm that even one blanket wasn't needed.

But I didn't go to sleep. The truth is, I've got a monkey on my back, a habit worse than marijuana though not as expensive as heroin. I can stiff it out and get to sleep anyway—but it wasn't helping that I could see light in Star's tent and a silhouette that was no longer troubled by a dress.

The fact is I am a compulsive reader. Thirty-five cents' worth of Gold Medal Original will put me right to sleep. Or Perry Mason. But I'll read the ads in an old *Paris-Match* that has been used to wrap herring before I'll do without.

I got up and went around the tent. "*Psst!* Rufo."

"Yes, milord." He was up fast, a dagger in his hand.

"Look, is there anything to read around this dump?"

"What sort of thing?"

"Anything, just anything. Words in a row."

"Just a moment." He was gone a while, using a flashlight around that beachhead dump of plunder. He came back and offered me a book and a small camp lamp. I thanked him, went back, and lay down.

It was an interesting book, written by Albertus Magnus and apparently stolen from the British Museum. Albert offered a long list of recipes for doing unlikely things: how to pacify storms and fly over clouds, how to overcome enemies, how to make a woman be true to you—

Here's that last one: "If thou wilt that a woman bee not visious nor desire men, take the private members of a Woolfe, and the haires which doe grow on the cheekes, or the eye-brows of him, and the hairs which bee under his beard, and burne it all, and give it to her. to drinke.

69

when she knowethe not, and she shal desire no other man."

This should annoy the "Woolfe." And if I were the gal, it would annoy me, too; it sounds like a nauseous mixture. But that's the exact formula, spelling and all, so if you are having trouble keeping her in line and have a "Woolfe" handy, try it. Let me know the results. By mail, not in person.

There were several recipes for making a woman love you who does not but a "Woolfe" was by far the simplest ingredient. Presently I put the book down and the light out and watched the moving silhouette on that translucent silk. Star was brushing her hair.

Then I quit tormenting myself and watched the stars. I've never learned the stars of the Southern Hemisphere; you seldom see stars in a place as wet as Southeast Asia and a man with a bump of direction doesn't need them.

But that southern sky was gorgeous.

I was staring at one very bright star or planet (it seemed to have a disk) when suddenly I realized it was moving.

I sat up. "Hey! Star!"

She called back, "Yes, Oscar?"

"Come see! A sputnik. A *big* one!"

"Coming." The light in her tent went out, she joined me quickly, and so did good old Pops Rufo, yawning and scratching his ribs. "Where, milord?" Star asked.

I pointed. "Right there! On second thought it may not be a sputnik; it might be one of our Echo series. It's awfully big and bright."

She glanced at me and looked away. Rufo said nothing. I stared at it a while longer, glanced at her. She was watching me, not it. I looked again, watched it move against the backdrop of stars.

"Star," I said, "that's not a sputnik. Nor an Echo balloon. That's a moon. A real moon."

"Yes, milord Oscar."

"Then this is not Earth."

"That is true."

70

"Hmm—" I looked back at the little moon, moving so fast among the stars, west to east.

Star said quietly, "You are not afraid, my hero?"

"Of what?"

"Of being in a strange world."

"Seems to be a pretty nice world."

"It is," she agreed, "in many ways."

"I like it," I agreed. "But maybe it's time I knew more about it. Where are we? How many light-years, or whatever it is, in what direction?"

She sighed. "I will try, milord. But it will not be easy; you have not studied metaphysical geometry—nor many other things. Think of the pages of a book—" I still had that cookbook of Albert the Great under my arm; she took it. "One page may resemble another very much. Or be very different. One page can be so close to another that it touches, at all points—yet have nothing to do with the page against it. We are as close to Earth—right now—as two pages in sequence in a book. And yet we are so far away that light-years cannot express it."

"Look," I said, "no need to get fancy about it. I used to watch 'Twilight Zone.' You mean another dimension. I dig it."

She looked troubled. "That's somewhat the idea but—"

Rufo interrupted. "There's still Igli in the morning."

"Yes," I agreed. "If we have to talk to Igli in the morning, maybe we need some sleep. I'm sorry. By the way, who *is* Igli?"

"You'll find out," said Rufo.

I looked up at that hurtling moon. "No doubt. Well, I'm sorry I disturbed you all with a silly mistake. Good night, folks."

So I crawled back into my sleeping silks, like a proper hero (all muscles and no gonads, usually), and they sacked in too. She didn't put the light back on, so I had nothing to look at but the hurtling moons of Barsoom. I had fallen into a book.

Well, I hoped it was a success and that the writer would keep me alive for lots of sequels. It was a pretty nice deal for the hero, up to this chapter at least. There was Dejah Thoris, curled up in her sleeping silks not twenty feet away.

I thought seriously of creeping up to the flap of her tent and whispering to her that I wanted to ask a few questions about metaphysical geometry and like matters. Love spells, maybe. Or maybe just tell her that it was cold outside and could I come in?

But I didn't. Good old faithful Rufo was curled up just the other side of that tent and he had a disconcerting habit of coming awake fast with a dagger in his hand. *And* he liked to shave corpses. As I've said, given a choice, I'm chicken.

I watched the hurtling moons of Barsoom and fell asleep.

VI

SINGING birds are better than alarm clocks and Barsoom was never like this. I stretched happily and smelled coffee and wondered if there was time for a dip before breakfast. It was another perfect day, blue and clear and the sun just up, and I felt like killing dragons before lunch. Small ones, that is.

I smothered a yawn and rolled to my feet. The lovely pavilion was gone and the black box mostly repacked; it was no bigger than a piano box. Star was kneeling before a fire, encouraging that coffee. She was a cavewoman this morning, dressed in a hide that was fancy but not as fancy as her own. From an ocelot, maybe. Or from du Pont.

"Howdy, Princess," I said. "What's for breakfast? And where's your chef?"

"Breakfast later," she said. "Just a cup of coffee for you now, too hot and too black—best you be bad tempered. Rufo is starting the talk with Igli." She served it to me in a paper cup.

I drank half a cup, burned my mouth and spat out grounds. Coffee comes in five descending stages: Coffee, Java, Jamoke, Joe, and Carbon Remover. This stuff was no better than grade four.

I stopped then, having caught sight of Rufo. And

company, lots of company. Along the edge of our terrace somebody had unloaded Noah's Ark. There was everything there from aardvarks to zebus, most of them with long yellow teeth.

Rufo was facing this picket line, ten feet this side and opposite a particularly large and uncouth citizen. About then that paper cup came apart and scalded my fingers.

"Want some more?" Star asked.

I blew on my fingers. "No, thanks. *This* is Igli?"

"Just the one in the middle that Rufo is baiting. The rest have come to see the fun, you can ignore them."

"Some of them look hungry."

"Most of the big ones are like Cuvier's devil, herbivorous. Those outsized lions would eat us—if Igli wins the argument. But only then. Igli is the problem."

I looked Igli over more carefully. He resembled that scion of the man from Dundee, all chin and no forehead, and he combined the less appetizing features of giants and ogres in *The Red Fairy Book*. I never liked that book much.

He was vaguely human, using the term loosely. He was a couple of feet taller than I am and outweighed me three or four hundred pounds but I am much prettier. Hair grew on him in clumps, like a discouraged lawn; and you just knew, without being told, that he had never used a man's deodorant for manly men. The knots of his muscles had knots on them and his toenails weren't trimmed.

"Star," I said, "what's the nature of the argument we have with him?"

"You must kill him, milord."

I looked back at him. "Can't we negotiate a peaceful coexistence? Mutual inspection, cultural exchange, and so forth?"

She shook her head. "He's not bright enough for that. He's here to stop us from going down into the valley—and either he dies, or we die."

I took a deep breath. "Princess, I've reached a decision. A man who always obeys the law is even stupider than one who breaks it every chance. This is no time to

74

worry about that local Sullivan Act. I want the flame-thrower, a bazooka, a few grenades, and the heaviest gun in that armory. Can you show me how to dig them out?"

She poked at the fire. "My hero," she said slowly, "I'm truly sorry—but it isn't that simple. Did you notice, last night when we were smoking, that Rufo lighted our cigarettes from candles? Not using even so much as a pocket lighter?"

"Well ... no. I didn't give it any thought."

"This rule against firearms and explosives is not a law such as you have back on Earth. It is more than that; it is impossible to use such things here. Else such things would be used against us."

"You mean they won't work?"

"They will not work. Perhaps 'hexed' is the word."

"Star. Look at me. Maybe you believe in hexes. I don't. And I'll give you seven to two that Tommy guns don't, either. I intend to find out. Will you give me a hand in unpacking?"

For the first time she looked really upset. "Oh, milord, I beg of you not to!"

"Why not?"

"Even the attempt would be disastrous. Do you believe that I know more about the hazards and dangers —and laws—of this world than you do? Will you believe me when I say that I would not have you die, that in solemn truth my own life and safety depend on yours? Please!"

It is impossible not to believe Star when she lays it on the line. I said thoughtfully, "Maybe you're right—or that character over there would be carrying a six-inch mortar as a side arm. Uh, Star, I've got a still better idea. Why don't we high-tail it back the way we came and homestead that spot where we caught the fish? In five years we'll have a nice little farm. In ten years, after the word gets around, we'll have a nice little motel, too, with a free-form swimming pool and a putting green."

She barely smiled. "Milord Oscar, there is no turning back."

"Why not? I could find it with my eyes closed."

"But *they* would find *us*. Not Igli but more like him would be sent to harry and kill us."

I sighed again. "As you say. They claim motels off the main highway are a poor risk anyhow. There's a battle-axe in that duffel. Maybe I can chop his feet off before he notices me."

She shook her head again. I said, "What's the matter now? Do I have to fight him with one foot in a bucket? I thought anything that cut or stabbed—anything I did with my own muscles—was okay?"

"It is okay, milord. But it won't work."

"Why not?"

"Igli can't be killed. You see, he is not really alive. He is a construct, made invulnerable for this one purpose. Swords or knives or even axes will not cut him; they bounce off. I have seen it."

"You mean he is a robot?"

"Not if you are thinking of gears and wheels and printed circuits. 'Golem' would be closer. The Igli is an imitation of life." Star added, "Better than life in some ways, since there is no way—none that I know of—to kill him. But worse, too, as Igli isn't very bright nor well balanced. He has conceit without judgment. Rufo is working on that now, warming him up for you, getting him so mad he can't think straight."

"He is? Gosh! I must be sure to thank Rufo for that. Thank him too much. I think. Well, Princess, what am I supposed to do now?"

She spread her hands as if it were all self-evident. "When you are ready, I will loose the wards—and then you will kill him."

"But you just said—" I stopped. When they abolished the French Foreign Legion very few cushy billets were left for us romantic types. Umbopa could have handled this. Conan, certainly. Or Hawk Carse. Or even Don Quixote, for that thing was about the size of a windmill. "All right, Princess, let's get on with it. Is it okay for me to spit on my hands? Or is that cheating?"

She smiled without dimpling and said gravely, "Milord Oscar, we will all spit on our hands; Rufo and I will be fighting right beside you. Either we win . . . or we all die."

We walked over and joined Rufo. He was making donkey's ears at Igli and shouting, "Who's your father, Igli? Your mother was a garbage can but *who's your father?* Look at him! No belly button! Yaaa!"

Igli retorted, *"Your* mother barks! Your sister gives green stamps!"—but rather feebly, I thought. It was plain that that remark about belly buttons had cut him to the quick—he didn't have one. Only reasonable, I suppose.

The above is not quite what either of them said, except the remark about the belly button. I wish I could put it in the original because, in the Nevian language, the insult is a high art at least equal to poetry. In fact the epitome of literary grace is to address your enemy (publicly) in some difficult verse form, say the sestina, with every word dripping vitriol.

Rufo cackled gleefully. "Make one, Igli! Push your finger in and make one. They left you out in the rain and you ran. They forgot to finish you. Call that thing a *nose?*" He said in aside to me, in English, "How do you want him, Boss? Rare? Or well done?"

"Keep him busy while I study the matter. He doesn't understand English?"

"Not a bit."

"Good. How close can I go to him without getting grabbed?"

"Close as you like as long as the wards are up. But, Boss—look, I'm not supposed to advise you—but when we get down to work, don't let him get you by the plums."

"I'll try not to."

"You be careful." Rufo turned his head and shouted, "Yaaa! Igli picks his nose and eats it!" He added, *"She* is a good doctor, the best, but just the same, you be careful."

"I will." I stepped closer to the invisible barrier, looked up at this creature. He glared down at me and made growling noises, so I thumbed my nose at him and gave him a wet, fruity Bronx cheer. I was downwind and it seemed likely that he hadn't had a bath in thirty or forty years; he smelled worse than a locker room at the half.

It gave me a seed of an idea. "Star, can this cherub swim?"

She looked surprised. "I really don't know."

"Maybe they forgot to program him for it. How about you, Rufo?"

Rufo looked smug. "Try me, just try me. I could teach fish. Igli! Tell us why the sow wouldn't kiss you!"

Star could swim like a seal. My style is more like a ferry boat but I get there. "Star, maybe that thing can't be killed but it breathes. It's got some sort of oxygen metabolism, even if it burns kerosene. If we held his head underwater for a while—as long as necessary—I'll bet the fire would go out."

She looked wide-eyed. "Milord Oscar . . . my champion . . . I was not mistaken in you."

"It's going to take some doing. Ever play water polo, Rufo?"

"I invented it."

I hoped he had. I had played it—once. Like being ridden on a rail, it is an interesting experience—once. "Rufo, can you lure our chum down toward the bank? I take it that the barrier follows this line of furry and feathery friends? It it does, we can get him almost to that high piece of bank with the deep pool under it— you know, Star, where you ducked me the first time."

"Nothing to it," said Rufo. "We move, he'll come along."

"I'd like to get him running. Star, how long does it take you to unswitch your fence?"

"I can loose the wards in an instant, milord."

"Okay, here's the plan. Rufo, I want you to get Igli to chasing you, as fast as possible—and you cut out and head for that high bank just before you reach the stream. Star, when Rufo does that, you chop off the barrier—loose the wards—instantly. Don't wait for me to say so. Rufo, you dive in and swim like hell; don't let him grab you. With any luck, if Igli is moving fast, as big and clumsy as he is he'll go in, too, whether he means to or not. But I'll be pacing you, flanking you and a bit behind you.

If Igli manages to put on the brakes, I'll hit him with a low tackle and knock him in. Then we all play water polo."

"Water polo I have never seen," Star said doubtfully.

"There won't be any referee. All it means this time is that all three of us jump him, in the water, and shove his head under and keep it there—and help each other to keep him from shoving *our* heads under. Big as he is, unless he can outswim us he'll be at a terrible disadvantage. We go on doing this until he is limp and stays limp, never let him get a breath. Then, to make sure, we'll weigh him down with stones—it won't matter whether he's really dead or not. Any questions?"

Rufo grinned like a gargoyle. "This is going to be fun!"

Both those pessimists seemed to think that it would work, so we got started. Rufo shouted an allegation about Igli's personal habits that even Olympia Press would censor, then dared Igli to race him, offering an obscene improbability as a wager.

It took Igli a lumbering long time to get that carcass moving but when he did get rolling, he was faster than Rufo and left a wake of panicked animals and birds behind him. I'm pretty fast but I was hard pushed to hold position on the giant, flanking and a few paces back, and I hoped that Star would not loose the wards if it appeared that Igli might catch Rufo on dry land.

However, Star did loose the wards just as Rufo cut away from the barrier, and Rufo reached the bank and made a perfect racing dive without slowing down, all to plan.

But nothing else was.

I think Igli was too stupid to twig at once that the barrier was down. He kept on a few paces after Rufo had gone left oblique, then did cut left rather sharply. But he had lost speed and he didn't have any trouble stopping on dry land.

I hit him a diving tackle, illegal and low, and down he went—but *not* over into the water. And suddenly I had a double armful of struggling and very smelly golem.

But I had a wildcat helping me at once, and quickly thereafter Rufo, dripping wet, added his vote.

But it was a stalemate and one that we were bound to lose in time. Igli outweighed all of us put together and seemed to be nothing but muscle and stink and nails and teeth. We were suffering bruises, contusions, and flesh wounds—and we weren't doing Igli any damage. Oh, he screamed like a TV grunt & groaner every time one of us twisted an ear or bent back a finger, but we weren't really hurting him and he was decidedly hurting us. There wasn't a chance of dragging that hulk into the water.

I had started with my arms around his knees and I stayed that way, of necessity, as long as I could, while Star tried to weigh down one of his arms and Rufo the other. But the situation was fluid; Igli thrashed like a rattler with its back broken and was forever getting one limb or another free and trying to gouge and bite. It got us into odd positions and I found myself hanging onto one calloused foot, trying to twist it off, while I stared into his open mouth, wide as a bear trap and less appetizing. His teeth needed cleaning.

So I shoved the toe of his foot into his mouth.

Igli screamed, so I kept on shoving, and pretty soon he didn't have room to scream. I kept on pushing.

When he had swallowed his own left leg up to the knee, he managed to wrench his right arm loose from Star and grabbed at his disappearing leg—and I grabbed his wrist. "Help me!" I yelped to Star. *"Push!"*

She got the idea and shoved with me. That arm went into his mouth to the elbow and the leg went farther in, quite a bit of the thigh. By then Rufo was working with us and forced Igli's left hand in past his cheek and into the jaws. Igli wasn't struggling so hard by then, short on air probably, so getting the toe of his right foot started into his mouth simply required determination, with Rufo hauling back on his hairy nostrils while I bore down with a knee on his chin and Star pushed.

We kept on feeding him into his mouth, gaining an inch at a time and never letting up. He was still quivering and trying to get loose when we had him rolled up clear to his hips, and his rank armpits about to disappear.

It was like rolling a snowball in reverse; the more we pushed, the smaller he got and the more his mouth stretched—ugliest sight I ever have seen. Soon he was down to the size of a medicine ball ... and then a soccer ball ... then a baseball and I rolled him between my palms and kept pushing, hard.

—a golf ball, a marble, a pea ... and finally there was nothing but some dirty grease on my hands.

Rufo took a deep breath. "I guess that'll teach him not to put his foot in his mouth with his betters. Who's ready for breakfast?"

"I want to wash my hands first," I said.

We all bathed, using plenty of soap, then Star took care of our wounds and had Rufo treat hers, under her instructions. Rufo is right; Star is the best medic. The stuff she used on us did not sting, the cuts closed up, the flexible dressings she put over them did not have to be changed, and fell off in time with no infection and no scars. Rufo had one very bad bite, about forty cents' worth of hamburger out of his left buttock, but when Star was through with him, he could sit down and it didn't seem to bother him.

Rufo fed us little golden pancakes and big German sausages, popping with fat, and gallons of *good* coffee. It was almost noon before Star loosed the wards again and we set out for our descent down the cliff.

VII

THE descent beside the great waterfall into Nevia valley is a thousand feet and more than sheer; the cliff overhangs and you go down on a line, spinning slowly like a spider. I don't advise this; it is dizzy-making and I almost lost those wonderful pancakes.

The view is stupendous. You see the waterfall from the side, free-springing, not wetting the cliff, and falling so far that it shrouds itself in mist before it hits bottom. Then as you turn you face frowning cliff, then a long look out over a valley too lush and green and beautiful to be believed—marsh and forest at the foot of the cliff, cultivated fields in middle distance a few miles away, then far beyond and hazy at the base but sharp at the peaks a mighty wall of snow-covered mountains.

Star had sketched the valley for me. "First we fight our way through the marsh. After that it is easy going—we simply have to look sharp for blood kites. Because we come to a brick road, very nice."

"A yellow brick road?" I asked.

"Yes. That's the clay they have. Does it matter?"

"I guess not. Just don't make a hobbit of it. Then what?"

"After that we'll stop overnight with a family, the squire of the countryside there. Good people, you'll enjoy them."

"And then the going gets tough," Rufo added.

"Rufo, don't borrow trouble!" Star scolded. "You will please refrain from comments and allow Oscar to cope with his problems as he comes to them, rested, clear-eyed, and unworried. Do you know anyone else who could have handled Igli?"

"Well, since you put it that way ... no."

"I do put it that way. We all sleep in comfort tonight. Isn't that enough? You'll enjoy it as much as anyone."

"So will you."

"When did I ever fail to enjoy anything? Hold your tongue. Now, Oscar, at the foot of the cliff are the Horned Ghosts—no way to avoid them, they'll see us coming down. With luck we won't see any of the Cold Water Gang; they stay back in the mists. But if we have the bad luck to encounter both, we may have the good luck that they will fight each other and let us slip away. The path through the marsh is tricky; you had best study this sketch until you know it. Solid footing is only where little yellow flowers grow no matter how solid and dry a piece looks. But, as you can see, even if you stay carefully on the safe bits, there are so many side trails and dead ends that we could wander all day and be trapped by darkness—and never get out."

So here I was, coming down first, because the Horned Ghosts would be waiting at the bottom. My privilege. Wasn't I a "Hero"? Hadn't I made Igli swallow himself?

But I wished that the Horned Ghosts really were ghosts. They were two-legged animals, omnivorous. They ate anything, including each other, and especially travelers. From the belly up they were described to me as much like the Minotaur; from there down they were splay-footed satyrs. Their upper limbs were short arms but without real hands—no thumbs.

But oh those horns! They had horns like Texas long-horns, but sticking up and forward.

However, there is one way of converting a Horned Ghost into a real ghost. It has a soft place on its skull, like a baby's soft spot, between those horns. Since the brute charges head down, attempting to impale you, this is the only vulnerable spot that can be reached. All it takes is to stand your ground, don't flinch, aim for that one little spot—and hit it.

So my task was simple. Go down first, kill as many as necessary to insure that Star would have a safe spot to land, then stand fast and protect her until Rufo was down. After that we were free to carve our way through the marsh to safety. If the Cold Water Gang didn't join the party—

I tried to ease my position in the sling I was riding—my left leg had gone to sleep—and looked down. A hundred feet below the reception committee had gathered.

It looked like an asparagus patch. Of bayonets.

I signaled to stop lowering. Far above me, Rufo checked the line; I hung there, swaying, and tried to think. If I had them lower me straight into that mob, I might stick one or two before I myself was impaled. Or maybe none— The only certainty was that I would be dead long before my friends could join me.

On the other hand, besides that soft spot between the horns, each of these geeks had a soft underbelly, just made for arrows. If Rufo would lower me a bit—

I signaled to him. I started slowly down, a bit jerkily, and he almost missed my signal to stop again. I had to pull up my feet; some of those babies were a-snorting and a-ramping around and shoving each other for a chance to gore me. One Nijinsky among them did manage to scrape the sole of my left buskin, giving me goose flesh clear to my chin.

Under that strong inducement I pulled myself hand over hand up the line far enough to let me get my feet into the sling instead of my fanny. I stood in it, hanging onto the line and standing on one foot and then on the other to work pins and needles out. Then I unslung my bow and strung it. This feat would have been worthy of a trained acrobat—but have you ever tried to bend a bow and let fly while standing in a bight at one end of a thousand-foot line and clinging to the line with one hand?

You lose arrows that way. I lost three and almost lost me.

I tried buckling my belt around the line. That caused me to hang upside down and lost me my Robin Hood hat and more arrows. My audience liked that one; they applauded—I think it was applause—so, for an encore, I tried to shift the belt up around my chest to enable me to hang more or less straight down—and maybe get off an arrow or two.

I didn't quite lose my sword.

So far, my only results had been to attract customers ("Mama, see the funny man!") and to make myself swing back and forth like a pendulum.

Bad as the latter was, it did give me an idea. I started increasing that swing, pumping it up like a playground swing. This was slow work and it took a while to get the hang of it, as the period of that pendulum of which I was the weight was over a minute—and it does no good to try to hurry a pendulum; you have to work with it, not against it. I hoped my friends could see well enough to guess what I was doing and not foul it up.

After an unreasonably long time I was swinging back and forth in a flattish arc about a hundred feet long, passing very fast over the heads of my audience at the bottom of each swing, slowing to a stop at the end of each swing. At first those spike heads tried to move with me, but they tired of that and squatted near the mid-point and watched, their heads moving as I swung, like spectators of a slow-motion tennis match.

But there is always some confounded innovator. My notion was to drop off at one end of this arc where it just missed the cliff and make a stand there with my back to the wall. The ground was higher there, I would not have so far to drop. But one of those horned horrors figured it out and trotted over to that end of the swing. He was followed by two or three more.

That settled it; I would have to drop off at the other end. But young Archimedes figured that out, too. He left his buddies at the cliff face and trotted after me. I pulled ahead of him at the low point of the swing—but slowed down and he caught up with me long before I reached the dead point at the end. He had only a hundred feet to do in about thirty seconds—a slow walk. He was under me when I got there.

The odds wouldn't improve; I kicked my feet clear, hung by one hand and drew sword during that too-slow traverse, and dropped off anyway. My notion was to spit that tender spot on his head before my feet touched the ground.

Instead, I missed and he missed and I knocked him sprawling and sprawled right after him and rolled to my feet and ran for the cliff face nearest me, poking that genius in his belly with my sword without stopping.

That foul blow saved me. His friends and relatives stopped to quarrel over who got the prime ribs before a clot of them moved in my direction. This gave me time to set my feet on a pile of scree at the base of the cliff, where I could play "King of the Castle," and return my sword and nock an arrow.

I didn't wait for them to rush me. I simply waited until they were close enough that I could not miss, took a bead on the wishbone of the old bull who was leading them, if he had a wishbone, and let that shaft go with every pound of that heavy bow.

It passed through him and stuck into one behind him.

This led to another quarrel over the price of chops. They ate them, teeth and toenails. That was their weakness: all appetite and too little brain. If they had co-operated, they could have had me in one rush when I first hit the ground. Instead they stopped for lunch.

I glanced up. High above me, Star was a tiny spider on a thread; she grew rapidly larger. I moved crabwise along the wall until I was opposite the point, forty feet from the cliff, where she would touch ground.

When she was about fifty feet up, she signaled Rufo to stop lowering, drew her sword and saluted me. "Magnificent, my Hero!" We were all wearing swords; Star had chosen a dueling sword with a 34" blade—a big sword for a woman but Star is a big woman. She had also packed her belt pouch with medic's supplies, an ominous touch had I noticed, but did not, at the time.

I drew and returned her salute. They were not bothering me yet, although some, having finished lunch or having been crowded out, were milling around and looking me over. Then I sheathed again, and nocked an arrow. "Start pumping it up, Star, right toward me. Have Rufo lower you a bit more."

She returned sword and signaled Rufo. He let her down slowly until she was about nine feet off the ground, where she signaled a stop. "Now pump it up!" I called out. Those bloodthirsty natives had forgotten me; they were watching Star, those not still busy eating Cousin Abbie or Great-Uncle John.

"All right," she answered. "But I have a throwing line. Can you catch it?"

"Oh!" The smart darling had watched my maneuvers and had figured out what would be needed. "Hold it a moment! I'll make a diversion." I reached over my shoulder, counted arrows by touch—seven. I had started with twenty and made use of one; the rest were scattered, lost.

I used three in a hurry, right, left, and ahead, picking targets as far away as I dared risk, aiming at midpoint and depending on that wonderful bow to take those shafts straight and flat. Sure enough, the crowd went for fresh meat like a government handout. "Now!"

Ten seconds later I caught her in my arms and collected a split-second kiss for toll.

Ten minutes later Rufo was down by the same tactics, at a cost of three of my arrows and two of Star's smaller ones. He had to lower himself, sitting in the bight and checking the free end of the line under both armpits; he would have been a sitting duck without help. As soon as he was untangled from the line, he started jerking it down off the cliff, and faking it into a coil.

"Leave that!" Star said sharply. "We haven't time and it's too heavy to carry."

"I'll put it in the pack."

"No."

"It's a good line," Rufo persisted. "We'll need it."

"You'll need a shroud if we're not through the marsh by nightfall." Star turned to me. "How shall we march, milord?"

I looked around. In front of us and to the left a few jokers still milled around, apparently hesitant about getting closer. To our right and above us the great cloud at the base of the falls made iridescent lace in the sky. About three hundred yards in front of us was where we would enter the trees and just beyond the marsh started.

We went downhill in a tight wedge, myself on point, Rufo and Star following on flank, all of us with arrows nocked. I had told them to draw swords if any Horned Ghost got within fifty feet.

None did. One idiot came straight toward us, alone, and Rufo knocked him over with an arrow at twice that distance. As we came up on the corpse Rufo drew his dagger. "Let it be!" said Star. She seemed edgy.

"I'm just going to get the nuggets and give them to Oscar."

"And get us all killed. If Oscar wants nuggets, he shall have them."

"What sort of nuggets?" I asked, without stopping.

"Gold, Boss. Those blighters have gizzards like a chicken. But gold is all they swallow for it. Old ones yield maybe twenty, thirty pounds."

I whistled.

"Gold is common here," Star explained. "There is a great heap of it at the base of the falls, inside the cloud, washed down over eons. It causes fights between the Ghosts and the Cold Water Gang, because the Ghosts have this odd appetite and sometimes risk entering the cloud to satisfy it."

"I haven't seen any of the Cold Water Gang yet," I commented.

"Pray God you don't," Rufo answered.

"All the more reason to get deep into the marsh," Star added. "The Gang doesn't go into it and even the Ghosts don't go far in. Despite their splay feet, they can be sucked under."

"Anything dangerous in the swamp itself?"

"Plenty," Rufo told me. "So be sure you step on the yellow flowers."

"Watch where you put your own feet. If that map was right, I won't lose us. What does a Cold Water Gangster look like?"

Rufo said thoughtfully, "Ever seen a man who had been drowned for a week?" I let the matter drop.

Before we got to the trees I had us sling bows and draw swords. Just inside the cover of trees, they jumped us. Horned Ghosts, I mean, not the Cold Water Gang. An ambush from all sides, I don't know how many. Rufo killed four or five and Star at least two and I danced around, looking active and trying to survive.

We had to climb up and over bodies to move on, too many to count.

We kept on into the swamp, following the little golden pathfinder flowers and the twists and turns of the map in my head. In about half an hour we came to a clearing, big as a double garage. Star said faintly, "This is far enough." She had been holding one hand pressed to her side but had not been willing to stop until then, although blood stained her tunic and all down the left leg of her tights.

She let Rufo attend her first, while I guarded the bottleneck into the clearing. I was relieved not to be asked to help, as, after we gently removed her tunic, I felt sick at seeing how badly she had been gored—and never a peep out of her. That golden body—hurt!

As a knight errant, I felt like a slob.

But she was chipper again, once Rufo had followed her instructions. She treated Rufo, then treated me— half a dozen wounds each but scratches compared with the rough one she had taken.

Once she had me patched up she said, "Milord Oscar, how long will it be until we are out of the marsh?"

I ran through it in my head. "Does the going get any worse?"

"Slightly better."

"Not over an hour."

"Good. Don't put those filthy clothes back on. Rufo, unpack a bit and we'll have clean clothes and more arrows. Oscar, we'll need them for the blood kites, once we are out of the trees."

The little black box filled most of the clearing before it was unfolded enough to let Rufo get out clothes and reach the arsenal. But clean clothes and full quiver made me feel like a new man, especially after Rufo dug out a half liter of brandy and we split it three ways, gurgle-gurgle! Star replenished her medic's pouch, then I helped Rufo fold up the luggage.

Maybe Rufo was giddy from brandy and no lunch. Or perhaps from loss of blood. It could have been just the bad luck of an unnoticed patch of slippery mud. He had the box in his arms, about to make the last closure that would fold it to knapsack size, when he slipped, recovered violently, and the box sailed out of his arms into a chocolate-brown pool.

It was far out of reach. I yelled, "Rufo, off with your belt!" I was reaching for the buckle of mine.

"No, no!" screamed Rufo. "Stand back! Get clear!"

A corner of the box was still in sight. With a safety line on me I *knew* I could get it, even if there was no bottom to the pool. I said so, angrily.

"No, Oscar!" Star said urgently. "He's right. We march. Quickly."

So we marched—me leading, Star breathing on my neck, Rufo crowding her heels.

We had gone a hundred yards when there was a mud volcano behind us. Not much noise, just a bass rumble and a slight earthquake, then some very dirty rain. Star quit hurrying and said pleasantly, "Well, that's that."

Rufo said, "And all the liquor was in it!"

"I don't mind that," Star answered. "Liquor is every-where. But I had new clothes in there, pretty ones, Oscar.

90

I wanted you to see them; I bought them with you in mind."

I didn't answer. I was thinking about a flamethrower and an M-1 and a couple of cases of ammo. And the liquor, of course.

"Did you hear me, milord?" she persisted. "I wanted to wear them for you."

"Princess," I answered, "you have your prettiest clothes right with you, always."

I heard the happy chuckle that goes with her dimples. "I'm sure that you have often said that before. And no doubt with great success."

We were out of the swamp long before dark and hit the brick road soon after. Blood kites are no problem. They are such murderous things that if you shoot an arrow in the direction of one of their dives, a kite will swerve and pluck it out of the air, getting the shaft right down its gullet. We usually recovered the arrows.

We were among plowed fields soon after we reached the road and soon the blood kites thinned out. Just at sundown we could see outbuildings and the lights in the manor where Star said that we would spend the night.

VIII

MILORD Doral 't Giuk Dorali should have been a Texan. I don't mean that the Doral could have been mistaken for a Texan but he had that you-paid-for-the-lunch-I'll-pay-for-the-Cadillacs expansiveness.

His farmhouse was the size of a circus tent and as lavish as a Thanksgiving dinner—rich, sumptuous, fine carvings and inlaid jewels. Nevertheless it had a sloppy, lived-in look and if you didn't watch where you put your feet, you would step on a child's toy on a broad, sweeping staircase and wind up with a broken collarbone. There were children and dogs underfoot everywhere and the youngest of each weren't housebroken. It didn't worry the Doral. Nothing worried the Doral, he enjoyed life.

We had been passing through his fields for miles (rich as the best Iowa farmland and no winters; Star told me they produced four crops a year)—but it was late in the day and an occasional field hand was all we saw save for one wagon we met on the road. I thought that it was pulled by a team of two pairs of horses. I was mistaken the team was but one pair and the animals were not horses, they had eight legs each.

All of Nevia valley is like that, the commonplace mixed with the wildly different. Humans were humans, dogs were dogs—but horses weren't horses. Like Alice trying to cope with the Flamingo, every time I thought I had it licked, it would wiggle loose.

The man driving those equine centipedes stared but not because we were dressed oddly; he was dressed as I was. He was staring at Star, as who wouldn't? The people working in fields had mostly been dressed in sort of a lava-lava. This garment, a simple wraparound tied off at the waist, is the equivalent in Nevia of overalls or blue jeans for both men and women; what we were wearing was equal to the Gray Flannel Suit or to a woman's basic black. Party or formal clothes—well, that's another matter.

As we turned into the grounds of the manor we picked up a wake of children and dogs. One kid ran ahead and, when we reached the broad terrace in front of the main house, milord Doral himself came out the great front door. I didn't pick him for lord of the manor; he was wearing one of those short sarongs, was barefooted and bareheaded. He had thick hair, shot with gray, an imposing beard, and looked like General U. S. Grant.

Star waved and called out, "Jock! Oh, Jocko!" (The name was "Giuk," but I caught it as "Jock" and Jock he is.)

The Doral stared at us, then lumbered forward like a tank, "Ettyboo! Bless your beautiful blue eyes! Bless your bouncy little bottom! Why didn't you let me *know?*" (I have to launder this because Nevian idioms don't parallel ours. Try translating certain French idioms literally into English and you'll see what I mean. The Doral was not being vulgar; he was being formally and gallantly polite to an old and highly respected friend.)

He grabbed Star in a hug, lifted her off her feet, kissed her on both cheeks and on the mouth, gnawed one ear, then set her down with an arm around her. "Games and celebrations! Three months of holiday! Races and rassling every day, orgies every night! Prizes for the strongest, the fairest, the wittiest—"

Star stopped him. "Milord Doral—"

"Eh? And a prize of all prizes for the first baby born—"

"Jocko darling! I love you dearly, but tomorrow we must ride. All we ask is a bone to gnaw and a corner to sleep in."

"Nonsense! You can't do this to me."

"You know that I must."

"Politics be damned! I'll die at your feet, Sugar Pie. Poor old Jocko's heart will stop. I feel an attack coming right now." He felt around his chest. "Someplace here—"

She poked him in the belly. "You old fraud. You'll die as you've lived, and not of heartbreak. Milord Doral—"

"Yes, milady?"

"I bring you a Hero."

He blinked. "You're not talking about Rufo? Hi, Rufe, you old polecat! Heard any good ones lately? Get back to the kitchen and pick yourself a lively one."

"Thank you, milord Doral." Rufo "made a leg," bowing deeply, and left us.

Star said firmly, "If the Doral please."

"I hear."

Star untangled his arm, stood straight and tall and started to chant:

> "By the Singing Laughing Waters
> "Came a Hero Fair and Fearless.
> "Oscar hight this noble warrior,
> "Wise and Strong and never daunted,
> "Trapped the Igli with a question,
> "Caught him out with paradoxes,
> "Shut the Igli's mouth with Igli.
> "Fed him to him, feet and fingers!
> "Nevermore the Singing Waters . . ."

It went on and on, none of it lies yet none of it quite true—colored like a press agent's handout. For example, Star told him that I had killed twenty-seven Horned Ghosts, one with my bare hands. I don't remember that many and as for "bare hands," that was an accident. I had just stabbed one of those vermin as another one tumbled at my feet, shoved from behind. I didn't have time to get my sword clear, so I set a foot on one horn and pulled hard on the other with my left hand and his head came apart like snapping a wishbone. But I had done it from desperation, not choice.

Star even ad-libbed a long excursus about my father's heroism and alleged that my grandaddy had led the charge at San Juan Hill and then started in on my great-grandfathers. But when she told him how I had picked up that scar that runs from left eye to right jaw, she pulled out all the stops.

Now look, Star had quizzed me the first time I met her and she had encouraged me to tell her more during that long hike the day before. But I did *not* give her most of the guff she was handing the Doral. She must have had the Sûreté, the F.B.I., the Archie Goodwin on me for months. She even named the team we had played against when I busted my nose and I never told her *that*.

I stood there blushing while the Doral looked me up and down with whistles and snorts of appreciation. When Star ended, with a simple: "Thus it happened," he let out a long sigh and said, "Could we have that part about Igli over again?"

Star complied, chanting different words and more detail. The Doral listened, frowning and nodding approval. "A heroic solution," he said. "So he's a mathematician, too. Where did he study?"

"A natural genius, Jock."

"It figures." He stepped up to me, looked me in the eye and put his hands on my shoulders. "The Hero who confounds Igli may choose any house. But he will honor my home by accepting hospitality of roof . . . and table . . . and bed?"

He spoke with great earnestness, holding my eye; I had no chance to look at Star for a hint. And I wanted a hint. The person who says smugly that good manners are the same everywhere and people are just people hasn't been farther out of Podunk than the next whistle stop.

I'm no sophisticate but I had been around enough to learn that. It was a formal speech, stuffed with protocol, and called for a formal answer.

I did the best I could. I put my hands on his shoulders and answered solemnly, "I am honored far beyond any merit of mine, sir."

"But you accept?" he said anxiously.

"I accept with all my heart." ("Heart" is close enough. I was having trouble with language.)

He seemed to sigh with relief. "Glorious!" He grabbed me in a bear hug, kissed me on both cheeks, and only some fast dodging kept me from being kissed on the mouth.

Then he straightened up and shouted, "Wine! Beer! Schnaps! Who the dadratted tomfoolery is supposed to be chasing? I'll skin somebody alive with a rusty file! Chairs! Service for a Hero! Where *is* everybody?"

That last was uncalled for; while Star was reciting what a great guy I am, some eighteen or fifty people had gathered on the terrace, pushing and shoving and trying to get a better look. Among them must have been the personnel with the day's duty because a mug of ale was shoved into my hand and a four-ounce glass of 110-proof firewater into the other before the boss stopped yelling. Jocko drank boilermaker style, so I followed suit, then was happy to sit down on a chair that was already behind me, with my teeth loosened, my scalp lifted, and the beer just starting to put out the fire.

Other people plied me with bits of cheese, cold meats, pickled this and that, and unidentified drinking food all tasty, not waiting for me to accept it but shoving it into my mouth if I opened it even to say *"Gesundheit!"* I ate as offered and soon it blotted up the hydrofluoric acid.

In the meantime the Doral was presenting his household to me. It would have been better had they worn chevrons because I never did get them straightened out as to rank. Clothes didn't help because, just as the squire was dressed like a field hand, the second scullery maid might (and sometimes did) duck back in and load herself with golden ornaments and her best party dress. Nor were they presented in order of rank.

I barely twigged as to which was the lady of the manor, Jocko's wife—his senior wife. She was a very comely older woman, a brunette carrying a few pounds extra but with that dividend most fetchingly distributed. She was dressed as casually as Jocko but, fortunately, I noticed her because she went at once to greet Star and they embraced warmly, two old friends. So I had my ears spread when she was presented to me a moment later—as (and I caught it) *the* Doral (just as Jocko was *the* Doral) but with the feminine ending.

I jumped to my feet, grabbed her hand, bowed over it and pressed it to my lips. This isn't even faintly a Nevian custom but it brought cheers and Mrs. Doral blushed and looked pleased and Jocko grinned proudly.

She was the only one I stood up for. Each of the men and boys made a leg to me, with a bow; all the gals from six to sixty curtsied—not as we know it, but Nevian style. It looked more like a step of the Twist. Balance on one foot and lean back as far as possible, then balance on the other while leaning forward, all the while undulating slowly. This doesn't sound graceful but it is, and it proved that there was not a case of arthritis nor a slipped disk anywhere on the Doral spread.

Jocko hardly ever bothered with names. The females were "Sweetheart" and "Honeylamb" and "Pretty Puss" and he called all the males, even those who seemed to be older than he was, "Son."

Possibly most of them were his sons. The setup in Nevia I don't fully understand. This looked like a feudalism out of our own history—and maybe it was—but whether this mob was the Doral's slaves, his serfs, his hired hands, or all members of one big family I never got straight. A mixture, I think. Titles didn't mean anything. The only title Jocko held was that he was singled out by a grammatical inflection as being *the* Doral instead of just any of a couple of hundred Dorals. I've scattered the tag "milord" here and there in this memoir because Star and Rufo used it, but it was simply a courteous form of address paralleling one in Nevian. "Freiherr" does not mean "free man," and "monsieur" does not mean "my lord"—these things don't translate well. Star sprinkled her speech with "milords" because she was much too polite to say "Hey, Mac!" even with her intimates.

(The very politest endearments in Nevian would win you a clout in the teeth in the USA.)

Once all hands had been presented to the Gordon, Hero First Class, we adjourned to get ready for the banquet that Jocko, cheated of his three months of revelry, had swapped for his first intention. It split me off from Star as well as from Rufo; I was escorted to my chambers by my two valettes.

That's what I said. Female. Plural. It is a good thing that I had become relaxed to female attendants in men's washrooms, European style, and still more relaxed by Southeast Asia and l'Île du Levant; they don't teach you how to cope with valettes in American public schools. Especially when they are young and cute and terribly anxious to please . . . and I had had a long, dangerous day. I learned, first time out on patrol, that nothing hikes up that old biological urge like being shot at and living through it.

It there had been only one, I might have been late to dinner. As it was, they chaperoned each other, though not intentionally, I believe. I patted the redhead on her fanny when the other one wasn't looking and reached, I thought, an understanding for a later time.

Well, having your back scrubbed is fun, too. Shorn, shampooed, shined, shaved, showered, smelling like a belligerent rose, decked out in the fanciest finery since Cecil B. deMille rewrote the Bible, I was delivered by them to the banquet hall on time.

But the proconsul's dress uniform I wore was a suit of fatigues compared with Star's getup. She had lost all her pretty clothes earlier in the day but our hostess had been able to dig up something.

First a dress that covered Star from chin to ankle—like plate glass. It seemed to be blue smoke, it clung to her

and billowed out behind. Underneath was "underwear."
She appeared to be wrapped in twining ivy—but this ivy
was gold, picked out in sapphires. It curved across her
beautiful belly, divided into strands and cupped her
breasts, the coverage being about like a bikini minimum
but more startling and much more effective.

Her shoes were sandals in an S-curve of something
transparent and springy. Nothing appeared to hold them
on, no straps, no clips; her lovely feet, bare, rested on
them. It made her appear as if she were on tiptoe about
four inches off the floor.

Her great mane of blond hair was built up into a structure as complex as a full-rigged ship, and studded with
sapphires. She was wearing a fortune or two of sapphires
here and there on her body, too; I won't itemize.

She spotted me just as I caught sight of her. Her face
lit up and she called out, in English, "My Hero, you are
beautiful!"

I said "Uh—"

Then I added, "You haven't been wasting your time,
either. Do I sit with you? I'll need coaching."

"No, no! You sit with the gentlemen, I sit with the
ladies. You won't have any trouble."

This is not a bad way to arrange a banquet. We each
had separate low tables, the men in a row facing the
ladies, with about fifteen feet between them. It wasn't
necessary to make chitchat with the ladies and they all
were worth looking at. The Lady Doral was opposite
me and was giving Star a run for the Golden Apple. Her
costume was opaque some places but not the usual places.
Most of it was diamonds. I believe they were diamonds;
I don't think they make rhinestones that big.

About twenty were seated; two or three times that
many were serving, entertaining, or milling around. Three
girls did nothing but see to it that I did not starve nor
die of thirst—I didn't have to learn how to use their
table tools; I never touched them. The girls knelt by
me; I sat on a big cushion. Later in the evening Jocko
lay flat on his back with his head in a lap so that his

maids could pop food into his mouth or hold a cup to his lips.

Jocko had three maids as I did; Star and Mrs. Jocko had two each; the rest struggled along with one apiece. These serving maids illustrate why I had trouble telling the players without a program. My hostess and my Princess were dressed fit to kill, sure—but one of my flunkies, a sixteen-year-old strong contender for Miss Nevia, was dressed only in jewelry but so much of it that she was more "modestly" dressed than Star or Doral Letva, the Lady Doral.

Nor did they act like servants except for their impassioned determination to see that I got drunk and stuffed. They chattered among themselves in teen-age argot and made wisecracks about how big my muscles were, etc., as if I had not been present. Apparently heroes are not expected to talk, for every time I opened my mouth something went into it.

There was always something doing—dancers, jugglers, recitations of poetry—in the space between the tables. Kids wandered around and grabbed tidbits from platters before they reached the tables. One little doll about three years old squatted down in front of me, all big eyes and open mouth, and stared, letting dancers avoid her as best they could. I tried to get her to come to me, but she just stared and played with her toes.

A damsel with a dulcimer strolled among the tables, singing and playing. It could have been a dulcimer, she might have been a damsel.

About two hours along in the feast, Jocko stood up, roared for silence, belched loudly, shook off maids who were trying to steady him, and started to recite.

Same verse, different tune—he was reciting my exploits. I would have thought that he was too drunk to recite a limerick but he sounded off endlessly, in perfect scansion with complex inner rhymes and rippling alliterations, an astounding feat of virtuosity in rhetoric.

He stuck to Star's story line but embroidered it. I listened with growing admiration, both for him as a poet and for good old Scar Gordon, the one-man army. I decided that I must be a purty goddam hot hero, so when he sat down, I stood up.

The girls had been more successful in getting me drunk than in getting me fed. Most of the food was strange and it was usually tasty. But a cold dish had been fetched in, little froglike creatures in ice, served whole. You dipped them in a sauce and took them in two bites.

The gal in the jewels grabbed one, dipped it and put it up for me to bite. And it woke up.

This little fellow—call him "Elmer"—Elmer rolled his eyes and *looked* at me, just as I was about to bite him.

I suddenly wasn't hungry and jerked my head back.

Miss Jewelry Shop laughed heartily, dipped him again, and showed me how to do it. No more Elmer—

I didn't eat for quite a while and drank more than too much. Every time a bite was offered me I would see Elmer's feet disappearing, and gulp, and have another drink.

That's why I stood up.

Once up, there was dead silence. The music stopped because the musicians were waiting to see what to improvise as background to my poem.

I suddenly realized that I didn't have anything to say.

Not anything. There wasn't a prayer that I could ad-lib a poem of thanks, a graceful compliment to my host —in Nevian. Hell, I couldn't have done it in English.

Star's eyes were on me. She looked gravely confident.

That did it. I didn't risk Nevian; I couldn't even remember how to ask my way to the men's room. So I gave it to 'em, both barrels, in English. Vachel Lindsay's "Congo."

As much of it as I could remember, say about four pages. What I did give them was that compelling rhythm and rhyme scheme, double-talking and faking on any fluffs and really slamming it on "beating on a table with the handle of a broom! Boom! Boom! Boomlay boom!" and the orchestra caught the spirit and we rattled the dishes.

The applause was wonderful and Miss Tiffany grabbed my ankle and kissed it.

So I gave them Mr. E. A. Poe's "Bells" for dessert. Jocko kissed me on my left eye and slobbered on my shoulder.

Then Star stood up and explained, in scansion and rhyme, that in my own land, in my own language, among my own people, warriors and artists all, I was as famous a poet as I was a hero (Which was true. Zero equals zero), and that I had done them the honor of composing my greatest work, in the jewels of my native tongue, a fitting thanks to the Doral and house Doral for hospitality of roof, of table, of bed—and that she would, in time, do her poor best to render my music into their language.

Between us we got the Oscar.

Then they brought in the *pièce de résistance*, a carcass roasted whole and carried by four men. From the size and shape it might have been roast peasant under glass. But it was dead and it smelled wonderful and I ate a lot of it and sobered up. After the roast there were only eight or nine other things, soups and sherbets and similar shilly-shallying. The party got looser and people didn't stay at their own tables. One of my girls fell asleep and spilled my wine cup and about then I realized that most of the crowd had gone.

Doral Letva, flanked by two girls, led me to my chambers and put me to bed. They dimmed the lights and withdrew while I was still trying to phrase a gallant good night in their language.

They came back, having shucked all jewelry and other encumbrances and posed at my bedside, the Three Graces. I had decided that the younger ones were mama's daughters. The older girl was maybe eighteen, full ripe, and a picture of what mama must have been at that age; the younger one seemed five years younger, barely nubile, as pretty for her own age and quite self-conscious. She blushed and dropped her eyes when I looked at her. But her sister stared back with sultry eyes, boldly provocative.

Their mother, an arm around each waist, explained

102

simply but in rhyme that I had honored their roof and their table—and now their bed. What was a Hero's pleasure? One? Or two? Or all three?

I'm chicken. We know that. If it hadn't been that little sister was about the size of the little brown sisters who had scared me in the past, maybe I could have shown aplomb.

But, hell, those doors didn't close. Just arches. And Jocko me bucko might wake up anytime; I didn't know where he was. I won't say I've never bedded a married woman nor a man's daughter in his own house—but I've followed American cover-up conventions in such matters. This flat-footed proposition scared me worse than the Horned Goats. I mean "Ghosts."

I struggled to put my decision in poetic language.

I didn't manage it but I put over the idea of negative.

The little girl started to bawl and fled. Her sister looked daggers, snorted, *"Hero!"* and went after her. Mama just looked at me and left.

She came back in about two minutes. She spoke very formally, obviously exercising great control, and prayed to know if any woman in this house had met with the Hero's favor? Her name, please? Or could I describe her? Or would I have them paraded so that I might point her out?

I did my best to explain that, were a choice to be made, she herself would be my choice—but that I was tired and wished to sleep alone.

Letva blinked back tears, wished me a hero's rest, and left a second time, even faster. For an instant I thought she was going to slap me.

Five seconds later I got up and tried to catch her. But she was gone, the gallery was dark.

I fell asleep and dreamt about the Cold Water Gang. They were even uglier than Rufo had suggested and they were trying to make me eat big gold nuggets, all with the eyes of Elmer.

IX

RUFO shook me awake. "Boss! Get up. Right now!"

I buried my head in the covers. "Go 'way!" My mouth tasted of spoiled cabbage, my head buzzed, and my ears were on crooked.

"Right *now! She* says to."

I got up. Rufo was dressed in our Merry Men clothes and wearing sword, so I dressed the same way and buckled on mine. My valettes were not in sight, nor my borrowed finery. I stumbled after Rufo into the great dining hall. There was Star, dressed to travel, and looking grim. The fancy furnishings of the night before were gone; it was as bleak as an abandoned barn. A bare table was all, and on it a joint of meat, cold in congealed grease, and a knife beside it.

I looked at it without relish. "What's that?"

"Your breakfast, if you want it. But *I* shall not stay under this roof and eat cold shoulder." It was a tone, a manner, I had never heard from her.

Rufo touched my sleeve. "Boss. Let's get out of here. Now."

So we did. Not a soul was in sight, indoors or out, not even children or dogs. But three dashing steeds were waiting. Those eight-legged tandem ponies, I mean, the horse version of a dachshund, saddled and ready to go. The saddle rigs were complex; each pair of legs had a leather yoke over it and the load was distributed by poles flexing laterally, one on each side, and mounted on this was a chair with a back, a padded seat, and arm rests. A tiller rope ran to each arm rest.

A lever on the left was both brake and accelerator and I hate to say how suggestions were conveyed to the beast. However, the "horses" didn't seem to mind.

They weren't horses. Their heads were slightly equine but they had pads rather than hoofs and were omnivores, not hayburners. But you grow to like these beasties. Mine was black with white points—beautiful. I named her "Ars Longa." She had soulful eyes.

Rufo lashed my bow and quiver to a baggage rack behind my chair and showed me how to get aboard, adjust my seat belt, and get comfortable with feet on foot rests rather than stirrups and my back supported—as comfy as first-class seats in an airliner. We took off fast and hit a steady pace of ten miles an hour, single-footing (the only gait longhorses have) but smoothed by that eight-point suspension so that it was like a car on a gravel road.

Star rode ahead, she hadn't spoken another word. I tried to speak to her but Rufo touched my arm. "Boss, don't," he said quietly. "When *She* is like this, all you can do is wait."

Once we were underway, Rufo and I knee to knee and Star out of earshot ahead, I said, "Rufo, what in the the world happened?"

He frowned. "We'll never know. *She* and the Doral had a row, that's clear. But best we pretend it never happened."

He shut up and so did I. Had Jocko been obnoxious to Star? Drunk he certainly was and amorous he might have been. But I couldn't visualize Star not being able to handle a man so as to avoid rape without hurting his feelings.

That led to further grim thoughts. If the older sister had come in alone— If Miss Tiffany hadn't passed out— If my valette with the fiery hair had showed up to undress me as I had understood she would— Oh, hell!

Presently Rufo eased his seat belt, lowered his back rest and raised his foot rests to reclining position, covered his face with a kerchief and started to snore. After a while I did the same; it had been a short night, no breakfast, and I had a kingsize hangover. My "horse" didn't need any help; the two held position on Star's mount.

When I woke I felt better, aside from hunger and thirst. Rufo was still sleeping; Star's steed was still fifty paces ahead. The countryside was still lush, and ahead perhaps a half mile was a house—not a lordly manor but a farmhouse. I could see a well sweep and thought of moss-covered buckets, cool and wet and reeking of typhoid—well, I had had my booster shots in Heidlebérg; I wanted a drink. Water, I mean. Better yet, beer—they made fine beer hereabouts.

Rufo yawned, put away his kerchief, and raised his seat. "Must have dozed off," he said with a silly grin.

"Rufo, you see that house?"

"Yes. What about it?"

"Lunch, that's what. I've gone far enough on an empty stomach. And I'm so thirsty that I could squeeze a stone and drink the whey from it."

"Then best you do so."

"Huh?"

"Milord, I'm sorry—I'm thirsty, too—but we aren't stopping there. *She* wouldn't like it."

"She wouldn't, eh? Rufo, let me set you straight. Just because milady Star is in a pet is no reason for me to ride all day with no food or water. You do as you see fit; I'm stopping for lunch. Uh, do you have any money on you? Local money?"

He shook his head. "You don't do it that way, not here. Boss. Wait another hour. Please."

106

"Why?"

"Because we are still on the Doral's land, that's why. I don't know that he has sent word ahead to have us shot on sight; Jock is a goodhearted old blackguard. But I would rather be wearing full armor; a flight of arrows wouldn't surprise me. Or a drop net just as we turned in among those trees."

"You really think so?"

"Depends on how angry he is. I mind once, when a man *really* offended him, the Doral had this poor rube stripped down and tied by his family jewels and placed —no, I can't tell that one." Rufo gulped and looked sick. "Big night last night, I'm not myself. Better we speak of pleasant things. You mentioned squeezing whey from a rock. No doubt you were thinking of the Strong Muldoon?"

"Damn it, don't change the subject!" My head was throbbing. "I won't ride under those trees and the man who lets fly a shaft at me had better check his own skin for punctures. I'm thirsty."

"Boss," Rufo pleaded. *"She* will neither eat nor drink on the Doral's land—even if they begged her to. And *She's* right. You don't know the customs. Here one accepts what is freely given ... but even a child is too proud to touch anything begrudged. Five miles more. Can't the hero who killed Igli before breakfast hold out another five miles?"

"Well ... all right, all right! But this is a crazy sort of country, you must admit. Utterly insane."

"Mmmm ..." he answered. "Have you ever been in Washington, D.C.?"

"Well—" I grinned wryly. *"Touché!* And I forgot that this is your native land. No offense intended."

"Oh, but it's not. What made you think so?"

"Why—" I tried to think. Neither Rufo nor Star had said so, but— "You know the customs, you speak the language like a native."

"Milord Oscar, I've forgotten how many languages I speak. When I hear one of them, I speak it."

"Well, you're not an American. Nor a Frenchman, I think."

He grinned merrily. "I could show you birth certificates from both countries—or could until we lost our baggage. But, no, I'm not from Earth."

"Then where are you from?"

Rufo hesitated. "Best you get your facts from *Her*."

"Tripe! I've got both feet hobbled and a sack over my head. This is ridiculous."

"Boss," he said earnestly, "*She* will answer any question you ask. But you must ask them."

"I certainly shall!"

"So let's speak of other matters. You mentioned the Strong Muldoon—"

"*You* mentioned him."

"Well, perhaps I did. I never met Muldoon myself, though I've been in that part of Ireland. A fine country and the only really logical people on Earth. Facts won't sway them in the face of higher truth. An admirable people. I heard of Muldoon from one of my uncles, a truthful man who for many years was a ghost writer of political speeches. But at this time, due to a mischance while writing speeches for rival candidates, he was enjoying a vacation as a free-lance correspondent for an American syndicate specializing in Sunday feature stories. He heard of the Strong Muldoon and tracked him down, taking train from Dublin, then a local bus, and at last Shank's Mares. He encountered a man plowing a field with a one-horse plow ... but this man was shoving the plow ahead of himself without benefit of horse, turning a neat eight-inch furrow. 'Aha!' said my uncle and called out, 'Mr. Muldoon!'

"The farmer stopped and called back, 'Bless you for the mistake, friend!'—picked up the plow in one hand, pointed with it and said, 'You'll be finding Muldoon that way. Strong, he is.'

"So my uncle thanked him and went on until he found another man setting out fence posts by shoving them into the ground with his bare hand ... and in stony soil, it's true. So again my uncle hailed him as Muldoon.

"The man was so startled he dropped the ten or dozen six-inch posts he had tucked under the other arm. 'Get along with your blarney, now!' he called back. 'You must know that Muldoon lives farther on down this very same road. He's *strong*.'

"The next local my uncle saw was building a stone fence. Dry-stone work it was and very neat. This man was trimming the rock without hammer or trowel, splitting them with the edge of his hand and doing the fine trim by pinching off bits with his fingers. So again my uncle addressed a man by that glorious name.

"The man started to speak but his throat was dry from all that stone dust; his voice failed him. So he grabbed up a large rock, squeezed it the way you squeezed Igli—forced water out of it as if it had been a goatskin, drank. Then he said, 'Not me, my friend. He's *strong*, as everyone knows. Why, many is the time that I have seen him insert his little finger—' "

My mind was distracted from this string of lies by a wench pitching hay just across the ditch from the road. She had remarkable pectoral muscles and a lava-lava just suited her. She saw me eyeing her and gave me the eye right back, with a wiggle tossed in.

"You were saying?" I asked.

"Eh? '—just to the first joint . . . and hold himself at arm's length for *hours!*"

"Rufo," I said, "I don't believe it could have been more than a few minutes. Strain on the tissues, and so forth."

"Boss," he answered in a hurt tone, "I could take you to the very spot where the Mighty Dugan used to perform this stunt."

"You said his name was Muldoon."

"He was a Dugan on his mother's side, very proud of her he was. You'll be pleased to know, milord, that the boundary of the Doral's land is now in sight. Lunch in minutes only."

"I can use it. With a gallon of anything, even water."

"Passed by acclamation. Truthfully, milord, I'm not at my best today. I need food and drink and a long siesta before the fighting starts, or I'll yawn when I should parry. Too large a night."

"I didn't see you at the banquet."

"I was there in spirit. In the kitchen the food is hotter, the choice is better, and the company less formal. But I had no intention of making a night of it. Early to bed is my motto. Moderation in all things. Epictetus. But the pastry cook— Well, she reminds me of another girl I once knew, my partner in a legitimate business, smuggling. But *her* motto was that anything worth doing at all is worth overdoing—and she did. She smuggled on top of smuggling, a side line of her own unmentioned to me and not taken into account—for I was listing every item with the customs officers, a copy with the bribe, so that they would know I was honest.

"But a girl can't walk through the gates fat as a stuffed goose and walk back through them twenty minutes later skinny as the figure one—not that she was, just a manner of speaking—without causing thoughtful glances. If it hadn't been for the strange thing the dog did in the night, the busies would have nabbed us."

"What was the strange thing the dog did in the night?"

"Just what I was doing last night. The noise woke us and we were out over the roof and free, but with nothing to show for six months' hard work but skinned knees. But that pastry cook— You saw her, milord. Brown hair, blue eyes, a widow's peak and the rest remarkably like Sophia Loren."

"I have a vague memory of someone like that."

"Then you didn't see her, there is nothing vague about Nalia. As may be, I had intended to lead the life sanitary last night, knowing that there would be bloodshed today. You know:

'Once at night and outen the light;
'Once in the morning, a new day a-borning'

"—as the Scholar advised. But I hadn't reckoned with Nalia. So here I am with no sleep and no breakfast and

110

if I'm dead before nightfall in a pool of my own blood, it'll be partly Nalia's doing."

"I'll shave your corpse, Rufo; that's a promise." We had passed the marker into the next county but Star didn't slow down. "Bye the bye, where did you learn the undertaker's trade?"

"The what? Oh! That was a far place indeed. The top of that rise, behind those trees, is a house and that's where we'll be having lunch. Nice people."

"Good!" The thought of lunch was a bright spot as I was again regretting my Boy Scout behavior of the night before. "Rufo, you had it all wrong about the strange thing the dog did in the night."

"Milord?"

"The dog did nothing in the night, that was the strange thing."

"Well, it certainly didn't *sound* that way," Rufo said doubtfully.

"Another dog, another far place. Sorry. What I started to say was: A funny thing happened to me on the way to bed last night—and I *did* lead the life sanitary."

"Indeed, milord?"

"In deed, if not in thought." I needed to tell somebody and Rufo was the sort of scoundrel I could trust. I told him the Story of the Three Bares.

"I should have risked it," I concluded. "And, swelp me, I would have, if that kid had been put to bed—alone—when she should have been. Or I think I would have, regardless of White Shotgun or jumping out windows. Rufo, why do the prettiest gals always have fathers or husbands? But I tell you the truth, there they were—the Big Bare, the Middle-Sized Bare, and the Littlest Bare, close enough to touch and all of them anxious to keep my bed warm—and I didn't do a damn thing! Go ahead and laugh. I deserve it."

He didn't laugh. I turned to look at him and his expression was piteous. "Milord! Oscar my comrade! *Tell me it isn't true!*"

"It is true," I said huffily. "And I regretted it at once. Too late. And *you* complained about *your* night!"

111

"Oh, my God!" He threw his mount into high gear and took off. Ars Longa looked back inquiringly over her shoulder, then continued on.

Rufo caught up with Star; they stopped, short of the house where lunch was to be expected. They waited and I joined them. Star was wearing no expression; Rufo looked unbearably embarrassed.

Star said, "Rufo, go beg lunch for us. Fetch it here. I would speak with milord alone."

"Yes, milady!" He got out fast.

Star said to me, still with no expression, "Milord Hero, is this true? What your groom reports to me?"

"I don't know what he reported."

"It concerned your failure—your alleged failure—last night."

"I don't know what you mean by 'failure.' If you want to know what I did after the banquet . . . I slept alone. Period."

She sighed but her expression did not change. "I wanted to hear it from your lips. To be just." Then her expression did change and I have never seen such anger. In a low, almost passionless voice she began chewing me out:

"You hero. You incredible butter-brained dolt. Clumsy, bumbling, loutish, pimple-pocked, underdone, over-muscled, idiotic—"

"Stop it!"

"Quiet, I am not finished with you. Insulting three innocent ladies, offending a staunch—"

"SHUT UP!!!"

The blast blew her hair back. I started in before she could rev up again. "Don't ever again speak to me that way, Star. Never."

"But—"

"Hold your tongue, you bad-tempered brat! You have not earned the right to speak to me that way. Nor will any girl ever earn the right. You will always—*always!*—address me politely and with respect. One more word of your nasty rudeness and I'll spank you until the tears fly."

112

"You wouldn't *dare!*"

"Get your hand away from that sword or I'll take it away from you, down your pants right here on the road, and spank you with *it*. Till your arse is red and you beg for mercy. Star, I do not fight females—but I do punish naughty children. Ladies I treat as ladies. Spoiled brats I treat as spoiled brats. Star, you could be the Queen of England and the Galactic Overlord all rolled into one— but ONE MORE WORD out of line from you, and down come your tights and you won't be able to sit for a week. Understand me?"

At last she said in a small voice, "I understand, milord."

"And besides that, I'm resigning from the hero business. I won't listen to such talk twice, I won't work for a person who treats me that way even once." I sighed, realizing that I had just lost my corporal's stripes again. But I always felt easier and freer without them.

"Yes, milord." I could barely hear her. It occurred to me that it was a long way back to Nice. But it didn't worry me.

"All right, let's forget it."

"Yes, milord." She added quietly, "But may I explain *why* I spoke as I did?"

"No."

"Yes, milord."

A long silent time later Rufo returned. He stopped out of earshot, I motioned him to join us.

We ate silently and I didn't eat much but the beer was good. Rufo tried once to make chitchat with an impossibility about another of his uncles. It couldn't have fallen flatter in Boston.

After lunch Star turned her mount—those "horses" have a small turning circle for their wheelbase but it's easier to bring them full circle in a tight place by leading them. Rufo said, "Milady?"

She said impassively, "I am returning to the Doral."

"*Milady!* Please not!"

"Dear Rufo," she said warmly but sadly. "You can wait up at that house—and if I'm not back in three days,

113

you are free." She looked at me, looked away. "I hope that milord Oscar will see fit to escort me. But I do not ask it. I have not the right." She started off.

I was slow in getting Ars Longa turned; I didn't have the hang of it. Star was a good many bricks down the road; I started after her.

Rufo waited until I was turned, biting his nails, then suddenly climbed aboard and caught up with me. We rode knee to knee, a careful fifty paces behind Star. Finally he said, "This is suicide. You know that, don't you?"

"No, I didn't know it."

"Well, it is."

I said, "Is that why you are not bothering to say 'sir'?"

"Milord?" He laughed shortly and said, "I guess it is. No point in that nonsense when you are going to die soon."

"You're mistaken."

"Huh?"

" 'Huh, milord,' if you please. Just for practice. But from now on, even if we last only thirty minutes. Because *I* am running the show now—and not just as her stooge. I don't want any doubt in your mind as to who is boss once the fighting starts. Otherwise turn around and I'll give your mount a slap on the rump to get you moving. Hear me?"

"Yes, milord Oscar." He added thoughtfully, "I knew you were boss as soon as I got back. But I don't see how you did it. Milord, I have never seen *Her* meek before. May one ask?"

"One may not. But you have my permission to ask her. If you think it is safe. Now tell me about this 'suicide' matter—and don't say she doesn't want you to give me advice. From here on you'll give advice any time I ask—and keep your lip buttoned if I don't."

"Yes, milord. All right, the suicide prospects. No way to figure the odds. It depends on how angry the Doral is. But it won't be a fight, can't be. Either we get clobbered the instant we poke our noses in . . . or we are safe until we leave his land again, even if he tells us to turn around and ride away." Rufo looked very thoughtful. "Milord, if you want a blind guess— Well, I figure you've insulted the Doral the worst he has ever been hurt in the course of a long and touchy life. So it's about ninety to ten that, two shakes after we turn off the road, we are all going to be sprouting more arrows than Saint Sebastian."

"Star, too? She hasn't done anything. Nor have you." (Nor I, either, I added to myself. What a country!)

Rufo sighed. "Milord, each world has its own ways. Jock won't *want* to hurt Her. He likes Her. He's terribly fond of Her. You could say that he loves Her. But if he kills you, he has *got* to kill Her. Anything else would be inhumane by his standards—and he's a very moral bloke; he's noted for it. And kill me, too, of course, but I don't count. He *must* kill *Her* even though it will start a chain of events that will wipe him out just as dead once the news gets out. The question is: Does he have to kill *you?* I figure he has to, knowing these people. Sorry ... milord."

I mulled it over. "Then why are you here, Rufo?"

"Milord?"

"You can cut the 'sirs' down to one an hour. Why are you here? If your estimate is correct, your one sword and one bow can't affect the outcome. She gave you a fair chance to chicken out. So what is it? Pride? Or are *you* in love with her?"

"Oh, my God, no!"

Again I saw Rufo really shocked. "Excuse me," he went on. "You caught me with my guard down." He thought about it. "Two reasons, I suppose. The first is that if Jock allows us to parley—well, *She* is quite a talker. In the second place"—he glanced at me—"I'm superstitious, I admit it. You're a man with luck. I've seen it. So I want to be close to you even when reason tells me to run. You could fall in a cesspool and—"

"Nonsense. You should hear my hard-luck story."

"Maybe in the past. But I'm betting the dice as they roll." He shut up.

A bit later I said, "You stay here." I speeded up and

115

joined Star. "Here are the plans," I told her. "When we get there, you stay out on the road with Rufo. I'm going in alone."

She gasped. "Oh, milord! No!"

"Yes."

"But—"

"Star, do you want me back? As your champion?"

"With all my heart!"

"All right. Then do it my way."

She waited before answering. "Oscar—"

"Yes, Star."

"I will do as you say. But will you let me explain before you decide what you will say?"

"Go on."

"In this world, the place for a lady to ride is by her champion. And that is where I would want to be, my Hero, when in peril. Especially when in peril. But I'm not pleading for sentiment, nor for empty form. Knowing what I now know I can prophesy with certainty that, if you go in first, you will die at once, and I will die—and Rufo—as soon as they can chase us down. That will be quickly, our mounts are tired. On the other hand, if I go in alone—"

"No."

"Please, milord. I was not proposing it. If I were to go in alone, I would be almost as likely to die at once as you would be. Or perhaps, instead of feeding me to the pigs, he would simply have me feed the pigs and be a plaything of the pig boys—a fate merciful rather than cold justice in view of my utter degradation in returning without you. But the Doral is fond of me and I think he might let me live . . . as a pig girl and no better than pigs. This I would risk if necessary and wait my chance to escape, for I cannot afford pride; I have no pride, only necessity." Her voice was husky with tears.

"Star, Star!"

"My darling!"

"Huh? You said—"

"May I say it? We may not have much time. My Hero . . . my darling." She reached out blindly, I took her

116

hand; she leaned toward me and pressed it to her breast.

Then she straightened up but kept my hand. "I'm all right now. I am a woman when I least expect it. No, my darling Hero, there is only one way for us to go in and that is side by side, proudly. It is not only safest, it is the only way I would wish it—could I afford pride. I can afford anything else. I could buy you the Eiffel Tower for a trinket, and replace it when you broke it. But not pride."

"Why is it safest?"

"Because he may—I say 'may'—let us parley. If I can get in ten words, he'll grant a hundred. Then a thousand. I may be able to heal his hurt."

"All right. But— Star, what *did* I do to hurt him? I *didn't!* I went to a lot of trouble *not* to hurt him."

She was silent a while, then—"You are an American."

"What's that got to do with it? Jock doesn't know it."

"It has, perhaps, everything to do with it. No, America is at most a name to the Doral for, although he has studied the Universes, he has never traveled. But— You will not be angry with me again?"

"Uh ... let's call a King's-X on that. Say anything you need to say but explain things. Just don't chew me out. Oh, hell, chew me out if you like—this once. Just don't let it be a habit ... my darling."

She squeezed my hand. "Never will I again! The error lay in *my* not realizing that you are American. I don't know America, not the way Rufo does. If Rufo had been present— But he wasn't; he was wenching in the kitchen. I suppose I assumed, when you were offered table and roof and bed, that you would behave as a Frenchman would. I never dreamed that you would refuse it. Had I known, I could have spun a thousand excuses for you. An oath taken. A holy day in your religion. Jock would have been disappointed but not hurt; he is a man of honor."

"But— Damn it, I still don't see why he wants to shoot me for *not* doing something I would expect, back home, that he might shoot me for *doing*. In this country, is a man forced to accept any proposition a gal makes? And why did she run and complain? Why didn't she keep it secret? Hell, she didn't even try. She dragged in her daughters."

"But, darling, it was *never* a secret. He asked you publicly and publicly you accepted. How would *you* feel if your bride, on your wedding night, kicked you out of the bedroom? 'Table, and roof, and bed.' You accepted."

" 'Bed.' Star, in America beds are multiple-purpose furniture. Sometimes we sleep in them. Just sleep. I didn't dig it."

"I know now. You didn't know the idiom. My fault. But do you now see why he was completely—and publicly —humiliated?"

"Well, yes, but he brought it on himself. He asked me in public. It would have been worse if I had said No then."

"Not at all. You didn't have to accept. You could have refused graciously. Perhaps the most graceful way, even though it be a white lie, is for the hero to protest his tragic inability—temporary or permanent—from wounds received in the very battle that proved him a hero."

"I'll remember that. But I still don't see why he was so astoundingly generous in the first place."

She turned and looked at me. "My darling, is it all right for me to say that *you* have astounded *me* every time I have talked with you? And I had thought I had passed beyond all surprises, years ago."

"It's mutual. You always astound me. However, I like it—except one time."

"My lord Hero, how often do you think a simple country squire has a chance to gain for his family a Hero's son, and raise it as his own? Can you not feel his gall-bitter disappointment at what you snatched from him after he thought you had promised this boon? His shame? His wrath?"

I considered it. "Well, I'll be dogged. It happens in America, too. But they don't boast about it."

"Other countries, other customs. At the very least, he had thought that he had the honor of a hero treating him as a brother. And with luck he expected the get of a hero. for house Doral."

"Wait a minute! Is that why he sent me *three?* To improve the odds?"

"Oscar, he would eagerly have sent you *thirty* . . . if you had hinted that you felt heroic enough to attempt it. As it was, he sent his chief wife and his two favorite daughters." She hesitated. "What I still don't understand—" She stopped and asked me a blunt question.

"Hell, no!" I protested, blushing. "Not since I was fifteen. But one thing that put me off was that mere child. She's one. I think."

Star shrugged. "She may be. But she is *not* a child; in Nevia she is a woman. And even if she is unbroached as yet, I'll wager she's a mother in another twelvemonth. But if you were loath to tap her, why didn't you shoo her out and take her older sister? That quaint hasn't been virgin since she's had breasts, to my certain knowledge—and I hear that Muri is 'some dish,' if that is the American idiom."

I muttered. I had been thinking the same thing. But I didn't want to discuss it with Star.

She said, *"Pardonne-moi, mon cher? Tu as dit?"*

"I said I had given up sex crimes for Lent!"

She looked puzzled. "But Lent is over, even on Earth. And it is not, here, at all."

"Sorry."

"Still, I'm pleased that you didn't pick Muri over Letva; Muri would have been unbearably stuck-up with her mother after such a thing. But I do understand that you *will* repair this, if I can straighten it out?" She added, "It makes great difference in how I handle the diplomacies."

(Star, Star—*you* are the one I want to bed!) "This is what you wish . . . my darling?"

"Oh, how much it would help!"

"Okay. You're the doctor. One . . . three . . . thirty— I'll die trying. But no little kids!"

"No problem. Let me think. If the Doral lets me get in just *five* words—" She fell silent. Her hand was pleasantly warm.

I did some thinking, too. These strange customs had

119

ramifications, some of which I had still shied away from. How was it, if Letva had immediately told her husband what a slob I was—

"Star? Where did *you* sleep last night?"

She looked around sharply. "Milord . . . is it permitted to ask you, please, to *mind your own business?*"

"I suppose so. But everybody seems to be minding mine."

"I am sorry. But I am very much worried and my heaviest worries you do not know as yet. It was a fair question and deserves a fair answer. Hospitality balances, always, and honors flow both ways. I slept in the Doral's bed. However, if it matters—and it may to you; I still do not understand Americans—I was wounded yesterday, it still bothered me. Jock is a sweet and gentle soul. We slept. Just slept."

I tried to make it nonchalant. "Sorry about the wound. Does it hurt now?"

"Not at all. The dressing will fall off by tomorrow. However— Last night was not the first time I enjoyed table and roof and bed at house Doral. Jock and I are old friends, beloved friends—which is why I think I can risk that he may grant me a few seconds before killing me."

"Well, I had figured out most of that."

"Oscar, by your standards—the way you have been raised—I am a bitch."

"Oh, never! A princess."

"A bitch. But I am not of your country and I was reared by another code. By my standards, and they seem good to me, I am a moral woman. Now . . . am I still 'your darling'?"

"My darling!"

"My darling Hero. My champion. Lean close and kiss me. If we die, I would my mouth be warm with your lips. The entrance is just around this bend."

"I know."

A few moments later we rode, swords sheathed and bows unstrung, proudly into the target area.

X

THREE days later we rode out again. This time breakfast was sumptuous. This time musicians lined our exit. This time the Doral rode with us.

This time Rufo reeled to his mount, each arm around a wench, a bottle in each hand, then, after busses from a dozen more, was lifted into his seat and belted in the reclining position. He fell asleep, snoring before we set out.

I was kissed good-bye more times than I could count and by some who had no reason to do it so thoroughly— for I was only an apprentice hero, still learning the trade.

It's not a bad trade, despite long hours, occupational hazards, and utter lack of security; it has fringe benefits, with many openings and rapid advancement for a man with push and willingness to learn. The Doral seemed well pleased with me.

At breakfast he had sung my prowess up to date in a thousand intricate lines. But I was sober and did not let his praises impress me with my own greatness; I knew better. Obviously a little bird had reported to him regularly—but that bird was a liar. John Henry the Steel-Drivin' Man couldn't have done what Jocko's ode said I did.

But I took it with my heroic features noble and impassive, then I stood up and gave them "Casey at the Bat," putting heart and soul into "Mighty Casey has struck OUT!"

Star gave it a free interpretation. I had (so she sang) praised the ladies of Doral, the ideas being ones associated with Madame Pompadour, Nell Gwyn, Theodora, Ninon de l'Enclos, and Rangy Lil. She didn't name these famous ladies; instead she was specific, in Nevian eulogy that would have startled François Villon.

So I had to come up with an encore. I gave them "Reilly's Daughter," then "Jabberwocky," with gestures.

Star had interpreted me in spirit; she had said what I would have said had I been capable of extemporizing poetry. Late on the second day I had chanced on Star in the steam room of the manor's baths. For an hour we lay wrapped in sheets on adjacent slabs, sweating it out and restoring the tissues. Presently I blurted out to her how surprised—and delighted—I was. I did it sheepishly but Star was one to whom I dared bare my soul.

She had listened gravely. When I ran down, she said quietly, "My Hero, as you know, I do not know America. But from what Rufo tells me your culture is unique, among all the Universes."

"Well, I realize that the USA is not sophisticated in such things, not the way France is."

" 'France!' " She shrugged, beautifully. " 'Latins are lousy lovers.' I heard that somewhere, I testify that it is true. Oscar, so far as I know, your culture is the only semicivilized one in which love is not recognized as the highest art and given the serious study it deserves."

"You mean the way they treat it here. Whew! 'Much too good for the common people!' "

"No, I do *not* mean the way it is treated here." She spoke in English. "Much as I love our friends here, this is a barbarous culture and their arts are barbaric. Oh, good art of its sort, very good; their approach is honest. But—if we live through this, after our troubles are over— I want you to travel among the Universes. You'll see what I mean." She got up, folding her sheet into a toga. "I'm glad you are pleased, my Hero. I'm proud of you."

I lay there a while longer, thinking about what she had said. The "highest art"—and back home we didn't even study it, much less make any attempt to teach it. Ballet takes years and years. Nor do they hire you to sing at the Met just because you have a loud voice.

Why should "love" be classed as an "instinct"?

Certainly the appetite for sex is an instinct—but did another appetite make every glutton a gourmet, every fry cook a Cordon Bleu? Hell, you had to *learn* even to be a fry cook.

I walked out of the steam room whistling "The Best Things in Life Are Free"—then chopped it off in sudden sorrow for all my poor, unhappy compatriots cheated of their birthright by the most mammoth hoax in history.

A mile out the Doral bade us good-bye, embracing me, kissing Star and mussing her hair; then he and his escort drew swords and remained at salute until we passed over the next rise. Star and I rode knee to knee while Rufo snored behind us.

I looked at her and her mouth twitched. She caught my eye and said demurely, "Good morning, milord."

"Good morning, milady. You slept well?"

"Very well, thank you, milord. And you?"

"The same, thank you."

"So? 'What was the strange thing the dog did in the night?'"

"'The dog did nothing in the night, that was the strange thing,'" I answered with a straight face.

"Really? So gay a dog? Then who was that knight I last saw with a lady?"

" 'Twasn't night, 'twas brillig."

"And your vorpal blade went snicker-snack! My beamish boy!"

"Don't try to pin your jabberwocking on *me*, you frolicsome wench," I said severely. "I've got friends, I have —I can prove an alibi. Besides, 'my strength is as the strength of ten because my heart is pure.' "

"And the line before that one. Yes, I know; your friends told me about it, milord." Suddenly she grinned and slapped me on the thigh and started bellowing the chorus of "Reilly's Daughter." Vita Brevis snorted; Ars Longa pricked up her ears and looked around reprovingly.

"Stop it," I said. "You're shocking the horses."

"They aren't horses and you can't shock them. Have you seen how *they* do it, milord? In spite of all those legs? First—"

"Hold your tongue! Ars Longa is a lady, even if you aren't."

"I warned you I was a bitch. First she sidles up—"

"I've seen it. Muri thought it would amuse me. Instead it gave me an inferiority complex that lasted all afternoon."

"I venture to disbelieve that it was *all* afternoon, milord Hero. Let's sing about Reilly then. You lead, I'll harmonize."

"Well— Not too loud, we'll wake Rufo."

"Not him, he's embalmed."

"Then you'll wake me, which is worse. Star darling, when and where was Rufo an undertaker? And how did he get from that into this business? Did they run him out of town?"

She looked puzzled. "Undertaker? Rufo? Not Rufo."

"He was most circumstantial."

"So? Milord, Rufo has many faults. But telling the truth is not one of them. Moreover, our people do not have undertakers."

"You don't? Then what do you do with leftover carcasses? Can't leave them cluttering the parlor. Untidy."

"I think so, too, but our people do just that: keep them in the parlor. For a few years at least. An overly sentimental custom but we are a sentimental people. Even so, it can be overdone. One of my great aunts kept all her former husbands in her bedchamber—a dreadful clutter and boring, too, because she talked about them, repeating herself and exaggerating. I quit going to see her."

"Well. Did she dust them?"

"Oh, yes. She was a fussy housekeeper."

"Uh— How many were there?"

"Seven or eight, I never counted."

"I see. Star? Is there black-widow blood in your family?"

"What? Oh! But, darling, there is black-widow blood in every woman." She dimpled, reached over and patted my knee. "But Auntie didn't kill them. Believe me, my Hero, the women in my family are much too fond of men to waste them. No, Auntie just hated to let them go. I think that is foolish. Look forward, not back."

" 'And let the dead past bury its dead.' Look, if your people keep dead bodies around the house, you must have undertakers. Embalmers at least. Or doesn't the air get thick?"

"Embalming? Oh, no! Just place a stasis on them once you're sure they are dead. Or dying. Any schoolboy can do that." She added, "Perhaps I wronged Rufo. He has spent much time on your Earth—he likes the place, it fascinates him—and he may have tried undertaking. But it seems to me an occupation too honest and straightforward to attract him."

"You never did tell me what your people eventually do with a cadaver."

"Not bury it. That would shock them silly." Star shivered. "Even myself and I've traveled the Universes, learned to be indifferent to almost any custom."

"But what?"

"Much what you did to Igli. Apply a geometrical option and get rid of it."

"Oh. Star, where did Igli go?"

125

"I couldn't guess, milord. I had no chance to calculate it. Perhaps the ones who made him know. But I think they were even more taken by surprise than I was."

"I guess I'm dense, Star. You call it geometry; Jocko referred to me as a 'mathematician.' But I did what was forced on me by circumstances; I didn't understand it."

"Forced on Igli, you should say, milord Hero. What happens when you place an insupportable strain on a mass, such that it cannot remain where it is? While leaving it nowhere to go? This is a schoolboy problem in metaphysical geometry and the oldest proto-paradox, the one about the irresistible force and the immovable body. The mass implodes. It is squeezed out of its own world into some other. This is often the way the people of a universe discover the Universes—but usually as disastrously as you forced it on Igli; it may take millennia before they control it. It may hover around the fringes as 'magic' for a long time, sometimes working, sometimes failing, sometimes backfiring on the magician."

"And you call this 'mathematics'?"

"How else?"

"I'd call it magic."

"Yes, surely. As I told Jocko, you have a natural genius. You could be a great warlock."

I shrugged uncomfortably. "I don't believe in magic."

"Nor do I," she answered, "the way you put it. I believe in what *is.*"

"That's what I mean, Star. I don't believe in hocus-pocus. What happened to Igli—I mean, 'what appeared to happen to Igli'—could not have happened because it would violate the law of conservation of mass-energy. There must be some other explanation."

She was politely silent.

So I brought to bear the sturdy common sense of ignorance and prejudice. "Look, Star, I'm not going to believe the impossible simply because I was there. A natural law is a natural law. You have to admit that."

We rode a few rods before she answered, "May it please milord Hero, the world is not what we wish it to be. It is what it is. No, I have over-assumed. Perhaps

126

it is indeed what we wish it to be. Either way, it is what it *is. Le voilà!* Behold it, self-demonstrating. *Das Ding an sich.* Bite it. It *is. Ai-je raison?* Do I speak truly?"

"That's what I was saying! The universe is what it is and can't be changed by jiggery-pokery. It works by exact rules, like a machine." (I hesitated, remembering a car we had had that was a hypochondriac. It would "fall sick," then "get well" as soon as a mechanic tried to touch it.) I went on firmly, "Natural law never takes a holiday. The invariability of natural law is the cornerstone of science."

"So it is."

"Well?" I demanded.

"So much the worse for science."

"But—" I shut up and rode in huffy silence.

Presently a slender hand touched my forearm, caressed it. "Such a strong sword arm," she said softly. "Milord Hero, may I explain?"

"Talk ahead," I said. "If you can sell me, you can convert the Pope to Mormonism. I'm stubborn."

"Would I have picked you out of hundreds of billions to be my champion were you not?"

" 'Hundreds of billions?' You mean millions, don't you?"

"Hear me, milord. Indulge me. Let us be Socratic. I'll frame the trick questions and you make the stupid answers—and we'll learn who shaved the barber. Then it will be your turn and I'll be the silly stooge. Okay?"

"All right, put a nickel in."

"Very well. Question: Are the customs at house Doral the customs you used at home?"

"What? You know they aren't. I've never been so flabbergasted since the time the preacher's daughter took me up into the steeple to show me the Holy Ghost." I chuckled sheepishly. "I'd be blushing yet but I've burned out my fuses."

"Yet the basic difference between Nevian customs and yours lies in only one postulate. Milord, there are worlds in which males kill females as soon as eggs are laid— and others in which females eat males even as they are

127

being fructified—like that black widow you made cousin to me."

"I didn't mean that, Star."

"I was not offended, my love. An insult is like a drink; it affects one only if accepted. And pride is too heavy baggage for my journey; I have none. Oscar, would you find such worlds stranger than this one?"

"You're talking about spiders or some such. Not people."

"I speak of people, the dominant race of each its world. Highly civilized."

"Ugh!"

"You will not say 'ugh' when you see them. They are so different from us that their home life cannot matter to us. Contrariwise, this planet is very like your Earth—yet your customs would shock old Jocko out of song. Darling, your world has a custom unique in the Universes. That is, the Twenty Universes known to me, out of thousands or millions or googols of universes. In the known Twenty Universes only Earth has this astounding custom."

"Do you mean 'War'?"

"Oh, no! Most worlds have warfare. This planet Nevia is on is one of the few where killing is retail, rather than wholesale. Here there be Heroes, killing is done with passion. This is a world of love and slaughter, both with gay abandon. No, I mean something much more shocking. Can you guess?"

"Uh . . . television commercials?"

"Close in spirit, but wide of the mark. You have an expression 'the oldest profession.' Here—and in all other known worlds—it isn't even the youngest. Nobody has heard of it and wouldn't believe it if he did. We few who visit Earth don't talk about it. Not that it would matter; most people don't believe travelers' tales."

"Star, are you telling me that there is *no* prostitution elsewhere in the Universe?"

"The Universes, my darling. None."

"You know," I said thoughtfully, "that's going to be a shock to my first sergeant. None at all?"

"I mean," she said bluntly, "that whoring seems to have been invented by Earth people and no others—and the idea would shock old Jocko into impotence. He's a straitlaced moralist."

"I'll be damned! We must be a bunch of slobs."

"I did not mean to offend, Oscar; I was reciting facts. But this oddity of Earth is not odd in its own context. Any commodity is certain to be sold—bought, sold, leased, rented, bartered, traded, discounted, price-stabilized, inflated, bootlegged, and legislated—and a woman's 'commodity' as it was called on Earth in franker days is no exception. The only wonder is the wild notion of thinking of it as a commodity. Why, it so surprised me that once I even— Never mind. Anything can be made a commodity. Someday I will show you cultures living in spaces, not on planets—nor on fundaments of any sort; not all universes have planets—cultures where the breath of life is sold like a kilo of butter in Provence. Other places so crowded that the privilege of staying alive is subject to tax—and delinquents are killed out of hand by the Department of Eternal Revenue and neighbors not only do not interfere, they are pleased."

"Good God! Why?"

"They solved death, milord, and most of them won't emigrate despite endless roomier planets. But we were speaking of Earth. Not only is whoring unknown elsewhere, but its permutations are unknown—dower, bridal price, alimony, separate maintenance, all the variations that color all Earth's institutions—every custom related even remotely to the incredible notion that what all women have an endless supply of is nevertheless merchandise, to be hoarded and auctioned."

Ars Longa gave a snort of disgust. No, I don't think she understood. She understands some Nevian but Star spoke English; Nevian lacks the vocabulary.

"Even your secondary customs," she went on, "are shaped by this unique institution. Clothing—you've noticed that there is no real difference here in how the two sexes dress. I'm in tights this morning and you are in shorts but had it been the other way around no one would have noticed."

"The hell they wouldn't! Your tights wouldn't fit me."

"They stretch. And body shyness, which is an aspect of sex-specialized clothing. Here nakedness is as unnoteworthy as on that pretty little island where I found you. All hairless peoples sometimes wear clothing and all peoples no matter how hirsute wear ornaments—but nakedness taboo is found *only* where flesh is merchandise to be packaged or displayed . . . that is to say, on Earth. It parallels 'Don't pinch the grapefruit' and putting false bottoms in berry boxes. If something is never haggled over, there is no need to make a mystery of it."

"So if we get rid of clothes we get rid of prostitution?"

"Heavens, no! You've got it backwards." She frowned. "I don't see how Earth could ever get rid of whoring; it's too much a part of everything you do."

"Star, you've got your facts wrong. There is almost no prostitution in America."

She looked startled. "Really? But— Isn't 'alimony' an American word? And 'gold digger'? And 'coming-out party'?"

"Yes, but prostitution has almost died out. Hell, I wouldn't know how to go about finding a whorehouse even in an Army town. I'm not saying that you don't wind up in the hay. But it's not commercialized. Star, even with an American girl who is well-known to be an easy make-out, if you offered her five bucks—or twenty —it's ten to one she would slap your face."

"Then how is it done?"

"You're nice to her instead. Take her to dinner, maybe to a show. Buy her flowers, girls are suckers for flowers. Then approach the subject politely."

"Oscar, doesn't this dinner and show, and possibly flowers, cost more than five dollars? Or even twenty? I understood that American prices were as high as French prices."

"Well, yes, but you can't just tip your hat and expect a girl to throw herself on her back. A tightwad—"

130

"I rest the case. All I was trying to show was that customs can be wildly different in different worlds."

"That's true, even on Earth. But—"

"Please, milord. I won't argue the virtue of American women, nor was I criticizing. Had I been reared in America I think I would want at least an emerald bracelet rather than dinner and a show. But I was leading up to the subject of 'natural law.' Is not the invariability of natural law an unproved assumption? Even on Earth?"

"Well— You haven't stated it fairly. It's an assumption, I suppose. But there has never been a case in which it failed to stand up."

"No black swans? Could it not be that an observer who saw an exception preferred not to believe his eyes? Just as you do not want to believe that Igli ate himself even though you, my Hero, forced him to? Never mind. Let's leave Socrates to his Xanthippe. Natural law may be invariable throughout a universe—and seems to be, in rigid universes. But it is certain that natural laws vary from universe to universe—and believe this you *must*, milord, else neither of us will live long!"

I considered it. Damn it, where *had* Igli gone? "Most unsettling."

"No more unsettling, once you get used to it, than shifting languages and customs as you shift countries. How many chemical elements are there on Earth?"

"Uh, ninety-two and a bunch of Johnny-Come-Latelies. A hundred and six or seven."

"Much the same here. Nevertheless a chemist from Earth would suffer some shocks. The elements aren't quite the same, nor do they behave quite the same way. H-bombs won't work here and dynamite won't explode."

I said sharply, "Now wait! Are you telling me that electrons and protons aren't the same here, to get down to basics?"

She shrugged. "Perhaps, perhaps not. What is an electron but a mathematical concept? Have you tasted one lately? Or put salt on the tail of a wavicle? Does it matter?"

"It damn' well would matter. A man can starve as

131

dead from lack of trace elements as from lack of bread."

"True. In some universes we humans must carry food if we visit them—which we sometimes must, if only to change trains. But here, and in each of the universes and countless planets where we humans live, you need not worry; local food will nourish you. Of course, if you lived here many years, then went back to Earth and died soon after and an autopsy were done with fussiest micro-analysis, the analyst might not believe his results. But your stomach wouldn't care."

I thought about this, my belly stuffed with wonderful food and the air around me sweet and good—certainly my body did not care if there were indeed the differences Star spoke of.

Then I recalled one aspect of life in which little differences cause big differences. I asked Star about it.

She looked blandly innocent. "Do you care, milord? You will be long gone before it matters to Doral. I thought your purpose these three days was simply to help me in my problem? With pleasure in your work, I realize—you threw yourself into the spirit of the oc-casion."

"Damn it, quit pulling my leg! I did it to help you. But a man can't help wondering."

She slapped my thigh and laughed. "Oh, my very darling! Stop wondering; human races throughout the Universes can crossbreed. Some crosses fruit but seldom and some mule out. But this is not one of them. You will live on here, even if you never return. You're not sterile; that was one of many things I checked when I examined your beautiful body in Nice. One is never sure how the dice will roll, but—I think the Doral will not be dis-appointed."

She leaned toward me. "Would you give your physician data more accurate than that which Jocko sang? I might offer a statistical probability. Or even a Sight."

"No, I would not! Nosy."

"It is a long nose, isn't it? As you wish, milord. In a less personal vein the fact of crossbreeding among hu-mans of different universes—and some animals such as

132

dogs and cats—is a most interesting question. The only certainty is that human beings flourish only in those universes having chemistries so similar that elements that make up deoxyribonucleic acids are so alike as not to matter. As for the rest, every scholar has his theory. Some hold to a teleologic explanation, asserting that Man evolves alike in all essential particulars in every universe that can support him because of Divine Plan—or through blind necessity, depending on whether the scholar takes his religion straight or chases it with soda.

"Some think that we evolved just once—or were created, as may be—and leaked across into other universes. Then they fight over which universe was the home of the race."

"How can there be any argument?" I objected. "Earth has fossil evidence covering the evolution of man. Other planets either have it or not, and that should settle it."

"Are you sure, milord? I thought that, on Earth, man's family tree has as many dotted lines as there are bastards in European royal lines."

I shut up. I had simply read some popular books. Perhaps she was right; a race that could not agree as to who did what to whom in a war only twenty years back probably didn't know what Alley Oop did to the upstairs maid a million years ago, when the evidence was only scattered bones. Hadn't there been hoaxes? The Piltdown Man, or some such?

Star went on, "Whatever the truth, there *are* leakages between worlds. On your own planet disappearances run to hundreds of thousands and not all are absconders or wife-deserters; see any police department's files. One usual place is the battlefield. The strain becomes too great and a man slides through a hole he didn't know was there and winds up 'missing in action.' Sometimes—not often—a man is seen to disappear. One of your American writers, Bierce or Pierce, got interested and collected such cases. He collected so many that he was collected, too. And your Earth experiences reverse leakage, the 'Kaspar Hausers,' persons from nowhere, speaking no known language and never able to account for themselves."

"Wait a minute? Why just people?"

"I didn't say 'just people.' Have you never heard of rains of frogs? Of stones? Of blood? Who questions a stray cat's origin? Are all flying saucers optical illusions? I promise you they are not; some are poor lost astronauts trying to find their way home. My people use space travel very little, as faster-than-light is the readiest way to lose yourself among the Universes. We prefer the safer method of metaphysical geometries—or 'magic' in the vulgar speech."

Star looked thoughtful. "Milord, your Earth may be the home of mankind. Some scholars think so."

"Why?"

"It touches so many other worlds. It's the top of the list as a transfer point. If its people render it unfit for life—unlikely, but possible—it will disrupt traffic of a dozen universes. Earth has had its fairy rings, and Gates, and Bifrost Bridges for ages; that one we used in Nice was there before the Romans came."

"Star, how can you talk about points on Earth 'touching' other planets—for centuries on end? The Earth moves around the Sun at twenty miles a second or such, and spins on its axis, not to mention other motions that add up to an involved curve at unthinkable speed. So how can it 'touch' other worlds?"

Again we rode in silence. At last Star said, "My Hero, how long did it take you to learn calculus?"

"Why, I haven't learned it. I've studied it a couple of years."

"Can you tell me how a particle can be a wave?"

"What? Star, that's quantum mechanics, not calculus. I could give an explanation but it wouldn't mean anything; I don't have the math. An engineer doesn't need it."

"It would be simplest," she said diffidently, "to answer your question by saying 'magic' just as you answered mine with 'quantum mechanics.' But you don't like that word, so all I can say is that after you study higher

134

geometries, metaphysical and conjectural as well as topological and judicial—if you care to make such study—I will gladly answer. But you won't need to ask."

(Ever been told: "Wait till you grow up, dear; then you will understand"? As a kid I didn't like it from grownups; I liked it still less from a girl I was in love with when I was fully grown.)

Star didn't let me sulk; she shifted the talk. "Some crossbreedings are from neither accidental slippages nor planned travel. You've heard of incubi and succubi?"

"Oh, sure. But I never bother my head with myths."

"Not myths, darling, no matter how often the legend has been used to explain embarrassing situations. Witches and warlocks are not always saints and some acquire a taste for rape. A person who has learned to open Gates can indulge such vice; he—or she—can sneak up on a sleeping person—maid, chaste wife, virgin boy—work his will and be long gone before cockcrow." She shuddered. "Sin at its nastiest. If we catch them, we kill them. I've caught a few, I killed them. Sin at its worst, even if the victim learns to like it." She shuddered again.

"Star, what is your definition of 'sin'?"

"Can there be more than one? Sin is cruelty and injustice, all else is peccadillo. Oh, a sense of sin comes from violating the customs of your tribe. But breaking custom is not sin even when it feels so; sin is wronging another person."

"How about 'sinning against God'?" I persisted.

She looked at me sharply. "So again we shave the barber? First, milord, tell me what you mean by 'God.'"

"I just wanted to see if you would walk into it."

"I haven't walked into that one in a mort of years. I'd as lief thrust with a bent wrist, or walk a pentacle in clothes. Speaking of pentacles, my Hero, our destination is not what it was three days ago. Now we go to a Gate I had not expected to use. More dangerous but it can't be helped."

"My fault! I'm sorry, Star."

"*My* fault, milord. But not all loss. When we lost our luggage I was more worried than I dared show—even though I was never easy about carrying firearms through a world where they may not be used. But our foldbox carried much more than firearms, things we are vulnerable without. The time you spent in soothing the hurt to the Doral's ladies I spent—in part—in wheedling the Doral for a new kit, almost everything heart could wish but firearms. Not all loss."

"We are going to another world now?"

"Not later than tomorrow dawn, if we live."

"Damn it, Star, both you and Rufo talk as if each breath might be our last."

"As it might be."

"You're not expecting an ambush now; we're still on Doral land. But Rufo is as full of dire forebodings as a cheap melodrama. And you are almost as bad."

"I'm sorry. Rufo does fret—but he is a good man at your back when trouble starts. As for me, I have been trying to be fair, milord, to let you know what to expect."

"Instead you confuse me. Don't you think it's time you put your cards face up?"

She looked troubled. "And if the Hanging Man is the first card turned?"

"I don't give a hoot! I can face trouble without fainting—"

"I know you can, my champion."

"Thanks. But not knowing makes me edgy. So talk."

"I will answer any question, milord Oscar. I have always been willing to."

"But you know that I don't know what questions to ask. Maybe a carrier pigeon doesn't need to know what the war is about—but I feel like a sparrow in a badminton game. So start from the beginning."

"As you say, milord. About seven thousand years ago—" Star stopped. "Oscar, do you want to know—now—all the interplay of politics of a myriad worlds and twenty universes over millennia in arriving at the present crisis? I'll try if you say, but just to outline it would take more time than remains until we *must* pass through that Gate. You are my true champion; my life hangs on your courage and skill. Do you want the politics behind my present helpless, almost hopeless predicament—save for you! Or shall I concentrate on the tactical situation?"

(Damn it! I did want the whole story.) "Let's stick to the tactical situation. For now."

"I promise," she said solemnly, "that if we live through it, you shall have every detail. The situation is this: I had intended us to cross Nevia by barge, then through the mountains to reach a Gate beyond the Eternal Peaks. That route is less risky but long.

"But now we must hurry. We will turn off the road late this afternoon and pass through some wild country, and country still worse after dark. The Gate there we must reach before dawn; with luck we may sleep. I hope so, because this Gate takes us to another world at a much more dangerous exit.

"Once there, in that world—Hokesh it is called, or Karth—in Karth-Hokesh we shall be close, too close, to a tall tower, mile high, and, if we win to it, our troubles start. In it is the Never-Born, the Eater of Souls—"

"Star, are you trying to scare me?"

"I would rather you were frightened now, if such is possible, than have you surprised later. My thought, milord, had been to advise you of each danger as we reached it, so that you could concentrate on one at a time. But you overruled me."

"Maybe you were right. Suppose you give me details on each as we come to it, just the outline now. So I'm to fight the Eater of Souls, am I? The name doesn't scare me; if he tries to eat *my* soul, he'll throw up. What do I fight him with? Spit?"

"That is one way," she said seriously, "but, with luck, we won't fight him—it—at all. We want what it guards."

"And what is that?"

"The Egg of the Phoenix."

"The Phoenix doesn't lay eggs."

"I know, milord. That makes it uniquely valuable."

"But—"

She hurried on. "That is its name. It is a small object, somewhat larger than an ostrich egg and black.

If I do not capture it, many bad things will happen. Among them is a small one: I will die. I mention that because it may not seem small to you—my darling!—and it is easier to tell you that one truth than it is to explain the issues."

"Okay. We steal the Egg. Then what?"

"Then we go home. To my home. After which you may return to yours. Or remain in mine. Or go where you list, through Twenty Universes and myriad worlds. Under any choice, whatever treasure you fancy is yours; you will have earned it and more . . . as well as my heartfelt thanks, milord Hero, and anything you ask of me."

(The biggest blank check ever written— If I could cash it.) "Star, you don't seem to think we will live through it."

She took a deep breath. "Not likely, milord. I tell you truth. My blunder has forced on us a most desperate alternative."

"I see. Star, will you marry me? Today?"

Then I said, "Easy there! Don't fall!" She hadn't been in danger of falling; the seat belt held her. But she sagged against it. I leaned over and put my arm around her shoulders. "Nothing to cry about. Just give me a yes or a no—and I fight for you anyway. Oh, I forgot. I love you. Anyhow I think it's love. A funny, fluttery feeling whenever I look at you or think about you—which is mostly."

"I love you, milord," she said huskily. "I have loved you since I first saw you. Yes, a 'funny, fluttery feeling' as if everything inside me were about to melt down."

"Well, not quite that," I admitted. "But it's probably opposite polarity for the same thing. Fluttery, anyhow. Chills and lightnings. How do we get married around here?"

"But, milord—my love—you always astound me. I knew you loved me. I hoped that you would tell me before—well, in time. Let me hear it once. I did not expect you to offer to *marry* me!"

"Why not? I'm a man, you're a woman. It's customary."

138

"But— Oh, my love, I told you! It isn't necessary to marry me. By your rules ... I'm a bitch."

"Bitch, witch, Sing Along with Mitch! What the hell, honey? That was *your* word, not mine. You have about convinced me that the rules I was taught are barbarous and yours are the straight goods. Better blow your nose —here, want my hanky?"

Star wiped her eyes and blew her nose but instead of the yes-darling I wanted to hear she sat up straight and did not smile. She said formally, "Milord Hero, had you not best sample the wine before you buy the barrel?"

I pretended not to understand.

"Please, milord love," she insisted. "I mean it. There's a grassy bit on your side of the road, just ahead. You can lead me to it this moment and willingly I will go."

I sat high and pretended to peer. "Looks like crab grass. Scratchy."

"Then p-p-pick your own grass! Milord ... I am willing, and eager, and not uncomely—but you will learn that I am a Sunday painter compared with artists you will someday meet. I am a working woman. I haven't been free to give the matter the dedicated study it deserves. Believe me! No, *try* me. You can't know that you want to marry me."

"So you're a cold and clumsy wench, eh?"

"Well ... I didn't say *that*. I'm only entirely unskilled —and I do have enthusiasm."

"Yes, like your auntie with the cluttered bedroom—it runs in your family, so you said. Let it stand that I want to marry you in spite of your obvious faults."

"But—"

"Star, you talk too much."

"Yes, milord," she said meekly.

"We're getting married. How do we do it? Is the local lord also justice of the peace? If he is, there will be no *droit du seigneur;* we haven't time for frivolities."

"Each squire is the local justice," Star agreed thoughtfully, "and does perform marriages, although most Nevians don't bother. But— Well, yes, he would expect *droit du seigneur* and, as you pointed out, we haven't time to waste."

"Nor is that my idea of a honeymoon. Star—look at me. I don't expect to keep you in a cage; I know you weren't raised that way. But we won't look up the squire. What's the local brand of preacher? A celibate brand, by choice."

"But the squire is the priest, too. Not that religion is an engrossing matter in Nevia; fertility rites are all they bother with. Milord love, the simplest way is to jump over your sword."

"Is that a marriage ceremony where you come from, Star?"

"No, it's from your world:

'Leap rogue, and jump whore,
'And married be forevermore—'

"—it's very old."

"Mmm— I don't care for the marriage lines. I may be a rogue but I know what you think of whores. What other chances are there?"

"Let me see. There's a rumormonger in a village we pass through soon after lunch. They sometimes marry townies who want it known far and wide; the service includes spreading the news."

"What sort of service?"

"I don't know. And I don't care, milord love. Married we will be!"

"That's the spirit! We won't stop for lunch."

"No, milord," she said firmly, "if wife I am to be, I shall be a good wife and not permit you to skip meals."

"Henpecking already. I think I'll beat you."

"As you will, milord. But you must eat, you are going to need your strength—"

"I certainly will!"

"—for fighting. For now I am ten times as anxious that we both live through it. Here is a place for lunch." She turned Vita Brevis off the road; Ars Longa followed. Star looked back over her shoulder and dimpled. "Have I told you today that you are beautiful . . . my love!"

XI

RUFO'S longhorse followed us onto the grassy verge Star picked for picnicking. He was still limp as a wet sock and snoring. I would have let him sleep but Star was shaking him.

He came awake fast, reaching for his sword and shouting, "*À moi! M'aidez! Les vaches!*" Fortunately some friend had stored his sword and belt out of reach on the baggage rack aft, along with bow, quiver, and our new foldbox.

Then he shook his head and said, "How many were there?"

"Down from there, old friend," Star said cheerfully. "We've stopped to eat."

"*Eat!*" Rufo gulped and shuddered. "Please, milady. No obscenity." He fumbled at his seat belt and fell out of his saddle; I steadied him.

Star was searching through her pouch; she pulled out a vial and offered it to Rufo. He shied back. "Milady!"

"Shall I hold your nose?" she said sweetly.

"I'll be all right. Just give me a moment ... and the hair of the dog."

"Certainly you'll be all right. Shall I ask milord Oscar to pin your arms?"

Rufo glanced at me appealingly; Star opened the little bottle. It fizzed and fumes rolled out and down. *"Now!"*

Rufo shuddered, held his nose, tossed it down.

I won't say smoke shot out of his ears. But he flapped like torn canvas in a gale and horrible noises came out.

Then he came into focus as suddenly as a TV picture. He appeared heavier and inches taller and had firmed out. His skin was a rosy glow instead of death pallor. "Thank you, milady," he said cheerfully, his voice resonant and virile. "Someday I hope to return the favor."

"When the Greeks reckon time by the kalends," she agreed.

Rufo led the longhorses aside and fed them, opening the foldbox and digging out haunches of bloody meat. Ars Longa ate a hundredweight and Vita Brevis and Mors Profunda even more; on the road these beasts need a high-protein diet. That done, he whistled as he set up table and chairs for Star and myself.

"Sugar pie," I said to Star, "what's in that pick-me-up?"

"An old family recipe:

> 'Eye of newt and toe of frog,
> 'Wool of bat and tongue of dog,
> 'Adder's fork and blind-worm's sting,
> 'Lizard's leg and howlet's wing—' "

"Shakespeare!" I said. "Macbeth."

" 'Cool it with a baboon's blood—' No, Will got it from me, milord love. That's the way with writers; they'll steal anything, file off the serial numbers, and claim it for their own. I got it from my aunt—another aunt—who was a professor of internal medicine. The rhyme is a mnemonic for the real ingredients which are much more complicated—never can tell when you'll need a hangover cure. I compounded it last night, knowing that Rufo, for the sake of our skins, would need to be at his sharpest today—two doses, in fact, in case you needed one. But you surprised me, my love; you break out with nobility at the oddest times."

"A family weakness. I can't help it."

"Luncheon is served, milady."

I offered Star my arm. Hot foods were hot, cold ones chilled; this new foldbox, in Lincoln green embossed with the Doral chop, had equipment that the lost box lacked. Everything was delicious and the wines were superb.

Rufo ate heartily from his serving board while keeping an eye on our needs. He had come over to pour the wine for the salad when I broke the news. "Rufo old comrade, milady Star and I are getting married today. I want you to be my best man and help prop me up."

He dropped the bottle.

Then he was busy wiping me and mopping the table. When at last he spoke, it was to Star. "Milady," he said tightly, "I have put up with much, uncomplaining, for reasons I need not state. But this is going too far. I won't let—"

"Hold your tongue!"

"Yes," I agreed, "hold it while I cut it out. Will you have it fried? Or boiled?"

Rufo looked at me and breathed heavily. Then he left abruptly, withdrawing beyond the serving board. Star said softly, "Milord love, I am sorry."

"What twisted *his* tail?" I said wonderingly. Then I thought of the obvious. "Star! Is Rufo jealous?"

She looked astounded, started to laugh and chopped it off. "No, no, darling! It's not that at all. Rufo— Well, Rufo has his foibles but he is utterly dependable where it counts. And we need him. Ignore it. Please, milord."

"As you say. It would take more than that to make me unhappy today."

Rufo came back, face impassive, and finished serving. He repacked without speaking and we hit the road.

The road skirted the village green; we left Rufo there and sought out the rumormonger. His shop, a crooked lane away, was easy to spot; an apprentice was beating a drum in front of it and shouting teasers of gossip to a crowd of locals. We pushed through and went inside.

The master rumormonger was reading something in each hand with a third scroll propped against his feet on a desk. He looked, dropped feet to floor, jumped up and made a leg while waving us to seats.

"Come in, come in, my gentles!" he sang out. "You do me great honor, my day is made! And yet if I may say so you have come to the right place whatever your problem whatever your need you have only to speak good news bad news every sort but sad news reputations restored events embellished history rewritten great deeds sung and all work guaranteed by the oldest established news agency in all Nevia news from all worlds all universes propaganda planted or uprooted offset or rechanneled satisfaction guaranteed honesty is the best policy but the client is always right don't tell me I know I know I have spies in every kitchen ears in every bedroom the Hero Gordon without a doubt and your fame needs no heralds milord but honored am I that you should seek me out a biography perhaps to match your matchless deeds complete with old nurse who recalls in her thin and ancient and oh so persuasive voice the signs and portents at your birth—"

Star chopped him off. "We want to get married."

His mouth shut, he looked sharply at Star's waistline and almost bought a punch in the nose. "It is a pleasure to do business with clients who know their own minds. And I must add that I heartily endorse such a public-spirited project. All this modern bundling and canoodling and scuttling without even three cheers or a by-your-leave sends taxes up and profits down that's logic. I only wish I had time to get married myself as I've told my wife many's the time. Now as to plans, if I may make a modest suggestion—"

"We want to be married by the customs of Earth."

"Ah, yes, certainly." He turned to a cabinet near his desk, spun dials. After a bit he said, "Your pardon, gentles, but my head is crammed with a billion facts, large and small, and—that name? Does it start with one 'R' or two?"

Star moved around, inspected the dials, made a setting.

The rumormonger blinked. *"That* universe? We seldom have a call for it. I've often wished I had time to travel but business business business—*LIBRARY!"*

"Yes, Master?" a voice answered.

"The planet Earth, Marriage Customs of—that's a capital 'Urr' and a soft theta." He added a five-group serial number. "Snap it up!"

In very short time an apprentice came running with a thin scroll. "Librarian says careful how you handle it, Master. Very brittle, he says. He says—"

"Shut up. Your pardon, gentles." He inserted the scroll in a reader and began to scan.

His eyes bugged out and he sat forward. "Unbeliev—" Then he muttered, "Amazing! Whatever made them think of *that!*" For several minutes he appeared to forget we were there, simply giving vent to: "Astounding! Fantastic!" and like expressions.

I tapped his elbow. "We're in a hurry."

"Eh? Yes, yes, milord Hero Gordon—milady." Reluctantly he left the scanner, fitted his palms together, and said, "You've come to the right place. Not another rumormonger in all Nevia could handle a project this size. Now my thought is—just a rough idea, talking off the top of my head—for the procession we'll need to call in the surrounding countryside although for the charivari we could make do with just townspeople if you want to keep it modest in accordance with your reputation for dignified simplicity—say one day for the procession and a nominal two nights of charivari with guaranteed noise levels of—"

"Hold it."

"Milord? I'm not going to make a profit on this; it will be a work of art, a labor of love—just expenses plus a little something for my overhead. It's my professional judgment, too, that a Samoan pre-ceremony would be more sincere, more touching really, than the optional Zulu rite. For a touch of comedy relief—at no extra charge; one of my file clerks just happens to be seven

145

months along, she'd be glad to run down the aisle and interrupt the ceremony—and of course there is the matter of witnesses to the consummation, how many for each of you, but that needn't be settled this week; we have the street decorations to think of first, and—"

I took her arm. "We're leaving."

"Yes, milord," Star agreed.

He chased after us, shouting about broken contracts. I put hand to sword and showed six inches of blade; his squawks shut off.

Rufo seemed to be all over his mad; he greeted us civilly, even cheerfully. We mounted and left. We had been riding south a mile or so when I said, "Star darling—"

"Milord love?"

"That 'jumping over the sword'—that really is a marriage ceremony?"

"A very old one, my darling. I think it dates back to the Crusades."

"I've thought of an updated wording:

'Jump rogue, and princess leap,
'My wife art thou and mine to keep!'

"—would that suit you?"

"Yes, yes!"

"But for the second line you say:

'—thy wife I vow and thine to keep.'

"Got it?"

Star gave a quick gasp. "Yes, my love!"

We left Rufo with the longhorses, giving no explanation, and climbed a little wooded hill. All of Nevia is beautiful, with never a beer can nor a dirty Kleenex to mar its Eden loveliness, but here we found an outdoor temple, a smooth grassy place surrounded by arching trees, an enchanted sanctuary.

I drew my sword and glanced along it, feeling its exquisite balance while noting again the faint ripples left by feather-soft hammer blows of some master swordsmith.

I tossed it and caught it by the forte. "Read the motto, Star."

She traced it out. " '*Dum vivimus, vivamus!*'—'While we live, let us *live!*' Yes, my love, yes!" She kissed it and handed it back; I placed it on the ground.

"Know your lines?" I asked.

"Graved in my heart."

I took her hand in mine. "Jump high. One ... two ... three!"

XII

WHEN I led my bride back down that blessed hill, arm around her waist, Rufo helped us mount without comment. But he could hardly miss that Star now addressed me as: "Milord husband." He mounted and tailed in, a respectful distance out of earshot.

We rode hand in hand for at least an hour. Whenever I glanced at her, she was smiling; whenever she caught my eye, the smile grew dimples. Once I asked, "How soon must we keep lookout?"

"Not until we leave the road, milord husband."

That held us another mile. At last she said timidly, "Milord husband?"

"Yes, wife?"

"Do you still think that I am 'a cold and clumsy wench'?"

"Mmm . . ." I answered thoughtfully, " 'cold'—no, I couldn't honestly say you were cold. But 'clumsy'— Well, compared with an artist like Muri, let us say—"

"Milord husband!"

"Yes? I was saying—"

"Are you honing for a kick in the belly?" She added, "American!"

"Wife . . . *would* you kick me in the belly?"

She was slow in answering and her voice was very low. "No, milord husband. Never."

"I'm pleased to hear it. But if you did, what would happen?"

"You—you would spank me. With my own sword. But not with your sword. Please, never with *your* sword . . . my husband."

"Not with your sword, either. With my hand. Hard. First I would spank you. And then—"

"And then what?"

I told her. "But don't give me cause. According to plans I have to fight later. And don't interrupt me in the future."

"Yes, milord husband."

"Very well. Now let's assign Muri an arbitrary score of ten. On that scale you would rate— Let me think."

"Three or four, perhaps? Or even five?"

"Quiet. I make it about a thousand. Yes, a thousand, give or take a point. I haven't a slide rule."

"Oh, what a beast you are, my darling! Lean close and kiss me—and just wait till I tell Muri."

"You'll say nothing to Muri, my bride, or you will be paddled. Quit fishing for compliments. You know what you are, you sword-jumping wench."

"And what am I?"

"My princess."

"Oh."

"And a mink with its tail on fire—and you know it."

"Is that good? I've studied American idiom most carefully but sometimes I am not sure."

"It's supposed to be tops. A figure of speech, I've never known a mink that well. Now get your mind on other matters, or you may be a widow on your bridal day. Dragons, you say?"

"Not until after nightfall, milord husband—and they aren't really dragons."

"As you described them, the difference could matter

149

only to another dragon. Eight feet high at the shoulders, a few tons each, and teeth as long as my forearm—all they need is to breathe flame."

"Oh, but they do! Didn't I say?"

I sighed. "No, you did not."

"They don't exactly *breathe* fire. That would kill them. They hold their breaths while flaming. It's swamp gas—methane—from the digestive tract. It's a controlled belch, with a hypergolic effect from an enzyme secreted between the first and second rows of teeth. The gas bursts into flame on the way out."

"I don't care how they do it; they're flamethrowers. Well? How do you expect me to handle them?"

"I had hoped that you would have ideas. You see," she added apologetically, "I hadn't planned on it, I didn't expect us to come this way."

"Well— Wife, let's go back to that village. Set up in competition with our friend the rumormonger—I'll bet we could outgabble him."

"Milord husband!"

"Never mind. If you want me to kill dragons every Wednesday and Saturday, I'll be on call. This flaming methane— Do they spout it from both ends?"

"Oh, just the front end. How could it be both?"

"Easy. See next year's model. Now quiet; I'm thinking over a tactic. I'll need Rufo. I suppose he has killed dragons before?"

"I don't know that a man has ever killed one, milord husband."

"So? My princess, I'm flattered by the confidence you place in me. Or is it desperation? Don't answer, I don't want to know. Keep quiet and let me think."

At the next farmhouse Rufo was sent in to arrange returning the longhorses. They were ours, gifts from the Doral, but we had to send them home as they could not live where we were going—Muri had promised me that she would keep an eye on Ars Longa and exercise her. Rufo came back with a bumpkin mounted on a heavy draft animal, bareback—he kept shifting numbly between second and third pairs of legs to spare the animal's back and controlled it by voice.

When we dismounted, retrieved our bows and quivers, and prepared to hoof it, Rufo came up. "Boss, Manure Foot craves to meet the hero and touch his sword. Brush him off?"

Rank hath its duties as well as its privileges. "Fetch him."

The lad, overgrown and fuzz on his chin, approached eagerly, stumbling over his feet, then made a leg so long he almost fell. "Straighten up, son," I said. "What's your name?"

"Pug, milord Hero," he answered shrilly. ("Pug" will do. The Nevian meaning was as rugged as Jocko's jokes.)

"A stout name. What do you want to be when you grow up?"

"A hero, milord! Like yourself."

I thought of telling him about those rocks on the Glory Road. But he would find them soon enough if ever he tramped it—and either not mind, or turn back and forget the silly business. I nodded approvingly and assured him that there was always room at the top in the Hero business for a lad with spirit—and that the lower the start, the greater the glory ... so work hard and study hard and wait his opportunity. Keep his guard up but always speak to strange ladies; adventure would come his way. Then I let him touch my sword—but not take it in hand. The Lady Vivamus is *mine* and I'd rather share my toothbrush.

Once, when I was young, I was presented to a Congressman. He had handed me the same fatherly guff I was now plagiarizing. Like prayer, it can't do any harm and might do some good, and I found that I was sincere when I said it and no doubt the Congressman was, too. Oh, possibly some harm, as the youngster might get himself killed on the first mile of that road. But that is better than sitting over the fire in your old age, sucking your gums and thinking about the chances you missed and the gals you didn't tumble. Isn't it?

I decided that the occasion seemed so important to

Pug that it should be marked, so I groped in my pouch and found a U.S. quarter. "What's the rest of your name, Pug?"

"Just 'Pug,' milord. Of house Lerdki, of course."

"Now you will have three names because I am giving you one of mine." I had one I didn't need, Oscar Gordon suited me fine. Not "Flash" as that name was never acknowledged by me. Not my Army nickname; I wouldn't write that one on the wall of a latrine. "Easy" was the name I could spare. I had always used "E. C. Gordon" rather than "Evelyn Cyril Gordon" and in school my name had shifted from "E. C." to "Easy" because of my style of broken-field running—I never ran harder nor dodged more than the occasion demanded.

"By authority vested in me by Headquarters United States Army Southeast Asia Command, I, the Hero Oscar, ordain that you shall be known henceforth as Lerdki 't Pug Easy. Wear it proudly."

I gave him the quarter and showed him George Washington on the obverse. "This is the father of my house, a greater hero than I will ever be. He stood tall and proud, spoke the truth, and fought for the right as he saw it, against fearful odds. Try to be like him. And here"—I turned it over—"is the chop of my house, the house he founded. The bird stands for courage, freedom, and ideals soaring high." (I didn't tell him that the American Eagle eats carrion, never tackles anything its own size, and will soon be extinct—it *does* stand for those ideals. A symbol means what you put into it.)

Pug Easy nodded violently and tears started to flow. I had not presented him to my bride; I didn't know that she would wish to meet him. But she stepped forward and said gently, "Pug Easy, remember the words of milord Hero. Treasure them and they will last you all your life."

The kid dropped to his knees. Star touched his hair and said, "Stand, Lerdki 't Pug Easy. Stand tall."

I said good-bye to Ars Longa, told her to be a good girl and I would be back someday. Pug Easy headed back with longhorses tailed up and we set out into the woods, arrows nocked and Rufo eyes-behind. There was a sign where we left the yellow brick road; freely translated it read: ALL HOPE ABANDON, YE WHO ENTER HERE.

(A literal translation is reminiscent of Yellowstone Park: "Warning—the varmints in these woods are *not* tame. Travelers are warned to stay on the road, as their remains will not be returned to their kin. The Lerdki, His Chop.")

Presently Star said, "Milord husband—"

"Yes, pretty foots?" I didn't look at her; I was watching my side and a bit of hers, and keeping an eye overhead as well, as we could be bombed here—something like blood kites but smaller and goes for the eyes.

"My Hero, you are truly noble and you have made your wife most proud."

"Huh? How?" I had my mind on targets—two kinds on the ground here: a rat big enough to eat cats and willing to eat people, and a wild hog about the same size and not a ham sandwich on him anyplace, all rawhide and bad temper. The hogs were easier targets, I had been told, because they charge straight at you. But don't miss. And have your sword loosened, you won't nock a second shaft.

"That lad, Pug Easy. What you did for him."

"Him? I fed him the old malarkey. Cost nothing."

"It was a kingly deed, milord husband."

"Oh, nonsense, diddycums. He expected big talk from a hero, so I did."

"Oscar my beloved, may a loyal wife point it out to her husband when he speaks nonsense of himself? I have known many heroes and some were such oafs that one would feed them at the back door if their deeds did not claim a place at the table. I have known few men who were noble, for nobility is scarcer far than heroism. But true nobility can always be recognized . . . even in one as belligerently shy about showing it as you are. The lad expected it, so you gave it to him—but *noblesse oblige* is an emotion felt only by those who are noble."

"Well, maybe. Star, you are talking too much again. Don't you think these varmints have ears?"

"Your pardon, milord. They have such good ears that they hear footsteps through the ground long before they hear voices. Let me have the last word, today being my bridal day. If you are—no, when you are gallant to some beauty, let us say Letva—or Muri, damn her lovely eyes! —I do not count it as nobility; it must be assumed to spring from a much commoner emotion than *noblesse oblige*. But when you speak to a country lout with pigsty on his feet, garlic on his breath, the stink of sweat all over him, and pimples on his face—speak gently and make *him* feel for the time as noble as you are and let him hope one day to be your equal—I know it is not because you hope to tumble him."

"Oh, I don't know. Boys that age are considered a treat in some circles. Give him a bath, perfume him, curl his hair—"

"Milord husband, is it permitted for me to *think* about kicking you in the belly?"

"Can't be court-martialed for thinking, that's the one thing they can't take away from you. Okay, I prefer girls; I'm a square and can't help it. What's this about Muri's eyes? Longlegs, are you jealous?"

I could hear dimples even though I couldn't stop to see them. "Only on my wedding day, milord husband; the other days are yours. If I catch you in sportiveness, I shall either not see it, or congratulate you, as may be."

"I don't expect you'll catch me."

"And I trust you'll not catch *me*, milord rogue," she answered serenely.

She did get the last word, for just then Rufo's bowstring went *Fwung!* He called out, "Got 'im!" and then we were very busy. Hogs so ugly they made razorbacks look like Poland-Chinas— I got one by arrow, down his slobbering throat, then fed steel to his brother a frozen second later. Star got a fair hit at hers but it deflected on bone and kept coming and I kicked it in the shoulder as I was still trying to free my blade from its cousin.

Steel between its ribs quieted it and Star coolly nocked another shaft and let fly while I was killing it. She got one more with her sword, leaning the point in like a matador at the moment of truth, dancing aside as it came on, dead and unwilling to admit it.

The fight was over. Old Rufo had got three unassisted and a nasty goring; I had a scratch and my bride was unhurt, which I made sure of as soon as things were quiet. Then I mounted guard while our surgeon took care of Rufo, after which she dressed my lesser cut.

"How about it, Rufo?" I asked. "Can you walk?"

"Boss, I won't stay in this forest if I have to crawl. Let's mush. Anyhow," he added, nodding at the worthless pork around us, "we won't be bothered by rats right away."

I rotated the formation, placing Rufo and Star ahead with his good leg on the outside and myself taking rear guard, where I should have been all along. Rear guard is slightly safer than point under most conditions but these weren't most conditions. I had let my blind need to protect personally my bride affect my judgment.

Having taken the hot spot I then went almost cross-eyed trying not only to see behind but ahead as well, so that I could close fast if Star—yes, and Rufo—got into trouble. Luckily we had a breathing spell in which I sobered down and took to heart the oldest lesson on patrol: You *can't* do the other man's job. Then I gave all my attention to our rear. Rufo, old as he was and wounded, would not die without slaughtering an honor guard to escort him to hell in style—and Star was no fainting heroine. I would bet long odds on her against anyone her own weight, name your weapon or bare-handed, and I pity the man who ever tried to rape her; he's probably still searching for his *cojones*.

Hogs didn't bother us again but as evening approached we began to see and oftener to hear those giant rats; they paced us, usually out of sight; they never attacked berserk the way the hogs had; they looked for the best of it, as rats always do.

Rats give me the horrors. Once when I was a kid, my

dad dead and Mother not yet remarried, we were flat broke and living in an attic in a condemned building. You could hear rats in the walls and twice rats ran over me in my sleep.

I still wake up screaming.

It doesn't improve a rat to blow it up to the size of a coyote. These were real rats, even to the whiskers, and shaped like rats save that their legs and pads were too large—perhaps the cube-square law on animal proportions works anywhere.

We didn't waste an arrow on one unless it was a fair shot and we zigzagged to take advantage of such openness as the forest had—which increased the hazard from above. However, the forest was so dense that attacks from the sky weren't our first worry.

I got one rat that tailed too closely and just missed another. We had to spend an arrow whenever they got bold; it caused the others to be more cautious. And once, while Rufo was drawing a bow on one and Star was ready with her sword to back him up, one of those vicious little hawks dived on Rufo.

Star cut him out of the air at the bottom of his stoop. Rufo hadn't even seen it; he was busy nailing brother rat.

We didn't have to worry about underbrush; this forest was parklike, trees and grass, no dense undergrowth. Not too bad, that stretch, except that we began to run out of arrows. I was fretting about that when I noticed something. "Hey, up ahead! You're off course. Cut to the right." Star had set course for me when we left the road but it was up to me to hold it; her bump of direction was erratic and Rufo's no better.

"Sorry, milord leader," Star called back. "The going was a trifle steep."

I closed in. "Rufo, how's the leg?" There was sweat on his forehead.

Instead of answering me, he said, "Milady, it will be dark soon."

"I know," she answered calmly, "so time for a bite of

156

supper. Milord husband, **that great flat rock** up ahead seems a nice place."

I thought she had slipped her gears and so did Rufo, but for another reason. "But, milady, we are far behind schedule."

"And much later we shall be unless I attend to your leg again."

"Better you leave me behind," he muttered.

"Better you keep quiet until your advice is asked," I told him. "I wouldn't leave a Horned Ghost to be eaten by rats. Star, how do we do this?"

The great flat rock sticking up like a skull in the trees ahead was the upper surface of a limestone boulder with its base buried. I stood guard in its center with Rufo seated beside me while Star set out wards at cardinal and semicardinal points. I didn't get to see what she did because my eyes had to be peeled for anything beyond her, shaft nocked and ready to knock it down or scare it off, while Rufo watched the other side. However, Star told me later that the wards weren't even faintly "magic" but were within reach of Earth technology once some bright boy got the idea—an "electrified fence" without the fence, as radio is a telephone without wires, an analogy that won't hold up.

But it was well that I kept honest lookout instead of trying to puzzle out how she set up that charmed circle, as she was attacked by the only rat we met that had no sense. He came straight at her, my arrow past her ear warned her, and she finished him off by sword. It was a very old male, missing teeth and white whiskers and likely weak in his mind. He was as large as a wolf, and with two death wounds still a red-eyed, mangy fury.

Once the last ward was placed Star told me that I could stop worrying about the sky; the wards roofed as well as fenced the circle. As Rufo says, if *She* says it, that settles it. Rufo had partly unfolded the foldbox while he watched; I got out her surgical case, more arrows for all of us, and food. No nonsense about manservant and gentlefolk, we ate together, sitting or sprawling and with Rufo lying flat to give his leg a chance while Star served

157

him, sometimes popping food into his mouth in Nevian hospitality. She had worked a long time on his leg while I held a light and handed her things. She packed the wound with a pale jelly before sealing a dressing over it. If it hurt, Rufo didn't mention it.

While we ate it grew dark and the invisible fence began to be lined with eyes, glowing back at us with the light we ate by, and almost as numerous as the crowd the morning Igli ate himself. Most of them I judged to be rats. One group kept to themselves with a break in the circle on each side; I decided these must be hogs; the eyes were higher off the ground.

"Milady love," I said, "will those wards hold all night?"

"Yes, milord husband."

"They had better. It is too dark for arrows and I can't see us hacking our way through that mob. I'm afraid you must revise your schedule again."

"I can't, milord Hero. But forget those beasts. Now we fly."

Rufo groaned. "I was afraid so. You know it makes me seasick."

"Poor Rufo," Star said softly. "Never fear, old friend, I have a surprise for you. Again such chance as this, I bought dramamine in Cannes—you know, the drug that saved the Normandy invasion back on Earth. Or perhaps you don't know."

Rufo answered, "'Know'? I was *in* that invasion, milady—and I'm allergic to dramamine; I fed fish all the way to Omaha Beach. Worst night I've ever had—why, I'd rather be *here!*"

"Rufo," I asked, "were you really at Omaha Beach?"

"Hell, yes, Boss. I did all of Eisenhower's thinking."

"But why? It wasn't your fight."

"You might ask yourself why you're in this fight, Boss. In my case it was French babes. Earthy and uninhibited and always cheerful about it and willing to learn. I remember one little mademoiselle from Armentières"—he pronounced it correctly—"who hadn't been—"

Star interrupted. "While you two pursue your bachelor

158

reminiscences, I'll get the flight gear ready." She got up and went to the foldbox.

"Go ahead, Rufo," I said, wondering how far he would stretch this one.

"No," he said sullenly. "*She* wouldn't like it. I can tell. Boss, you've had the damnedest effect on *Her*. More ladylike by the minute and that isn't like *Her* at all. First thing you know *She* will subscribe to *Vogue* and then there's no telling how far it will go. I don't understand it, it can't be your looks. No offense meant."

"And none taken. Well, tell me another time. If you can remember it."

"I'll never forget her. But, Boss, seasickness isn't the half of it. You think these woods are infested. Well, the ones we are coming to—wobbly in the knees, at least I will be—those woods have dragons."

"I know."

"So She told you? But you have to see it to believe it. The woods are full of 'em. More than there are Doyles in Boston. Big ones, little ones, and the two-ton teen-age size, hungry all the time. *You* may fancy being eaten by a dragon; I don't. It's humiliating. And final. They ought to spray the place with dragonbane, that's what they ought to do. There ought to be a law."

Star had returned. "No, there should not be a law," she said firmly. "Rufo, don't sound off about things you don't understand. Disturbing the ecological balance is the worst mistake any government can make."

Rufo shut up, muttering. I said, "My true love, what use is a dragon? Riddle me that."

"I've never cast a balance sheet on Nevia, it's not my responsibility. But I can suggest the imbalances that might follow any attempt to get rid of dragons—which the Nevians could do; you've seen that their technology is not to be sneered at. These rats and hogs destroy crops. Rats help to keep the hogs down by eating piglets. But rats are even worse than hogs, on food crops. The dragons graze through these very woods in the daytime—dragons are diurnal, rats are nocturnal and go into their holes in the heat of the day. The dragons and hogs keep the underbrush cropped back and the dragons keep the lower limbs trimmed off. But dragons also enjoy a tasty rat, so whenever one locates a rat hole, it gives it a shot of flame, not always killing adults as they dig two holes for each nest, but certainly killing any babies—and then the dragon digs in and has his favorite snack. There is a long-standing agreement, amounting to a treaty, that as long as the dragons stay in their own territory and keep the rats in check, humans will not bother them."

"But why not kill the rats, and then clean up the dragons?"

"And let the hogs run wild? Please, milord husband, I don't know all the answers in this case; I simply know that disturbing a natural balance is a matter to be approached with fear and trembling—and a very versatile computer. The Nevians seem content not to bother the dragons."

"Apparently we're going to bother them. Will that break the treaty?"

"It's not really a treaty, it's folk wisdom with the Nevians, and a conditioned reflex—or possibly instinct—with the dragons. And we aren't going to bother dragons if we can help it. Have you discussed tactics with Rufo? There won't be time when we get there."

So I discussed how to kill dragons with Rufo, while Star listened and finished her preparations. "All right," Rufo said glumly, "it beats sitting tight, like an oyster on the half shell waiting to be eaten. More dignified. I'm a better archer than you are—or at least as good—so I'll take the hind end, as I'm not as agile tonight as I should be."

"Be ready to switch jobs fast if he swings around."

"*You* be ready, Boss. I'll be ready for the best of reasons—my favorite skin."

Star was ready and Rufo had packed and reslung the foldbox while we conferred. She placed round garters above each knee of each of us, then had us sit on the rock facing our destination. "That oak arrow, Rufo."

"Star, isn't this out of the Albertus Magnus book?"

"Similar," she said. "My formula is more reliable and

the ingredients I use on the garters don't spoil. If you please, milord husband, I must concentrate on my witchery. Place the arrow so that it points at the cave."

I did so. "Is that precise?" she asked.

"If the map you showed me is correct, it is. That's aimed just the way I've been aiming since we left the road."

"How far away is the Forest of Dragons?"

"Uh, look, my love, as long as we're going by air why don't we go straight to the cave and skip the dragons?"

She said patiently, "I wish we could. But that forest is so dense at the top that we can't drop straight down at the cave, no elbow room. And the things that live in those trees, high up, are worse than dragons. They grow—"

"Please!" said Rufo. "I'm airsick already and we're not off the ground."

"Later, Oscar, if you still want to know. In any case we daren't risk encountering them—and won't; they stay up higher than the dragons can reach, they must. How far to the forest?"

"Mmm, eight and a half miles, by that map and how far we've come—and not more than two beyond that to the Cave of the Gate."

"All right. Arms tight around my waist, both of you, and as much body contact as possible; it's got to work on all of us equally." Rufo and I settled each an arm in a hug about her and clasped hands across her tummy. "That's good. Hang on tight." Star wrote figures on the rock beside the arrow.

It sailed away into the night with us after it.

I don't see how to avoid calling this magic, as I can't see any way to build Buck Rogers belts into elastic garters. Oh, if you like, Star hypnotized us, then used psi powers to teleport us eight and a half miles. "Psi" is a better word than "magic"; monosyllables are stronger than polysyllables—see Winston Churchill's speeches. I don't understand either word, any more than I can explain why I never get lost. I just think it's preposterous that other people can.

When I fly in dreams, I use two styles: one is a swan dive and I swoop and swirl and cut didos; the other is sitting Turk fashion like the Little Lame Prince and sailing along by sheer force of personality.

The latter is how we did it, like sailing in a glider with no glider. It was a fine night for flying (all nights in Nevia are fine; it rains just before dawn in the rainy season, they tell me) and the greater moon silvered the ground below us. The woods opened up and became clumps of trees; the forest we were heading for showed black against the distance, much higher and enormously more imposing than the pretty woods behind us. Far off to the left I could glimpse fields of house Lerdki.

We had been in the air about two minutes when Rufo said, "Pa'don me!" and turned his head away. He doesn't have a weak stomach; he didn't get a drop on us. It arched like a fountain. That was the only incident of a perfect flight.

Just before we reached the tall trees Star said crisply, *"Amech!"* We checked like a heli and settled straight down to a three-fanny landing. The arrow rested on the ground in front of us, again dead. Rufo returned it to his quiver. "How do you feel?" I asked. "And how's your leg?"

He gulped. "Leg's all right. Ground's going up and down."

"Hush!" Star whispered. "He'll be all right. But hush, for your lives!"

We set out moments later, myself leading with drawn sword, Star behind me, and Rufo dogging her, an arrow nocked and ready.

The change from moonlight to deep shadow was blinding and I crept along, feeling for tree trunks and praying that no dragon would be in the path my bump of direction led. Certainly I knew that the dragons slept at night, but I place no faith in dragons. Maybe the bachelors stood watches, the way bachelor baboons do. I wanted to surrender that place of honor to St. George and take a spot farther back.

Once my nose stopped me, a whiff of ancient musk. I

waited and slowly became aware of a shape the size of a real estate office—a dragon, sleeping with its head on its tail. I led them around it, making no noise and hoping that my heart wasn't as loud as it sounded.

My eyes were doing better now, reaching out for every stray moonbeam that trickled down—and something else developed. The ground was mossy and barely phosphorescent the way a rotten log sometimes is. Not much. Oh, very little. But it was the way a darkroom light, almost nothing when you go inside, later is plenty of light. I could see trees now and the ground—and dragons.

I had thought earlier, Oh, what's a dozen or so dragons in a big forest? Chances are we won't see one, any more than you catch sight of deer most days in deer country.

The man who gets the all-night parking concession in that forest will make a fortune if he figures out a way to make dragons pay up. We never were out of sight of one after we could see.

Of course these aren't dragons. No, they are uglier. They are saurians, more like *tyrannosaurus rex* than anything else—big hindquarters and heavy hind legs, heavy tail, and smaller front legs that they use either in walking or to grasp their prey. The head is mostly teeth. They are omnivores whereas I understand that *t. rex* ate only meat. This is no help; the dragons eat meat when they can get it, they prefer it. Furthermore, these not-so-fake dragons have evolved that charming trick of burning their own sewer gas. But no evolutionary quirk can be considered odd if you use the way octopi make love as a comparison.

Once, far off to the left, an enormous jet lighted up, with a grunting bellow like a very old alligator. The light stayed on several seconds, then died away. Don't ask me—two males arguing over a female, maybe. We kept going, but I slowed after the light went out, as even that much was enough to affect our eyes until our night sight recovered.

I'm allergic to dragons—literally, not just scared silly. Allergic the way poor old Rufo is to dramamine but more the way cat fur affects some people.

163

My eyes were watering as soon as we were in that forest, then my sinuses started to clog up and before we had gone half a mile I was using my left fist to rub my upper lip as hard as I could, trying to kill a sneeze with pain. At last I couldn't make it and jammed fingers up my nostrils and bit my lips and the contained explosion almost burst my eardrums. It happened as we were skirting the south end of a truck-and-trailer-size job; I stopped dead and they stopped and we waited. It didn't wake up.

When I started up, my beloved closed on me, grasped my arm; I stopped again. She reached into her pouch, silently found something, rubbed it on my nose and up my nostrils, then with a gentle push signed that we could move on.

First my nose burned cold, as with Vick's salve, then it felt numb, and presently it began to clear.

After more than an hour of this agelong spooky sneak through tall trees and giant shapes, I thought we were going to win "home free." The Cave of the Gate should be not more than a hundred yards ahead and I could see the rise in ground where the entrance would be—and only one dragon in our way and that not in direct line.

I hurried.

There was this little fellow, no bigger than a wallaby and about the same shape, aside from baby teeth four inches long. Maybe he was so young he had to wake to potty in the night, I don't know. All I know is that I passed close to a tree he was behind and stepped on his tail, and he *squealed!*

He had every right to. But that's when it hit the fan. The adult dragon between us and the cave woke up at once. Not a big one—say about forty feet, including the tail.

Good old Rufo went into action as if he had had endless time to rehearse, dashing around to the brute's south end, arrow nocked and bow bent, ready to loose in a hurry. "Get its tail up!" he called out.

I ran to the front end and tried to antagonize the beast by shouting and waving my sword while wondering how far that flamethrower could throw. There are only four places to put an arrow into a Nevian dragon; the rest is armored like a rhino only heavier. Those four are his mouth (when open), his eyes (a difficult shot; they are little and piggish), and that spot right under his tail where almost any animal is vulnerable. I had figured that an arrow placed in that tender area should add mightily to that "itching, burning" sensation featured in small ads in the backs of newspapers, the ones that say AVOID SURGERY!

My notion was that, if the dragon, not too bright, was unbearably annoyed at both ends at once, his coordination should go all to hell and we could peck away at him until he was useless, or until he got sick of it and ran. But I had to get his tail up, to let Rufo get in a shot. These creatures, satchel-heavy like old *t. rex*, charge head up and front legs up and balance this by lifting the tail.

The dragon was weaving its head back and forth and I was trying to weave the other way, so as not to be lined up if it turned on the flame—when suddenly I got my first blast of methane, whiffing it before it lighted, and retreated so fast that I backed into that baby I had stepped on before, went clear over it, landed on my shoulders and rolled, and that saved me. Those flames shoot out about twenty feet. The grown-up dragon had reared up and still could have fried me, but the baby was in the way. It chopped off the flame—but Rufo yelled, "Bull's-eye!"

The reason that I backed away in time was halitosis. It says here that "pure methane is a colorless, odorless gas." This G.I.-tract methane wasn't pure; it was so loaded with homemade ketones and aldehydes that it made an unlimed outhouse smell like Shalimar.

I figure that Star's giving me that salve to open up my nose saved my life. When my nose clamps down I can't even smell my upper lip.

The action didn't stop while I figured this out; I did all my thinking either before or after, not during. Shortly after Rufo shot it in the bull's-eye, the beast got a look of utter indignation, opened its mouth again without flaming and tried to reach its fanny with both hands. It couldn't—forelegs too short—but it tried. I had returned sword in a hurry once I saw the length of that flame jet and had grabbed my bow. I had time to get one arrow into its mouth, left tonsil maybe.

This message got through faster. With a scream of rage that shook the ground it started for me, belching flame—and Rufo yelled, "A wart seven!"

I was too busy to congratulate him; those critters are fast for their size. But I'm fast, too, and had more incentive. A thing that big can't change course very fast, but it can swing its head and with it the flame. I got my pants scorched and moved still faster, trying to cut around it.

Star carefully put an arrow into the other tonsil, right where the flame came out, while I was dodging. Then the poor thing tried so hard to turn *both* ways at *both* of us that it got tangled in its feet and fell over, a small earthquake. Rufo sank another arrow in its tender behind, and Star loosed one that passed through its tongue and stuck on the fletching, not damaging it but annoying it dreadfully.

It pulled itself into a ball, got to its feet, reared up and tried to flame me again. I could tell it didn't like me.

And the flame went out.

This was something I had hoped for. A proper dragon, with castles and captive princesses, has as much fire as it needs, like six-shooters in TV oaters. But these creatures fermented their own methane and couldn't have too big a reserve tank nor under too high pressure—I hoped. If we could nag one into using all its ammo fast, there was bound to be a lag before it recharged.

Meanwhile Rufo and Star were giving it no peace with the pincushion routine. It made a real effort to light up again while I was traversing rapidly, trying to keep that squealing baby dragon between me and the big one, and it behaved like an almost dry Ronson; the flame flickered and caught, shot out a pitiful six feet and went out. But it tried so hard to get me with that last flicker that it fell over again.

I took a chance that it would be sluggy for a second or two like a man who's been tackled hard, ran in and stuck my sword in its right eye.

It gave one mighty convulsion and quit.

(A lucky poke. They say dinosaurs that big have brains the size of chestnuts. Let's credit this beast with one the size of a cantaloupe—but it's still luck if you thrust through an eye socket and get the brain right off. Nothing we had done up to then was more than mosquito bites. But it died from that one poke. St. Michael *and* St. George guided my blade.)

And Rufo yelled, "Boss! Git fer home!"

A drag race of dragons was closing on us. It felt like that drill in basic where you have to dig a foxhole, then let a tank pass over you.

"This way!" I yelled. "Rufo! This way, not that! *Star!*" Rufo skidded to a stop, we got headed the same way and I saw the mouth of the cave, black as sin and inviting as a mother's arms. Star hung back; I shoved her in and Rufo stumbled after her and I turned to face more dragons for my lady love.

But she was yelling, "Milord! Oscar! Inside, you idiot! *I must set the wards!*"

So I got inside fast and she did, and I never did chew her out for calling her husband an idiot.

XIII

THE littlest dragon followed us to the cave, not belligerently (although I don't trust anything with teeth that size) but more, I think, the way a baby duck follows anyone who leads. It tried to come in after us, drew back suddenly as its snout touched the invisible curtain, like a kitten hit by a static spark. Then it hung around outside, making wheepling noises.

I began to wonder whether or not Star's wards could stop flame. I found out as an old dragon arrived right after that, shoved his head into the opening, jerked it back indignantly just as the kid had, then eyed us and switched on his flame-thrower.

No, the wards don't stop flame.

We were far enough inside that we didn't get singed but the smoke and stink and heat were ghastly and just as deadly if it went on long.

An arrow whoofed past my ear and that dragon gave up interest in us. He was replaced by another who wasn't convinced. Rufo, or possibly Star, convinced him before he had time to light his blowtorch. The air cleared; from somewhere inside there was an outward draft.

Meanwhile Star had made a light and the dragons were holding an indignation meeting. I glanced behind me —a narrow, low passage that dropped and turned. I stopped paying attention to Star and Rufo and the inside of the cave; another committee was calling.

I got the chairman in his soft palate before he could belch. The vice-chairman took over and got in a brief remark about fifteen feet long before he, too, changed his mind. The committee backed off and bellowed bad advice at each other.

The baby dragon hung around all during this. When the adults withdrew he again came to the door, just short of where he had burned his nose. "Koo-werp?" he said plaintively. "Koo-werp? Keet!" Plainly he wanted to come in.

Star touched my arm. "If milord husband pleases, we are ready."

"*Keet!*"

"Right away," I agreed, then yelled, "Beat it, kid! Back to your mama."

Rufo stuck his head alongside mine. "Probably can't," he commented. "Likely that was its mama we ruined."

I didn't answer as it made sense; the adult dragon we had finished off had come awake instantly when I stepped on the kid's tail. This sounds like mother love, if dragons go in for mother love—I wouldn't know.

But it's a hell of a note when you can't even kill a dragon and feel lighthearted afterwards.

We meandered back into that hill, ducking stalactites and stepping around stalagmites while Rufo led with a torch. We arrived in a domed chamber with a floor glazed smooth by unknown years of calcified deposit. It had stalactites in soft pastel shades near the walls and a lovely, almost symmetrical chandelier from the center but no stalagmite under it. Star and Rufo had stuck lumps of the luminescent putty which is the common night light in Nevia at a dozen points around the room;

it bathed the room in a soft light and pointed up the stalactites.

Among them Rufo showed me webs. "Those spinners are harmless," he said. "Just big and ugly. They don't even bite like a spider. But—mind your step!" He pulled me back. "These things are poisonous even to touch. Blindworms. That's what took us so long. Had to be sure the place was clean before warding it. But now that *She* is setting wards at the entrances I'll give it one more check."

The so-called blindworms were translucent, irridescent things the size of large rattlesnakes and slimy-soft like angleworms; I was glad they were dead. Rufo speared them on his sword, a grisly shishkebab, and carried them out through the entrance we had come in.

He was back quickly and Star finished warding. "That's better," he said with a sigh as he started cleaning his blade. "Don't want their perfume around the house. They rot pretty fast and puts me in mind of green hides. Or copra. Did I ever tell you about the time I shipped as a cook out of Sydney? We had a second mate aboard who never bathed and kept a penguin in his stateroom. Female, of course. This bird was no more cleanly than he was and it used to—"

"Rufo," said Star, "will you help with the baggage?"

"Coming, milady."

We got out food, sleeping mats, more arrows, things that Star needed for her witching or whatever, and canteens to fill with water, also from the foldbox. Star had warned me earlier that Karth-Hokesh was a place where the local chemistry was not compatible with human life; everything we ate or drank we must fetch with us.

I eyed those one-liter canteens with disfavor. "Baby girl, I think we are cutting rations and water too fine."

She shook her head. "We won't need more, truly."

"Lindbergh flew the Atlantic on just a peanut butter sandwich," Rufo put in. "But I urged him to take more."

"How do you know we won't need more?" I persisted. "Water especially."

"I'm filling mine with brandy," Rufo said. "You divvy with me, I'll divvy with you."

"Milord love, water is heavy. If we try to hang everything on us against any emergency, like the White Knight, we'll be too weighted down to fight. I'm going to have to strain to usher through three people, weapons, and a minimum of clothing. Living bodies are easiest; I can borrow power from you both. Once-living materials are next; you've noticed, I think, that our clothing is wool, our bows of wood, and strings are of gut. Things never living are hardest, steel especially, yet we must have swords and, if we still had firearms, I would strain to the limit to get them through, for now we need them. However, milord Hero, I am simply informing you. You must decide—and I feel sure I can handle, oh, even half a hundredweight more of dead things if necessary. If you will select what your genius tells you."

"My genius has gone fishing. But, Star my love, there is a simple answer. Take everything."

"Milord?"

"Jocko set us out with half a ton of food, looks like, and enough wine to float a loan, and a little water. Plus a wide variety of Nevia's best tools for killing, stabbing, and mayhem. Even armor. And more things. In that foldbox is enough to survive a siege, without eating or drinking anything from Karth-Hokesh. The beauty of it is that it weighs only about fifteen pounds, packed—not the fifty pounds you said you could swing by straining. I'll strap it on my own back and won't notice it. It won't slow me down; it may armor me against a swing at my back. Suits?"

Star's expression would have fitted a mother whose child has just caught onto the Stork hoax and is wondering how to tackle an awkward subject. "Milord husband, the mass is much too great. I doubt if any witch or warlock could move it unassisted."

"But folded up?"

"It does not change it, milord; the mass is still there —still more dangerously there. Think of a powerful spring, wound very tight and small, thus storing much

171

energy. It takes enormous power to put a foldbox through a transition in its compacted form, or it explodes."

I recalled a mud volcano that had drenched us and quit arguing. "All right, I'm wrong. But one question— If the mass is there always, why does it weigh so little when folded?"

Star got the same troubled expression. "Your pardon, milord, but we do not share the language—the mathematical language—that would permit me to answer. As yet, I mean; I promise you chance to study if you wish. As a tag, think of it as a tame spacewarp. Or think of the mass being so extremely far away—in a new direction —from the sides of the foldbox that local gravitation hardly matters."

(I remembered a time when my grandmother had asked me to explain television to her—the guts, not the funny pictures. There are things which cannot be taught in ten easy lessons, nor popularized for the masses; they take years of skull sweat. This be treason in an age when ignorance has come into its own and one man's opinion is as good as another's. But there it is. As Star says, the world is what it is—and doesn't forgive ignorance.)

But I was still curious. "Star, is there any way to tell me why some things go through easier than others? Wood easier than iron, for example?"

She looked rueful. "No, because I don't know myself. Magic is not science, it is a collection of ways to do things—ways that work but often we don't know why."

"Much like engineering. Design by theory, then beef it up anyhow."

"Yes, milord husband. A magician is a rule-of-thumb engineer."

"And," put in Rufo, "a philosopher is a scientist with no thumbs. I'm a philosopher. Best of all professions."

Star ignored him and got out a sketch block, showed me what she knew of the great tower from which we must steal the Egg of Phoenix. This block appeared to be a big cube of Plexiglas; it looked like it, felt like it, and took thumb prints like it.

But she had a long pointer which sank into it as if the block were air. With its tip she could sketch in three dimensions; it left a thin glowing line wherever she wanted it—a 3-dimensional blackboard.

This wasn't magic; it was advanced technology—and it will beat the hell out of our methods of engineering drawing when we learn how, especially for complex assemblies such as aviation engines and UHF circuitry— even better than exploded isometric with transparent overlays. The block was about thirty inches on a side and the sketch inside could be looked at from any angle— even turned over and studied from underneath.

The Mile-High Tower was not a spire but a massy block, somewhat like those stepped-back buildings in New York, but enormously larger.

Its interior was a maze.

"Milord champion," Star said apologetically, "when we left Nice there was in our baggage a finished sketch of the Tower. Now I must work from memory. However, I had studied the sketch so very long that I believe I can get relations right even if proportions suffer. I feel sure of the true paths, the paths that lead to the Egg. It is possible that false paths and dead ends will not be as complete; I did not study them as hard."

"Can't see that it matters," I assured her. "If I know the true paths, any I don't know are false ones. Which we won't use. Except to hide in, in a pinch."

She drew the true paths in glowing red, false ones in green—and there was a lot more green than red. The critter who designed that tower had a twisty mind. What appeared to be the main entrance went in, up, branched and converged, passed close to the Chamber of the Egg —then went back down by a devious route and dumped you out, like P. T. Barnum's "This Way to the Egress."

Other routes went inside and lost you in mazes that could not be solved by follow-the-left-wall. If you did, you'd starve. Even routes marked in red were very complex. Unless you knew where the Egg was guarded, you could enter correctly and still spend this year and next January in fruitless search.

173

"Star, have you been in the Tower?"

"No, milord. I have been in Karth-Hokesh. But far back in the Grotto Hills. I've seen the Tower only from great distance."

"Somebody must have been in it. Surely your—opponents—didn't send you a map."

She said soberly, "Milord, sixty-three brave men have died getting the information I now offer you."

(So now we try for sixty-four!) I said, "Is there any way to study just the red paths?"

"Certainly, milord." She touched a control, green lines faded. The red paths started each from one of the three openings, one "door" and two "windows."

I pointed to the lowest level. "This is the only one of thirty or forty doors that leads to the Egg?"

"That is true."

"Then just inside that door they'll be waiting to clobber us."

"That would seem likely, milord."

"Hmmm . . ." I turned to Rufo. "Rufe, got any long, strong, lightweight line in that plunder?"

"I've got some Jocko uses for hoisting. About like heavy fishing line, breaking strength around fifteen hundred pounds."

"Good boy!"

"Figured you might want it. A thousand yards enough?"

"Yes. Anything lighter than that?"

"Some silk trout line."

In an hour we had made all preparations I could think of and that maze was as firmly in my head as the alphabet. "Star hon, we're ready to roll. Want to whomp up your spell?"

"No, milord."

"Why not? 'Twere best done quickly."

"Because I can't, my darling. These Gates are not true gates; there is always a matter of timing. This one will be ready to open, for a few minutes, about seven hours from now, then cannot be opened again for several weeks."

I had a sour thought. "If the buckos we are after know this, they'll hit us as we come out."

"I hope not, milord champion. They should be watching for us to appear from the Grotto Hills, as they know we have a Gate somewhere in those hills—and indeed that is the Gate I planned to use. But this Gate, even if they know of it, is so badly located—for us—that I do not think they would expect us to dare it."

"You cheer me up more all the time. Have you thought of anything to tell me about what to expect? Tanks? Cavalry? Big green giants with hairy ears?"

She looked troubled. "Anything I say would mislead you, milord. We can assume that their troops will be constructs rather than truly living creatures . . . which means they can be anything. Also, anything may be illusion. I told you about the gravity?"

"I don't think so."

"Forgive me, I'm tired and my mind isn't sharp. The gravity varies, sometimes erratically. A level stretch will seem to be downhill, then quickly uphill. Other things . . . any of which may be illusion."

Rufo said, "Boss, if it moves, shoot it. If it speaks, cut its throat. That spoils most illusions. You don't need a program; there'll be just us—and all the others. So when in doubt, kill it. No sweat."

I grinned at him. "No sweat. Okay, we'll worry when we get there. So let's quit talking."

"Yes, milord husband," Star seconded. "We had best get several hours' sleep."

Something in her voice had changed. I looked at her and she was subtly different, too. She seemed smaller, softer, more feminine and compliant than the Amazon who had fired arrows into a beast a hundred times her weight less than two hours before.

"A good idea," I said slowly and looked around. While Star had been sketching the mazes of the Tower, Rufo had repacked what we couldn't take and—I now noticed—put one sleeping pad on one side of the cave and the other two side by side as far from the first as possible.

I silently questioned her by glancing at Rufo and shrugging an implied, "What now?"

Her answering glance said neither yes nor no. Instead she called out, "Rufo, go to bed and give that leg a chance. Don't lie on it. Either belly down or face the wall."

For the first time Rufo showed his disapproval of what we had done. He answered abruptly, not what Star said but what she may have implied: "You couldn't *hire* me to look!"

Star said to me in a voice so low I barely heard it, "Forgive him, milord husband. He is an old man, he has his quirks. Once he is in bed I will take down the lights."

I whispered, "Star my beloved, it still isn't my idea of how to run a honeymoon."

She searched my eyes. "This is your will, milord love?"

"Yes. The recipe calls for a jug of wine and a loaf of bread. Not a word about a chaperon. I'm sorry."

She put a slender hand against my chest, looked up at me. "I am glad, milord."

"You are?" I didn't see why she had to say so.

"Yes. We both need sleep. Against the morrow. That your strong sword arm may grant us many morrows."

I felt better and smiled down at her. "Okay, my princess. But I doubt if I'll sleep."

"Ah, but you will!"

"Want to bet?"

"Hear me out, milord darling. Tomorrow ... after you have won ... we go quickly to my home. No more waitings, no more troubles. I would that you knew the language of my home, so that you will not feel a stranger. I want it to be *your* home, at once. So? Will milord husband dispose himself for bed? Lie back and let me give him a language lesson? You will sleep, you know that you will."

"Well ... it's a fine idea. But you need sleep even more than I do."

"Your pardon, milord, but not so. Four hours' sleep puts spring in my step and a song on my lips."

"Well..."

Five minutes later I was stretched out, staring into the most beautiful eyes in any world and listening to her beloved voice speak softly in a language strange to me. . . .

XIV

RUFO was shaking my shoulder. "Breakfast, Boss!" He shoved a sandwich into my hand and a pot of beer into the other. "That's enough to fight on and lunch is packed. I've laid out fresh clothes and your weapons and I'll dress you as soon as you finish. But snap it up. We're on in a few minutes." He was already dressed and belted.

I yawned and took a bite of sandwich (anchovies, ham and mayonnaise, with something that wasn't quite tomato and lettuce)—and looked around. The place beside me was empty but Star seemed to have just gotten up; she was not dressed. She was on her knees in the center of the room, drawing some large design on the floor.

"Morning, chatterbox," I said. "Pentacle?"

"Mmm—" she answered, not looking up.

I went over and watched her work. Whatever it was, it was not based on a five-cornered star. It had three major centers, was very intricate, had notations here and there —I recognized neither language nor script—and the only sense I could abstract from it was what appeared to be a hypercube seen face on. "Had breakfast, hon?"

"I fast this morning."

"You're skinny now. Is that a tesseract?"

"Stop it!"

Then she pushed back her hair, looked up, and smiled ruefully. "I'm sorry, darling. The witch is a bitch, that's certain. But please don't look over my shoulder. I'm having to do this by memory; I lost my books in the marsh—and it's difficult. And no questions now, please, please. You might shake my confidence—and I *must* be utterly confident."

I made a leg. "Your pardon, milady."

"Don't be formal with me, darling. Love me anyhow and give me a quick kiss—then let me be."

So I leaned over and gave her a high-caloric kiss, with mayonnaise, and let her be. I dressed while I finished the sandwich and beer, then sought out a natural alcove just short of the wards in the passage, one which had been designated the men's room. When I came back Rufo was waiting with my sword belt. "Boss, you'd be late for your own hanging."

"I hope so."

A few minutes later we were standing on that diagram, Star on pitcher's mound with Rufo and myself at first and third bases. He and I were much hung about, myself with two canteens and Star's sword belt (on its last notch) as well as my own, Rufo with Star's bow slung and with two quivers, plus her medic's kit and lunch. We each had longbow strung and tucked under left arm; we each had drawn sword. Star's tights were under my belt behind in an untidy tail, her jacket was crumpled under Rufo's belt, while her buskins and hat were crammed into pockets—etc. We looked like a rummage sale.

But this did leave Rufo's left hand and mine free. We faced outward with swords at ready, reached behind us and Star clasped us each firmly by hand. She stood in the exact center, feet apart and planted solidly and was wearing that required professionally of witches when

179

engaged in heavy work, i.e., not even a bobby pin. She looked magnificent, hair shaggy, eyes shining, and face flushed, and I was sorry to turn my back.

"Ready, my gallants?" she demanded, excitement in her voice.

"Ready," I confirmed.

"*Ave, Imperatrix, nos morituri te—*"

"Stop that, Rufo! *Silence!*" She began to chant in a language unknown to me. The back of my neck prickled.

She stopped, squeezed our hands much harder, and shouted, *"Now!"*

Sudden as a slammed door, I find I'm a Booth Tarkington hero in a Mickey Spillane situation.

I don't have time to moan. Here is this *thing* in front of me, about to chop me down, so I run my blade through his guts and yank it free while he makes up his mind which way to fall; then I dose his buddy the same way. Another one is squatting and trying to get a shot at my legs past the legs of his squad mates. I'm as busy as a one-armed beaver with paper hangers and hardly notice a yank at my belt as Star recovers her sword.

Then I do notice as she kills the hostile who wants to shoot me. Star is everywhere at once, naked as a frog and twice as lively. There was a dropped-elevator sensation at transition, and suddenly reduced gravitation could have been bothersome had we time to indulge it.

Star makes use of it. After stabbing the laddie who tries to shoot me, she sails over my head and the head of a new nuisance, poking him in the neck as she passes and he isn't a nuisance any longer.

I think she helps Rufo, but I can't stop to look. I hear his grunts behind me and that tells me that he is still handing out more than he's catching.

Suddenly he yells, *"Down!"* and something hits the back of my knees and I go down—land properly limp and am about to roll to my feet when I realize Rufo is the cause. He is belly down by me and shooting what has to be a gun at a moving target out across the plain, himself behind the dead body of one of our playmates.

Star is down, too, but not fighting. Something has poked a hole through her right arm between elbow and shoulder.

Nothing else seemed to be alive around me, but there were targets four to five hundred feet away and opening rapidly. I saw one fall, heard *Zzzzt*, smelled burning flesh near me. One of those guns was lying across a body to my left; I grabbed it and tried to figure it out. There was a shoulder brace and a tube which should be a barrel; nothing else looked familiar.

"Like this, my Hero." Star squirmed to me, dragging her wounded arm and leaving a trail of blood. "Place it like a rifle and sight it so. There is a stud under your left thumb. Press it. That's all—no windage, no elevation."

And no recoil, as I found when I tracked one of the running figures with the sights and pressed the stud. There was a spurt of smoke and down he went. "Death ray," or Laser beam, or whatever—line it up, press the stud, and anyone on the far end quit the party with a hole burned in him.

I got a couple more, working right to left, and by then Rufo had done me out of targets. Nothing moved, so far as I could see, anywhere.

Rufo looked around. "Better stay down, Boss." He rolled to Star, opened her medic's kit at his own belt, and put a rough and hasty compress on her arm.

Then he turned to me. "How bad are you hurt, Boss?"

"Me? Not a scratch."

"What's that on your tunic? Ketchup? Someday somebody is going to offer you a pinch of snuff. Let's see it."

I let him open my jacket. Somebody, using a sawtooth edge, had opened a hole in me on my left side below the ribs. I had not noticed it and hadn't felt it—until I saw it and then it hurt and I felt queasy. I strongly disapprove of violence done to me. While Rufo dressed it, I looked around to avoid looking at it.

We had killed about a dozen of them right around us, plus maybe half that many who had fled—and had

181

shot all who fled, I think. How? How can a 60-lb. dog armed only with teeth take on, knock down, and hold prisoner an armed man? Ans: By all-out attack.

I think we arrived as they were changing the guard at that spot known to be a Gate—and had we arrived even with swords sheathed we would have been cut down. As it was, we killed a slew before most of them knew a fight was on. They were routed, demoralized, and we slaughtered the rest, including those who tried to bug out. Karate and many serious forms of combat (boxing isn't serious, nor anything with rules)—all these work that same way: go-for-broke, all-out attack with no wind up. These are not so much skills as an attitude.

I had time to examine our late foes; one was faced toward me with his belly open. "Iglis" I would call them, but of the economy model. No beauty and no belly buttons and not much brain—presumably constructed to do one thing: fight, and try to stay alive. Which describes us, too—but we did it faster.

Looking at them upset my stomach, so I looked at the sky. No improvement—it wasn't decent sky and wouldn't come into focus. It crawled and the colors were wrong, as jarring as some abstract paintings. I looked back at our victims, who seemed almost wholesome compared with that "sky."

While Rufo was doctoring me, Star squirmed into her tights and put on her buskins. "Is it all right for me to sit up to get into my jacket?" she asked.

"No," I said. "Maybe they'll think we're dead." Rufo and I helped her finish dressing without any of us rising up above the barricade of flesh. I'm sure we hurt her arm but all she said was, "Sling my sword left-handed. What now, Oscar?"

"Where are the garters?"

"Got 'em. But I'm not sure they will work. This is a very odd place."

"Confidence," I told her. "That's what you told me a few minutes ago. Put your little mind to work *believing* you can do it." We ranged ourselves and our plunder, now enhanced by three "rifles" plus side arms of the

182

same sort, then laid out the oaken arrow for the top of the Mile-High Tower. It dominated one whole side of the scene, more a mountain than a building, black and monstrous.

"Ready?" asked Star. "Now you two believe, too!" She scrawled with her finger in the sand. "Go!"

We went. Once in the air, I realized what a naked target we were—but we were a target on the ground, too, for anyone up on that tower, and worse if we had hoofed it. "Faster!" I yelled in Star's ear. "Make us go faster!"

We did. Air shrilled past our ears and we bucked and dipped and sideslipped as we passed over those gravitational changes Star had warned me about—and perhaps that saved us; we made an evasive target. However, if we got all of that guard party, it was possible that no one in the Tower knew we had arrived.

The ground below was gray-black desert surrounded by a mountain ringwall like a lunar crater and the Tower filled the place of a central peak. I risked another look at the sky and tried to figure it out. No sun. No stars. No black sky nor blue—light came from all over and the "sky" was ribbons and boiling shapes and shadow holes of all colors.

"What in God's name kind of planet is this?" I demanded.

"It's not a planet," she yelled back. "It's a *place*, in a different sort of universe. It's not fit to live in."

"Somebody lives here." I indicated the Tower.

"No, no, nobody lives here. That was built just to guard the Egg."

The monstrousness of that idea didn't soak in right then. I suddenly recalled that we didn't dare eat or drink here—and started wondering how we could breathe the air if the chemistry was that poisonous. My chest felt tight and started to burn. So I asked Star and Rufo moaned. (He rated a moan or two; he hadn't thrown up. I don't think he had.)

"Oh, at least twelve hours," she said. "Forget it. No importance."

Whereupon my chest really hurt and I moaned, too.

We were dumped on top of the Tower right after that; Star barely got out *"Amech!"* in time to keep us from zooming past.

The top was flat, seemed to be black glass, was about two hundred yards square—and there wasn't a fiddle-winking thing to fasten a line to. I had counted on at least a ventilator stack.

The Egg of the Phoenix was about a hundred yards straight down. I had had two plans in mind if we ever reached the Tower. There were three openings (out of hundreds) which led to true paths to the Egg—and to the Never-Born, the Eater of Souls, the M.P. guarding it. One was at ground level and I never considered it. A second was a couple of hundred feet off the ground and I had given that serious thought: loose an arrow with a messenger line so that the line passed over any projection above that hole; use that to get the strong line up, then go up the line—no trick for any crack Alpinist, which I wasn't but Rufo was.

But the great Tower turned out to have no projections, real modern simplicity of design—carried too far.

The third plan was, if we could reach the top, to let ourselves down by a line to the third non-fake entrance, almost on level with the Egg. So here we were, all set—and no place to hitch.

Second thoughts are wonderful thoughts—why hadn't I had Star drive us straight into that hole in the wall?

Well, it would take very fine sighting of that silly arrow; we might hit the wrong pigeonhole. But the important reason was that I hadn't thought of it.

Star was sitting and nursing her wounded arm. I said, "Honey, can you fly us, slow and easy, down a couple of setbacks and into that hole we want?"

She looked up with drawn face. "No."

"Well. Too bad."

"I hate to tell you—but I burned out the garters on that speed run. They won't be any good until I can re-charge them. Not things I can get here. Green mugwort, blood of a hare—things like that."

"Boss," said Rufo, "how about using the whole top of the Tower as a hitching post?"

"How do you mean?"

"We've got lots of line."

It was a workable notion—walk the line around the top while somebody else held the bitter end, then tie it and go down what hung over. We did it—and finished up with only a hundred feet too little of line out of a thousand yards.

Star watched us. When I was forced to admit that a hundred feet short was as bad as no line at all, she said thoughtfully, "I wonder if Aaron's Rod would help?"

"Sure, if it was stuck in the top of this overgrown ping-pong table. What's Aaron's Rod?"

"It makes stiff things limp and limp things stiff. No, no, not *that*. Well, that, too, but what I mean is to lay this line across the roof with about ten feet hanging over the far side. Then make that end and the crossing part of the line steel hard—sort of a hook."

"Can you do it?"

"I don't know. It's from The Key of Solomon and it's an incantation. It depends on whether I can remember it—and on whether such things work in this universe."

"Confidence, confidence! Of course you can."

"I can't even think how it starts. Darling, can you hypnotize? Rufo can't—or at least not me."

"I don't know a thing about it."

"Do just the way I do with you for a language lesson. Look me in the eye, talk softly, and tell me to remember the words. Perhaps you had better lay out the line first."

We did so and I used a hundred feet instead of ten for the bill of the hook, on the more-is-better principle. Star lay back and I started talking to her, softly (and without conviction) but over and over again.

Star closed her eyes and appeared to sleep. Suddenly she started to mumble in tongues.

"Hey, Boss! Damn thing is hard as rock and stiff as a life sentence!"

I told Star to wake up and we slid down to the set-

185

back below as fast as we could, praying that it wouldn't go limp on us. We didn't shift the line; I simply had Star cause more of it to starch up, then I went on down, made certain that I had the right opening, three rows down and fourteen over, then Star slid down and I caught her in my arms; Rufo lowered the baggage, weapons mostly, and followed. We were in the Tower and had been on the planet—correction: the "place"—we had been in the place called Karth-Hokesh not more than forty minutes.

I stopped, got the building matched in my mind with the sketch block map, fixed the direction and location of the Egg, and the "red line" route to it, the true path.

Okay, go on in a few hundred yards, snag the Egg of the Phoenix and *go!* My chest stopped hurting.

XV

"BOSS," said Rufo, "Look out over the plain."

"At what?"

"At nothing," he answered. "Those bodies are gone. You sure as hell ought to be able to see them, against black sand and not even a bush to break the view."

I didn't look. "That's the moose's problem, damn it! We've got work to do. Star, can you shoot left-handed? One of these pistol things?"

"Certainly, milord."

"You stay ten feet behind me and shoot anything that moves. Rufo, you follow Star, bow ready and an arrow nocked. Try for anything you see. Sling one of those guns—make a sling out of a bit of line." I frowned. "We'll have to abandon most of this. Star, you can't bend a bow, so leave it behind, pretty as it is, and your quiver. Rufo can sling my quiver with his; we use the same arrows. I hate to abandon my bow, it suits me so. But I must. Damn."

"I'll carry it, my Hero."

"No, any clutter we can't use must be junked." I unhooked my canteen, drank deeply, passed it over. "You two finish it and throw it away."

While Rufo drank, Star slung my bow. "Milord husband? It weighs nothing this way and doesn't hamper my shooting arm. So?"

"Well— If it gets in your way, cut the string and forget it. Now drink your fill and we go." I peered down the corridor we were in—fifteen feet wide and the same high, lighted from nowhere and curving away to the right, which matched the picture in my mind. "Ready? Stay closed up. If we can't slice it, shoot it, or shaft it, we'll salute it." I drew sword and we set out, quick march.

Why my sword, rather than one of those "death ray" guns? Star was carrying one of those and knew more about one than I did. I didn't even know how to tell if one was charged, nor had I judgment in how long to press the button. She could shoot, her bowmanship proved that, and she was at least as cool in a fight as Rufo or myself.

I had disposed weapons and troops as well as I knew how. Rufo, behind with a stock of arrows, could use them if needed and his position gave him time to shift to either sword or Buck Rogers "rifle" if his judgment said to—and I didn't need to advise him; he would.

So I was backed up by long-range weapons ancient and ultramodern in the hands of people who knew how to use them and temperament to match—the latter being the more important. (Do you know how many men in a platoon actually *shoot* in combat? Maybe six. More likely three. The rest freeze up.)

Still, why didn't I sheathe my sword and carry one of those wonder weapons?

A properly balanced sword is the most versatile weapon for close quarters ever devised. Pistols and guns are all offense, no defense; close on him fast and a man with a gun can't shoot, he has to stop you before you reach him. Close on a man carrying a blade and you'll be spitted like a roast pigeon—unless you have a blade and can use it better than he can.

A sword never jams, never has to be reloaded, is always ready. Its worst shortcoming is that it takes great skill and patient, loving practice to gain that skill; it can't be taught to raw recruits in weeks, nor even months.

But most of all (and this was the real reason) to grasp the Lady Vivamus and feel her eagerness to bite gave me courage in a spot where I was scared spitless.

They (whoever "they" were) could shoot us from ambush, gas us, booby-trap us, many things. But they could do those things even if I carried one of those strange guns. Sword in hand, I was relaxed and unafraid—and that made my tiny "command" more nearly safe. If a C.O. needs to carry a rabbit's foot, he should—and the grip of that sweet sword was bigger medicine than all the rabbits' feet in Kansas.

The corridor stretched ahead, no break, no sound, no threat. Soon the opening to the outside could no longer be seen. The great Tower felt empty but not dead; it was alive the way a museum is alive at night, with crowding presence and ancient evil. I gripped my sword tightly, then consciously relaxed and flexed my fingers.

We came to a sharp left turn. I stopped short. "Star, this wasn't on your sketch."

She didn't answer. I persisted, "Well, it wasn't. Was it?"

"I am not sure, milord."

"Well, *I* am. Hmm—"

"Boss," said Rufo, "are you dead sure we entered by the right pigeonhole?"

"I'm certain. I may be wrong but I'm not uncertain—and if I'm wrong, we're dead pigeons anyhow. Mmm—Rufo, take your bow, put your hat on it, stick it out where a man would look around that corner if he were standing—and time it as I do look out, but lower down." I got on my belly.

"Ready . . . *now!*" I sneaked a look six inches above the floor while Rufo tried to draw fire higher up.

Nothing in sight, just bare corridor, straight now.

"Okay, follow me!" We hurried around the corner

I stopped after a few paces. "What the hell?"

"Something wrong Boss?"

"Plenty." I turned and sniffed. "Wrong as can be. The Egg is up that way," I said, pointing, "maybe two hundred yards—by the sketch block map."

"Is that bad?"

"I'm not sure. Because it was that same direction and angle, off on the left, *before* we turned that corner. So now it ought to be on the right."

Rufo said, "Look, Boss, why don't we just follow the passageways you memorized? You may not remember every little—"

"Shut up. Watch ahead, down the corridor. Star, stand there in the corner and watch me. I'm going to try something."

They placed themselves, Rufo "eyes ahead" and Star where she could see both ways, at the right-angle bend. I went back into the first reach of corridor, then returned. Just short of the bend I closed my eyes and kept on.

I stopped after another dozen steps and opened my eyes. "That proves it," I said to Rufo.

"Proves what?"

"There isn't any bend in the corridor." I pointed to the bend.

Rufo looked worried. "Boss, how do you feel?" He tried to touch my cheek.

I pulled back. "I'm not feverish. Come with me, both of you." I led them back around that right angle some fifty feet and stopped. "Rufo, loose an arrow at that wall ahead of us at the bend. Lob it so that it hits the wall about ten feet up."

Rufo sighed but did so. The arrow rose true, disappeared in the wall. Rufo shrugged. "Must be pretty soft up there. You've lost us an arrow, Boss."

"Maybe. Places and follow me." We took that corner again and here was the spent arrow on the floor somewhat farther along than the distance from loosing to bend. I let Rufo pick it up; he looked closely at the Doral chop by the fletching, returned it to quiver. He said nothing. We kept going.

We came to a place where steps led downward—but where the sketch in my head called for steps leading up. "Mind the first step," I called back. "Feel for it and don't fall."

The steps felt normal, for steps leading downward—with the exception that my bump of direction told me that we were *climbing*, and our destination changed angle and distance accordingly. I closed my eyes for a quick test and found that I was indeed climbing, only my eyes were deceived. It was like one of those "crooked houses" in amusement parks, in which a "level' floor is anything but level—like that but cubed.

I quit questioning the accuracy of Star's sketch and tracked its trace in my head regardless of what my eyes told me. When the passageway branched four ways while my memory showed only a simple branching, one being a dead end, I unhesitatingly closed my eyes and followed my nose—and the Egg stayed where it should stay, in my mind.

But the Egg did not necessarily get closer with each twist and turn save in the sense that a straight line is not the shortest distance between two points—is it ever? The path was as twisted as guts in a belly; the architect had used a pretzel for a straight edge. Worse yet, another time when we were climbing "up" stairs—at a piece level by the sketch—a gravitational anomaly caught us with a full turn and we were suddenly sliding down the ceiling.

No harm done save that it twisted again as we hit bottom and dumped us from ceiling to floor. With both eyes peeled I helped Rufo gather up arrows and off we set again. We were getting close to the lair of the Never-Born—and the Egg.

Passageways began to be narrow and rocky, the false twists tight and hard to negotiate—and the light began to fail.

That wasn't the worst. I'm not afraid of dark nor of tight places; it takes a department store elevator on Dollar Day to give me claustrophobia. But I began to hear rats.

Rats, lots of rats, running and squeaking in the walls

around us, under us, over us. I started to sweat and was sorry I had taken that big drink of water. Darkness and closeness got worse, until we were crawling through a rough tunnel in rock, then inching along on our bellies in total darkness as if tunneling out of Château d'If . . . and rats brushed past us now, squeaking and chittering.

No, I didn't scream. Star was behind me and she didn't scream and she didn't complain about her wounded arm —so I couldn't scream. She patted me on the foot each time she inched forward, to tell me that she was all right and to report that Rufo was okay, too. We didn't waste strength on talk.

I saw a faint something, two ghosts of light ahead, and stopped and stared and blinked and stared again. Then I whispered to Star, "I see something. Stay put, while I move up and see what it is. Hear me?"

"Yes, milord Hero."

"Tell Rufo."

Then I did the only really brave thing I have ever done in my life: I inched forward. Bravery is going on anyhow when you are so terrified your sphincters won't hold and you can't breathe and your heart threatens to stop, and that is an exact description for that moment of E. C. Gordon, ex-Pfc. and hero by trade. I was fairly certain what those two faint lights were and the closer I got the more certain I was—I could smell the damned thing and place its outlines.

A rat. Not the common rat that lives in city dumps and sometimes gnaws babies, but a giant rat, big enough to block that rat hole but enough smaller than I am to have room to maneuver in attacking me—room I didn't have at all. The best I could do was to wriggle forward with my sword in front of me and try to keep the point aimed so that I would catch him with it, make him eat steel—because if he dodged past that point I would have nothing but bare hands and no room to use them. He would be at my face.

I gulped sour vomit and inched forward. His eyes seemed to drop a little as if he were crouching to charge. But no rush came. The lights got more definite and wider apart, and when I had squeezed a foot or two farther I realized with shaking relief that they were not rat's eyes but something else—anything, I didn't care what.

I continued to inch forward. Not only was the Egg in that direction but I still didn't know what it was and I had best see before telling Star to move up.

The "eyes" were twin pinholes in a tapestry that covered the end of that rat hole. I could see its embroidered texture and I found I could look through one of its imperfections when I got up to it.

There was a large room beyond, the floor a couple of feet lower than where I was. At the far end, fifty feet away, a man was standing by a bench, reading a book. Even as I watched he raised his eyes and glanced my way. He seemed to hesitate.

I didn't. The hole had eased enough so that I managed one foot under and lunged forward, brushing the arras aside with my sword. I stumbled and bounced to my feet, on guard.

He was at least as fast. He had slapped the book down on the bench and drawn sword himself, advanced toward me, while I was popping out of that hole. He stopped, knees bent, wrist straight, left arm back, and point for me, perfect as a fencing master, and looked me over, not yet engaged by three or four feet between our steels.

I did not rush him. There is a go-for-broke tactic, "the target," taught by the best swordmasters, which consists in headlong advance with arm, wrist, and blade in full extension—all attack and no attempt to parry. But it works only by perfect timing when you see your opponent slacken up momentarily. Otherwise it is suicide.

This time it would have been suicide; he was as ready as a tomcat with his back up. So I sized him up while he looked me over. He was a smallish neat man with arms long for his height—I might or might not have reach on him, especially as his rapier was an old style, longer than Lady Vivamus (but slower thereby, unless he had a much stronger wrist)—and he was dressed more for the Paris of Richelieu than for Karth-Hokesh. No, that's not fair; the great black Tower had no styles, else I would have been as out of style in my fake Robin Hood getup. The Iglis we had killed had worn no clothes.

He was an ugly cocky little man with a merry grin and the biggest nose west of Durante—made me think of my first sergeant's nose, very sensitive he was about being called "Schnozzola." But the resemblance stopped there; my first sergeant never smiled and had mean, piggish eyes; this man's eyes were merry and proud.

"Are you Christian?" he demanded.

"What's it to you?"

"Nothing. Blood's blood, either way. If Christian you be, confess. If pagan, call your false gods. I'll allow you no more than three stanzas. But I'm sentimental, I like to know what I'm killing."

"I'm American."

"Is that a country? Or a disease? And what are you doing in Hoax?"

" 'Hoax'? Hokesh?"

He shrugged only with his eyes, his point never moved. "Hoax, Hokesh—a matter of geography and accent; this château was once in the Carpathians, so 'Hokesh' it is, if 'twill make your death merrier. Come now, let us sing."

He advanced so fast and smoothly that he seemed to apport and our blades rang as I parried his attack in sixte and riposted, was countered—remise, reprise, beat-and-attack—the phrase ran so smoothly, so long, and in such variation that a spectator might have thought that we were running through Grand Salute.

But *I* knew! That first lunge was meant to kill me, and so was his every move throughout the phrase. At the same time he was feeling me out, trying my wrist, looking for weaknesses, whether I was afraid of low line and always returned to high or perhaps was a sucker for a disarm. I never lunged, never had a chance to; every part of the phrase was forced on me, I simply replied, tried to stay alive.

I knew in three seconds that I was up against a better swordsman than myself, with a wrist like steel yet

194

supple as a striking snake. He was the only swordsman I have ever met who used prime and octave—*used* them, I mean, as readily as sixte and carte. Everyone learns them and my own master made me practice them as much as the other six—but most fencers don't *use* them; they simply may be forced into them, awkwardly and just before losing a point.

I would lose, not a point, but my life—and I knew, long before the end of that first long phrase, that my life was what I was about to lose, by all odds.

Yet at first clash the idiot began to sing!

"Lunge and counter and thrust,
"Sing me the logic of steel!
"Tell me, sir, how do you feel?
"Riposte and remise if you must
"In logic long known to be just.

"Shall we argue, rebut and refute
"In enthymeme clear as your eye?
"Tell me, sir, why do you sigh?
"*Tu es fatigué, sans doute?*
"Then sleep while I'm counting the loot."

The above was long enough for at least thirty almost-successful attempts on my life, and on the last word he disengaged as smoothly and unexpectedly as he had engaged.

"Come, come, lad!" he said. "Pick it up! Would let me sing alone? Would die as a clown with ladies watching? Sing!—and say good-bye gracefully, with your last rhyme racing your death rattle." He banged his right boot in a flamenco stomp. "Try! The price is the same either way."

I didn't drop my eyes at the sound of his boot; it's an old gambit, some fencers stomp on every advance, every feint, on the chance that the noise will startle opponent out of timing, or into rocking back, and thus gain a point. I had last fallen for it before I could shave.

But his words gave me an idea. His lunges were short —full extension is fancy play for foils, too dangerous for real work. But I had been retreating, slowly, with the wall behind me. Shortly, when he re-engaged, I would either be a butterfly pinned to that wall, or stumble over something unseen, go arsy-versy, then spiked like wastepaper in the park. I didn't dare leave that wall behind me.

Worst, Star would be coming out of that rat hole behind me any moment now and might be killed as she emerged even if I managed to kill him at the same time. But if I could turn him around— My beloved was a practical woman; no "sportsmanship" would keep her steel stinger out of his back.

But the happy counterthought was that if I went along with his madness, tried to rhyme and sing, he might play me along, amused to hear what I could do, before he killed me.

But I couldn't afford to stretch it out. Unfelt, he had pinked me in the forearm. Just a bloody scratch that Star could make good as new in minutes—but it would weaken my wrist before long and it disadvantaged me for low line: Blood makes a slippery grip.

"First stanza," I announced, advancing and barely engaging, foible-à-foible. He respected it, not attacking, playing with the end of my blade, tiny counters and feather-touch parries.

That was what I wanted. I started circling right as I began to recite—and he let me:

> "Tweedledum and Tweedledee
> "Agreed to rustle cattle.
> "Said Tweedledum to Tweedledee
> "I'll use my nice new saddle."

"Come, come, my old!" he said chidingly. "No stealing. Honor among beeves, always. And rhyme and scansion limp. Let your Carroll fall trippingly off the tongue."

"I'll try," I agreed, still moving right. "Second stanza—

> "I sing of two lasses in Birmingham,
> "Shall we weep at the scandal concerning them?"—

196

—and I rushed him.

It didn't quite work. He had, as I hoped, relaxed the tiniest bit, evidently expecting that I would go on with mock play, tips of blades alone, while I was reciting.

It caught him barely off guard but he failed to fall back, parrying strongly instead and suddenly we were in an untenable position, corps-à-corps, forte-à-forte, almost tête-à-tête.

He laughed in my face and sprang back as I did, landing us back *en garde*. But I added something. We had been fencing point only. The point is mightier than the edge but my weapon had both and a man used to the point is sometimes a sucker for a cut. As we separated I flipped my blade at his head.

I meant to split it open. No time for that, no force behind it, but it sliced his right forehead almost to eyebrow.

"Touché!" he shouted. "Well struck. And well sung. Let's have the rest of it."

"All right," I agreed, fencing cautiously and waiting for blood to run into his eyes. A scalp wound is the bloodiest of flesh wounds and I had great hopes for this one. And sword-play is an odd thing; you don't really use your mind, it is much too fast for that. Your wrist thinks and tells your feet and body what to do, bypassing your brain—any thinking *you* do is for later, stored instructions, like a programed computer.

I went on:

> "They're now in the dock
> "For lifting the—"

I got him in the forearm, the way he got me, but worse. I thought I had him and pressed home. But he did something I had heard of, never seen: He retreated very fast, flipped his blade and changed hands.

No help to me— A right-handed fencer hates to take on a southpaw; it throws everything out of balance, whereas a southpaw is used to the foibles of the right-handed majority—and this son of a witch was just as strong, just as skilled, with his left hand. Worse, he now had toward me the eye undimmed by blood.

He pinked me again, in the kneecap, hurting like fire and slowing me. Despite *his* wounds, much worse than mine, I knew I couldn't go on much longer. We settled down to grim work.

There is a riposte in seconde, desperately dangerous but brilliant—if you bring it off. It had won me several matches in *épée* with nothing at stake but a score. It starts from sixte; first your opponent counters. Instead of parrying to carte, you press and bind, sliding all the way down and around his blade and corkscrewing in till your point finds flesh. Or you can beat, counter, and bind, starting from sixte, thus setting it off yourself.

Its shortcoming is that, unless it is done perfectly, it is too late for parry and riposte; you run your own chest against his point.

I didn't try to initiate it, not against *this* swordsman; I just thought about it.

We continued to fence, perfectly each of us. Then he stepped back slightly while countering and barely skidded in his own blood.

My wrist took charge; I corkscrewed in with a perfect bind to seconde—and my blade went through his body.

He looked surprised, brought his bell up in salute, and crumpled at the knees as the grip fell from his hand. I had to move forward with my blade as he fell, then started to pull it out of him.

He grasped it. "No, no, my friend, please leave it there. It corks the wine, for a time. Your logic is sharp and touches my heart. Your name, sir?"

"Oscar of Gordon."

"A good name. One should never be killed by a stranger. Tell me, Oscar of Gordon, have you seen Carcassonne?"

"No."

"See it. Love a lass, kill a man, write a book, fly to the Moon—I have done all these." He gasped and foam came out of his mouth, pink. "I've even had a house fall on me. What devastating wit! What price honor when

198

timber taps thy top? 'Top?' tap? taupe, tape—tonsor!—
when timber taps thy tonsor. You shaved mine."

He choked and went on: "It grows dark. Let us exchange gifts and part friends, if you will. My gift first,
in two parts: Item: You are lucky, you shall not die in
bed."

"I guess not."

"Please. Item: Friar Guillaume's razor ne'er shaved the
barber, it is much too dull. And now your gift, my old—
and be quick, I need it. But first—how did that limerick
end?"

I told him. He said, very weakly, almost in rattle,
"Very good. Keep trying. Now grant me your gift, I am
more than ready." He tried to Sign himself.

So I granted him grace, stood wearily up, went to the
bench and collapsed on it, then cleaned both blades, first
wiping the little Solingen, then most carefully grooming
the Lady Vivamus. I managed to stand and salute him
with a clean sword. It had been an honor to know him.

I was sorry I hadn't asked him his name. He seemed
to think I knew it.

I sat heavily down and looked at the arras covering
the rat hole at the end of the room and wondered why
Star and Rufo hadn't come out? All that clashing steel
and talk—

I thought about walking over and shouting for them.
But I was too weary to move just yet. I sighed and closed
my eyes—

Through sheer boyish high spirits (and carelessness I
had been chided for, time and again) I had broken a
dozen eggs. My mother looked down at the mess and I
could see that she was about to cry. So I clouded up too.
She stopped her tears, took me gently by the shoulder,
and said, "It's all right, son. Eggs aren't that important."
But I was ashamed, so I twisted away and ran.

Downhill I ran, heedless and almost flying—then was
shockingly aware that I was at the wheel and the car was
out of control. I groped for the brake pedal, couldn't
find it and felt panic . . . then did find it—and felt it

sink with that mushiness that means you've lost brake-fluid pressure. Something ahead in the road and I couldn't *see*. Couldn't even turn my head and my eyes were clouded with something running down into them. I twisted the wheel and nothing happened—radius rod gone.

Screams in my ear as we hit!—and I woke up in bed with a jerk and the screams were my own. I was going to be late to school, disgrace not to be borne. Never born, agony shameful, for the schoolyard was empty; the other kids, scrubbed and virtuous, were in their seats and I couldn't find my classroom. Hadn't even had time to go to the bathroom and here I was at my desk with my pants down about to do what I had been too hurried to do before I left home and all the other kids had their hands up but teacher was calling on *me*. I *couldn't* stand up to recite; my pants were not only down I didn't have any on at all if I stood up they would see it the boys would laugh at me the girls would giggle and look away and tilt their noses. But the unbearable disgrace was that *I didn't know the answer!*

"Come, come!" my teacher said sharply. "Don't waste the class's time, E.C. You Haven't Studied Your Lesson."

Well, no, I hadn't. Yes, I had, but she had written "Problems 1-6" on the blackboard and I had taken that as "1 *and* 6"—and this was number 4. But *She* would never believe me; the excuse was too thin. We pay off on touchdowns, not excuses.

"That's how it is, Easy," my Coach went on, his voice more in sorrow than in anger. "Yardage is all very well but you don't make a nickel unless you cross that old goal line with the egg tucked underneath your arm." He pointed at the football on his desk. "There it is. I had it gilded and lettered clear back at the beginning of the season, you looked so good and I had so much confidence in you—it was meant to be yours at the end of the season, at a victory banquet." His brow wrinkled and he spoke as if trying to be fair. "I won't say you could have saved things all by yourself. But you do take things too easy, Easy—maybe you need another name. When the road gets rough, you could try harder." He sighed. "My fault, I should have cracked down. Instead, I tried to be a father to you. But I want you to know you aren't the only one who loses by this—at my age it's not easy to find a new job."

I pulled the covers up over my head; I couldn't stand to look at him. But they wouldn't let me alone; somebody started shaking my shoulder. "Gordon!"

"Le'me 'lone!"

"Wake up, Gordon, and get your ass inside. You're in trouble."

I certainly was, I could tell that as soon as I stepped into the office. There was a sour taste of vomit in my mouth and I felt awful—as if a herd of buffaloes had walked over me, stepping on me here and there. Dirty ones.

The First Sergeant didn't look at me when I came in; he let me stand and sweat first. When he did look up, he examined me up and down before speaking.

Then he spoke slowly, letting me taste each word. "Absent Over Leave, terrorizing and insulting native women, unauthorized use of government property ... scandalous conduct ... insubordinate and obscene language ... resisting arrest ... striking an M.P.—Gordon, why didn't you steal a horse? We hang horse thieves in these parts. It would make it all so much simpler."

He smiled at his own wit. The old bastard always had thought he was a wit. He was half right.

But I didn't give a damn what he said. I realized dully that it had all been a dream, just another of those dreams I had had too often lately, wanting to get out of this aching jungle. Even *She* hadn't been real. My—what was her name?—even her name I had made up. Star. My Lucky Star— Oh, Star, my darling, you *aren't!*"

He went on: "I see you took off your chevrons. Well, that saves time but that's the only thing good about it. Out of uniform. No shave. And your clothes are filthy! Gordon, you are a disgrace to the Army of the United States. You know that, don't you? And you can't sing your way out of this one. No I.D. on you, no pass, using a name not your own. Well, Evelyn Cyril my fine lad, we'll use your right name now. Officially."

He swung around in his swivel chair—he hadn't had his fat ass out of it since they sent him to Asia, no patrols for him. "Just one thing I'm curious about. Where did you get *that?* And whatever possessed you to try to steal it?" He nodded at a file case behind his desk.

I recognized what was sitting on it, even though it had been painted with gold gilt the last time I recalled seeing it whereas now it was covered with the special black gluey mud they grow in Southeast Asia. I started toward it. "That's mine!"

"No, no!" he said sharply. "Burny, burny, boy." He moved the football farther back. "Stealing it doesn't make it yours. I've taken charge of it as evidence. For your information, you phony hero, the docs think he's going to die."

"Who?"

"Why should you care who? Two bits to a Bangkok tickul you didn't know his name when you clobbered him. You can't go around clobbering natives just because you're feeling brisk—they've got rights, maybe you hadn't heard. You're supposed to clobber them only when and where you are told to."

Suddenly he smiled. It didn't improve him. With his long, sharp nose and his little bloodshot eyes I suddenly realized how much he looked like a rat.

But he went on smiling and said, "Evelyn my boy, maybe you took off those chevrons too soon."

"Huh?"

"Yes. There may be a way out of this mess. Sit down." He repeated sharply, " 'Sit down,' I said. If I had my way, we'd simply Section-Eight you and forget you —anything to get rid of you. But the Company Commander has other ideas—a really brilliant idea that could close your whole file. There's a raid planned for tonight. So"—he leaned over, got a bottle of Four Roses and two cups out of his desk, poured two drinks— "have a drink."

Everybody knew about that bottle—everybody but the

Company Commander, maybe. But the top sergeant had never been known to offer anyone a drink—save one time when he had followed it by telling his victim that he was being recommended for a general court-martial.

"No, thanks."

"Come on, take it. Hair of the dog. You're going to need it. Then go take a shower and get yourself looking decent even if you aren't, before you see the Company Commander."

I stood up. I wanted that drink, I needed it. I would have settled for the worst rotgut—and Four Roses is pretty smooth—but I would have settled for the fire-water old—what was his name?—had used to burst my eardrums.

But I didn't want to drink with him. I should not drink anything at all here. Nor eat any—

I spat in his face.

He looked utterly shocked and started to melt. I drew my sword and had at him.

It got dark but I kept on laying about me, sometimes connecting, sometimes not.

XVI

SOMEONE was shaking my shoulder. "Wake up!"

"Le'me 'lone!"

"You've got to wake up. Boss, please wake up."

"Yes, my Hero—*please!*"

I opened my eyes, smiled at her, then tried to look around. Kee-*ripes*, what a shambles! In the middle of it, close to me, was a black glass pillar, thick and about five feet high. On top was the Egg. "Is that it?"

"Yep!" agreed Rufo. "That's it!" He looked battered but gay.

"Yes, my Hero champion," Star confirmed, "that is the true Egg of the Phoenix. I have tested."

"Uh—" I looked around. "Then where's old Soul-Eater?"

"You killed it. Before we got here. You still had sword in hand and the Egg tucked tightly under your left arm. We had much trouble getting them loose so that I could work on you."

I looked down my front, saw what she meant, and

looked away. Red just isn't my color. To take my mind off surgery I said to Rufo, "What took you so long?"

Star answered, "I thought we would never find you!"

"How did you find me?"

Rufo said, "Boss, we couldn't exactly lose you. We simply followed your trail of blood—even when it dead-ended into blank walls. *She* is stubborn."

"Uh ... see any dead men?"

"Three or four. Strangers, no business of ours. Constructs, most likely. We didn't dally." He added, "And we won't dally getting out, either, once you're patched up enough to walk. Time is short."

I flexed my right knee, cautiously. It still hurt where I had been pinked on the kneecap, but what Star had done was taking the soreness out. "My legs are all right. I'll be able to walk as soon as Star is through. But"—I frowned—"I don't relish going through that rat tunnel again. Rats give me the willies."

"What rats, Boss? In which tunnel?"

So I told him.

Star made no comment, just went on plastering me and sticking on dressings. Rufo said, "Boss, you did get down on your knees and crawl—in a passage just like all the others. I couldn't see any sense to it but you had proved that you knew what you were doing, so we didn't argue, we did it. When you told us to wait while you scouted, we did that, too—until we had waited a long time and *She* decided that we had better try to find you."

I let it drop.

We left almost at once, going out the "front" way and had no trouble, no illusions, no traps, nothing but the fact that the "true path" was long and tedious. Rufo and I stayed alert, same formation, with Star in the middle carrying the Egg.

Neither Star nor Rufo knew whether we were still likely to be attacked, nor could we have held off anything stronger than a Cub Scout pack. Only Rufo could bend a bow and I could no longer wield a sword. However, the single necessity was to give Star time to destroy the Egg rather than let it be captured. "But that's nothing to worry about," Rufo assured me. "About like being at ground-zero with an A-weapon. You'll never notice it."

Once we were outside it was a longish hike to the Grotto Hills and the other Gate. We lunched as we hiked—I was terribly hungry—and shared Rufo's brandy and Star's water without too much water. I felt pretty good by the time we reached the cave of this Gate; I didn't even mind sky that wasn't sky but some sort of roof, nor the odd shifts in gravitation.

A diagram or "pentacle" was already in this cave. Star had only to freshen it, then we waited a bit—that had been the rush, to get there before that "Gate" could be opened; it wouldn't be available for weeks or perhaps months thereafter—much too long for any human to live in Karth-Hokesh.

We were in position a few minutes early. I was dressed like the Warlord of Mars—just me and sword belt and sword. We all lightened ship to the limit as Star was tired and pulling live things through would be strain enough. Star wanted to save my pet longbow but I vetoed it. She did insist that I keep the Lady Vivamus and I didn't argue very hard; I didn't want ever to be separated from my sword again. She touched it and told me that it was *not* dead metal, but now part of me.

Rufo wore only his unpretty pink skin, plus dressings; his attitude was that a sword was a sword and he had better ones at home. Star was, for professional reasons, wearing no more.

"How long?" asked Rufo, as we joined hands.

"Count down is minus two minutes," she answered. The clock in Star's head is as accurate as my bump of direction. She never used a watch.

"You've told him?" said Rufo.

"No."

Rufo said, "Haven't you any shame? Don't you think you've conned him long enough?" He spoke with surprising roughness and I was about to tell him that he must not speak to her that way. But Star cut him off.

"QUIET!"

206

She began to chant. Then—*"Now!"*

Suddenly it was a different cave. "Where are we?" I asked. I felt heavier.

"On Nevia's planet," Rufo answered. "Other side of the Eternal Peaks—and I've got a good mind to get off and see Jocko."

"Do it," Star said angrily. "You talk too much."

"Only if my pal Oscar comes along. Want to, old comrade? I can get us there, take about a week. No dragons. They'll be glad to see you—especially Muri."

"You leave Muri out of this!" Star was actually shrill.

"Can't take it, huh?" he said sourly. "Younger woman and all that."

"You know that's not it!"

"Oh, how very much it is!" he retorted. "And how long do you think you can get away with it? It's not fair, it never was fair. It—"

"Silence! Count down right now!" We joined hands again and whambo! we were in another place. This was still another cave with one side partly open to the outdoors; the air was very thin and bitterly cold and snow had sifted in. The diagram was let into rock in raw gold. "Where is this?" I wanted to know.

"On your planet," Star answered. "A place called Tibet."

"And you could change trains here," Rufo added, "if *She* weren't so stubborn. Or you could walk out—although it's a long, tough walk; I did it once."

I wasn't tempted. The last I had heard, Tibet was in the hands of unfriendly peace-lovers. "Will we be here long?" I asked. "This place needs central heating." I wanted to hear anything but more argument. Star was my beloved and I couldn't stand by and hear anyone be rude to her—but Rufo was my blood brother by much lost blood; I owed my life to him several times over.

"Not long," answered Star. She looked drawn and tired.

"But time enough to get this straightened out," added Rufo, "so that you can make up your own mind and not be carried around like a cat in a sack. *She* should have told you long since. *She*—"

"Positions!" snapped Star. "Count down coming up. Rufo, if you don't shut up, I'll leave you here and let you walk out again—in deep snow barefooted to your chin."

"Go ahead," he said. "Threats make me as stubborn as you are. Which is surprising. Oscar. *She* is—"

"SILENCE!"

"—Empress of the Twenty Universes—"

XVII

WE were in a large octagonal room, with lavishly beautiful silvery walls.

"—and my grandmother," Rufo finished.

"Not 'Empress,' " Star protested. "That's a silly word for it."

"Near enough."

"And as for the other, that's my misfortune, not my fault." Star jumped to her feet, no longer looking tired, and put one arm around my waist as I got up, while she held the Egg of the Phoenix with the other. "Oh, darling, I'm so happy! We made it! Welcome home, my Hero!"

"Where?" I was sluggy—too many time zones, too many ideas, too fast.

"Home. My home. Your home now—if you'll have it. *Our* home."

"Uh, I see . . . my Empress."

She stomped her foot. "Don't call me that!"

"The proper form of address," said Rufo, "is 'Your Wisdom.' Isn't it, Your Wisdom?"

"Oh, Rufo, shut up. Go fetch clothes for us."

He shook his head. "War's over and I just got paid off. Fetch 'em yourself, Granny."

"Rufo, you're impossible."

"Sore at me, Granny?"

"I will be if you don't stop calling me 'Granny.'" Suddenly she handed the Egg to me, put her arms around Rufo and kissed him. "No, Granny's not sore at you," she said softly. "You always were a naughty child and I'll never quite forget the time you put oysters in my bed. But I guess you came by it honestly—from your grandmother." She kissed him again and mussed his fringe of white hair. "Granny loves you. Granny always will. Next to Oscar, I think you are about perfect— aside from being an unbearable, untruthful, spoiled, disobedient, disrespectful brat."

"That's better," he said. "Come to think of it, I feel the same way about you. What do you want to wear?"

"Mmm . . . get out a lot of things. It's been so long since I had a decent wardrobe." She turned back to me. "What would you like to wear, my Hero?"

"I don't know. I don't know anything. Whatever you think is appropriate—Your Wisdom."

"Oh, darling, please don't call me that. Not ever." She seemed suddenly about to cry.

"All right. What shall I call you?"

"Star is the name you gave me. If you must call me something else, you could call me your 'princess.' I'm not a princess—and I'm not an 'empress' either; that's a poor translation. But I *like* being 'your princess'—the way you say it. Or it can be 'lively wench' or any of lots of things you've been calling me." She looked up at me very soberly. "Just like before. Forever."

"I'll try . . . my princess."

"My Hero."

"But there seems to be a lot I don't know."

She shifted from English to Nevian. "Milord husband, I wished to tell all. I sighed to tell you. And milord will be told everything. But I held mortal fear that milord, if

210

told too soon, would refuse to come with me. Not to the Black Tower, but to here. Our home."

"Perhaps you chanced wisely," I answered in the same language. "But I am here, milady wife—my princess. So tell me. I wish it."

She shifted back to English. "I'll talk, I'll talk. But it will take time. Darling, will you hold your horses just a bit longer? Having been patient with me—so very patient, my love!—for so long?"

"Okay," I agreed. "I'll string along. But, look, I don't know the streets in this neighborhood, I'll need some hints. Remember the mistake I made with old Jocko just from not knowing local customs."

"Yes, dear, I will. But don't worry, customs are simple here. Primitive societies are always more complex than civilized ones—and this one isn't primitive." Rufo dumped then a great heap of clothing at her feet. She turned away, a hand still on my arm, put a finger to her mouth with a very intent, almost worried look. "Now let me see. What shall I wear?"

"Complex" is a relative matter; I'll sketch only the outlines.

Center is the capital planet of the Twenty Universes. But Star was not "Empress" and it is not an empire.

I'll go on calling her "Star" as hundreds of names were hers and I'll call it an "empire" because no other word is close, and I'll refer to "emperors" and "empresses"—and to the Empress, my wife.

Nobody knows how many universes there are. Theory places no limit: any and all possibilities in unlimited number of combinations of "natural" laws, each sheaf appropriate to its own universe. But this is just theory and Occam's Razor is much too dull. All that is known in Twenty Universes is that twenty have been discovered, that each has its own laws, and that most of them have planets, or sometimes "places," where human beings live. I won't try to say what lives elsewhere.

The Twenty Universes include many real empires. Our Galaxy in our universe has its stellar empires—yet so huge is our Galaxy that our human race may never meet another, save through the Gates that link the universes. Some planets have no known Gates. Earth has many and that is its single importance; otherwise it rates as a backward slum.

Seven thousand years ago a notion was born for coping with political problems too big to handle. It was modest at first: How could a planet be run without ruining it? This planet's people included expert cyberneticists but otherwise were hardly farther along than we are; they were still burning the barn to get the rats and catching their thumbs in machinery. These experimenters picked an outstanding ruler and tried to help him.

Nobody knew why this bloke was so successful but he was and that was enough; they weren't hipped on theory. They gave him cybernetic help, taping for him all crises in their history, all known details, what was done, and the outcomes of each, all organized so that he could consult it almost as you consult your memory.

It worked. In time he was supervising the whole planet—Center it was, with another name then. He didn't rule it, he just untangled hard cases.

They taped also everything this first "Emperor" did, good and bad, for guidance of his successor.

The Egg of the Phoenix is a cybernetic record of the experiences of two hundred and three "emperors" and "empresses," most of whom "ruled" all the known universes. Like a foldbox, it is bigger inside than out. In use, it is more the size of the Great Pyramid.

Phoenix legends abound throughout the Universes: the creature that dies but is immortal, rising ever young from its own ashes. The Egg *is* such a wonder, for it is far more than a taped library now; it is a print, right down to their unique personalities, of *all* experience of *all* that line from His Wisdom IX through Her Wisdom CCIV, Mrs. Oscar Gordon.

The office is not hereditary. Star's ancestors include His Wisdom I and most of the other wisdoms—but millions of others have as much "royal" blood. Her grandson Rufo was not picked although he shares all her ancestors. Or perhaps he turned it down. I never asked, it would have reminded him of a time one of his uncles did something obscene and improbable. Nor is it a question one asks.

Once tapped, a candidate's education includes everything from how to cook tripe to highest mathematics—including all forms of personal combat for it was realized millennia ago that, no matter how well he was guarded, the victim would wear better if he himself could fight like an angry buzz saw. I stumbled on this through asking my beloved an awkward question.

I was still trying to get used to the fact that I had married a grandmother, whose grandson looked older than I did and was even older than he looked. The people of Center live longer than we do anyway and both Star and Rufo had received "Long-Life" treatment. This takes getting used to. I asked Star, "How long do you 'wisdoms' live?"

"Not too long," she answered almost harshly. "Usually we are assassinated."

(My big mouth—)

A candidate's training includes travel in many worlds —not all planets-places inhabited by human beings; nobody lives that long. But many. After a candidate completes all this and if selected as heir, postgraduate work begins: the Egg itself. The heir has imprinted in him (her) the memories, the very personalities, of past emperors. He (*She*) becomes an integration of them. Star-Plus. A supernova. Her Wisdom.

The living personality is dominant but all that mob is there, too. Without using the Egg, Star could recall experiences that happened to people dead many centuries. *With* the Egg—herself hooked into the cybernet —she had seven thousand years of sharp, just-yesterday memories.

Star admitted to me that she had hesitated ten years before accepting the nomination. She hadn't *wanted* to be all those people; she had wanted to go on being herself, living as she pleased. But the methods used to pick

213

candidates (I don't know them, they are lodged in the Egg) seem almost infallible; only three have ever refused.

When Star became Empress she had barely started the second half of her training, having had imprinted in her only seven of her predecessors. Imprinting does not take long but the victim needs recovery time between prints—for she gets every damned thing that ever happened to him, bad and good: the time he was cruel to a pet as a child and his recalled shame of it in his mature years, the loss of his virginity, the unbearably tragic time that he goofed a really serious one—*all* of it.

"I *must* experience their mistakes," Star told me. "Mistakes are the only certain way to learn."

So the whole weary structure is based on subjecting *one person* to all the miserable errors of seven thousand years.

Mercifully the Egg doesn't have to be used often. Most of the time Star could be herself, no more bothered by imprinted memories than you are over that nasty remark in second grade. Most problems Star could solve shooting from the hip—no recourse to the Black Room and a full hookup.

For the one thing that stood out as this empirical way of running an empire grew up was that the answer to most problems was: *Don't do anything*.

Always King Log, never King Stork—"Live and let live." "Let well enough alone." "Time is the best physician." "Let sleeping dogs lie." "Leave them alone and they'll come home, wagging their tails behind them."

Even positive edicts of the Imperium were usually negative in form: Thou Shalt Not Blow Up Thy Neighbors' Planet. (Blow your own if you wish.) Hands off the guardians of the Gates. Don't demand justice, you too will be judged.

Above all, don't put serious problems to a popular vote. Oh, there is no rule against local democracy, just in imperial matters. Old Rufo—excuse me; *Doctor* Rufo, a most distinguished comparative culturologist (with a

214

low taste for slumming)—Rufe told me that every human race tries every political form and that democracy is used in many primitive societies...but he didn't know of any civilized planet using it, as *Vox Populi, Vox Dei* translates as: "My God! How did we get in *this* mess!"

But Rufe claimed to enjoy democracy—any time he felt depressed he sampled Washington, and the antics of the French Parliament were second only to the antics of French women.

I asked him how advanced societies ran things?

His brow wrinkled. "Mostly they don't."

That described the Empress of Twenty Universes: Mostly she didn't.

But sometimes she did. She might say: "This mess will clear up if you will take that troublemaker there— What's your name? You with the goatee—out and shoot him. Do it now." (I was present. They did it now. He was head of the delegation which had brought the problem to her—some fuss between intergalactic trading empires in the VIIth Universe—and his chief deputy pinned his arms and his own delegates dragged him outside and killed him. Star went on drinking coffee. It's better coffee than we get back home and I was so upset that I poured myself a cup.)

An Emperor has no power. Yet, if Star decided that a certain planet should be removed, people would get busy and there would be a nova in that sky. Star has never done this but it has been done in the past. Not often— His Wisdom will search his soul (and the Egg) a long time before decreeing anything so final even when his hypertrophied horse sense tells him that there is no other solution.

The Emperor is sole source of Imperial law, sole judge, sole executive—and does very little and has no way to enforce his rulings. What he or she does have is enormous prestige from a system that has worked for seven millennia. This non-system holds together by having no togetherness, no uniformity, never seeking perfection, no utopias—just answers good enough to get

215

by, with lots of looseness and room for many ways and attitudes.

Local affairs are local. Infanticide?—they're your babies, your planet. PTAs, movie censorship, disaster relief—the Empire is ponderously unhelpful.

The Crisis of the Egg started long before I was born. His Wisdom CCIII was assassinated and the Egg stolen at the same time. Some baddies wanted power—and the Egg, by its unique resources, has latent in it key to such power as Genghis Khan never dreamed.

Why should anybody want power? I can't understand it. But some do, and they did.

So Star came to office half-trained, faced by the greatest crisis the Empire had ever suffered, and cut off from her storehouse of Wisdom.

But not helpless. Imprinted in her was the experience of seven hypersensible men and she had all the cyber-computer system save that unique part known as the Egg. First she had to find out what had been done with the Egg. It wasn't safe to mount an attack on the planet of the baddies; it might destroy the Egg.

Available were ways to make a man talk if one didn't mind using him up. Star didn't mind. I don't mean anything so crude as rack and tongs. This was more like peeling an onion, and they peeled several.

Karth-Hokesh is so deadly that it was named for the only explorers to visit it and come back alive. (We were in a "garden subdivision," the rest is much worse). The baddies made no attempt to stay there; they just cached the Egg and set guards and booby traps around it and on the routes to it.

I asked Rufo, "What use was the Egg *there?*"

"None," he agreed. "But they soon learned that it was no use anywhere—without *Her*. They needed either its staff of cyberneticists . . . or they needed Her Wisdom. They couldn't open the Egg. *She* is the only one who can do that unassisted. So they baited a trap for *Her*. Capture Her Wisdom, or kill Her—capture by preference, kill Her if need be and then try for key people

216

here at Center. But they didn't dare risk the second while *She* was alive."

Star started a search to determine the best chance of recovering the Egg. Invade Karth-Hokesh? The machines said, "Hell, no!" I would say no, too. How do you mount an invasion into a place where a man not only can't eat or drink anything local but can't breathe the air more than a few hours? When a massive assault will destroy what you are after? When your beachheads are two limited Gates?

The computers kept coming up with a silly answer, no matter how the question was framed.

Me.

A "Hero," that is—a man with a strong back, a weak mind, and a high regard for his own skin. Plus other traits. A raid by a thus-and-so man, if aided by Star herself, might succeed. Rufo was added by a hunch Star had (hunches of Their Wisdoms being equal to strokes of genius) and the machines confirmed this. "I was drafted," said Rufo. "So I refused. But I never have had any sense where *She* is concerned, damn it; She spoiled me when I was a kid."

There followed years of search for the specified man. (Me, again—I'll never know why.) Meanwhile brave men were feeling out the situation and, eventually, mapping the Tower. Star herself reconnoitered, and got acquainted in Nevia, too.

(Is Nevia part of the "Empire?" It is and it isn't. Nevia's planet has the only Gates to Karth-Hokesh other than one from the planet of the baddies; that is its importance to the Empire—and the Empire isn't important to Nevia at all.)

This "Hero" was most likely to be found on a barbaric planet such as Earth. Star checked, and turned down, endless candidates winnowed from many rough peoples before her nose told her that I might do.

I asked Rufo what chance the machines gave us.

"What makes you say that?" he demanded.

"Well, I know a little of cybernetics."

"You think you do. Still— There was a prediction.

217

Thirteen percent success, seventeen percent no game—and seventy percent death for us all."

I whistled. *"You* should whistle!" he said indignantly. "You didn't know any more than a cavalry horse knows. You had nothing to be scared of."

"I was scared."

"You didn't have time to be. It was planned so. Our one chance lay in reckless speed and utter surprise. But I *knew.* Son, when you told us to wait, there in the Tower, and disappeared and didn't come back, why, I was so scared I caught up on my regretting."

Once set up, the raid happened as I told it. Or pretty much so, although I may have seen what my mind could accept rather than exactly what happened. I mean "magic." How many times have savages concluded "magic" when a "civilized" man came along with something the savage couldn't understand? How often is some tag, such as "television," accepted by cultural savages (who nevertheless twist dials) when "magic" would be the honest word?

Still, Star never insisted on that word. She accepted it when *I* insisted on it.

But I would be disappointed if *everything* I saw turned out to be something Western Electric will build once Bell Labs works the bugs out. There ought to be *some* magic, somewhere, just for flavor.

Oh, yes, putting me to sleep for the first transition was to keep from scaring a savage silly. Nor did the "black biers" cross over—that was posthypnotic suggestion, by an expert: my wife.

Did I say what happened to the baddies? Nothing. Their Gates were destroyed; they are isolated until they develop star travel. Good enough, by the sloppy standards of the Empire. Their Wisdoms never carry grudges.

XVIII

CENTER is a lovely planet, Earth-like but lacking Earth's faults. It has been retailored over millennia to make it a Never-Never Land. Desert and snow and jungle were saved enough for pleasure; floods and other disasters were engineered out of existence.

It is uncrowded but has a large population for its size—that of Mars but with oceans. Surface gravity is almost that of Earth. (A higher constant, I understand.) About half the population is transient, as its great beauty and unique cultural assets—focus of twenty universes— make it a tourist's paradise. Everything is done for the comfort of visitors with an all-out thoroughness like that of the Swiss but with technology not known on Earth.

Star and I had residences a dozen places around the planet (and endless others in other universes); they ranged from palaces to a tiny fishing lodge where Star did her own cooking. Mostly we lived in apartments in an artificial mountain that housed the Egg and its staff; adjacent were halls, conference rooms, secretariat, etc. If Star felt like working she wanted such things at hand.

But a system ambassador or visiting emperor of a hundred systems had as much chance of being invited into our private home as a hobo at the back door of a Beverly Hills mansion has of being invited into the drawing room.

But if Star happened to like him, she might fetch him home for a midnight snack. She did that once—a funny little leprechaun with four arms and a habit of tap-dancing his gestures. But she did no official entertaining and felt no obligation to attend social affairs. She did not hold press conferences, make speeches, receive delegations of Girl Scouts, lay cornerstones, proclaim special "Days," make ceremonial appearances, sign papers, deny rumors, nor any of the time-gnawing things that sovereigns and V.I.P.'s do on Earth.

She consulted individuals, often summoning them from other universes, and she had at her disposal all the news from everywhere, organized in a system that had been developed over centuries. It was through this system that she decided what problems to consider. One chronic complaint was that the Imperium ignored "vital questions"—and so it did. Her Wisdom passed judgment only on problems she selected; the bedrock of the system was that most problems solved themselves.

We often went to social events; we both enjoyed parties and, for Her Wisdom and Consort, there was endless choice. There was one negative protocol: Star neither accepted nor regretted invitations, showed up when she pleased and refused to be fussed over. This was a drastic change for capital society as her predecessor had imposed protocol more formal than of the Vatican.

One hostess complained to me about how *dull* society had become under the new rules—maybe I could do something?

I did. I looked up Star and told her the remark, whereupon we left and joined a drunken artists' ball—a luau!

Center is such a hash of cultures, races, customs, and styles that it has few rules. The one invariant custom was: Don't impose *your* customs on *me*. People wore what they did at home, or experimented with other styles; any social affair looked like a free-choice costume ball. A guest could show up at a swank party stark-naked without causing talk—and some did, a small minority. I don't mean non-humans or hirsute humans; clothes are not for them. I mean humans who would look at home in New York in American clothes—and others who would attract notice even in l'Île du Levant because they have no hair at all, not even eyebrows. This is a source of pride to them; it shows their "superiority" to us hairy apes, they are as proud as a Georgia cracker is of his deficiency in melanin. So they go naked oftener than other human races. I found their appearance startling but one gets used to it.

Star wore clothes outside our home, so I did. Star would never miss a chance to dress up, an endearing weakness that made it possible to forget, at times, her Imperial status. She never dressed twice alike and was ever trying something new—and disappointed if I didn't notice. Some of her choices would cause heart failure even on a Riviera beach. She believed that a woman's costume was a failure unless it made men want to tear it off.

One of Star's most effective outfits was the simplest. Rufo happened to be with us and she got a sudden notion to dress as we had on the Quest of the Egg—and biff, bang, costumes were available, or manufactured to order, as may be; Nevian clothes are most uncommon in Center.

Bows, arrows, and quivers were produced with the same speed and Merry Men were we. It made me feel good to buckle on the Lady Vivamus; she had been hanging untouched on a wall of my study ever since the great black Tower.

Star stood, feet planted wide, fists on hips, head thrown back, eyes bright, and cheeks flushed. "Oh, this is fun! I feel good, I feel *young!* Darling, promise me, promise me truly, that someday we will again go on an adventure! I get so damn' sick of being sensible."

She spoke English, as the language of Center is ill suited to such ideas. It's a pidgin language with thousands of years of imports and changes and is uninflected, positional, and flat.

"Suits," I agreed. "How about it, Rufo? Want to walk that Glory Road?"

"After they pave it."

"Guff. You'll come, I know you. Where and when, Star? Never mind 'where'—just 'when.' Skip the party and start right now!"

Suddenly she was not merry. "Darling, you know I can't. I'm less than a third of the way through my training."

"I should have busted that Egg when I found it."

"Don't be cross, darling. Let's go to the party and have fun."

We did. Travel on Center is by apports, artificial "Gates" that require no "magic" (or perhaps still more); one sets destination like punching buttons in an elevator, so there is no traffic problem in cities—nor a thousand other unpleasant things; they don't let the bones show in their cities. Tonight Star chose to get off short of destination, swagger through a park, and make an entrance. She knows how well tights suit her long legs and solid buttocks; she rolled her hips like a Hindu woman.

Folks, we were a sensation! Swords aren't worn in Center, save possibly by visitors. Bows and arrows are hen's teeth, too. We were as conspicuous as a knight in armor on Fifth Avenue.

Star was as happy as a kid playing trick-or-treat. So was I. I felt two axe handles across the shoulders and wanted to hunt dragons.

It was a ball not unlike one on Earth. (According to Rufo, all our races everywhere have the same basic entertainment: get together in mobs to dance, drink, and gossip. He claimed that the stag affair and the hen party are symptoms of a sick culture. I won't argue.) We swaggered down a grand staircase, music stopped, people stared and gasped—and Star enjoyed being noticed. Musicians got raggedly back to work and guests went back to the negative politeness the Empress usually demanded. But we still got attention. I had thought that the story of the Quest of the Egg was a state secret as I had never heard it mentioned. But, even if known, I still would have expected the details to be known only to us three.

Not so. Everyone knew what those costumes meant, and more. I was at the buffet, sopping up brandy and a Dagwood of my own invention, when I was cornered by Scheherazade's sister, the pretty one. She was of one of the human-but-not-like-us races. She was dressed in rubies the size of your thumb and reasonably opaque cloth. She stood about five-five, barefooted, weighed maybe one twenty and her waist couldn't have been over fifteen inches, which exaggerated two other measurements that did not need it. She was brunette, with the slantiest eyes I've ever seen. She looked like a beautiful cat and looked at me the way a cat looks at a bird.

"Self," she announced.

"Speak."

"Sverlani. World—" (Name and code—I had never heard of it.) "Student food designer, mathematico-sybaritic."

"Oscar Gordon. Earth. Soldier." I omitted the I.D. for Earth; she knew who I was.

"Questions?"

"Ask."

"Is sword?"

"Is."

She looked at it and her pupils dilated. "Is-was sword destroy construct guard Egg?" ("Is this sword now present the direct successor in space-time sequential change, aside from theoretical anomalies involved in between-universe transitions, of the sword used to kill the Never-Born?" The double tense of the verb, present-past, stipulates and brushes aside the concept that identity is a meaningless abstraction—is this the sword you actually used, in the everyday meaning, and don't kid me, soldier, I'm no child.)

"Was-is," I agreed. ("I was there and I guarantee that I followed it all the way here, so it still is.")

223

She gave a little gasp and her nipples stood up. Around each was painted, or perhaps tattooed, the multi-universal design we call "Wall of Troy"—and so strong was her reaction that Ilium's ramparts crumbled again.

"Touch?" she said pleadingly.

"Touch."

"Touch *twice?*" ("Please, may I handle it enough to get the feel of it? Pretty please, with sugar on it! I ask too much and it is your right to refuse, but I guarantee not to hurt it"—they get mileage out of words, but the flavor is in the manner.)

I didn't want to, not the Lady Vivamus. But I'm a sucker for pretty girls. "Touch ... twice," I grudged. I drew it and handed it to her guard foremost, alert to grab it before she put somebody's eye out or stabbed herself in the foot.

She accepted it gingerly, eyes and mouth big, grasping it by the guard instead of the grip. I had to show her. Her hand was far too small for it; her hands and feet, like her waist, were ultra slender.

She spotted the inscription. "Means?"

Dum vivimus, vivamus doesn't translate well, not because they can't understand the idea but because it's water to a fish. How else would one live? But I tried. "Touch-twice life. Eat. Drink. Laugh."

She nodded thoughtfully, then poked the air, wrist bent and elbow out. I couldn't stand it, so I took it from her, dropped slowly into a foil guard, lunged in high line, recovered—a move so graceful that big hairy men look good in it. It's why ballerinas study fencing.

I saluted and gave it back to her, then adjusted her right elbow and wrist and left arm—this is why ballerinas get half rates, it's fun for the swordmaster. She lunged, almost pinking a guest in his starboard ham.

I took it back, wiped the blade, sheathed it. We had gathered a solid gallery. I picked up my Dagwood from the buffet, but she wasn't done with me. "Self jump sword?"

I choked. If she understood the meaning—or if I did —I was being propositioned the most gently I had ever been, in Center. Usually it's blunt. But surely Star hadn't spread the details of our wedding ceremony? Rufo? I hadn't told him but Star might have.

When I didn't answer, she made herself clear and did not keep her voice down. "Self unvirgin unmother unpregnant fertile."

I explained as politely as the language permits, which isn't very, that I was dated up. She dropped the subject, looked at the Dagwood. "Bite touch taste?"

That was another matter; I passed it over. She took a hearty bite, chewed thoughtfully, looked pleased. "Xenic. Primitive. Robust. Strong dissonance. Good art." Then she drifted away, leaving me wondering.

Inside of ten minutes the question was put to me again. I received more propositions than at any other party in Center and I'm sure the sword accounted for the bull market. To be sure, propositions came my way at every social event; I was Her Wisdom's consort. I could have been an orangutan and offers still would have been made. Some hirsutes looked like orangutans and were socially acceptable but I could have smelled like one. And behaved worse. The truth was that many ladies were curious about what the Empress took to bed, and the fact that I was a savage, or at best a barbarian, made them more curious. There wasn't any taboo against laying it on the line and quite a few did.

But I was still on my honeymoon. Anyhow, if I had accepted all those offers, I would have gone up with the window shade. But I enjoyed hearing them once I quit cringing at the "Soda?—or ginger ale?" bluntness; it's good for anybody's morale to be asked.

As we were undressing that night I said, "Have fun, pretty things?"

Star yawned and grinned. "I certainly did. And so did you, old Eagle Scout. Why didn't you bring that kitten home?"

"What kitten?"

"You know what kitten. The one you were teaching to fence."

"Meeow!"

"No, no, dear. You should send for her. I heard her state her profession, and there is a strong connection between good cooking and good—"

"Woman, you talk too much!"

She switched from English to Nevian. "Yes, milord husband. No sound I shall utter that does not break unbidden from love-anguished lips."

"Milady wife beloved . . . sprite elemental of the Singing Waters—"

Nevian is more useful than the jargon they talk on Center.

Center is a fun place and a Wisdom's consort has a cushy time. After our first visit to Star's fishing lodge, I mentioned how nice it would be to go back someday and tickle a few trout at that lovely place, the Gate where we had entered Nevia. "I wish it were on Center."

"It shall be."

"Star. You would move it? I know that some Gates, commercial ones, can handle real mass, but, even so—"

"No, no. But just as good. Let me see. It will take a day or so to have it stereoed and measured and air-typed and so forth. Water flow, those things. But meanwhile— There's nothing much beyond this wall, just a power plant and such. Say a door here and the place where we broiled the fish a hundred yards beyond. Be finished in a week, or we'll have a new architect. Suits?"

"Star, you'll do no such thing."

"Why not, darling?"

"Tear up the whole house to give me a trout stream? Fantastic!"

"I don't think so."

"Well, it is. Anyhow, sweet, the idea is not to move that stream here, but to go *there*. A vacation."

She sighed. "How I would love a vacation."

"You took an imprint today. Your voice is different."

"It wears off, Oscar."

"Star, you're taking them too fast. You're wearing yourself out."

Perhaps. But I must be the judge of that, as you know."

"As I *don't* know! You can judge the whole goddam creation—as you do and I know it—but *I*, your husband, must judge whether you are overworking—and stop it."

"Darling, darling!"

There were too many incidents like that.

I was not jealous of her. That ghost of my savage past had been laid in Nevia, I was not haunted by it again.

Nor is Center a place such ghost is likely to walk. Center has as many marriage customs as it has cultures —thousands. They cancel out. Some humans there are monogamous by instinct, as swans are said to be. So it can't be classed as "virtue." As courage is bravery in the face of fear, virtue is right conduct in the face of temptation. If there is no temptation, there can be no virtue. But these inflexible monogamists were no hazard. If someone, through ignorance, propositioned one of these chaste ladies, he risked neither a slap nor a knife; she would turn him down and go right on talking. Nor would it matter if her husband overheard; jealousy is never learned in a race automatically monogamous. Not that I ever tested it; to me they looked—and smelled— like spoiled bread dough. Where there is no temptation there is no virtue.

But I had chances to show "virtue." That kitten with the wasp waist tempted me—and I learned that she was of a culture in which females may not marry until they prove themselves pregnable, as in parts of the South Seas and certain places in Europe; she was breaking no taboos of her tribe. I was tempted more by another gal, a sweetie with a lovely figure, a delightful sense of humor, and one of the best dancers in any universe. She didn't write it on the sidewalk; she just let me know that she was neither too busy nor uninterested, using that argot with skillful indirection.

This was refreshing. Downright "American." I did inquire (elsewhere) into the customs of her tribe and found that, while they were rigid as to marriage, they were permissive otherwise. I would never do as a son-

227

in-law but the window was open even though the door was locked.

So I chickened. I gave myself a soul-searching and admitted curiosity as morbid as that of any female who propositioned me simply because I was Star's consort. Sweet little Zhai-ee-van was one of those who didn't wear clothes. She grew them on the spot; from tip of her nose to her tiny toes she was covered in soft, sleek, gray fur, remarkably like chinchilla. Gorgeous!

I didn't have the heart, she was too nice a kid.

But this temptation I admitted to Star—and Star implied gently that I must have muscles between my ears; Zhai-ee-van was an outstanding artiste even among her own people, who were esteemed as most talented devotees of Eros.

I stayed chicken. A romp with a kid that sweet should involve love, some at least, and it wasn't love, just that beautiful fur—along with a fear that a romp with Zhai-ee-van could turn into love and she couldn't marry me even if Star turned me loose.

Or didn't turn me loose— Center has no rule against polygamy. Some religions there have rules for and against this and that but this mixture of cultures has endless religions and they cancel each other the way conflicting customs do. Culturologists state a "law" of religious freedom which they say is invariant: Religious freedom in a cultural complex is inversely proportional to the strength of the strongest religion. This is supposed to be one case of a general invariant, that all freedoms arise from cultural conflicts because a custom which is not opposed by its negative is mandatory and always regarded as a "law of nature."

Rufo didn't agree; he said his colleagues stated as equations things which are not mensurate and not definable—holes in their heads!—and that freedom was never more than a happy accident because the common jerk, all human races, hates and fears all freedom, not only for his neighbors but for himself, and stamps it out whenever possible.

Back to Topic "A"— Centrists use every sort of marriage contract. Or none. They practice domestic partnership, coition, propagation, friendship, and love—but not necessarily all at once nor with the same person. Contracts could be as complex as a corporate merger, specifying duration, purposes, duties, responsibilities, number and sex of children, genetic selection methods, whether host mothers were to be hired, conditions for canceling and options for extension—anything but "marital fidelity." It is axiomatic there that this is unenforceable and therefore not contractual.

But marital fidelity is commoner there than it is on Earth; it simply is not legislated. They have an ancient proverb reading *Women and Cats*. It means: "Women and Cats do as they please, and men and dogs might as well relax to it." It has its opposite: *Men and Weather* which is blunter and at least as old, since the weather has long been under control.

The usual contract is no contract; he moves his clothes into her home and stays—until she dumps them outside the door. This form is highly thought of because of its stability: A woman who "tosses his shoes" has a tough time finding another man brave enough to risk her temper.

My "contract" with Star was no more than that, if contracts, laws, and customs applied to the Empress, which they did not and could not. But that was not the source of my increasing unease.

Believe me, I was *not* jealous.

But I was increasingly fretted by those dead men crowding her mind.

One evening as we were dressing for some whingding she snapped at me. I had been prattling about how I had spent my day, being tutored in mathematics, and no doubt had been as entertaining as a child reporting a day in kindergarten. But I was enthusiastic, a new world was opening to me—and Star was always patient.

But she snapped at me in a baritone voice.

I stopped cold. "You were imprinted today!"

I could feel her shift gears. "Oh, forgive me, darling! No, I'm not myself. I'm His Wisdom CLXXXII."

I did a fast sum. "That's fourteen you've taken since the Quest—and you took only seven in all the years before that. What the hell are you trying to do? Burn yourself out? Become an idiot?"

She started to scorch me. Then she answered gently, "No, I am not risking anything of the sort."

"That isn't what I hear."

"What you may have heard has no weight, Oscar, as no one else can judge—either my capacity, or what it means to accept an imprint. Unless you have been talking to my heir?"

"No." I knew she had selected him and I assumed that he had taken a print or two—a standard precaution against assassination. But I hadn't met him, didn't want to, and didn't know who he was.

"Then forget what you've been told. It is meaningless." She sighed. "But, darling, if you don't mind, I won't go tonight; best I go to bed and sleep. Old Stinky CLXXXII is the nastiest person I've ever been—a brilliant success in a critical age, you must read about him. But inside he was a bad-tempered beast who hated the very people he helped. He's fresh in me now, I must keep him chained."

"Okay, let's go to bed."

Star shook her head. " 'Sleep,' I said. I'll use autosuggestion and by morning you won't know he's been here. You go to the party. Find an adventure and forget that you have a difficult wife."

I went but I was too bad-tempered even to consider "adventures."

Old Nasty wasn't the worst. I can hold my own in a row—and Star, Amazon though she is, is not big enough to handle me. If she got rough, she would at last get that spanking. Nor would I fear interference from guards; that had been settled from scratch: When we two were alone together, we were private. Any third person changed that, nor did Star have privacy alone, even in her bath. Whether her guards were male or female I don't know, nor would she have cared. Guards were never in sight.

230

So our spats were private and perhaps did us both good, as temporary relief.

But "the Saint" was harder to take than Old Nasty. He was His Wisdom CXLI and was so goddam noble and spiritual and holier-than-thou that I went fishing for three days. Star herself was robust and full of ginger and joy in life; this bloke didn't drink, smoke, chew gum, nor utter an unkind word. You could almost see Star's halo while she was under his influence.

Worse, he had renounced sex when he consecrated himself to the Universes and this had a shocking effect on Star; sweet submissiveness wasn't her style. So I went fishing.

I've one good thing to say for the Saint. Star says that he was the most unsuccessful emperor in all that long line, with genius for doing the wrong thing from pious motives, so she learned more from him than any other; he made every mistake in the book. He was assassinated by disgusted customers after only fifteen years, which isn't long enough to louse up anything as ponderous as a multi-universe empire.

His Wisdom CXXXVII was a Her—and Star was absent two days. When she came home she explained. "Had to, dear. I've always thought I was a rowdy bitch —but she shocked even me."

"How?"

"I ain't talkin', Guv'nor. I gave myself intensive treatment to bury her where you'll never meet her."

"I'm curious."

"I know you are and that's why I drove a stake through her heart—rough job, she's my direct ancestor. But I was afraid you might like her better than you do me. That unspeakable trull!"

I'm still curious.

Most of them weren't bad Joes. But our marriage would have been smoother if I had never known they were there. It's easier to have a wife who is a touch batty than one who is several platoons—most of them men. To be aware of their ghostly presence even when Star's own personality was in charge did my libido no

231

good. But I must concede that Star knew the male viewpoint better than any other woman in any history. She didn't have to guess what would please a man; she knew more about it than I did, from "experience"—and was explosively uninhibited about sharing her unique knowledge.

I shouldn't complain.

But I did, I blamed her for being those other people. She endured my unjust complaints better than I endured what I felt to be the injustice in my situation vis-à-vis all that mob of ghosts.

Those ghosts weren't the worst fly in the soup.

I did not have a job. I don't mean nine-to-five and cut the grass on Saturdays and get drunk at the country club that night; I mean I didn't have any purpose. Ever look at a male lion in a zoo? Fresh meat on time, females supplied, no hunters to worry about— He's got it made, hasn't he?

Then why does he look bored!

I didn't know I had a problem, at first. I had a beautiful and loving wife; I was so wealthy that there was no way to count it; I lived in a most luxurious home in a city more lovely than any on Earth; everybody I met was nice to me; and best second only to my wonderful wife, I had endless chance to "go to college" in a marvelous and un-Earthly sense, with no need to chase a pigskin. Nor a sheepskin. I need never stop and had any conceivable help. I mean, suppose Albert Einstein drops everything to help with your algebra, pal, or Rand Corporation and General Electric team up to devise visual aids to make something easier for you.

This is luxury greater than riches.

I soon found that I could not drink the ocean even held to my lips. Knowledge on Earth alone has grown so out of hand that no man can grasp it—so guess what the bulk is in Twenty Universes, each with its laws, its histories, and Star alone knows how many civilizations.

In a candy factory, employees are urged to eat all they want. They soon stop.

I never stopped entirely; knowledge has more variety.

232

But my studies lacked purpose. The Secret Name of God is no more to be found in twenty universes than in one— and all other subjects are the same size unless you have a natural bent.

I had no bent, I was a dilettante—and I realized it when I saw that my tutors were bored with me. So I let most of them go, stuck with math and multi-universe history, quit trying to know it all.

I thought about going into business. But to enjoy business you must be a businessman at heart (I'm not), or you have to need dough. I had dough; all I could do was lose it—or, if I won, I would never know whether word had gone out (from any government anywhere): Don't buck the Empress's consort, we will make good your losses.

Same with poker. I introduced the game and it caught on fast—and I found that I could no longer play it. Poker must be serious or it's nothing—but when you own an ocean of money, adding or losing a few drops mean *nothing*.

I should explain— Her Wisdom's "civil list" may not have been as large as the expenditures of many big spenders in Center; the place is rich. But it was as big as Star wanted it to be, a bottomless well of wealth. I don't know how many worlds split the tab, but call it twenty thousand with three billion people each—it was more than that.

A penny each from 60,000,000,000,000 people is six hundred billion dollars. The figures mean nothing except to show that spreading it so thin that nobody could feel it still meant more money than I could dent. Star's non-government of her un-Empire was an expense, I suppose —but her personal expenses, and mine, *no matter how lavish*, were irrelevant.

King Midas lost interest in his piggy bank. So did I. Oh, I spent money. (I never touched any—unnecessary.) Our "flat" (I won't call it a palace)—our home had a gymnasium more imaginative than any university gym; I had a *salle d'armes* added and did a lot of fencing, almost every day with all sorts of weapons. I ordered foils made to match the Lady Vivamus and the best swordmasters in several worlds took turns helping me. I had a range added, too, and had my bow picked up from that Gate cave in Karth-Hokesh, and trained in archery and in other aimed weapons. Oh, I spent money as I pleased.

But it wasn't much fun.

I was sitting in my study one day, doing not a damn thing but brood, while I played with a bowlful of jewels.

I had fiddled with jewelry design a while. It had interested me in high school; I had worked for a jeweler one summer. I can sketch and was fascinated by lovely stones. He lent me books, I got others from the library—and once he made up one of my designs.

I had a Calling.

But jewelers are not draft-deferred so I dropped it—until Center.

You see, there was no way for me to give Star a present unless I made it. So I did. I made costume jewelry of real stones, studying it (expert help, as usual), sending for a lavish selection of stones, drawing designs, sending stones and drawings out to be made up.

I knew that Star enjoyed jeweled costumes; I knew she liked them naughty—not in the sense of crowding the taboos, there weren't any—but provocative, gilding the lily, accentuating what hardly needs it.

The things I designed would have seemed at home in a French revue—but of real gems. Sapphires and gold suited Star's blond beauty and I used them. But she could wear any color and I used other gems, too.

Star was delighted with my first try and wore it that evening. I was proud of it; I had swiped the design from memory of a costume worn by a showgirl in a Frankfurt night club my first night out of the Army—a G-string deal, transparent long skirt open from the hip on one side and with sequins on it (*I* used sapphires), a thing that wasn't a bra but an emphasizer, completely jeweled, and a doohickey in her hair to match. High golden sandals with sapphire heels.

Star was warmly grateful for others that followed

234

But I learned something. I'm not a jewelry designer. I saw no hope of matching the professionals who catered to the wealthy in Center. I soon realized that Star wore my designs because they were my gift, just as mama pins up the kindergarten drawings that sonny brings home. So I quit.

This bowl of gems had been kicking around my study for weeks—fire opals, sardonyx, carnelians, diamonds and turquoise and rubies, moonstones and sapphires and garnets, peridot, emeralds, chrysolite—many with no English names. I ran them through my fingers, watching the many-colored fire falls, and felt sorry for myself. I wondered how much these pretty marbles would cost on Earth? I couldn't guess within a million dollars.

I didn't bother to lock them up at night. And *I* was the bloke who had quit college for lack of tuition and hamburgers.

I pushed them aside and went to my window—there because I had told Star that I didn't like not having a window in my study. That was on arrival and I didn't find out for months how much had been torn down to please me; I had thought they had just cut through a wall.

It was a beautiful view, more a park than a city, studded but not cluttered with lovely buildings. It was hard to realize that it was a city bigger than Tokyo; its "bones" didn't show and its people worked even half a planet away.

There was a murmur soft as bees, like the muted roar one can never escape in New York—but softer, just enough to make me realize that I was surrounded by people, each with his job, his purpose, his function.

My function? Consort.

Gigolo!

Star, without realizing it, had introduced prostitution into a world that had never known it. An innocent world, where man and woman bedded together only for the reason that they both wanted to.

A prince consort is not a prostitute. He has his work and it is often tedious, representing his sovereign mate,

235

laying cornerstones, making speeches. Besides that, he has his duty as royal stud to ensure that the line does not die.

I had none of these. Not even the duty of entertaining Star—hell, within ten miles of me were millions of men who would jump at the chance.

The night before had been bad. It started badly and went on into one of those weary pillow conferences which married couples sometimes have, and aren't as healthy as a bang-up row. We had had one, as domestic as any working stiff worried over bills and the boss.

Star had done something she had never done before: brought work home. Five men, concerned with some intergalactic hassle—I never knew what as the discussion had been going on for hours and they sometimes spoke a language not known to me.

They ignored me, I was furniture. On Center introductions are rare; if you want to talk to someone, you say "Self," and wait. If he doesn't answer, walk off. If he does, exchange identities.

None of them did, and I was damned if I would start it. As strangers in my home it was up to them. But they didn't act as if it was *my* home.

I sat there, the Invisible Man, getting madder and madder.

They went on arguing, while Star listened. Presently she summoned maids and they started undressing her, brushing her hair. Center is not America, I had no reason to feel shocked. What she was doing was being rude to them, treating *them* as furniture (she hadn't missed how they treated me).

One said pettishly, "Your Wisdom, I do wish you would listen as you agreed to." (I've expanded the argot.)

Star said coldly, "I am judge of my conduct. No one else is capable."

True. She could judge her conduct, they could not. Nor, I realized bitterly, could I. I had been feeling angry at her (even though I knew it didn't matter) for calling in her maids and starting to ready for bed with these lunks present—and I had intended to tell her not

236

to let it happen again. I resolved not to raise that issue.

Shortly Star chopped them off. "He's right. You're wrong. Settle it that way. Get out."

But I did intend to sneak it in by objecting to her bringing "tradespeople" home.

Star beat me to the punch. The instant we were alone she said, "My love, forgive me. I agreed to hear this silly mix-up and it dragged on and on, then I thought I could finish it quickly if I got them out of chairs, made them stand up here, and made clear that I was bored. I never thought they would wrangle another hour before I could squeeze out the real issue. And I knew that, if I put it over till tomorrow, they would stretch it into hours. But the problem was important, I couldn't drop it." She sighed. "That ridiculous man— Yet such people scramble to high places. I considered having him fool-killed. Instead I must let him correct his error, or the situation will break out anew."

I couldn't even hint that she had ruled the way she had out of annoyance; the man she had chewed out was the one in whose favor she had ruled. So I said, "Let's go to bed, you're tired"—and then didn't have sense enough to refrain from judging her myself.

XIX

WE went to bed.

Presently she said, "Oscar, you are displeased."

"I didn't say so."

"I feel it. Nor is just tonight and those tedious clowns. You have been withdrawing yourself, unhappy." She waited.

"It's nothing."

"Oscar, anything which troubles you can never be 'nothing' to me. Although I may not realize it until I know what it is."

"Well—I feel so damn *useless!*"

She put her soft, strong hand on my chest. "To me you are not useless. Why do you feel useless to yourself?"

"Well—look at this bed!" It was a bed the like of which Americans never dream; it could do everything but kiss you good night—and, like the city, it was beautiful, its bones did not show. "This sack, at home, would cost more—if they could build it—than the best house my mother ever lived in."

She thought about that. "Would you like to send

money to your mother?" She beckoned the bedside communicator. "Is Elmendorf Air Force Base of America address enough?"

(I don't recall ever telling her where Mother lived.) "No, no!" I gestured at the talker, shutting it off. "I do *not* want to send her money. Her husband supports her. He won't take money from me. That's not the point."

"Then I don't see the point as yet. Beds do not matter, it is who is in a bed that counts. My darling, if you don't like this bed, we can get another. Or sleep on the floor. Beds do not matter."

"This bed is okay. The only thing wrong is that I didn't pay for it. You did. This house. My clothes. The food I eat. My—my *toys!* Every damned thing I have you gave me. Know what I am, Star? A gigolo! Do you know what a gigolo is? A somewhat-male prostitute."

One of my wife's most exasperating habits was, sometimes, to refuse to snap back at me when she knew I was spoiling for a row. She looked at me thoughtfully. "America is a busy place, isn't it? People work all the time, especially men."

"Well . . . yes."

"It isn't the custom everywhere, even on Earth. A Frenchman isn't unhappy if he has free time; he orders another *café au lait* and lets the saucers pile up. Nor am I fond of work. Oscar, I ruined our evening from laziness, too anxious to avoid having to redo a weary task tomorrow. I will not make that mistake twice."

"Star, that doesn't matter. That's over with."

"I know. The first issue is rarely the key. Nor the second. Nor, sometimes, the twenty-second. Oscar, you are not a gigolo."

"What do you call it? When it looks like a duck and quacks like a duck and acts like a duck, I call it a duck. Call it a bunch of roses. It still quacks."

"No. All this around us—" She waved. "Bed. This beautiful chamber. The food we eat. My clothes and yours. Our lovely pools. The night majordomo on watch against the chance that you or I might demand a singing

239

bird or a ripe melon. Our captive gardens. All we see or touch or use or fancy—and a thousand times as much in distant places, all these you earned with your own strong hands; they are yours, by right."

I snorted. "They are," she insisted. "That was our contract. I promised you great adventure, and greater treasure, and even greater danger. You agreed. You said, 'Princess, you've hired yourself a boy.'" She smiled. "Such a big boy. Darling, I think the dangers were greater than you guessed . . . so it has pleased me, until now, that the treasure is greater than you were likely to have guessed. Please don't be shy about accepting it. You have earned it and more—as much as you are ever willing to accept."

"Uh— Even if you are right, it's too much. I'm drowning in marshmallows!"

"But, Oscar, you don't have to take one bit you don't want. We can live simply. In one room with bed folded into wall if it pleases you."

"That's no solution."

"Perhaps you would like bachelor digs, out in town?"

"'Tossing my shoes,' eh?"

She said levelly, "My husband, if your shoes are ever tossed, you must toss them. I jumped over your sword. I shall not jump back."

"Take it easy!" I said. "It was your suggestion. If I took it wrong, I'm sorry. I know you don't go back on your word. But you might be regretting it."

"I am not regretting it. Are *you?*"

"No, Star, no! But—"

"That's a long pause for so short a word," she said gravely. "Will you tell me?"

"Uh . . . that's just it. Why didn't *you* tell *me?*"

"Tell what, Oscar? There are so many things to tell."

"Well, a lot of things. What I was getting into. About you being the Empress of the whole works, in particular . . . before you let me jump over the sword with you."

Her face did not change but tears rolled down her cheeks. "I could answer that you did not ask me—"

"I didn't know what to ask!"

"That is true. I could assert, truthfully, that had you asked I would have answered. I could protest that I did not 'let you' jump over the sword, that you overruled my protests that it was not necessary to offer me the honor of marriage by the laws of your people . . . that I was a wench you could tumble at will. I could point out that I am not an empress, not royal, but a working woman whose job does not permit her even the luxury of being noble. All these are true. But I will not hide behind them; I will meet your question." She slipped into Nevian. "Milord Hero, I feared sorely that if I did not bend to your will, you would leave me!"

"Milady wife, truly did you think that your champion would desert you in your peril?" I went on in English, "Well, that nails it to the barn. You married me because the Egg damned well had to be recovered and Your Wisdom told you that I was necessary to the job—and might bug out if you didn't. Well, Your Wisdom wasn't sharp on that point; I don't bug out. Stupid of me but I'm stubborn." I started to get out of bed.

"Milord love!" She was crying openly.

"Excuse me. Got to find a pair of shoes. See how far I can throw them." I was being nasty as only a man can be who has had his pride wounded.

"Please, Oscar, please! Hear me first."

I heaved a sigh. "Talk ahead."

She grabbed my hand so hard I would have lost fingers had I tried to pull loose. "Hear me out. My beloved, it was not that at all. I knew that you would not give up our quest until it was finished or we were dead. I *knew!* Not only had I reports reaching back years before I ever saw you but also we had shared joy and danger and hardship; I knew your mettle. But, had it been needed, I could have bound you with a net of words, persuaded you to agree to betrothal only—until the quest was over. You are a romantic, you would have agreed. But, darling, darling! I *wanted* to marry you . . . bind you to me by *your* rules, so that"—she stopped to sniff back tears—"so that, when you saw all this, and this, and this, and the things you call 'your toys,' you *still* would stay with me. It was not politics, it was *love*—love romantic and unreasoned, love for your own sweet self."

She dropped her face into her hands and I could barely hear her. "But I know so little of love. Love is a butterfly that lights when it listeth, leaves as it chooses; it is never bound with chains. I sinned. I tried to bind you. Unjust I knew it was, cruel to you I now see it to be." Star looked up with crooked smile. "Even Her Wisdom has no wisdom when it comes to being a woman. But, though silly wench I be, I am not too stubborn to know that I have wronged my beloved when my face is rubbed in it. Go, go, get your sword; I will jump back over it and my champion will be free of his silken cage. Go, milord Hero, while my heart is firm."

"Go fetch your own sword, wench. That paddling is long overdue."

Suddenly she grinned, all hoyden. "But, darling, my sword is in Karth-Hokesh. Don't you remember?"

"You can't avoid it this time!" I grabbed her. Star is a handful and slippery, with amazing muscles. But I'm bigger and she didn't fight as hard as she could have. Still I lost skin and picked up bruises before I got her legs pinned and one arm twisted behind her. I gave her a couple of hearty spanks, hard enough to print each finger in pink, then lost interest.

Now tell me, were those words straight from her heart—or was it acting by the smartest woman in twenty universes?

Later, Star said, "I'm glad your chest is not a scratchy rug, like some men, my beautiful."

"I was a pretty baby, too. How many chests have you checked?"

"A random sample. Darling, have you decided to keep me?"

"A while. On good behavior, you understand."

"I'd rather be kept on bad behavior. But—while you're feeling mellow—if you are—I had best tell you another thing—and take my spanking if I must."

242

"You're too anxious. One a day is maximum, hear me?"

"As you will, sir. Yassuh, Boss man. I'll have my sword fetched in the morning and you can spank me with it at your leisure. If you think you can catch me. But I must tell this and get it off my chest."

"There's nothing on your chest. Unless you count—"

"Please! You've been going to our therapists."

"Once a week." The first thing Star had ordered was an examination for me so complete as to make an Army physical seem perfunctory. "The Head Sawbones insists that my wounds aren't healed but I don't believe him; I've never felt better."

"He is stalling, Oscar—by my order. You're healed, I am not unskilled, I was most careful. But—darling, I did this for selfish reasons and now you must tell me if I have been cruel and unjust to you again. I admit I was sneaky. But my intentions were good. However, I know, as the prime lesson of my profession, that good intentions are the source of more folly than all other causes put together."

"Star, what are you prattling about? Women are the source of all folly."

"Yes, dearest. Because they always have good intentions—and can prove it. Men sometimes act from rational self-interest, which is safer. But not often."

"That's because half their ancestors are female. Why have I been keeping doctor's appointments if I don't need them?"

"I didn't say you don't need them. But you may not think so. Oscar, you are far advanced with Long-Life treatments." She eyed me as if ready to parry or retreat.

"Well, I'll be damned!"

"You object? At this stage it can be reversed."

"I hadn't thought about it." I knew that Long-Life was available on Center but knew also that it was rigidly restricted. Anybody could have it—just before emigrating to a sparsely settled planet. Permanent residents must grow old and die. This was one matter in which one of Star's predecessors had interfered in local government.

Center, with disease practically conquered, great prosperity, and lodestone of a myriad peoples, had grown too crowded, especially when Long-Life sent skyward the average age of death.

This stern rule had thinned the crowds. Some people took Long-Life early, went through a Gate and took their chances in wilderness. More waited until that first twinge that brings awareness of death, then decided that they weren't too old for a change. And some sat tight and died when their time came.

I knew that twinge; it had been handed to me by a bolo in a jungle. "I guess I have no objection."

She sighed with relief. "I didn't know and should not have slipped it into your coffee. Do I rate a spanking?"

"We'll add it to the list you already rate and give them to you all at once. Probably cripple you. Star, how long is 'Long-Life'?"

"That's hard to answer. Very few who have had it have died in bed. If you live as active a life as I know you will—from your temperament—you are most unlikely to die of old age. Nor of disease."

"And I never grow old?" It takes getting used to.

"Oh, yes, you can grow old. Worse yet, senility stretches in proportion. If you let it. If those around you allow it. However— Darling, how old do I look? Don't tell me with your heart, tell me with your eyes. By Earth standards. Be truthful, I know the answer."

It was ever a joy to look at Star but I tried to look at her freshly, for hints of autumn—outer corners of eyes, her hands, for tiny changes in skin—hell, not even a stretch mark, yet I knew she had a grandchild.

"Star, when I first saw you, I guessed eighteen. You turned around and I upped the ante a little. Now, looking closely and not giving you any breaks—not over twenty-five. And that is because your features seem mature. When you laugh, you're a teen-ager; when you wheedle, or look awestruck, or suddenly delighted with a puppy or kitten or something, you're about twelve. From the chin up, I mean; from the chin down you can't pass for less than eighteen."

"A buxom eighteen," she added. "Twenty-five Earth years—by rates of growth on Earth—is right on the mark I was shooting at. The age when a woman stops growing and starts aging. Oscar, your apparent age under Long-Life is a matter of choice. Take my Uncle Joseph— the one who sometimes calls himself 'Count Cagliostro.' He set himself at thirty-five, because he says that anything younger is a boy. Rufo prefers to look older. He says it gets him respectful treatment, keeps him out of brawls with younger men—and still lets him give a younger man a shock if one does pick a fight because, as you know, Rufo's older age is mostly from chin up."

"Or the shock he can give younger women," I suggested.

"With Rufo one never knows. Dearest, I didn't finish telling you. Part of it is teaching the body to repair itself. Your language lessons here—there hasn't been a one but what a hypnotherapist was waiting to give your body a lesson through your sleeping mind, after your language lesson. Part of apparent age is cosmetic therapy—Rufo need not be bald—but more is controlled by the mind. When you decide what age you like, they can start imprinting it."

"I'll think about it. I don't want to look too much older than you."

Star looked delighted. "Thank you, dear! You see how selfish I've been."

"How? I missed that point."

She put a hand over mine. "I didn't want you to grow old—and die!—while I stayed young."

I blinked at her. "Gosh, lady, that *was* selfish of you, wasn't it? But you could varnish me and keep me in the bedroom. Like your aunt."

She made a face. "You're a nasty man. She didn't varnish them."

"Star, I haven't seen any of those keepsake corpses around here."

She looked surprised. "But that's on the planet where I was born. This universe, another star. Very pretty place. Didn't I ever say?"

"Star, my darling, mostly you've never said."

"I'm sorry. Oscar, I don't want to hand you surprises. Ask me. Tonight. Anything."

I considered it. One thing I had wondered about, a certain lack. Or perhaps the women of her part of the race had another rhythm. But I had been stopped by the fact that I had married a grandmother—how old? "Star, are you pregnant?"

"Why, no, dear. *Oh!* Do you want me to be? You want us to have children?"

I stumbled, trying to explain that I hadn't been sure it was possible—or maybe she was. Star looked troubled. "I'm going to upset you again. I had best tell it all. Oscar, I was no more brought up to luxury than you were. A pleasant childhood, my people were ranchers. I married young and was a simple mathematics teacher, with a hobby research in conjectural and optional geometries. Magic, I mean. Three children. My husband and I got along well . . . until I was nominated. Not selected, just named for examination and possible training. He knew I was a genetic candidate when he married me—but so many millions are. It didn't seem important.

"He wanted me to refuse. I almost did. But when I accepted, he- well, he 'tossed my shoes.' We do it formally there; he published a notice that I was no longer his wife."

"He did, eh? Mind if I look him up and break his arms?"

"Dear, dear! That was many years ago and far away; he is long dead. It doesn't matter."

"In any case he's dead. Your three kids—one of them is Rufo's father? Or mother?"

"Oh, no! That was later."

"Well?"

Star took a deep breath. "Oscar, I have about fifty children."

That did it. Too many shocks and I guess I showed it, for Star's face reflected deep concern. She rushed through the explanation.

When she was named heir, changes were made in her,

246

surgical, biochemical, and endocrinal. Nothing as drastic as spaying and to different ends and by techniques more subtle than ours. But the result was that about two hundred tiny bits of Star—ova alive and latent—were stored near absolute zero.

Some fifty had been quickened, mostly by emperors long dead but "alive" in their stored seed—genetic gambles on getting one or more future emperors. Star had not borne them; an heir's time is too precious. She had never seen most of them; Rufo's father was an exception. She didn't say, but I think Star liked to have a child around to play with and love—until the strenuous first years of her reign and the Quest for the Egg left her no time.

This change had a double purpose: to get some hundreds of star-line children from a single mother, and to leave the mother free. By endocrine control of some sort, Star was left free of Eve's rhythm but in all ways young—not pills nor hormone injections; this was permanent. She was simply a healthy woman who never had "bad days." This not for her convenience but to insure that her judgment as the Great Judge would never be whipsawed by her glands. "This is sensible," she said seriously. "I can remember there used to be days when I would bite the head off my dearest friend for no reason, then burst into tears. One can't be judicial in that sort of storm."

"Uh, did it affect your interest? I mean your desire for—"

She gave me a hearty grin. "What do *you* think?" She added seriously, "The *only* thing that affects my libido—changes it for the worse, I mean—are . . . is?— English has the oddest structure—is-are those pesky imprintings. Sometimes up, sometimes down—and you'll remember one woman whose name we won't mention who affected me so carnivorously that I didn't dare come near you until I had exorcised her black soul! A fresh imprint affects my judgment as well, so I never hear a case until I have digested the latest one. I'll be glad when they're over!"

"So will I."

"Not as glad as *I* will be. But, aside from that, darling, I don't vary much as a female and you know it. Just my usual bawdy self who eats young boys for breakfast and seduces them into jumping over swords."

"How many swords?"

She looked at me sharply. "Since my first husband kicked me out I have not been married until I married *you*, Mr. Gordon. If that is not what you meant, I don't think you should hold against me things that happened before you were born. If you want details since then, I'll satisfy your curiosity. Your morbid curiosity, if I may say so."

"You want to boast. Wench, I won't pamper it."

"I do *not* want to boast! I've little to boast about. The Crisis of the Egg left me almost no time in which to be a woman, damn it! Until Oscar the Rooster came along. Thank you, sir."

"And keep a civil tongue in your head."

"Yes, sir. Nice Rooster! But you've led us far from our muttons, dear. If you want children—*yes*, darling! There are about two hundred and thirty eggs left and they belong to *me*. Not to posterity. Not to the dear people, bless their greedy little hearts. Not to those God-playing genetic manipulators. *Me!* It's all I own. All else is *ex officio*. But these are *mine* ... and if you want them, they are yours, my only dear."

I should have said, *"Yes!"* and kissed her. What I did say was, "Uh, let's not rush it."

Her face fell. "As milord Hero husband pleases."

"Look, don't get Nevian and formal. I mean, well, it takes getting used to. Syringes and things, I suppose, and monkeying by technicians. And, while I realize you don't have time to have a baby yourself—"

I was trying to·say that, ever since I got straightened out about the Stork, I had taken for granted the usual setup, and artificial insemination was a dirty trick to play even on a cow—and that this job, subcontracted on both sides, made me think of slots in a Horn & Hardart, or a mail-order suit. But give me time and I would adjust.

Just as she had adjusted to those damned imprints—

She gripped my hands. "Darling, you needn't!"

"Needn't what?"

"Be monkeyed with by technicians. And I will *take* time to have your baby. If you don't mind seeing my body get gross and huge—it does, it does, I remember— then happily I will do it. All will be as with other people so far as you are concerned. No syringes. No technicians. Nothing to offend your pride. Oh, I'll have to be worked on. But I'm used to being handled like a prize cow; it means no more than having my hair shampooed."

"Star, you would go through nine months of inconvenience—and maybe die in childbirth—to save me a few moments' annoyance?"

"I shall not die. Three children, remember? Normal deliveries, no trouble."

"But, as you pointed out, that was 'many years ago.' "

"No matter."

"Uh, how many years?" ("How old are you, my woman?" The question I never dared ask.)

She looked upset. "Does it matter, Oscar?"

"Uh, I suppose not. You know more about medicine than I do—"

She said slowly, "You were asking how old I am, were you not?"

I didn't say anything. She waited, then went on, "An old saw from your world says that a woman is as young as she feels. And I feel young and I *am* young and I have zest for life and I can bear a baby—or many babies—in my own belly. But I know—oh, I know!—that your worry is not just that I am too rich and occupy a position not easy for a husband. Yes, I know that part too well; my first husband rejected me for that. But he was my age. The most cruel and unjust thing I have done is that I *knew* that my age could matter to you—and I kept still. That was why Rufo was so outraged. After you were asleep that night in the cave of the Forest of Dragons he told me so, in biting words. He said he knew I was not above enticing young boys but he never thought that I would sink so low as to trap one into marriage without

249

first telling him. He's never had a high opinion of his old granny, he said, but this time—"

"Shut up, Star!"

"Yes, milord."

"It doesn't make a damn bit of difference!"—and I said it so flatly that I believed it—and do now. "Rufo doesn't know what I think. You are younger than tomorrow's dawn—you always will be. That's the last I want to hear about it!"

"Yes, milord."

"And knock that off, too. Just say, 'Okay, Oscar.'"

"Yes, Oscar! Okay!"

"Better. Unless you're honing for another spanking. And I'm too tired." I changed the subject. "About this other matter— There's no reason to stretch your pretty tummy if other ways are at hand. I'm a country jake, that's all; I'm not used to big city ways. When you suggested that you do it yourself, did you mean that they could put you back together the way you were?"

"No. I would simply be host-mother as well as genetic mother." She smiled and I knew I was making progress. "But saving a tidy sum of that money you don't want to spend. Those healthy, sturdy women who have other people's babies charge high. Four babies, they can retire —ten makes them wealthy."

"I should think they would charge high! Star, I don't object to spending money. I'll concede, if you say so, that I've earned more than I spend, by my work as a professional hero. That's a tough racket, too."

"You've earned it."

"This citified way of having babies— Can you pick it? Boy, or girl?"

"Of course. Male-giving wigglers swim faster, they can be sorted out. That's why Wisdoms are usually men—I was an unplanned candidate. You shall have a son, Oscar."

"Might prefer a girl. I've a weakness for little girls."

"A boy, a girl—or both. Or as many as you want."

"Star, let me study it. Lots of angles—and I don't think as well as you do."

250

"Pooh!"

"If you don't think better than I do, the cash customers are getting rooked. Mmm, male seed can be stored as easily as eggs?"

"Much easier."

"That's all the answer we need now. I'm not too jumpy about syringes; I've stood in enough Army queues. I'll go to the clinic or whatever it is, then we can settle it slowly. When we decide"—I shrugged—"mail the postcard and when it goes *clunk!*—we're parents. Or some such. From there on the technicians and those husky gals can handle it."

"Yes, milo— Okay, darling!"

All better. Almost her little girl face. Certainly her sixteen-year-old face, with new party dress and boys a shivery, delightful danger. "Star, you said earlier that it was often not the second issue but even the twenty-second that matters."

"Yes."

"I know what's wrong with me. I can tell you—and maybe Her Wisdom knows the answer."

She blinked. "If you can tell me, sweetheart—Her Wisdom will solve it, even if I have to tear the place down and put it back up differently—from here to the next galaxy—or I'll go out of the Wisdom business!"

"That sounds more like my Lucky Star. All right, it's not that I'm a gigolo. I've earned my coffee and cakes, at least; the Soul-Eater did damn near eat my soul, he knew its exact shape—he . . . it—it knew things I had long forgotten. It was rough and the pay ought to be high. It's not your age, dearest. Who cares how old Helen of Troy is? You're the right age forever—can a man be luckier? I'm not jealous of your position; I wouldn't want it with chocolate icing. I'm not jealous of the men in your life—the lucky stiffs! Not even now, as long as I don't stumble over them getting to the bathroom."

"There are no other men in my life now, milord husband."

"I had no reason to think so. But there is always next week, and even you can't have a Sight about *that*, my beloved. You've taught me that marriage is not a form of death—and you obviously aren't dead, you lively wench."

"Perhaps not a Sight," she admitted. "But a feeling."

"I won't bet on it. I've read the Kinsey Report."

"What report?"

"He disproved the Mermaid theory. About married women. Forget it. Hypothetical question: If Jocko visited Center, would you still have the same feeling? We should have to invite him to sleep here."

"The Doral will never leave Nevia."

"Don't blame him, Nevia is wonderful. I said 'If'— If he does, will you offer him 'roof, table, and bed'?"

"That," she said firmly, "is *your* decision, milord."

"Rephrase it: Will you expect *me* to humiliate Jocko by not returning his hospitality? Gallant old Jocko, who let us live when he was entitled to kill us? Whose bounty —arrows and many things, including a new medic's kit— kept us alive and let us win back the Egg?"

"By Nevian customs of roof and table and bed," she insisted, "the *husband* decides, milord husband."

"We aren't in Nevia and here a wife has a mind of her own. You're dodging, wench."

She grinned naughtily. "Does that 'if' of yours include Muri? And Letva? They're his favorites, he wouldn't travel without them. And how about little what's-her-name?—the nymphet?"

"I give up. I was just trying to prove that jumping over a sword does not turn a lively wench into a nun."

"I am aware of it, my Hero," she said levelly. "All I can say is that I intend that *this* wench shall never give her Hero a moment's unease—and my intentions are usually carried out. I am not 'Her Wisdom' for nothing."

"Fair enough. I never thought you would cause me that sort of unease. I was trying to show that the task may not be too difficult. Damn it, we've wandered off. Here's my real problem. I'm not good for anything. I'm worthless."

"Why, my dearest! You're good for *me*."

"But not for myself. Star, gigolo or not, I can't be a pet poodle. Not even yours. Look, you've got a job.

It keeps you busy and it's important. But me? There is nothing for me to do, nothing *at all!*—nothing better than designing bad jewelry. You know what I am? A hero by trade, so you told me; you recruited me. Now I'm retired. Do you know anything in all twenty universes more useless than a *retired* hero?"

She mentioned a couple. I said, "You're stalling. Anyhow they break up the blankness of the male chest. I'm serious, Star. This *is* the issue that has made me unfit to live with. Darling, I'm asking you to put your whole mind on it—and all those ghostly helpers. Treat it the way you treat an Imperial problem. Forget I'm your husband. Consider my total situation, all you know about me—and tell me what I can do with hands and head and time that is worth doing. *Me,* being what I am."

She held still for long minutes, her face in that professional calm she had worn the times I had audited her work. "You are right," she said at last. "There is nothing worth your powers on this planet."

"Then what *do* I do?"

She said tonelessly, "You must leave."

"Huh?"

"You think I like the answer, my husband? Do you think I like most answers I must give? But you asked me to consider it professionally. I obeyed. That is the answer. You must leave this planet—and me."

"So my shoes get tossed anyhow?"

"Be not bitter, milord. That *is* the answer. I can evade and be womanish only in my private life; I cannot refuse to think if I agree to do so as 'Her Wisdom.' You must leave me. But, no, no, no, your shoes are not tossed! You *will* leave, because you must. Not because *I* wish it." Her face stayed calm but tears streamed again. "One cannot ride a cat . . . nor hurry a snail . . . nor teach a snake to fly. Nor make a poodle of a Hero. I knew it, I refused to look at it. You will do what you must do. But your shoes will remain ever by my bed, *I* am not sending you away!" She blinked back tears. "I cannot lie to you, even by silence. I will not say that no other shoes will rest here . . . if you are gone a long time. I have been lonely. There are no words to say how lonely this job is. When you go . . . I shall be lonelier than ever. But you will find your shoes here when you return."

"When I return? You have a Sight?"

"No, milord Hero. I have only a feeling . . . that if you live . . . you will return. Perhaps many times. But Heroes do not die in bed. Not even this one." She blinked and tears stopped and her voice was steady. "Now, milord husband, if it please you, shall we dim the lights and rest?"

We did and she put her head on my shoulder and did not cry. But we did not sleep. After an aching time I said, "Star, do you hear what I hear?"

She raised her head. "I hear nothing."

"The City. Can't you hear it? People. Machines. Even thoughts so thick your bones feel it and your ear almost catches it."

"Yes. I know that sound."

"Star, do you *like* it here?"

"No. It was never necessary that I like it."

"Look, damn it! You said that I would leave. *Come with me!*"

"Oh, Oscar!"

"What do you owe them? Isn't recovering the Egg enough? Let them take a new victim. Come walk the Glory Road with me again! There must be work in my line somewhere."

"There is always work for Heroes."

"Okay, we set up in business, you and I. Heroing isn't a bad job. The meals are irregular and the pay uncertain —but it's never dull. We'll run ads: 'Gordon & Gordon, Heroing Done Reasonable. No job too large, no job too small. Dragons exterminated by contract, satisfaction guaranteed or no pay. Free estimates on other work. Questing, maiden-rescuing, golden fleece located night or day?' "

I was trying to jolly her but Star doesn't jolly. She answered in sober earnest. "Oscar, if I am to retire, I should train my heir first. True, no one can order me to do anything—but I have a duty to train my replacement."

"How long will that take?"

"Not long. Thirty years, about."

"Thirty years!"

"I could force it to twenty-five, I think."

I sighed. "Star, do you know how old I am?"

"Yes. Not yet twenty-five. *But you will get no older!*"

"But right now I'm still that age. That's all the time there has *ever* been for *me*. Twenty-five years as a pet poodle and I won't be a hero, nor anything. I'll be out of my silly mind."

She thought about it. "Yes. That is true."

She turned over, we made a spoon and pretended to sleep.

Later I felt her shoulders shaking and knew that she was sobbing. "Star?"

She didn't turn her head. All I heard was a choking voice, "Oh, my dear, my very dear! If I were even a *hundred* years younger!"

XX

I LET the precious, useless gems dribble through my fingers, listlessly pushed them aside. If *I* were only a hundred years *older*—

But Star was right. She could not leave her post without relief. Her notion of proper relief, not mine nor anyone's else. And I couldn't stay in this upholstered jail much longer without beating my head on the bars.

Yet both of us wanted to stay together.

The real nasty hell of it was that I knew—just as she knew—that each of us would forget. Some, anyhow. Enough so that there would be other shoes, other men, and she would laugh again.

And so would I— She had seen that and had gravely, gently, with subtle consideration for another's feelings, told me indirectly that I need not feel guilty when next I courted some other girl, in some other land, somewhere.

Then why did I feel like a heel?

How did I get trapped with no way to turn without

being forced to choose between hurting my beloved and going clean off my rocker?

I read somewhere about a man who lived on a high mountain, because of asthma, the choking, killing kind, while his wife lived on the coast below him, because of heart trouble that could not stand altitude. Sometimes they looked at each other through telescopes.

In the morning there had been no talk of Star's retiring. The unstated *quid-pro-quo* was that, if she planned to retire, I would hang around (*thirty years!*) until she did. Her Wisdom had concluded that I could not, and did not speak of it. We had a luxurious breakfast and were cheerful, each with his secret thoughts.

Nor were children mentioned. Oh, I would find that clinic, do what was needed. If she wanted to mix her star line with my common blood, she could, tomorrow or a hundred years hence. Or smile tenderly and have it cleaned out with the rest of the trash. None of *my* people had even been mayor of Podunk and a plow horse isn't groomed for the Irish Sweepstakes. If Star put a child together from our genes, it would be sentiment, a living valentine—a younger poodle she could pet before she let it run free. But sentiment only, as sticky if not as morbid as that of her aunt with the dead husbands, for the Imperium could not use my bend sinister.

I looked up at my sword, hanging opposite me. I hadn't touched it since the party, long past, when Star chose to dress for the Glory Road. I took it down, buckled it on and drew it—felt that surge of liveness and had a sudden vision of a long road and a castle on a hill.

What does a champion owe his lady when the quest is done?

Quit dodging, Gordon! What does a *husband* owe his *wife?* This very sword— "Jump Rogue and Princess leap, My wife art thou and mine to *keep.*" "—for richer, for poorer, for better, for worse . . . to love and to cherish, till death do us part." *That* was what I meant by that doggerel and Star had known it and I had known it and knew it now.

When we vowed, it had seemed likely that we would be

257

parted by death that same day. But that didn't reduce the vow nor the deepness with which I had meant it. I hadn't jumped the sword to catch a tumble on the grass before I died; I could have had that free. No, I had wanted "—to have and to hold, to love and to cherish, till death do us part"!

Star had kept her vow to the letter. Why did *I* have itchy feet?

Scratch a hero and find a bum.

And a *retired* hero was as silly as those out-of-work kings that clutter Europe.

I slammed out of our "flat," wearing sword and not giving a damn about stares, apported to our therapists, found where I should go, went there, did what was necessary, told the boss biotechnician that Her Wisdom must be told, and jumped down his throat when he asked questions.

Then back to the nearest apport booth and hesitated—I needed companionship the way an Alcoholics-Anonymous needs his hand held. But I had no intimates, just hundreds of acquaintances. It isn't easy for the Empress's consort to have friends.

Rufo it had to be. But in all the months I had been on Center I had never been in Rufo's home. Center does not practice the barbarous custom of dropping in on people and I had seen Rufo only at the Residence, or on parties; Rufo had never invited me to his home. No, no coldness there; we saw him often, but always he had come to us.

I looked for him in apport listings—no luck. Then as little with see-speak lists. I called the Residence, got the communication officer. He said that "Rufo" was not a surname and tried to brush me off. I said, "Hold it, you overpaid clerk! Switch me off and you'll be in charge of smoke signals in Timbuctu an hour from now. Now listen. This bloke is elderly, bald-headed, one of his names is 'Rufo' I think, and he is a distinguished comparative culturologist. *And* he is a grandson of Her Wisdom. I think you know who he is and have been dragging your feet from bureaucratic arrogance. You have five minutes.

Then I talk to Her Wisdom and ask *her,* while *you* pack!"

("Stop! Danger you! Other old bald Rufo (?) top compculturist. Wisdom egg-sperm-egg. Five-minutes. Liar and/or fool. Wisdom? Catastrophe!")

In less than five minutes Rufo's image filled the tank. "Well!" he said. "I wondered who had enough weight to crash my shutoff."

"Rufo, may I come see you?"

His scalp wrinkled. "Mice in the pantry, son? Your face reminds me of the time my uncle—"

"Please, Rufo!"

"Yes, son," he said gently. "I'll send the dancing girls home. Or shall I keep them?"

"I don't care. How do I find you?"

He told me, I punched his code, added my charge number, and I was there, a thousand miles around the horizon. Rufo's place was a mansion as lavish as Jocko's and thousands of years more sophisticated. I gathered an impression that Rufo had the biggest household on Center, all female. I was wrong. But all female servants, visitors, cousins, daughters, made themselves a reception committee—to look at Her Wisdom's bedmate. Rufo shooed them away and took me to his study. A dancing girl (evidently a secretary) was fussing over papers and tapes. Rufo slapped her fanny out, gave me a comfortable chair, a drink, put cigarettes near me, sat down and said nothing.

Smoking isn't popular on Center, what they use as tobacco is the reason. I picked up a cigarette. "Chesterfields! Good God!"

"Have 'em smuggled," he said. "But they don't make anything like Sweet Caps anymore. Bridge sweepings and chopped hay."

I hadn't smoked in months. But Star had told me that cancer and such I could now forget. So I lit it—and coughed like a Nevian dragon. Vice requires constant practice.

" 'What news on the Rialto?' " Rufo inquired. He glanced at my sword.

"Oh, nothing." Having interrupted Rufo's work, I now shied at baring my domestic troubles.

Rufo sat and smoked and waited. I needed to say something and the American cigarette reminded me of an incident, one that had added to my unstable condition. At a party a week earlier, I had met a man thirty-five in appearance, smooth, polite, but with that supercilious air that says: "Your fly is unzipped, old man, but I'm too urbane to mention it."

But I had been delighted to meet him, he had spoken *English!*

I had thought that Star, Rufo, and myself were the only ones on Center who spoke English. We often spoke it, Star on my account, Rufo because he liked to practice. He spoke Cockney like a costermonger, Bostonese like Beacon Hill, Aussie like a kangaroo; Rufo knew all English languages.

This chap spoke good General American. "Nebbi is the name," he said, shaking hands where no one shakes hands, "and you're Gordon, I know. Delighted to meet you."

"Me, too," I agreed. "It's a surprise and a pleasure to hear my own language."

"Professional knowledge, my dear chap. Comparative culturologist, linguisto-historo-political. You're American, I know. Let me place it—Deep South, not born there. Possibly New England. Overlaid with displaced Middle Western, California perhaps. Basic speech, lower-middle class, mixed."

The smooth oaf was good. Mother and I lived in Boston while my father was away, 1942-45. I'll never forget those winters; I wore overshoes from November to April. I had lived Deep South, Georgia and Florida, and in California at La Jolla during the Korean unWar and, later, in college. "Lower-middle class"? Mother had not thought so.

"Near enough," I agreed. "I know one of your colleagues."

"I know whom you mean, 'the Mad Scientist.' Wonderfully wacky theories. But tell me: How were things when

260

you left? Especially, how is the United States getting along with its Noble Experiment?"

" 'Noble Experiment'?" I had to think; Prohibition was gone before I was born. "Oh, that was repealed."

"Really? I must go back for a field trip. What have you now? A king? I could see that your country was headed that way but I did not expect it so soon."

"Oh, no," I said. "I was talking about Prohibition."

"Oh, that. Symptomatic but not basic. I was speaking of the amusing notion of chatter rule. 'Democracy.' A curious delusion—as if adding zeros could produce a sum. But it was tried in your tribal land on a mammoth scale. Before you were born, no doubt. I thought you meant that even the corpse had been swept away." He smiled. "Then they still have elections and all that?"

"The last time I looked, yes."

"Oh, wonderful. Fantastic, simply fantastic. Well, we must get together, I want to quiz you. I've been studying your planet a long time—the most amazing pathologies in the explored complex. So long. Don't take any wooden nickels, as your tribesmen say."

I told Rufo about it. "Rufe, I know I came from a barbarous planet. But does that excuse his rudeness? Or was it rudeness? I haven't really got the hang of good manners here."

Rufo frowned. "It is bad manners anywhere to sneer at a person's birthplace, tribe, or customs. A man does it at his own risk. If you kill him, nothing will happen to you. It might embarrass Her Wisdom a little. If *She* can be embarrassed."

"I won't kill him, it's not that important."

"Then forget it. Nebbi is a snob. He knows a little, understands nothing, and thinks the universes would be better if he had designed them. Ignore him."

"I will. It was just—look, Rufo, my country isn't perfect. But I don't enjoy hearing it from a stranger."

"Who does? I like your country, it has flavor. But— I'm not a stranger and this is not a sneer. Nebbi was right."

"Huh?"

"Except that he sees only the surface. Democracy can't work. Mathematicians, peasants, and animals, that's all there is—so democracy, a theory based on the assumption that mathematicians and peasants are equal, can never work. Wisdom is not additive; its maximum is that of the wisest man in a given group.

"But a democratic *form* of government is okay, as long as it doesn't work. Any social organization does well enough if it isn't rigid. The framework doesn't matter as long as there is enough looseness to permit that one man in a multitude to display his genius. Most so-called social scientists seem to think that organization is everything. It is almost nothing—except when it is a straitjacket. It is the incidence of heroes that counts, not the pattern of zeros."

He added, "Your country has a system free enough to let its heroes work at their trade. It should last a long time—unless its looseness is destroyed from inside."

"I hope you're right."

"I *am* right. This subject I know and I'm not stupid, as Nebbi thinks. He's right about the futility of 'adding zeros'—but he doesn't realize that he is a zero."

I grinned. "No point in letting a zero get my goat."

"None. Especially as you are not. Wherever you go, you will make yourself felt, you won't be one of the herd. I respect you, and I don't respect many. Never people as a whole, I could never be a democrat at heart. To claim to 'respect' and even to 'love' the great mass with their yaps at one end and smelly feet at the other requires the fatuous, uncritical, saccharine, blind, sentimental slobbishness found in some nursery supervisors, most spaniel dogs, and all missionaries. It isn't a political system, it's a disease. But be of good cheer; your American politicians are immune to this disease . . . and your customs allow the non-zero elbow room."

Rufo glanced at my sword again. "Old friend, you didn't come here to bitch about Nebbi."

"No." I looked down at that keen blade. "I fetched this to shave you, Rufo."

"*Eh?*"

"I promised I would shave your corpse. I owe it to you for the slick job you did on me. So here I am, to shave the barber."

He said slowly, "But I'm not yet a corpse." He did not move. But his eyes did, estimating distance between us. Rufo wasn't counting on my being "chivalrous"; he had lived too long.

"Oh, that can be arranged," I said cheerfully, "unless I get straight answers from you."

He relaxed a touch. "I'll try, Oscar."

"More than try, please. You're my last chance. Rufo, this must be private. Even from Star."

"Under the Rose. My word on it."

"With your fingers crossed, no doubt. But don't risk it, I'm serious. And straight answers, I need them. I want advice about my marriage."

He looked glum. "And I meant to go out today. Instead I worked. Oscar, I would rather criticize a woman's firstborn, or even her taste in hats. Much safer to teach a shark to bite. What if I refuse?"

"Then I shave you!"

"You would, you heavy-handed headsman!" He frowned. " 'Straight answers—' You don't want them, you want a shoulder to cry on."

"Maybe that, too. But I do want straight answers, not the lies you can tell in your sleep."

"So I lose either way. Telling a man the truth about his marriage is suicide. I think I'll sit tight and see if you have the heart to cut me down in cold blood."

"Oh, Rufo, I'll put my sword under your lock and key if you like. You know I would never draw against *you*."

"I know no such thing," he said querulously. "There's always that first time. Scoundrels are predictable, but you're a man of honor and that frightens me. Can't we handle this over the see-speak?"

"Come off it, Rufo. I've nobody else to turn to. I want you to speak frankly. I know that a marriage counselor has to lay it on the line, pull no punches. For the sake of blood we've lost together I ask you to advise me. And frankly, of course!"

" 'Of course,' is it? The last time I risked it you were for cutting the tongue out of me." He looked at me moodily. "But I was ever a fool where friendship speaks. Hear, I'll dicker ye a fair dicker. You talk, I'll listen ... and if it should come about that you're taking so long that my tired old kidneys complain and I'm forced to leave your welcome company for a moment ... why, then you'll misunderstand and go away in a huff and we'll say no more about it. Eh?"

"Okay."

"The Chair recognizes you. Proceed."

So I talked. I talked out my dilemma and frustration, sparing neither self nor Star (it was for her sake, too, and it wasn't necessary to speak of our most private matters; those, at least, were dandy). But I told our quarrels and many matters best kept in the family, I *had* to.

Rufo listened. Presently he stood up and paced, looking troubled. Once he tut-tutted over the men Star had brought home. "She shouldn't have called her maids in. But do forget it, lad. *She* never remembers that men are shy, whereas females merely have customs. Allow Her this."

Later he said, "No need to be jealous of Jocko, son. He drives a tack with a sledgehammer."

"I'm not jealous."

"That's what Menelaus said. But leave room for give and take. Every marriage needs it."

Finally I ran down, having told him Star's prediction that I would leave. "I'm not blaming her for anything and talking about it has straightened me out. I can sweat it out now, behave myself, and be a good husband. She does make terrible sacrifices to do her job—and the least I can do is make it easier. She's so sweet and gentle and good."

Rufo stopped, some distance away with his back to his desk. "You think so?"

"I know so."

"She's an old bag!"

I was out of my chair and at him at once. I didn't draw. Didn't think of it, wouldn't have anyhow. I wanted

264

to get my hands on him and punish him for talking that way about my beloved.

He bounced over the desk like a ball and by the time I covered the length of the room, Rufo was behind it, one hand in a drawer.

"Naughty, naughty," he said. "Oscar, I don't *want* to shave you."

"Come out and fight like a man!"

"Never, old friend. One step closer and you're dog meat. All your fine promises, your pleadings. 'Pull no punches' you said. 'Lay it on the line' you said. 'Speak frankly' you said. Sit down in that chair."

" 'Speaking frankly' doesn't mean being insulting!"

"Who's to judge? Can I submit my remarks for approval before I make them? Don't compound your broken promises with childish illogic. And would you force me to buy a new rug? I never keep one I've killed a friend on; the stains make me gloomy. Sit down in that chair."

I sat down.

"Now," said Rufo, staying where he was, "you will listen while *I* talk. Or perhaps you will get up and walk out. In which case I might be so pleased to see the last of your ugly face that that might be that. Or I might be so annoyed at being interrupted that you would drop dead in the doorway, for I've much pent up and ready to spill over. Suit yourself.

"I said," he went on, "that my grandmother is an old bag. I said it brutally, to discharge your tension—and now you're not likely to take too much offense at many offensive things I still must say. She's old, you know that, though no doubt you find it easy to forget, mostly. I forget it myself, mostly, even though She was old when I was a babe making messes on the floor and crowing at the dear sight of Her. Bag, She is, and you know it. I could have said 'experienced woman' but I had to rap your teeth with it; you've been dodging it even while you've been telling me how well you know it—and how you don't care. Granny is an old bag, we start from there.

"And why should *She* be anything else? Tell yourself the answer. You're not a fool, you're merely young. Ordinarily She has but two possible pleasures and the other She can't indulge."

"What's the other one?"

"Handing down bad decisions through sadistic spite, that's the one She dare not indulge. So let us be thankful that Her body has built into it this harmless safety valve, else we would all suffer grieviously before somebody managed to kill Her. Lad, dear lad, can you dream how mortal tired She must be of most things? Your own zest soured in only months. Think what it must be to hear the same old weary mistakes year after year with nothing to hope for but a clever assassin. Then be thankful that She still pleasures in one innocent pleasure. So She's an old bag and I mean no disrespect; I salute a beneficent balance between two things She must be to do her job.

"Nor did She stop being what She is by reciting a silly rhyme with you one bright day on a hilltop. You think She has taken a vacation from it since, sticking to you only. Possibly She has, if you have quoted Her exactly and I read the words rightly; She always tells the truth.

"But never *all* the truth—who can?—and She is the most skillful liar by telling the truth you'll ever meet. I misdoubt your memory missed some innocent-sounding word that gave an escape yet saved your feelings.

"If so, why should *She* do more than save your feelings? She's fond of you, that's clear—but must She be fanatic about it? All Her training, Her special bent, is to avoid fanaticism always, find practical answers. Even though She may not have mixed up the shoes, as yet, if you stay on a week or a year or twenty and time comes when She *wants* to, She can find ways, not lie to you in words—and hurt Her conscience not at all because She hasn't any. Just Wisdom, utterly pragmatic."

Rufo cleared his throat. "Now refutation and counterpoint and contrariwise. I like my grandmother and love Her as much as my meager nature permits and respect Her right down to Her sneaky soul—and I'll kill you or anyone who gets in Her way or causes Her unhappiness— and only part of this is that She has handed on to me a shadow of Her own self so that I understand Her. If

She is spared assassin's knife or blast or poison long enough, She'll go down in history as 'The Great.' But you spoke of Her 'terrible sacrifices.' Ridiculous! She *likes* being 'Her Wisdom,' the Hub around which all worlds turn. Nor do I believe that She would give it up for you or fifty better. Again, She didn't lie, as you've told it—She said *'if'* . . . knowing that much can happen in thirty years, or twenty-five, among which is the near certainly that you wouldn't stay that long. A swindle.

"But that's the least of swindles She's put over on you. She conned you from the moment you first saw Her and long before. She cheated both ways from the ace, forced you to pick the shell with the pea, sent you like any mark anxious for the best of it, cooled you off when you started to suspect, herded you back into line and to your planned fate—and made you like it. *She's* never fussy about methods and would con the Virgin Mary and make a pact with the Old One all in one breath, did it suit Her purpose. Oh, you got paid, yes, and good measure to boot; there's nothing small about *Her*. But it's time you knew you were conned. Mind you, I'm not criticizing *Her*, I'm applauding—and I helped . . . save for one queasy moment when I felt sorry for the victim. But you were so conned you wouldn't listen, thank any saints who did. I lost my nerve for a bit, thinking that you were going to a sticky death with your innocent eyes wide. But *She* was smarter than I am, She always has been.

"Now! I like Her. I respect Her. I admire Her. I even love Her a bit. *All* of Her, not just Her pretty aspects but also all the impurities that make Her steel as hard as it *must* be. How about *you,* sir? What's *your* feeling about Her *now* . . . knowing She conned you, knowing what She is?"

I was still sitting. My drink was by me, untouched all this long harangue.

I took it and stood up. "Here's to the grandest old bag in twenty universes!"

Rufo bounced over the desk again, grabbed his glass. "Say that loud and often! And to Her, She'd love it! May She be blessed by God, Whoever He is, and kept safe. We'll never see another like *Her*, more's the pity! —for we need them by the gross!"

We tossed it down and smashed our glasses. Rufo fetched fresh ones, poured, settled in his chair, and said, "Now for serious drinking. Did I ever tell you about the time my—"

"You did. Rufo, I want to know about this swindle."

"Such as?"

"Well, I can see much of it. Take that first time we flew—"

He shuddered. "Let's not."

"I never wondered then. But, since Star can do this, we could have skipped Igli, the Horned Ghosts, the marsh, the time wasted with Jocko—"

"Wasted?"

"For her purpose. And the rats and hogs and possibly the dragons. Flown directly from that first Gate to the second. Right?"

He shook his head. "Wrong."

"I don't see it."

"Assuming that She could fly us that far, a question I hope never to settle, She could have flown us to the Gate She preferred. What would you have done then? If popped almost directly from Nice to Karth-Hokesh? Charged out and fought like a wolverine, as you did? Or said, 'Miss, you've made a mistake. Show me the exit from this Fun House—I'm not laughing.' "

"Well—I wouldn't have bugged out."

"But would you have *won?* Would you have been at that keen edge of readiness it took?"

"I see. Those first rounds were live-ammo exercises in my training. Or was it live ammo? Was all that first part swindle? Maybe with hypnotism, to make it feel right? God knows she's expert. No danger till we reached the Black Tower?"

He shuddered again. "No, no! Oscar, *any* of that could have killed us. I never fought harder in my life, nor was ever more frightened. *None* of it could be skipped. I don't understand all Her reasons, I'm not Her Wisdom. But She would never risk *Herself* unless necessary. She would

268

sacrifice ten million brave men, were it needed, as the cheaper price. She knows what She's worth. But She fought beside us with all She has—you *saw!* Because it had to be."

"I still don't understand all of it."

"Nor will you. Nor will I. She would have sent you in alone, had it been possible. And at that last supreme danger, that thing called 'Eater of Souls' because it had done just that to many braves before you ... had you lost to it, She and I would have tried to fight our way out —I was ready, any moment; I couldn't tell you—and if we had escaped—unlikely—She would have shed no tears for you. Or not many. Then worked another twenty or thirty or a hundred years to find and con and train another champion—and fought just as hard by *his* side. She has courage, that cabbage. She knew how thin our chances were; you didn't. Did *She* flinch?"

"No."

"But you were the key, first to be found, then ground to fit. You yourself *act,* you're never a puppet, or you could never have won. *She* was the only one who could nudge and wheedle such a man and place him where he *would* act; no lesser person than *She* could handle the scale of hero *She* needed. So She searched until She found him ... and honed him fine. Tell me, why did you take up the sword? It's not common in America."

"What?" I had to think. Reading *King Arthur* and *The Three Musketeers,* and Burroughs' wonderful Mars stories — But every kid does that. "When we moved to Florida, I was a Scout. The Scoutmaster was a Frenchman, taught high school. He started some of us kids. I liked it, it was something I did well. Then in college—"

"Ever wonder why that immigrant got that job in that town? And volunteered for Scout work? Or why your college had a fencing team when many don't? No matter, if you had gone elsewhere, there would have been fencing in a YMCA or something. Didn't you have more combat than most of your category?"

"Hell, yes!"

'Could have been killed anytime, too—and *She* would

have turned to another candidate already being honed. Son, I don't know how you were selected, nor how you were converted from a young punk into the hero you potentially were. Not my job. Mine was, simpler—just more dangerous—your groom and your 'eyes-behind.' Look around. Fancy quarters for a servant, eh?"

"Well, yes. I had almost forgotten that you were supposed to be my groom."

" 'Supposed,' hell! I *was*. I went three times to Nevia as *Her* servant, training for it. Jocko doesn't know to this day. If I went back, I would be welcome, I think. But only in the kitchen."

"But *why?* That part seems silly."

"Was it? When we snared you, your ego was in feeble shape; it had to be built up—and calling you 'Boss' and serving your meals while I stood and you sat, with *Her*, was part of it." He gnawed a knuckle and looked annoyed. "I still think She witched your first two arrows. Someday I'd like a return match—with *Her* not around."

"I may fool you. I've been practicing."

"Well, forget it. We got the Egg, that's the important thing. And here's this bottle and that's important, too." He poured again. "Will that be all, 'Boss'?"

"Damn you, Rufo! Yes, you sweet old scoundrel. You've straightened me out. Or conned me again, I don't know which."

"No con, Oscar, by the blood we've shed. I've told the truth as straight as I know it, though it hurt me. I didn't want to, you're my friend. Walking that rocky road with you I shall treasure all the days of my life."

"Uh . . . yes. Me, too. All of it."

"Then why are you frowning?"

"Rufo, I understand her now—as well as an ordinary person can—and respect her utterly . . . and love her more than ever. But I can't be anybody's fancy man. Not even hers."

"I'm glad I didn't have to say that. Yes. She's right. She's always right, damn Her! You must leave. For both of you. Oh, *She* wouldn't be hurt too much but staying would ruin you, in time. Destroy you, if you're stubborn."

some I mailed ahead and some I carried, for I had no intention of paying Uncle Sugar 91 percent.

You lose track of time on a different day and calendar; there was a week or two left on that free ride home my orders called for. It seemed smart to take it—less conspicuous. So I did—an old four-engine transport, Prestwick to Gander to New York.

Streets looked dirtier, buildings not as tall—and headlines worse than ever. I quit reading newspapers, didn't stay long; California I thought of as "home." I phoned Mother; she was reproachful about my not having written and I promised to visit Alaska as soon as I could. How were they all? (I had in mind that my half brothers and sisters might need college help someday.)

They weren't hurting. My stepfather was on flight orders and had made permanent grade. I asked her to forward any mail to my aunt.

California looked better than New York. But it wasn't Nevia. Not even Center. It was more crowded than I remembered. All you can say for California towns is that they aren't as bad as other places. I visited my aunt and uncle because they had been good to me and I was thinking of using some of that gold in Switzerland to buy him free from his first wife. But she had died and they were talking about a swimming pool.

So I kept quiet. I had been almost ruined by too much money, it had grown me up a bit. I followed the rule of Their Wisdoms: Leave well enough alone.

The campus felt smaller and the students looked so *young*. Reciprocal, I guess. I was coming out of the malt shop across from Administration when two Letter sweaters came in, shoving me aside. The second said, "Watch it, Dad!"

I let him live.

Football had been re-emphasized, new coach, new dressing rooms, stands painted, talk about a stadium. The coach knew who I was; he knew the records and was out to make a name. "You're coming back, aren't you?" I told him I didn't think so.

"Nonsense!" he said. "Gotta get that old sheepskin!

Silliest thing on earth to let your hitch in the Army stop you. Now look—" His voice dropped.

No nonsense about "sweeping the gym," stuff the Conference didn't like. But a boy could live with a family— and one could be found. If he paid his fees in cash, who cared? Quiet as an undertaker—"That leaves your G.I. benefits for pocket money."

"I don't have any."

"Man, don't you read the papers?" He had it on file: While I was gone, that unWar had been made eligible for G.I. benefits.

I promised to think it over.

But I had no such intention. I had indeed decided to finish my engineering degree, I like to finish things. But not there.

That evening I heard from Joan, the girl who had given me such a fine sendoff, then "Dear-Johnned" me. I intended to look her up, call on her and her husband; I just hadn't found out her married name yet. But she ran across my aunt, shopping, and phoned me. "Easy!" she said and sounded delighted.

"Who— Wait a minute. *Joan!*"

I must come to dinner that very night. I told her "Fine," and that I was looking forward to meeting· the lucky galoot she had married.

Joan looked sweet as ever and gave me a hearty arms-around-my-neck smack, a welcome-home kiss, sisterly but good. Then I met the kids, one crib size and the other toddling.

Her husband was in L.A.

I should have reached for my hat. But it was all right think nothing of it Jim had phoned after she talked to me to say that he had to stay over one more night and *of course* it was all right for me to take her out to dinner he had seen me play football and maybe I would like to bowl tomorrow night she hadn't been able to get a baby sitter but her sister and brother-in-law were stopping in for drinks couldn't stay for dinner they were tied up after all dear it isn't like we hadn't known each other a long time oh you do too remember my sister there they are stopping out in front and I don't have the children in bed.

Her sister and brother-in-law stayed for one drink; Joan and her sister put the kids to bed while the brother-in-law sat with me and asked how things were in Europe he understood I was just back and then he told me how things were in Europe and what should be done about them. "You know, Mr. Jordan," he told me, tapping my knee, "a man in the real estate business like I am gets to be a pretty shrewd judge of human nature has to be and while I haven't actually been in Europe the way you have haven't had time somebody has to stay home and pay taxes and keep an eye on things while you lucky young fellows are seeing the world but human nature is the same anywhere and if we dropped just one little bomb on Minsk or Pinsk or one of those places they would see the light right quick and we could stop all this diddling around that's making it tough on the businessman. Don't you agree?"

I said he had a point. They left and he said that he would ring me tomorrow and show me some choice lots that could be handled on almost nothing down and were certain to go way up what with a new missile plant coming in here soon. "Nice listening to your experiences, Mr. Jordan, real pleasant. Sometime I must tell you about something that happened to me in Tijuana but not with the wife around ha ha!"

Joan said to me, "I can't see why she married him. Pour me another drink, hon, a double, I need it. I'm going to turn the oven down, dinner will keep."

We both had a double and then another, and had dinner about eleven. Joan got tearful when I insisted on going home around three. She told me I was chicken and I agreed; she told me things could have been so different if I hadn't insisted on going into the Army and I agreed again; she told me to go out the back way and not turn on any lights and she never wanted to see me again and Jim was going to Sausalito the seventeenth.

I caught a plane for Los Angeles next day.

Now look— I am *not* blaming Joan. I like Joan. I

respect her and will always be grateful to her. She is a fine person. With superior early advantages—say in Nevia—she'd be a *wow!* She's quite a gal, even so. Her house was clean, her babies were clean and healthy and well cared for. She's generous and thoughtful and good-tempered.

Nor do I feel guilty. If a man has any regard for a girl's feelings, there is one thing he cannot refuse: a return bout if she wants one. Nor will I pretend that I didn't want it, too.

But I felt upset all the way to Los Angeles. Not over her husband, he wasn't hurt. Not over Joanie, she was neither swept off her feet nor likely to suffer remorse. Joanie is a good kid and had made a good adjustment between her nature and an impossible society.

Still, I was upset.

A man must not criticize a woman's most womanly quality. I must make it clear that little Joanie was just as sweet and just as generous as the younger Joanie who had sent me off to the Army feeling grand. The fault lay with me; *I* had changed.

My complaints are against the whole culture with no individual sharing more than a speck of blame. Let me quote that widely traveled culturologist and rake, Dr. Rufo:

"Oscar, when you get home, don't expect too much of your feminine compatriots. You're sure to be disappointed and the poor dears aren't to blame. American women, having been conditioned out of their sex instincts, compensate by compulsive interest in rituals over the dead husk of sex...and each one is sure she knows 'intuitively' the right ritual for conjuring the corpse. She *knows* and nobody can tell her any different... especially a man unlucky enough to be in bed with her. So don't try. You will either make her furious or crush her spirit. You'll be attacking that most Sacred of Cows: the myth that women know all about sex, just from being women."

Rufo had frowned. "The typical American female is sure that she has genius as a couturière, as an interior decorator, as a gourmet cook, and, always, as a courtesan. Usually she is wrong on four counts. But don't try to tell her so."

He had added, "Unless you can catch one not over twelve and segregate her, especially from her mother—and even that may be too late. But don't misunderstand me; it evens out. The American male is convinced that he is a great warrior, a great statesman, and a great lover. Spot checks prove that he is as deluded as she is. Or worse. Historo-culturally speaking, there is strong evidence that the American male, rather than the female, murdered sex in your country."

"What can *I* do about it?"

"Slip over to France now and then. French women are almost as ignorant but not nearly as conceited and often are teachable."

When my plane landed, I put the subject out of mind as I planned to be an anchorite a while. I learned in the Army that no sex is easier than a starvation allowance—and I had serious plans.

I had decided to be the square I naturally am, with hard work and a purpose in life. I could have used those Swiss bank accounts to be a playboy. But I had been a playboy, it wasn't my style.

I had been on the biggest binge in history—one I wouldn't believe if I didn't have so much loot. Now was time to settle down and join Heroes Anonymous. *Being* a hero is okay. But a *retired* hero—first he's a bore, then he's a bum.

My first stop was Caltech. I could now afford the best and Caltech's only rival is where they tried to outlaw sex entirely. I had seen enough of the dreary graveyard in 1942-45.

The Dean of Admissions was not encouraging. "Mr. Gordon, you know that we turn down more than we accept? Nor could we give you full credit on this transcript. No slur on your former school—and we do like to give ex-servicemen a break—but this school has higher standards. Another thing, you won't find Pasadena a cheap place to live."

I said I would be happy to take whatever standing I merited, and showed him my bank balance (one of them) and offered a check for a year's fees. He wouldn't take it but loosened up. I left with the impression that a place might be found for E. C. "Oscar" Gordon.

I went downtown and started the process to make me legally "Oscar" instead of "Evelyn Cyril." Then I started job hunting.

I found one out in the Valley, as a junior draftsman in a division of a subsidiary of a corporation that made tires, food machinery, and other things—missiles in this case. This was part of the Gordon Rehabilitation Plan. A few months over the drafting board would get me into the swing again and I planned to study evenings and behave myself. I found a furnished apartment in Sawtelle and bought a used Ford for commuting.

I felt relaxed then; "Milord Hero" was buried. All that was left was the Lady Vivamus, hanging over the television. But I balanced her in hand first and got a thrill out of it. I decided to find a *salle d'armes* and join its club. I had seen an archery range in the Valley, too, and there ought to be someplace where American Rifle Association members fired on Sundays. No need to get flabby—

Meanwhile I would forget the loot in Switzerland. It was payable in gold, not funny money, and if I let it sit, it might be worth more—maybe much more—from inflation than from investing it. Someday it would be capital, when I opened my own firm.

That's what I had my sights on: Boss. A wage slave, even in brackets where Uncle Sugar takes more than half, is still a slave. But I had learned from Her Wisdom that a boss must train; I could not buy "Boss" with gold.

So I settled down. My name change came through; Caltech conceded that I could look forward to moving to Pasadena—and mail caught up with me.

Mother sent it to my aunt, she forwarded it to the hotel address I had first given, eventually it reached my flat. Some were letters mailed in the States over a year ago, sent on to Southeast Asia, then Germany, then

278

Alaska, then more changes before I read them in Sawtelle.

One offered that bargain on investment service again; this time I could knock off 10 percent more. Another was from the coach at college—on plain stationery and signed in a scrawl. He said certain parties were determined to see the season start off with a bang. Would $250 per month change my mind? Phone his home number, collect. I tore it up.

The next was from the Veterans Administration, dated just after my discharge, telling me that as a result of *Barton vs. United States,* et al., it had been found that I was legally a "war orphan" and entitled to $110/month for schooling until age twenty-three.

I laughed so hard I hurt.

After some junk was one from a Congressman. He had the honor to inform me that, in cooperation with the Veterans of Foreign Wars, he had submitted a group of special bills to correct injustices resulting from failure to classify correctly person who were "war orphans," that the bills had passed under consent, and that he was happy to say that one affecting me allowed me to my twenty-seventh birthday to complete my education inasmuch as my twenty-third birthday had passed before the error was rectified. I am, sir, sincerely, etc.

I couldn't laugh. I thought how much dirt I would have eaten, or—you name it—the summer I was conscripted if I had been sure of $110 a month. I wrote that Congressman a thank-you letter, the best I knew how.

The next item looked like junk. It was from Hospitals' Trust, Ltd., therefore a pitch for a donation or a hospital insurance ad—but I couldn't see why anyone in Dublin would have me on their list.

Hospitals' Trust asked if I had Irish Hospitals' Sweepstakes ticket number such-and-such, and its official receipt? This ticket had been sold to J. L. Weatherby, Esq. Its number had been drawn in the second unit drawing, and had been a ticket of the winning horse. J. L. Weatherby had been informed and had notified Hospitals' Trust, Ltd., that he had disposed of ticket to E. C. Gordon, and, on receiving receipt, had mailed it to such party.

Was I the "E. C. Gordon," did I have the ticket, did I have the receipt? H. T. Ltd. would appreciate an early reply.

The last item in the stack had an A.P.O. return address. In it was an Irish Sweepstakes receipt—and a note: *This should teach me not to play poker. Hope it wins you something*—J. L. WEATHERBY. The cancellation was over a year old.

I stared at it, then got the papers I had carried through the Universes. I found the matching ticket. It was bloodstained but the number was clear.

I looked at the letter. *Second* unit drawing—

I started examining tickets under bright light. The others were counterfeit. But the engraving of *this* ticket and *this* receipt was sharp as paper money. I don't know where Weatherby bought that ticket, but he did not buy it from the thief who sold me mine.

Second drawing— I hadn't known there was more than one. But drawings depend on the number of tickets sold, in units of £120,000. I had seen the results of only the *first*.

Weatherby had mailed the receipt care of Mother, to Wiesbaden, and it must have been in Elmendorf when I was in Nice—then had gone to Nice, and back to Elmendorf because Rufo had left a forwarding address with American Express; Rufo had known all about me of course and had taken steps to cover my disappearance.

On that morning over a year earlier while I sat in a café in Nice, I held a winning ticket with the receipt in the mail. If I had looked farther in that *Herald-Tribune* than the "Personal" ads I would have found the results of the Second Unit drawing and never answered that ad.

I would have collected $140,000, never have seen Star a second time—

Or would Her Wisdom have been balked?

Would I have refused to follow my "Helen of Troy" simply because my pockets were lined with money?

I gave myself the benefit of doubt. *I would have walked the Glory Road anyhow!*

At least, I hoped so.

Next morning I phoned the plant, then went to a bank and through a routine I had gone through twice in Nice.

Yes, it was a good ticket. Could the bank be of service in collecting it? I thanked them and left.

A little man from Internal Revenue was on my doorstep—

Almost— He buzzed from below while I was writing to Hospitals' Trust, Ltd.

Presently I was telling him that I was damned if I would! I'd leave the money in Europe and they could whistle! He said mildly not to take that attitude, as I was just blowing off steam because the I.R.S. didn't like paying informers' fees but would if my actions showed that I was trying to evade the tax.

They had me boxed. I collected $140,000 and paid $103,000 to Uncle Sugar. The mild little man pointed out that it was better that way; so often people put off paying and got into trouble.

Had I been in Europe, it would have been $140,000 *in gold*—but now it was $37,000 in paper—because free and sovereign Americans can't have gold. They might start a war, or turn Communist, or something. No, I couldn't leave the $37,000 in Europe as gold; that was illegal, too. They were very polite.

I mailed 10 percent, $3,700, to Sgt. Weatherby and told him the story. I took $33,000 and set up a college trust for my siblings, handled so that my folks wouldn't know until it was needed. I crossed my fingers and hoped that news about this ticket would not reach Alaska. The L.A. papers never had it, but word got around somehow; I found myself on endless sucker lists, got letters offering golden opportunities, begging loans, or demanding gifts.

It was a month before I realized I had forgotten the California State Income Tax. I never did sort out the red ink.

XXII

I GOT back to the old drawing board, slugged away at books in the evening, watched a little television, weekends some fencing.

But I kept having this dream—

I had it first right after I took that job and now I was having it every night—

I'm heading along this long, long road and I round a curve and there's a castle up ahead. It's beautiful, pennants flying from turrets and a winding climb to its drawbridge. But I know, I just *know*, that there is a princess captive in its dungeon.

That part is always the same. Details vary. Lately the mild little man from Internal Revenue steps into the road and tells me that toll is paid here—10 percent more than whatever I've got.

Other times it's a cop and he leans against my horse (sometimes it has four legs, sometimes eight) and writes a ticket for obstructing traffic, riding with out-of-date license, failing to observe stop sign, and gross insubordination. He wants to know if I have a permit to carry that lance?—and tells me that game laws require me to tag any dragons killed.

Other times I round that turn and a solid wave of

freeway traffic, five lanes wide, is coming at me. That one is worst.

I started writing this after the dreams started. I couldn't see going to a headshrinker and saying, "Look, Doc, I'm a hero by trade and my wife is Empress in another universe—" I had even less desire to lie on his couch and tell how my parents mistreated me as a child (they didn't) and how I found out about little girls (that's *my* business).

I decided to talk it out to a typewriter.

It made me feel better but didn't stop the dreams. But I learned a new word: "acculturated." It's what happens when a member of one culture shifts to another, with a sad period when he doesn't fit. Those Indians you see in Arizona towns, not doing anything, looking in shop windows or just standing. Acculturation. They don't fit.

I was taking a bus down to see my ear, nose, and throat doctor—Star promised me that her therapy plus that at Center would free me of the common cold—and it has; I don't catch *anything*. But even therapists that administer Long-Life can't protect human tissues against poison gas; L.A. smog was getting me. Eyes burning, nose stopped up—twice a week I went down to get horrid things done to my nose. I used to park my car and go down Wilshire by bus, as parking was impossible close in.

In the bus I overheard two ladies: "—much as I despise them, you *can't* give a cocktail party without inviting the Sylvesters."

It sounded like a foreign language. Then I played it back and understood the words.

But *why* did she have to invite the Sylvesters?

If she despised them, why didn't she either ignore them, or drop a rock on their heads?

In God's name, why give a "cocktail party"? People who don't like each other particularly, standing around (never enough chairs), talking about things they aren't interested in, drinking drinks they don't want (why set a *time* to take a drink?) and getting high so that they won't notice they aren't having fun. *Why?*

283

I realized that acculturation had set in. I didn't fit.

I avoided buses thereafter and picked up five traffic tickets and a smashed fender. I quit studying, too. Books didn't seem to make sense. It warn't the way I larned it back in dear old Center.

But I stuck to my job as a draftsman. I always have been able to draw and soon I was promoted to major work.

One day the Chief Draftsman called me over. "Here, Gordon, this assembly you did—"

I was proud of that job. I had remembered something I had seen on Center and had designed it in, reducing moving parts and improving a clumsy design into one that made me feel good. It was tricky and I had added an extra view. "Well?"

He handed it back. "Do it over. Do it right."

I explained the improvement and that I had done the drawing a better way to—

He cut me off. "We don't want it done a better way, we want it done *our* way."

"Your privilege," I agreed and resigned by walking out.

My flat seemed strange at that time on a working day. I started to study *Strength of Materials*—and chucked the book aside. Then I stood and looked at the Lady Vivamus.

"Dum Vivimus, Vivamus!" Whistling, I buckled her on, drew blade, felt that thrill run up my arm.

I returned sword, got a few things, traveler's checks and cash mostly, walked out. I wasn't going anywhere, just thataway!

I had been striding along maybe twenty minutes when a prowl car pulled up and took me to the station.

Why was I wearing that thing? I explained that gentlemen wore swords.

If I would tell them what movie company I was with, a phone call could clear it up. Or was it television? The Department cooperated but liked to be notified.

Did I have a license for concealed weapons? I said it wasn't concealed. They told me it was—by that scabbard.

284

I mentioned the Constitution; I was told that the Constitution sure as hell didn't mean walking around city streets with a toad sticker like that. A cop whispered to the sergeant, "Here's what we got him on, Sarge. The blade is longer than—" I think it was three inches. There was trouble when they tried to take the Lady Vivamus away from me. Finally I was locked up, sword and all.

Two hours later my lawyer got it changed to "disorderly conduct" and I was released, with talk of a sanity hearing.

I paid him and thanked him and took a cab to the airport and a plane to San Francisco. At the port I bought a large bag, one that would take the Lady Vivamus catercornered.

That night in San Francisco I went to a party. I met this chap in a bar and bought him a drink and he bought me one and I stood him to dinner and we picked up a gallon of wine and went to this party. I had been explaining to him that what sense was there in going to school to learn one way when there was already a better way? As silly as an Indian studying buffalo calling! Buffalos are in zoos! Acculturated, that's what it was!

Charlie said he agreed perfectly and his friends would like to hear it. So we went and I paid the driver to wait but took my suitcase inside.

Charlie's friends didn't want to hear my theories but the wine was welcome and I sat on the floor and listened to folk singing. The men wore beards and didn't comb their hair. The beards helped, it made it easy to tell which were girls. One beard stood up and recited a poem. Old Jocko could do better blind drunk but I didn't say so.

It wasn't like a party in Nevia and certainly not in Center, except this: I got propositioned. I might have considered it if this girl hadn't been wearing sandals. Her toes were dirty. I thought of Zhai-ee-van and her dainty, clean fur, and told her thanks, I was under a vow.

The beard who had recited the poem came over and stood in front of me. "Man, like what rumble you picked up that scar?"

285

I said it had been in Southeast Asia. He looked at me scornfully. "Mercenary!"

"Well, not always," I told him. "Sometimes I fight for free. Like right now."

I tossed him against a wall and took my suitcase outside and went to the airport—and then Seattle and Anchorage, Alaska, and wound up at Elmendorf AFB, clean, sober, and with the Lady Vivamus disguised as fishing tackle.

Mother was glad to see me and the kids seemed pleased —I had bought presents between planes in Seattle—and my stepdaddy and I swapped yarns.

I did one important thing in Alaska; I flew to Point Barrow. There I found part of what I was looking for: no pressure, no sweat, not many people. You look out across the ice and know that only the North Pole is over that way, and a few Eskimos and fewer white people here. Eskimos are every bit as nice as they have been pictured. Their babies never cry, the adults never seem cross—only the dogs staked-out between the huts are bad-tempered.

But Eskimos are "civilized" now; the old ways are going. You can buy a choc malt at Barrow and airplanes fly daily in a sky that may hold missiles tomorrow.

But they still seal amongst the ice floes, the village is rich when they take a whale, half starved if they don't. They don't count time and they don't seem to worry about anything—ask a man how old he is, he answers: "Oh, I'm quite of an age." That's how old Rufo is. Instead of good-bye, they say, "Sometime again!" No particular time and again we'll see you.

They let me dance with them. You must wear gloves (in their way they are as formal as the Doral) and you stomp and sing with the drums—and I found myself weeping. I don't know why. It was a dance about a little old man who doesn't have a wife and now he sees a seal—

I said, "Sometime again!"—went back to Anchorage and to Copenhagen. From 30,000 feet the North Pole looks like prairie covered with snow, except black lines that are water. I never expected to see the North Pole.

From Copenhagen I went to Stockholm, Majatta was

not with her parents but was only a square away. She cooked me that Swedish dinner, and her husband is a good Joe. From Stockholm I phoned a "Personal" ad to the Paris edition of the *Herald-Tribune,* then went to Paris.

I kept the ad in daily and sat across from the Two Maggots and stacked saucers and tried not to fret. I watched the ma'm'selles and thought about what I might do.

If a man wanted to settle down for forty years or so, wouldn't Nevia be a nice place? Okay, it has dragons. It doesn't have flies, nor mosquitoes, nor smog. Nor parking problems, nor freeway complexes that look like diagrams for abdominal surgery. Not a traffic light anywhere.

Muri would be glad to see me. I might marry her. And maybe little whatever-her-name was, her kid sister, too. Why not? Marriage customs aren't everywhere those they use in Paducah. Star would be pleased; she would like being related to Jocko by marriage.

But I would go see Star first, or soon anyhow, and kick that pile of strange shoes aside. But I wouldn't stay; it would be "sometime again" which would suit Star. It is a phrase, one of the few, that translates exactly into Centrist jargon—and means exactly the same.

"Sometime again," because there are other maidens, or pleasing facsimiles, elsewhere, in need of rescuing. Somewhere. And a man must work at his trade, which wise wives know.

"I cannot rest from travel; I will drink life to the lees." A long road, a trail, a "Tramp Royal," with no certainty of what you'll eat or where or if, nor where you'll sleep, nor with whom. But somewhere is Helen of Troy and all her many sisters and there is still noble work to be done.

A man can stack a lot of saucers in a month and I began to fume instead of dream. Why the hell didn't Rufo show up? I brought this account up to date from sheer nerves. Has Rufo gone back? Or is he dead?

Or was he "never born"? Am I a psycho discharge and what is in this case I carry with me wherever I go?

A sword? I'm afraid to look, so I do—and now I'm afraid to ask. I met an old sergeant once, a thirty-year man, who was convinced that he owned all the diamond mines in Africa; he spent his evenings keeping books on them. Am I just as happily deluded? Are these francs what is left of my monthly disability check?

Does anyone ever get two chances? Is the Door in the Wall always gone when next you look? Where do you catch the boat for Bridgadoon? Brother, it's like the post office in Brooklyn: *You can't get there from here!*

I'm going to give Rufo two more weeks—

I've heard from Rufo! A clipping of my ad was forwarded to him but he had a little trouble. He wouldn't say much by phone but I gather he was mixed up with a carnivorous Fräulein and got over the border almost *sans culottes*. But he'll be here tonight. He is quite agreeable to a change in planets and universes and says he has something interesting in mind. A little risky perhaps, but not dull. I'm sure he's right both ways. Rufo might steal your cigarettes and certainly your wench but things aren't dull around him—and he would die defending your rear.

So tomorrow we are heading up that Glory Road, rocks and all!

Got any dragons you need killed?